# Brewed

## A Life's Journey

A Novel

Michael C. Aquilino

Brewed A Life's Journey, is a work of fiction. Any reference to any historical event, to any real person, or to any location are used fictitiously. Other names, places, or events are from the author's imagination, and any resemblance to any actual person, place, or event, living or dead, is purely coincidental.



ISBN: 978-0-578-36323-3 (paperback)
ISBN: 978-0-578-36324-0 (Ebook)

To my wife Giovanna for all her help and support in making this book possible, and to our loving children and grandchildren.

"I start Monday in the brewhouse. My dreams are all coming true. I don't know why I am so blessed. I feel like I have been reborn."

## Chapter 1

# Beginnings

It's June 20, 1933, in the town of Kelheim, which is situated at the confluence of the river Altmuhl and the river Danube in Bavaria. Helmut awakens for another day at his new job at the Baumer Brewery. The brewery has existed since the early 1800s and has been an important part of the town of Kelheim ever since. The wonderful aroma of the beer brewing permeates the entire town. He is quite excited at the opportunities this new position can provide him. Helmut's primary job since starting at the brewery six months ago is taking care of loading the delivery trucks and horse-drawn wagons. But Helmut dreams of someday being promoted into the brewhouse and learning the art of brewing. The only thing Helmut knows about brewing beer is something called the Reinheitsgebot (what a great Scrabble word!) or German Purity Law. It has been in effect for over 500 years. It states the only ingredients that can be used to brew beer are water, malt, hops, and yeast.

Helmut grew up on a small farm just outside of Kelheim. His family has farmed the same land for several generations. They were cabbage farmers and what they grew would be pickled and turned into sauerkraut, which is a traditional side dish throughout Germany. Helmut's parents had recently died, and he wanted to move into the city and try something new. He dreaded the long days on the farm and the continued isolation. Fortunately, he was able to sell the farm to his neighbor to the north. As the farm had some value when he sold it, Helmut was happy to have money in his pocket for the first time in his life.

As Helmut walks from his small apartment overlooking Kelheim Square, he thinks to himself, "Is it ever going to stop raining?" In Bavaria, June & July is the wettest time of the year. As he walks to work, Helmut changes his routine and stops at a bakery for a treat before work. He smiles as he enters, thinking, "pastries for breakfast and lunch, hmmmm, why not!" One of the best bakeries in all of Kelheim was located just a block from the brewery. It was definitely a favorite of Helmut and his co-workers at the factory. They spend many lunches and breaks sitting outside at the brewery's beer garten, eating bratwurst or snacking on the delicious German cookies & pastries, all of which are washed down with a stein of fresh beer. For now, Helmut asks Mr. Meyer the baker for a slice of his famous kuchen. He wolfs it down before leaving the shop and says to Mr. Meyer, "I will see you again at lunchtime, if the rain lets up." Helmut leaves and rushes off to the brewery for another long day of work. It turns out to be a hectic morning as one horse has thrown a shoe, and one of the delivery trucks had a flat tire. This set Helmut back in his duties, but the problems are quickly resolved. Mr. Baumer has said by next year they would no longer have a need for the horses, and they would be eliminated from the brewery.

Beer sales have been strong, and Helmut was told to plan on loading an extra delivery truck this afternoon. Usually the Baumer Brewery supplied Kelheim, but it has been increasing its territory into the surrounding towns. It's around noon and it looks like a break in the weather, as the rain has finally stopped. Helmut looks up, and the sun warms his face and dries his wet clothes. Today, as on many other occasions, Helmut and his best friend Josef go to the bakery to pick something up to have with lunch. Josef works in the brewery's packaging department and has for a couple of years. Helmut asks, "What's new, Josef?" He replies, "I received an overseas cable from my Uncle Otto in the United States of America and he has invited me to visit." It would be quite an adventure, as Josef had never left the town of Kelheim his entire life. Helmut asks, "Josef, are you thinking of taking him up on his offer?" He replies, "Yes, someday for sure." On the way, they pass a couple of street vendors cooking a variety of wursts, which they will get on the way back to the brewery.

When they got there, they were shocked to see the bakery window marked with a large white star. Helmut asks Josef if he knew what that star represents. Josef replies, "It is the Jewish Star of David." Josef tells him that many of the small shops in Kelheim were owned by Jewish people. They really did not understand why this symbol was put on the window, but they were about to find out.

They enter the bakery and look to see what Mr. Meyer has for sale today. Perhaps some more kuchen, or schneeballen, or just some crusty bread. However, to their surprise and dismay, Mr. Meyer was not there. They ask the man in the store, where is Mr. Meyer? He replies, "I am the new owner of the bakery. I am Garth, a proud Aryan, and Lutheran. That Jew Meyer has been taken away and will not be returning." Helmut and Yosef did not know how to respond to this. Josef, who grew up in Kelheim, said since they were children, they would go to Mr. Meyers' shop for a cookie. Mr. Meyer always enjoyed giving cookies to the neighborhood children, probably because he and his wife could never have children of their own. Garth barks at them, "Well, what do you want? Please decide as I am very busy. As soon as you leave, I have to wash that damn star off of the shop window. Then I have to prepare some more bread for baking, so what will it be?" Both Helmut and Josef have lost their appetites, as they were upset at what happened to Mr. Meyer. They tell Garth, "Nothing today, thank you." as they hurry out of the shop. In the coming days, they began to realize that many familiar shopkeepers and tradesmen they had known were being replaced, just like what happened with Mr. Meyer, the baker. But why, they ask themselves, what have they done, other than be a Jew?

It was a time of great political upheaval throughout Germany. Adolf Hitler was the leader of a formal political party, The National Socialist German Workers Party. The nickname for the "NSGWP" was the "NAZI" party. In January 1933, the President of Germany, Paul von Hindenburg, named Hitler as Chancellor of Germany. Hitler preached national unity and racial purity. To him, Jewish people, as well as many other groups such as gypsies, were deemed to be inferior. He dreamed of a Germany populated by a master race, as he called it. He and his Nazi party were very popular throughout Bavaria, as well as the rest of Germany. Through their reign of terror, any freedoms the German people thought they once had are being rapidly eliminated. Every aspect of their lives was being dominated and controlled by the Nazi party. Adolf Hitler had just officially formed the Gestapo (secret police) as spies and enforcers of his policies a few months earlier. Josef had always been an outstanding student and had a love of reading. A recent phenomenon of the Nazi's burning books in enormous bonfires in the town square was becoming an all too frequent occurrence. Helmut and Josef quietly wondered amongst themselves when life would get back to normal. Sadly, things were about to get a lot worse.

It's a new day in Kelheim and the rain has started again. It would have been nice to see the sun again, Helmut thought. The river has risen and is very near overflowing its banks. Nobody in Kelheim had ever remembered any flooding in the area, so they were very unconcerned. Helmut and Josef asked Mr. Baumer if the brewery should shut down? They tell him it would be a good idea to move what equipment they can to higher ground, and more importantly to put sandbags around the brewery. Mr. Baumer said that it was nonsense and to get back to work. Later that day, Helmut went back to his apartment in the square, exhausted from a long day of work. He bought a wurst from a street vendor for dinner and he washed it down with a couple of mugs of beer. Before long, Helmut dozed off for the night. Now it's around three a.m. when he is awakened by a ferocious clap of thunder. He looks out his window and there is a violent thunderstorm raging. He looks off in the distance and the lightning is illuminating the brewery. "Oh no, it looks like there is water in the street," he exclaims. As he runs through the empty tavern downstairs, he yells, "The river had overflowed its banks! I have to get to the brewery and see if I can help." The rain and wind are so strong Helmut cannot make it more than a few feet from the tavern door. He goes back in and prays that the rain will stop. He is fortunate because they built the town square where he lives on a hill, and it is the high ground in Kelheim. The storm continues through the night and into the next day.

The flood waters have risen so fast that a quarter of the town of Kelheim is now underwater and the Baumer Brewery has been completely destroyed. Raging flood waters had undermined the foundation and most of the brewery had collapsed in on itself. The malt house, underground caves beneath the brewery used to store and age beer (called lagering) in a cool environment, were also lost, as was the case with the horse stables and truck garage. It was a surreal landscape. There were hundreds of bodies, animals, and beer kegs floating everywhere. Tragically, the owner of the brewery, Max Baumer, and his daughter Greta, died in the flood. Helmut grieved not only for the loss of his job but also for Greta, as Helmut was very fond of her. Greta was known for her wonderful smile and the kindness she showed towards her father's employees. Helmut had hoped that someday he could prove himself worthy of Mr. Baumer's daughter so he could marry her. Unfortunately, that was not going to happen. The strain on Helmut was profound, and with a heavy heart, it almost brought him to the brink of suicide. Fortunately for him, his best friend Josef had survived the flooding as well. "Please don't give up Helmut," Josef told him. "We will face this together. Let me help you." They spent the coming days and weeks leaning on each other for emotional support and pooling their savings in an attempt to survive. Josef was not aware that Helmut still had the money from the sale of the farm hidden away. That money was going to change their lives.

The devastation was extensive, but again the worst was yet to come. Because of the already poor sanitation in the town, it faced another crisis. The wet conditions caused a large amount of mold growth on any structure that remained. The moldy odor, along with the decomposition of the dead, made for unbearable living conditions. The water and sewage system have failed and so the availability of safe potable water was very limited. The only hospital in Kelheim was located fortunately on high ground and was spared. However, the surviving residents were coming down with typhus and dysentery, and the hospital was rapidly running out of beds.

The local burgermeister showed up in the town square and was nailing posters to the wall. This was being done throughout Bavaria. The government was hiring anyone capable of assisting to help bury the dead and clean up the town, now that the flood waters had receded. Helmut and Josef jumped at the chance to have a job, even such a sad one, such as they were offered.

After a couple of months of hard labor, the many hundreds of workers had left Kelheim, although a few made Kelheim their home. Any structures in the low-lying areas that had been flooded were demolished, as it was impossible to clean them properly so people could live in them. Fortunately, many weeks after the flood, the weather has turned uncharacteristically sunny and dry. This certainly helped to dry out all the previously flooded areas. The hundreds of poor victims of the flood had been laid to rest. This included all the people that died initially in the floodwaters and the ones that died later in the hospitals of disease. Unfortunately, many were buried in mass graves, as it was the expedient thing to do. The aftermath of this tragedy has certainly tested the faith and fortitude of the survivors.

It's now the middle of August and the weather is still looking good, quite warm and pleasant. Now that they have completed the cleanup of the flood damaged areas of Kelheim, you can once again smell the lovely aroma of baking bread. Because of all the workers that were brought into Kelheim for the cleanup, the bakeries, pastry shops, and all the surviving merchants have done a brisk business. What is missing is that heavy malty aroma from the Baumer Brewery that always wafted through the town. With the brewery being destroyed, beer had to be brought into Kelheim from other regional breweries. The availability and quality were not as good as it used to be when Baumer was in business.

Helmut and Josef were walking back to the town square to get some lunch and talk about what they would do next. Helmut asks, "Why are there so many Nazi soldiers in the square?" Josef replies, "I don't know, but it looks like they are making everyone get into a line over by the tavern." They decided they better not try to resist and got on the end of the line. As they looked at the table that was set up at the front of the line, they recognized the burgermeister (the mayor), the local priest, as well as the tavern owner. The other man at the table was from the Gestapo. As they stood in line, they could read the new posters on the wall. They were from the Nazi party in Berlin directing that all German citizens would immediately have to carry government identity documents at all times.

As their turn had arrived, they stood in front of the table of dignitaries. "What are your names?" asked the burgermeister. They responded, "I am Helmut Lang" and "I am Josef Vogel." He then asked if anyone else at the table besides himself can verify the true identity of Helmut and Josef. The local priest said, "I can, as they both had been baptized in my church." The Nazi Gestapo agent asked the priest to show him the records that proved Helmut and Josef were indeed descended from Christian parents. The priest confirmed they were, as the church records were meticulous. The tavern owner said that both of their fathers would stop at the tavern and were both well- known to the townspeople. He said Helmut's father was a farmer just outside of town, and Josef's father was a stonemason in Kelheim. All of their parents are deceased now. "Very well," said the Nazi, "Issue them their papers." They were instructed to carry them at all times, as it was now their duty as German citizens. Not having them would make them subject to arrest. "Remember to contact the burgermeister, if you are planning on leaving town for any reason," said the Nazi. The guard barks at them, "You can go on your way." As they left the square, they turned and saw an elderly couple being led away. They wondered what they had done wrong to be arrested, but then they saw a white Star of David had been painted on their backs!

Josef asked Helmut if he wanted to come over to his apartment next to the local theater. Helmut said that would be fine. Josef then asks "What do you think of getting tickets to the theater tonight?" Helmut replies, "That sounds like fun, but right now, let's get some beer." After a few mugs each, they were both passed out on the floor. The rest of the afternoon had passed, and it was now early evening. Helmut awakens and yells out, "Hey Josef, wake up! It's getting dark out. Where did the day go? We have to get cleaned up and get dinner before the show." Josef replies as he slowly awakens and rubs his face. "Alright! We definitely had one too many mugs of beer today, my friend."

Josef says, "There is a very fine restaurant down the block from the theater. It may be expensive, but we deserve to splurge a little. This has turned out to be a terrible year." Helmut replies "Maybe a night out on the town would lift our spirits. The time has come to start making some hard choices. Do we stay in Kelheim or try our fortunes somewhere else?" They arrived at Klippers Restaurant just before 7:00 p.m. and it appeared to be quite busy. Probably many other theater patrons had the same idea as Helmut & Josef. As they approached the oberkellner (waiter), he looked at them strangely. "Can I help you tonight? Have you ever been to our establishment before?" he said. Josef replies, "This is our first time. Do you have any tables left?" he inquired. The oberkellner said, "I have a small table near the back entrance I can give you, but I must ask you to not bother the other patrons." As they looked around the restaurant, they realized they were underdressed for the occasion. I guess they are not used to serving working-class people in this restaurant, they thought. After just a couple of minutes, their waiter returns to the table. "I am Klaus and I will be serving you tonight. Would you like to start with a glass of wine tonight?" Helmut replies, "We will both have a glass of riesling please, why don't you let us see the menu while you are getting our wine?" Klaus returns with the wine and says "Do you know what you want to order?" Helmut had just finished looking at the menu and said "I would like the schweinebraten with a side of spaetzle and red cabbage." Very well, Klaus replied, "that is a good choice as the schweinebraten is our most popular entrée," Klaus says to Josef, "And you sir, what is your pleasure?" Josef replies, "I am in the mood for some sauerbraten, with a side of knodel and sauerkraut." Klaus says smirking, "Alright gentleman, I will get the orders right in." As they waited for their dinners, they thought, "They may think we don't belong in a place like this, but I'm sure our money is as good as anyone else's." The restaurant is quite noisy tonight. Besides all the tables being occupied, there are folk dancers performing on a small stage. Josef yells to Helmut, "Let's turn our chairs so we can enjoy the dancers." As is common in Bavaria and Austria, the dancers are performing the Schuhplattler. This is a traditional style of folk dance where the performers will slap their hands to their feet, knees, and thighs. The dancers are very good and seem to have a great time. Just as they finish their dance, the waiter arrives with their dinners. He quickly places their dinners on the table and storms off without a word. Josef says to Helmut, "Everything smells delicious. Let's eat." As they had not eaten since breakfast, just mugs of beer in the early afternoon, they cleaned their plates quickly. Helmut says, "That was wonderful, the meat was tender and flavorful with a wonderful aroma". Josef replied, "I agree with you, my friend. Mine was just as good." Their waiter, Klaus, came over and said it was time to pay their bill and leave as there were other patrons waiting for their table. Helmut says to Josef, "The dinner is on me; I appreciate your friendship and the help you have given me." Josef was quite surprised at the gesture, as he knew they had little money. Helmut said "Do not worry my friend, I have been able to save up a little." He still did not let on that he had the money from the sale of the farm. Josef replies "Alright, please let me reciprocate your kindness and I will purchase the theater tickets."

They arrived at the theater at about 8:15 p.m. for the 8:30 p.m. show. "Do you have any seats left?" they asked the attendant. She replies, "Yes, we have a couple of empty rows still available in the balcony." Josef says, "Alright, we will take two seats." As they made their way to their seats, they both remarked how hot and smokey it was in the theater. Maybe this wasn't such a good idea after all, they thought. They read their programs and realized the theater was putting on a variety show tonight. A delightful combination of some folk singers, yodelers, dancers, and a well-known Oompah band were performing. A young girl was coming up the aisle selling cigars. Helmut and Josef decided why not have one, as most of the people in the audience were smoking either a cigar or cigarette. This was the first time Helmut and Josef had gone to the theater in their lives. They were very pleased with the quality and professionalism of the performers. One act was just as good as the next, and there was a brief break between the acts. The variety show was well received by all in attendance, and the evening was hurrying by. It's a few minutes after 10:00 p.m. and the show has just concluded. The performers were met with a thunderous applause from the audience. As Helmut and Josef leave, they thought why not stop by the local tavern for a drink? The tavern was not that busy when they got there, but it will be when the other theater patrons arrive. The bar dame asks, "What can I get for you two?" Josef replies, "I think we had enough beer today, so how about a couple of glasses of zwetchgenwasser (plum brandy) for our nightcap." As Helmut and Josef drink their brandy, they remarked on what an enjoyable dinner and show they were fortunate to have had today. The last few months had certainly been terrible, so it was nice to have a night out. Helmut says to Josef, "Tomorrow we will have to go out and look for work. It will not be easy." Josef replies, "That is true, but for tonight, let's just try to enjoy the drinks. Tomorrow will come soon enough." Over in the corner of the tavern, there is a table with four German soldiers drinking beer. The more they drank, the louder and more obnoxious they became. "Let's toast to our beloved Fuhrer, Adolf Hitler. Raise a glass for our Fatherland, down with filthy gypsies and jews." Helmut and Josef hold no such belief that they are better than anyone else. Why do they act this way they thought to themselves? After listening to the soldiers for a while, Helmut and Josef decide it's best to call it a night before things turn violent. But it's too late, as the soldiers call out to them. Join us in a toast to the Fuhrer they yell. Helmut and Josef are startled at their proclamation. One of soldiers confronts them and says, "What's the matter with you two? Are you not loyal Germans? Show us your papers." Two of the soldiers then inspect their documents. As everything is in order, they say, "Finish your drinks and get the hell out, we only drink with loyal Germans, you scum. Don't let us see you in this tavern again." Helmut exclaims, "Hurry, let's get out of here before they change their minds. You are so lucky you live only a few buildings down from here. I have four or five blocks to get back to my place." Josef replies, "Get some rest and I will meet you in the morning and we can start looking for work."

Well, it's a new morning and a new month, September has arrived. Hopefully, new opportunities will come our way, Helmut thought. I wonder where Josef is this morning? He knows we are going to look for work today. Helmut is standing in front of the tavern he lives above, which is in the town square. He looks up and sees Josef slowly trudging his way down the street towards him. Helmut greets him, "Josef, you look terrible. What's wrong?" He replies, "I am hungover from yesterday's drinking and I feel terrible." Helmut is not surprised. "Well then, let's go sit at the cafe and get some coffee and some breakfast. That will help you feel better. Let's sit outside, as the fresh air will do you good." The waitress came over to take their orders. Helmut says he will order for them both. "Give my friend Josef some very strong coffee and an order of eiekuchen with fruit topping. No greasy sausage for you this morning, and I won't have any either." For you, sir, the waitress asks? Helmut replies, "I would like a bauer omelet and some eiekuchen, and of course coffee." As they are waiting for their breakfast, Helmut says, "You know, that was not an enjoyable experience with those soldiers last night. We better keep a low profile today, as we don't need the trouble." Josef replies, "That's right, we are going to have to be more careful!" As they consume their breakfast, they lament all the changes that are happening in Kelheim and throughout Germany. Is this Nazi thing really better than what we had before? Sure, things were tough, but now it seems if you are not of the right religion or believe differently than they do, you are looked down upon. Helmut says, "Josef, we must keep our voices low, so no one will overhear us." He replies, "Of course. Let's finish breakfast and be on our way."

As they leave the square, they decide to go over to the construction site at the other end of town. They have been building a cathedral for the last 10 years and it is slowly nearing completion. As they arrive, they seek out the construction manager. Josef says, "We are looking for work. My father was a stonemason all his life." The manager replies, "I could use you both for a couple of weeks. Your job will be to mix and deliver mortar to the masons. This is hard back-breaking work, but you two young Aryan men look like you can handle it." The mortar, which is a mixture of cement, sand and lime, is prepared in small batches and then delivered to the masons. Either job is very physical, and once the mortar is mixed, someone has to climb up the scaffold to deliver where needed. Josef starts out mixing, and Helmut does the delivering. At the end of the day, they are quite exhausted. Helmut says, "tomorrow we can ask the foreman if we can alternate both of our jobs each day." Josef smirks, "Sounds like a good idea. I think a couple of weeks of this is about all I can stand. One nice thing about this job is we get paid daily." The two weeks go by pretty fast, but they are so exhausted each night about all they can do is eat some dinner before passing out for the night. A couple of weeks pass and it is Friday night and they think, "Thank God this job is over." Helmut asks, "What do you want to do tonight, Josef?" He replies, "Tonight, we are going to get a hot bath and a massage before we hit the tavern. I know just the place. It is a popular bath house near the town square. Bring a clean change of clothes with you and we will meet there at 6:00 p.m." As they enter the bathhouse, they are directed to the locker room and told to strip out of your clothes and grab a large towel from the shelf. They are then brought to a room with multiple tubs set in the floor and told to use an open one. Helmut says to Josef, "This is not what I expected. Why do we have to be in here with all these naked men!!" Josef laughs hysterically and replies, "You were so sheltered, my friend. Please relax and enjoy, the best is yet to come!!" After bathing, they are sent to the steam room down the hall, which Helmut has never tried. Josef says "Give it a few minutes, the heat will open your pores, and relax your muscles." It is so steamy in the room and it is hard to see even the person sitting next to you. After about five minutes, Helmut calls it quits as the steam and heat make it hard to breathe. Josef says, "Alright, let's cool down a bit before we get our massage." The boys go back through the locker room to the other side of the bathhouse. There they meet their masseuse, Alfred. He says, "Come gentleman, who wants to go first?" Josef replies, "My friend Helmut can go. It's his first time." Helmut climbs on the table with a towel covering his backside and Alfred starts his massage working down from his shoulders to his legs. Helmut says to Josef, "I cannot believe how relaxed I feel. My muscles feel like jelly." He replies, "That's good. I'm glad you liked it. Would you like a happy ending?" Helmut responds, "I don't know what that is, but if you think I will like it, why not?" Alfred then tells them there will be an extra charge for that service. "No problem, I want to take care of my friend," Josef says. Alfred tells Helmut to relax and stay put as he leaves the room. A few minutes passed and a lovely, tall blonde woman enters the room. She says, "My name is Helga. I am here to give you a happy ending." She begins to massage Helmut, but it shocked him when she removes his towel. "Turn over," she orders. Josef tells Helmut it's alright, and to do as she says, as he steps out of the room. Helga says, "Close your eyes and relax," as she begins to message his genitals. Helmut quickly develops a raging hard on, which she makes fast work of. He thinks, "I have never had a woman touch me as he explodes into climax. After a few minutes, Josef steps back in the room. Helmut asks, "Have you done this before, Josef?" He replies, "Many times. Helmut there are showers in the next room. Go get cleaned up and change into your clean clothes. I will meet you outside in a few minutes. It's my turn now!!!"

Helmut waits outside the bathhouse nervously until Josef arrives. Helmut asks Josef, "What did you get me into?" Josef replies, "Did you not enjoy it, my friend? It's a safe, fun thing to do, no risk of pregnancy or disease. I have done it many times." Helmut was ashamed to admit how much he enjoyed it. After all, he is a 19 yr. old virgin who grew up a sheltered farm boy. Helmut admits to Josef they may have to come here again next week. Josef says, "Whatever you like, my friend. For now, let's get to the tavern. Remember, we should not go to the same tavern by the theater where those soldiers were." Helmut responds, "Not a problem, as there is a tavern on almost every block. Let's just go back to the square and go to the tavern I live above. I was talking with my landlord Heinrich this morning and he said they would be serving freshly made bratwurst tonight. And besides, if we drink too much, we can just go upstairs and crash at my place." As they arrive, they see the tavern is busy, so they take a couple of chairs at the bar. The bartender and owner Heinrich comes over and asks his favorite tenant what he and his friend want. Helmut says "We both want beer, brats, and kraut." Heinrich replies. "Jawohl, coming right up!"

Helmut was enjoying his mug of Munich style dunkel beer. This type of beer is dark in color, full-bodied, malty, with notes of toasted bread crust and not sweet. These dark, full-bodied beers are typical of beers brewed throughout Bavaria. Josef tried a mug of Pilsner Urquell, which is a light-colored blonde lager which differs from the traditional Munich style beer Helmut is drinking. Josef remarks, "I really like this pilsner. I think I can drink many more of these, as they are not as heavy as what you are having, Helmut." Everyone was having a great time and the piano player was keeping the atmosphere lively. Heinrich and his staff have just delivered a fresh round of beer to everyone. "Wait," the piano player calls out, and immediately starts playing and singing a short song that is used in the beer tents at Oktoberfest. "Ein Prosit, Ein Prosit, Der Gemutlichkeit, Ein Prosit, Ein Prosit, Der Gemutlichkeit." The phrase translates to, "A toast, A toast of comfort," The entire tavern raises their glasses and says, "Oans, Zwoa, Drei, Gsuffa!" which translates to, "One, Two, Three, Drink!"

Just as they complete their beer toast, their dinners arrive. Helmut says to Josef, "Heinrich was not lying. The bratwurst is quite fresh and delicious." Josef replies, "Everything is wonderful, great suggestion eating here." As they are just finishing their last bite of food, several German soldiers enter the tavern. Suddenly, one man at the end of the bar bolts from the room out the back door. The soldiers take chase and gunshots are heard from the alley. The patrons initially don't know if he was caught or killed. Evidently, it seems whoever it was has escaped, as the soldiers return to the tavern and start questioning the people at the bar. They say, "Do you know him? Where does he live? What were you talking about? Papers! Papers! All of you at the bar! Let me see your papers!

As they are at the opposite end of the bar, Helmut and Josef are the last to be questioned. They are asked what they know of this man. They reply, "Nothing. We were just having dinner and drinking a beer." One of the soldiers exclaims, "Wait a minute, aren't you the two Schweinhund from the tavern by the theater? We threw you out of there a couple of weeks ago." Helmut replies sheepishly, "Yes, it is true." The soldier replies, "I told you before, I don't think you are loyal Germans. What do you know about that man? Where do you live?" Helmut tells them he lives in the upstairs room above the tavern.

The soldier barks out, “Dieter and Yodel, go upstairs and search his room.” After a few minutes, they return and say, “We found nothing.” This only further enrages the soldier, and he screams at Helmut. “Tell me what you know about that man, tell me!” Helmut insists over and over that he does not know him. Suddenly, the soldier takes his rifle and, using the butt of the rifle, hits Helmut in the head. Helmut falls to the ground, unconscious. The soldiers yell to everyone that this is what will happen to them if someone does not offer information. “We have your names and we will be back,” they exclaim as they leave the tavern.

## CHAPTER 2

# FLIGHT

A couple of days have passed and Helmut is just waking up in his bed. He hears a voice tell him to get up very slowly. Helmut exclaims, "Why? What happened? My head hurts." Josef tells him, "It should hurt, as that soldier hit you in the head and gave you a concussion. The doctor said you will be better in a few more days. Let me run downstairs to the tavern and see if they have anything I can get for you to eat and drink." Helmut does not remember Josef and Heinrich carrying him to his room after the soldier's attack, as he slumps back into bed. Josef yells, "Hey Heinrich, can you send up some coffee and some bread and cheese? Our patient is awake." Heinrich replies, "Jawohl, right away, but Josef, I want to talk to you privately. This is not the first time you and Helmut have been hassled by the soldiers. I think as soon as Helmut can travel, you may want to get out of Kelheim." Josef says, "I was thinking the same thing. I have relatives down in Friedrichshafen that we could stay with. We will decide in a few days when Helmut is up to traveling."

A few more days pass and Helmut is feeling much better, although he cannot bend down as he gets light-headed when he does. Helmut says, "Josef, I need your help once again, my friend. Would you move the bed over from the wall?" Helmut still has most of the money from the sale of the farm hidden in the wall at the base of the bed. "Just press your hands on the wall and you will feel a loose board. Reach in and bring me the bag that is hidden inside." Josef does as instructed, but as he opens the small bag, he is astonished at what he finds. "Where did this money come from?" Josef asks. Helmut finally confides in Josef that he sold his farm after his parents passed and had been hiding it. He thought the soldiers may have found it when they searched his room. Josef shakes his head and says, "I was wondering why you were able to pay for both our dinners when we ate at Kleppers Restaurant?" Helmut says to Josef, "You and Heinrich are right in saying we should get out of Kelheim, but maybe out of Germany all together!! But how would we get the visas and travel documents needed to leave the country?"

Josef replies, "Helmut, I was telling Heinrich that I have relations that live down in Friedrichshafen. Maybe we could stay with them for a while. I will send them a telegram today and see what they think." Only a day goes by and a delivery boy shows up at his apartment with a telegram. Josef thinks to himself that was an awful quick response. The message is from Josef's Uncle Gerhart Vogel, who is his father's brother, and his Aunt Lena Vogel. It reads, "We anxiously await your arrival, Josef, and your friend is also welcome." Josef goes back to the tavern, "Helmut, I have wonderful news. We are going to stay at my uncle's house in Friedrichshafen." Helmut replies "That is great, but we must report to the burgermeister before we can leave town. Let's go right now!"

As they arrive at the City Hall, they are directed to wait as the burgermeister is busy with the Gestapo. After a few minutes, they recognize the Gestapo agent as he leaves the building as the one from the square who issued them their papers. The secretary then leads them into Herr Schmidt's office. He says, "I cannot believe you are here, as I needed to see you to update your papers. Well, what can I do for you two?" Josef replies, "Well, Herr Schmidt, my friend and I would like to travel down to Friedrichshafen." He replies, "For what purpose? You must give me a reason?" Josef tells him they have been invited to stay at his uncle's house. Herr Schmidt says, "The Gestapo have just updated the records. I heard about your altercation at the tavern with the soldiers." After double checking their records, he tells them, "Good news. You may travel, but neither of you is permitted to leave Germany. I think it is a good idea for you to get out of Kelheim for a while." Herr Schmidt then updates the stamps on their papers and they are sent on their way. As they leave the building, Helmut suggests to Josef that they gather his belongings first, and then go to Helmut's, as his apartment is closer to the train station. Josef tells Helmut, "After what happened to you, we need to leave Kelheim today!" Helmut replies "You will get no argument from me about that!" After they gather Helmut's things, they move the bed to get the cash. Helmut tells Josef, "I think it is a good idea that we split the money up in case one of us is arrested. It's not a lot of money, but it's something that will help us get started in a new city. There should be room to hide it in our boots in case they search us." Josef appreciates the trust Helmut has shown him and says, "If we get separated, we will meet at my uncle's house."

It's early afternoon as they arrive at the train station. It appears to be quite busy with many travelers, but unfortunately, many soldiers are standing guard there as well. Josef tells Helmut, "Do not worry, my friend. Our papers are all in order. Stay relaxed until we get on the train." They get in line at the ticket counter, but it takes a while as the line is quite long. When they finally get their turn, they ask for two tickets to Friedrichshafen on the next train. The attendant tells them seats are available on the 5:00 a.m. train if they want to wait. Helmut replies, "Jawohl, two tickets and we will wait." As the evening goes on, they patiently wait for the morning train. The station has a tiny restaurant and they can get a bratwurst and some beer to tide them over. As the evening drags on, people are coming and going, but pretty uneventful. It's about one o'clock in the morning now and they have been soundly sleeping on their bench. Suddenly, they are startled awake by shouting and loud whistles. The guards appear to be chasing someone by the trains. Several gunshots ring out and then quiet. Helmut remarks, "This can't be good. What should we do?" Josef replies, "What do we do? Nothing, of course. I told you before, stay calm." Well, Helmut was right to be concerned as the guards start going person to person checking their papers. On the other side of the room, the guards appear to have arrested someone. As they turn towards them, Helmut and Josef become even more apprehensive. Helmut is about to lose it and is on the verge of bolting. The guard approaches them and asks for their papers, which are found to be in order. The guards then search them and pats them down, looking for weapons. Josef was right to tell Helmut to stay calm. He knew everything was in order. Both were relieved they had hidden the money in their boots, as some of the more unscrupulous soldiers were known to steal people's valuables. Helmut tells Josef, "Thank God they have moved on. I can't wait to get on that train." Josef replies, "The train leaves in three hours. I'm too nervous to go back to sleep, but let's just try to calm down!" The next few hours pass without incident, and they can finally board the train. The conductor takes their tickets and checks their names off the manifest and they are on their way.

They first travel south to Munich. After changing trains, they will travel west to Memmingen and then turn south to Friedrichshafen. Altogether, the trip should take around 8-9 hours with stops and transfers included. It is Helmut's first time riding on a train. Josef had the good fortune to visit his aunt and uncle yearly while growing up in Kelheim, so he was quite familiar with train travel. Helmut and Josef are having a good time on their trip to Friedrichshafen. The weather is still good and they are enjoying the picturesque countryside. The route taken is mostly flat terrain as the Alps mountains lay to the south of Munich. Along the way, the passengers in their train car frequently break out into song to help pass the time. Fortunately, the trip was uneventful, and they reach their destination in the early afternoon.

The town of Friedrichshafen is the southwest German State of Baden-Wurttemberg. It lies about 200 miles southwest of Kelheim on Lake Constance. It is near the southern border of Germany, which adjoins both Switzerland and Austria. This is the town where Josef's father had grown up prior to moving to Kelheim in search of work. Friedrichshafen was well-known for its Maybach engine factory and the Zeppelin airship factory. The Zeppelin is an airship that has a rigid frame covered by fabric and filled with lighter than air gas. They named it for its inventor, Ferdinand von Zeppelin, who held the German patent starting in 1895 and started commercial service in 1910. The Zeppelin differed from the later developed Blimp in that the Zeppelin had a rigid metal frame. A major drawback of the Zeppelin's in service at this time, up to and including the Hindenburg tragedy on May 6, 1937, was they used hydrogen as their lighter Than air gas to give lift. The Germans used hydrogen, which is flammable instead of the rarer helium which is non-flammable. Most helium came from the United States oil industry, and the United States government would not allow it to be sold to Germany.

Helmut and Josef grab a taxi to take them to Josef's uncle's house. Josef tells Helmut, "My aunt is a wonderful cook and an excellent baker, so plan on putting on a few pounds during our stay." Helmut replies, "You know how much I love my pastries, so I'm looking forward to it." As the taxi stops in front of a tailor shop in the downtown business district, Helmut asks if they have arrived. Josef replies, "Yes, this is my uncle's store and they live in the back". As they enter, Josef's uncle greets them. "Welcome, Welcome, it is so good to see you Josef," as they hug. "It has been way too long." Then Uncle Gerhart turns to Helmut and tells him how happy he is to meet him, and that they can both stay as long as they wish. "I am going to close my shop early today. Come in the back as Aunt Lena has been waiting for you." As they enter the living quarters, Uncle Gerhart yells out, "Lena, Lena, the boys are here." She appears from the side room. "I was just getting your bedroom ready. Come, give me a hug." After they both embrace, they go sit in the parlor. Uncle Gerhart asks them if they would like to have some brandy. Before they can answer, he tells Lena, "Get four glasses and open a fresh bottle." They then spend the next few hours drinking and reminiscing about old times when Josef was younger, and getting acquainted with Helmut. At that point, Helmut asks to be excused. "Would you mind if I lay down for a few minutes before dinner? I seem to have a splitting headache." Uncle Gerhart chuckles and says, "Of course, I guess I got you a little drunk". After Helmut leaves the room, Josef confides with them. It's not the liquor, it's that Helmut suffered a concussion at the hands of the soldiers.

Helmut laid in bed and rested for about an hour until he heard Josef's Aunt Lena calling that dinner was ready. He sat up and realized that his headache was feeling much better. But now his stomach was growling, as he was quite hungry. As he left his room, Uncle Gerhart asked if he was feeling better. Helmut replies, "Yes, Dunka, just hungry now." Uncle Gerhart smiles and says, "My wife has prepared a feast for us to celebrate your visit, come let's go sit down in the dining room." Well, Uncle Gerhart was not exaggerating, as dinner was a combination of wiener schnitzel (veal cutlet), and spaetzle (fried noodle), kartoffelsalat (Bavarian potato salad), bratwurst, which is served with rotkohl (cooked red cabbage), and to wash it all down some lovely dry, fruity white wine. As they continue with their meal, Aunt Lena laughs out loud and says, "I cannot believe how much you boys are eating." Helmut and Josef reply "Sorry, Sorry." Lena says, "No need to apologize, I purposely made extra and I'm glad I did." After a leisurely dinner, Aunt Lena clears the table and cleans up. Uncle Gerhart takes Helmut and Josef out in the small garden behind their home. They each take a chair and Uncle Gerhart lights up his pipe and says, "I want to ask you something, and I would appreciate a straight answer. Why did you really come?" Josef replies, "Well, to be perfectly honest with you, we have found ourselves in a precarious position.

There is a group of soldiers that keep hassling us and we don't know the reason for it, other than they can." Uncle Gerhart says, "I thought it was something like that, but are you wanted men?" Josef replies, "Absolutely not, we have never been arrested, our record is clean and our papers are in order, but we thought it prudent to get out of Kelheim." Helmut interjects, "I tell you Herr Vogel, sometimes I wish we could leave Germany." Uncle Gerhart grows angry, "Lower your voice. Do not let anyone ever hear you talk like that, or you will be arrested. You are welcome to stay as long as you like, but you must be careful. I apologize for losing my temper, but the secret police have informants everywhere. Let's just sit out here and enjoy the evening. Aunt Lena will be out soon." They all sat out for another hour before calling it a night. Helmut says, "Thank you, Herr Vogel and Frau Vogel. The dinner was excellent and we appreciate your hospitality." Josef adds, "I have so missed visiting you as it has been too long. Thank you again." As they retire for the night, they think about how fortunate they are to have been taken in by such compassionate, loving people. Josef tells Helmut, "Tomorrow, why don't we spend the day sightseeing? We can think about looking for work in a day or two." Helmut replies, "Excellent idea. Maybe we can even take a boat ride on the lake." They both enter their shared bedroom and are fast asleep as soon as their heads hit the pillow.

Josef and Helmut awake the next morning around 9:00 a.m. feeling well rested. As they sit up in bed, they think to themselves, what is that wonderful aroma waffling into their bedroom. Josef says, "It must be my Aunt Lena, she loves to bake." Helmut replies, "What are we waiting for? Hurry and get dressed!" As they enter the kitchen, they find Aunt Lena at the stove. She looks at them and says, "I was wondering if you were ever going to wake up. Come sit at the table for breakfast." Josef asks, "Where is Uncle Gerhart?" She replies, "He had to open the shop, so he already ate. He wants to see you before you go out today." Josef asks, "What have you made this morning? It all smells wonderful." As she steps to the table, she tells them she has been up since 5:00

a.m. baking so she hopes they will enjoy it. Aunt Lena says to Josef, "Would you please pour coffee for all of us while I get the pastries on the table?" Helmut asks what she has made. She replies, "I made some apfelstrudel (apple strudel), pretzels and mustard, and some ausgezogene krapfen (yeast donuts covered with vanilla sugar)." After they try each of Aunt Lena's creations, Josef remarks on how wonderful everything is. "The donuts are soft and warm and melt in your mouth and the pretzels are salty and crunchy on the outside. The strudel is to die for, so flaky and full of flavor." She replies, "I am so happy that you are enjoying it so much. Eat as much as you want. Hopefully, it will sustain you until dinner." After breakfast is over, they help Aunt Lena clean up from breakfast. There is some strudel left that Uncle Gerhart will enjoy this evening, but the donuts are all gone. Aunt Lena says to them, "Here are the rest of the pretzels. You can have them for lunch if you get hungry. It's going to be a little cooler out today, so you will need a jacket if you go down to the lakeshore. I wrapped the pretzels in paper, so just tuck them in your jacket pocket." They both thanked Aunt Lena for the wonderful treats and then they both hugged her goodbye. "See you later," they exclaimed as they left the house and entered the tailor's shop.

As they walk through the shop, they are greeted by Uncle Gerhart, "Good morning boys, you look well rested. Did you fill up on Aunt Lena's pastries?" Josef replies, "Yes Uncle, we both are feeling fine this morning, although maybe a little sugar high after that breakfast," he chuckled. Uncle Gerhart says, "Look at me, can't you tell I love all the pastries she makes? Soon I will have to tailor myself a new suit!" Helmut thanks him again for everything and says, "We are planning on relaxing and sightseeing for a couple of days, would that be alright with you Herr Vogel?" He replies, "Of course it would, just be careful and don't forget your papers." They both reply, "We will be careful. See you tonight." As they leave the shop, they decide to walk down to the lake and take in the scenery there. It's only several blocks to the waterfront, and it is an unseasonably brisk morning. Josef says, "Aunt Lena was right when she told us to bring our jackets." As they walk the lake-front promenade, there is a slightly strong breeze blowing in from the lake. As they walk, they are struck by the large number of shops and taverns that line the promenade. Helmut tells Josef, "Look there. I see a couple of bakeries." Josef replies, "We will have no need of them with Aunt Lena around." The promenade is quite busy with shoppers and sightseers like them. Joseph says, "Hey, look there on the dock. A lot of people are boarding that ship. The sign says lake cruise." Helmut replies, "Let's do it. We were just talking about it yesterday." As they board the ship, there are a couple of soldiers checking papers, which were done without incident. The soldiers then join the passengers on the ship. Helmut mumbles out loud, "Why are they here?" The passenger next to him responds that since Lake Constance borders Germany, Austria, and Switzerland, they are on board to make sure no one tries to get off the ship. There are no stops allowed. It will just hug the coastline until returning to Friedrichshafen. The scenery is quite breathtaking, small towns, the forests, and the majestic Alps towering over the area. After several hours of cruising, the ship returned to Friedrichshafen's dock. It was a fantastic time had by all. As they exit the dock, Josef and Helmut decide to stop in one of the taverns on the promenade. Josef says, "Let's try this one. It doesn't look overly crowded." As they take a seat at the bar, the bar dame greets them. "I am Giselle. What can I get for you, gentleman, a dunkel, a pilsner, an ale, or a whit? Would you like to try a Belgium lambic?" Josef and Helmut both cry out at the same time, "Wait, Wait, we are so confused, what are you saying?" Giselle laughs out loud and tells them, "This is my father's tavern and when he was young, he worked in a brewery. He loves serving a variety of beers, and beer styles." Helmut replies, "I worked at a brewery taking care of loading the trucks. My friend Josef here worked in the breweries packaging department. But I never learned much about beer at all." Giselle asks, "While things are slow right now, would you like me to enlighten you with all things beer? I am not an expert on any of it, but I can give you some information." That sounds great, they both exclaim! Giselle starts to give them the breakdown. "The difference between a traditional German dark beer and a light-colored pilsner style beer is because of the water they brew with, and how dark they roast the malt. The difference between an ale and a lager is each uses a different type of yeast and the fermentation temps are different. They brew whit beer with wheat, instead of barley. In Belgium they brew a lambic with wild yeast." Josef replies, "I think I am just as confused as before, but you have made me thirstier. Let's try some ale." Giselle replies, "Good choice." and quickly fetches their drinks. Then they remember their pockets are stuffed with Aunt Lena's pretzels, which they happily eat and wash down with the delicious ale.

Giselle's father, Max, the tavern owner, has just returned from running an errand. "How are things, Giselle?" he exclaims. She replies, "Very well, I want you to meet Josef and Helmut, two of our new customers." Max greets them and asks where they are from. Josef replies, "We are from Kelheim and are visiting my Uncle Herr Gerhart, the tailor." Max responds, "I know who your uncle is. He did some tailoring for me a few years ago. Are you planning on staying in Friedrichshafen for a long time?" They tell him they are in town looking for work and if they don't find anything worthwhile, they will move on. Helmut tells him how Giselle mentioned her father had worked in a couple of breweries when he was younger. Helmut explains that he and Josef had worked at the Baumer Brewery. Max responds, "I worked in the brewhouse and fermenting cellars most of the time. I can tell you some stories." They both respond, "Yes. Please. We would love to hear them." Max explains, "One of my first jobs at the brewery was to collect the yeast when fermentation was finished, so they could reuse it. "The fermenting tanks were tall open top vessels which were quite dangerous. If you were not careful, the carbon dioxide being released could make you pass out or even kill you. As we were making ale, the yeast we used would float to the top when fermentation was complete.

My job was to scoop it out with a long-handled strainer and place it in buckets that we could pitch into the next fermenter. Well, I ran around that tank for hours and hours trying to scoop the yeast. I was so exhausted. The next day I was back doing the same job when my boss came to check on me. He laughed and told me they had played a joke on me as they usually do with the new guys. The trick to collecting the yeast, he explained, was to stand in one place, use your wrists to scoop in one direction, and grab the yeast as it floats past. No need to run yourself ragged!"

Helmut replies, "That is a great story. Thank you for sharing it." As they get up to leave the tavern, Josef says, "We really enjoyed the ale and the stories. Hopefully, we will see you again soon." Max and Giselle reply, "You are welcome here anytime!" As it is still midafternoon, they decide to keep walking and continue to check out the town. The temperature has warmed, so they removed their jackets. As they look out in the distance, they see a large Zeppelin tethered. Josef tells Helmut, "Let's walk over there and check out that airship." Helmut replies, "We may have to get a taxi if it is too far. Hard to tell from here." It turns out to be a little over an hour's walk from the waterfront tavern. As they arrive, they are amazed at the size of the Zeppelin. They could see the name on the fin. It said Graf Zeppelin. There was a fence around the field where it was tethered. Helmut yelled to the workers in the field, "Does anyone know how long the Zeppelin is?" The one closest to them replied, "It is 236.6 meters long (776 ft)." As Helmut and Josef circled the perimeter of the field, they came upon a ticket office. They went in to see if they could get some information on the airship. "Can I help you?" asked the attendant. Helmut asks "How far does the Zeppelin travel?" The attendant replies. "Four years ago, in 1929, it circumnavigated the world in about 3 weeks," but now it makes regular trips between Friedrichshafen and Rio de Janeiro, Brazil, as well as stops in other European cities." At the time, Brazil had a sizable German expatriate population, so The Graf Zeppelin provided passenger and mail service to them. He told them it was quite an expensive way to travel, so it was reserved for the rich. Josef asks, "What would it cost for us to travel to Brazil?" The attendant replies, "1500 Deutschemarks (about $590 dollars) each." Josef says, "I see what you mean about having to be rich. That's what I would make in one-year!" As they leave the ticket office, Helmut says to Josef, "Wouldn't it be something to go to Brazil, and then on to America." Josef replies, "I don't think we are ever getting out of Germany!"

Helmut says, "I think we should start heading back to your aunt and uncle's house." He replies, "Yes, let's get going as it will be a long walk, and we don't want to be late for dinner." As they arrive, they find Aunt Lena in the kitchen preparing dinner. Uncle Gerhart calls them to join him in the parlor for a sip of brandy, which was his nightly before dinner custom. Uncle Gerhart tells Helmut, "Go easy on the brandy tonight. We don't want you getting sick again." Helmut replies, "My head feels much better today. I did not have one headache and I think the worst may be over." Uncle Gerhart tells him that is good to hear, and then toasts to their health and success. As they finish their brandy, Aunt Lena calls them to dinner, "Come Gerhart, boys. Let's eat while it's still hot!" Josef asks, "What have you made us tonight, Aunt Lena?" She replies, "I fried some Fellchen, which is a nice light whitefish from Lake Constance, a side of Flammkuchen (quiche), which has eggs, bacon, and onions. For dessert, as I know you boys will still be hungry, I baked a wonderful Schwarzwälder Kirschtorte (black forest cake which is a chocolate cake with cream and cherries)." After dinner is over, the boys help Aunt Lena clean the table and wash the dishes. She thanks them for the help and tells them to join Uncle Gerhart in the parlor and she will bring them some dessert. Uncle Gerhart asks how their day of sightseeing went. Josef replies, "We took a boat ride on Lake Constance, stopped in a tavern, and saw the Graf Zeppelin." They tell him they have heard about Zeppelins, but don't think they had ever seen one before. Helmut says, "I am so impressed with how big it is." Uncle Gerhart says, "My childhood friend, Wolfgang, works as a foreman at the Zeppelin factory. He told me for all its size, it can only carry 20 passengers and about 36 crew members."

After a few minutes, Aunt Lena enters the parlor with a pot of hot coffee and they all take a cup. She asks "Is everyone having some Schwarzwälder Kirschtorte?" They all answer, "Of course." Once dessert is finished and she has cleaned the dishes, Uncle Gerhart asks her if she would play some songs on the piano. It turns out Aunt Lena is a wonderful piano player and they spend the evening singing songs and having her serenade them. She has grown quite weary and will be the first to retire for the evening. They all thank her as she hugs and kisses them goodnight.

Now that they are alone, Josef asks his uncle if they can speak confidentially with him. Uncle Gerhart replies, "Of course, but we must keep our voices low for the reasons we discussed earlier, and we don't want to disturb your aunt." Josef replies, "I have been corresponding with Uncle Otto, your brother, and he has invited me to visit him in the United States. Helmut and I are in agreement that we both want to get out of Germany. We don't want to just visit Uncle Otto in America, but want to go there permanently. But the Gestapo have put us on a list that prevents us from leaving Germany. Who knows what they will do to us next?" Uncle Gerhart confides in them, "You know, Aunt Lena and I were obviously sad to see Otto leave Germany. He left in 1914. Oh my, nineteen years ago, where has the time gone? He was always very adventurous, but how could we begrudge him a chance at a better life. Aunt Lena and I went through many hard times, especially after the war. But Germany was our home, and we never considered leaving." He tells them before the war, there was quite a lot of emigration to the United States from Germany and it was very easy to get a visa. In the last 10 years, that process has become harder and harder. Most times almost impossible to do legally. Josef and Helmut sit up in their chairs and say, "What do you mean legally? There is an illegal way? How would you know about such things?" Uncle Gerhart replies, "Look, boys, I am an old tailor now, but in my younger days, let's just say many of my friends were what you would call criminals!" He goes on to tell the boys that his childhood friend, Wolfgang, whom they spoke of earlier, is still involved in many illegal activities. If there is a way to get you out of Germany, he would be the one to talk to. He tells them getting out is only half the problem, it's finding a way to get into America. Since that country has been fighting an economic depression, new immigrants are unwanted by the government. Uncle Gerhart says, "I will call Wolfgang in the morning and see if we can set up a meeting. Now let's call it a night!" As they lay in bed, they are on the one hand happy to even have the possibility of leaving Germany, but are terrified of what will happen if they are caught.

It's early Friday morning as Uncle Gerhart creeps into the boy's room, "Josef, Helmut, wake up!" he whispers. They are both now awake and Josef replies, "What is it, Uncle?" He replies, "I have spoken to Wolfgang and he will come here tonight after dinner, but he wants you to stay in the house. Do not leave under any circumstances." Josef and Helmut agree to stay in and spend the day helping Aunt Lena clean the house and doing some minor repairs. It was good that they kept busy, as they were both apprehensive, but the day went by quickly. As they are about to sit down to dinner, Uncle Gerhart takes Aunt Lena aside and tells her that Wolfgang will come over after dinner. He asks her if she would mind going next door to the neighbors so they can talk privately. She replies, "I will do as you ask, but please do not get yourself into trouble. You know what happens to people that get involved with Wolfgang!" As they finish dinner, Aunt Lena makes note of how quiet everyone has been. She rises from her chair and asks them to do the cleanup, as she is going to visit the neighbor. As she opens the back door, she comes face to face with Wolfgang. He says, "Lena, you look wonderful. I have missed seeing you." She replies, "Thank you, Wolfy, as they embrace. Now don't you get Gerhart into any trouble, you hear!" Wolfgang laughs loudly and says, "You know me, Lena, would I do that?" She replies, "That's the problem Wolfy, I know you too well!" After she leaves, they all go into the parlor and have some brandy. Wolfgang says to Gerhardt, "You said on the phone that you needed my help. What is going on, my friend?" He replies, "Do you remember my nephew Josef, my brother Klaus's son." Wolfgang replies, "Of course I do. All grown up, I see, and who is your friend?" Helmut rises to greet him. "I am Helmut, Josef's friend from Kelheim." They sit back down and Gerhart explains that Josef and Helmut want to leave Germany and make their way to America so they can stay with my other brother, Otto. He explains that the Gestapo have put them on restriction and they may not travel outside of Germany, besides the fact that it is almost impossible to get a visa to go to the United States. Wolfgang listens intently and then tells them, "What you are asking is difficult for many reasons, but not impossible. In order to make this happen, we must act quickly. Every month that goes by, the Gestapo gets more and more powerful. The other major issue is money. There are many people that need to be paid off to get what we need. Off the top of my head, it could take up to a thousand Deutschmarks." Helmut interjects, "I have that available for Josef and I, so money should not be an issue." Wolfgang responds, "Should I ask where you got such a sum of money?" Helmut says, "It was from the sale of my parents' farm. It's all legitimate." Wolfgang tells them it will take a couple of days to figure things out, and he will return Sunday night with the plans. Wolfgang then instructs them not to leave the house, as he does not want them to get into trouble or draw any attention to themselves. Uncle Gerhart replies, "Thank you for coming, Wolfgang. The boys will do as you ask. See you Sunday night." Wolfgang thanks him for the brandy and leaves out the back door.

It has been a long couple of days for Josef and Helmut as they wait for Wolfgang's return. It's early October, and the weather has grown colder over the last few weeks. Now it's Sunday night and Aunt Lena has already gone to the neighbors as she knew the men would want to speak privately as they had done the other night. Just as they began Uncle Gerhart's nightly after dinner brandy ritual, Wolfgang arrives. They let him in and make sure the house is locked up before huddling in the parlor. "Have some brandy. It will warm you," Uncle Gerhart tells Wolfgang. He replies, "That sounds good. Make it a double." Wolfgang lays out his plan to get them to South America and, if all works out properly, ultimately to the United States. He explains, "The first thing that we must do is to get you both new identities. This can be accomplished easily as long as we get it done immediately. I have an associate, Dieter, who works in the municipal building preparing identity documents. He has worked for me for almost 20 years, but as far as the Gestapo knows, he is a totally loyal employee. Over the years, he has smuggled out paper, ink, and stamps and everything needed to prepare forged documents. Dieter has told me there is talk the Gestapo will be scrutinizing identity documents much more closely in the future, but rest assured what he will prepare for you will be perfect. He has already started work on them and will have them completed tomorrow night. Now the next part of the plan is the most dangerous. On Tuesday morning, you are to get a taxi and go directly to the train station and buy two tickets to Munich on the evening train. They will check your papers and record your names. You are to return immediately to your uncle's house. I again want you to stay home until it is time to leave for the train station. That evening, take the taxi to the station and once you are onboard the train, get seats in any car ahead of the dining car. The conductors will go car to car and stamp your ticket. They will then also check your name off of the travel manifest. This train is usually overcrowded, so you should just blend in with the rest of the passengers. It is critical that they record you as being on the train to Munich." Josef interjects, "Let me stop you right there. What are we going to do in Munich?" Wolfgang replies, "Let me finish. Let me finish. You will never arrive in Munich! The evening train you will be on does not make any stops along the way once it leaves Friedrichshafen. Once it arrives in Munich, the conductors do not check the manifest again, because there was no place anyone could have gotten off. Once you leave Friedrichshafen, one hour into your trip, the train will pass through a small village. Be alert to this and quietly make your way out onto the landing between cars facing towards the back of the train. If anyone asks where you are going, tell them you are going to the dining car. By this time of night, it will be quite dark and the train will slow considerably as it enters a curve before going into a small tunnel. This is your opportunity to jump as the train has slowed, and no one can see you from the train cars. Jump off the right side of the train and after it has passed, I want you to walk up the hill to the top. As you come down the bank, you will be on a dirt road. I will be waiting for you there. We will then burn your old papers and I will give you your new identities and travel documents. So, if anyone ever comes asking questions of your aunt and uncle, they can honestly tell them you took the train to Munich. This is easily verified from the records. You bought tickets and were recorded by the conductor as being on the train."

Wolfgang takes a sip of brandy and continues, "For the next part of the plan, we will rely on some good old-fashioned bribery, so to speak. After I pick you up, we will drive directly to the Zeppelin factory where I work. Along the way, I will fill you in on your alternative names and your background. It is critical that you memorize the information I will give you. Once we are at the factory, we will sleep in my office overnight. I have done this before, so me being there at night will not be a surprise to anyone. Wolfgang asks, "Have any of you heard of Ernst Peters?" Uncle Gerhart replies, "Of course, he is the captain of the Graf Zeppelin, a national hero". Wolfgang retorts back, "Yah a real national hero," he says sarcastically. "Ernst is the biggest womanizing, alcoholic, gambling, letch, in all of Germany! But that will work to our advantage. He owes me a considerable amount of money for his gambling debts, and let's just say I have paid off more than one irate husband so Ernst can keep his stoic image intact. So, when I leave here, I will pay him a visit. I will tell him you are going to pay off his debts, and by Wednesday morning, you will be the two newest members of the Graf Zeppelin crew." He explains that the Nazis have begun pulling workers from various backgrounds to go to work in military factories as they build up their offensive capabilities. As the Graf Zeppelin is held in high esteem by Adolf Hitler as a symbol of superior German technology and is used in their propaganda campaign, the workers that were relocated can be replaced.

Wolfgang goes on to tell them that on the following Monday, the Graf Zeppelin will make its next scheduled trip to Rio de Janeiro, Brazil. What the public does not know is that instead of returning directly to Germany, it will travel to the United States, and fly over a place called Chicago! Then it will land in a city in the state of Ohio called Akron. He continues to explain that the crew of the Zeppelin may not leave the landing areas at any of the stops that they make. The crew does not have travel visas that would allow them to formally enter whatever country they are in, so all their stops have facilities on the ground that the crew can use for their comfort.

So, he goes on, "Once you land in the United States, this is when you will make your escape. I will arrange to have my associates meet you and hide you from the authorities. Make sure you have a compass with you. When you land in Akron, I expect there will be quite a crowd gathered for the Zeppelin landing. As soon as you are moored, make a break for it. You are to use the crowd to cover you as you leave the landing area. The Zeppelin will only be on the ground for a short time to take on extra provisions and the American passengers, and will then depart. Once in the air, Captain Peters will radio the local authorities that two of his dummkopf crew members jumped ship and are loose in Akron. He will tell the crew that when you are arrested by the American authorities, you will both be deported back to Germany. Once on the ground, use your compass and you are to go to the north end of the field and look for two men wearing white suits with a red handkerchief in the breast pocket. They speak German, so ask them where you can get some good bratwurst. They will reply, "In Chicago, It's all good, Man!" This is how you will identify each other. You are to go with these men and they will then drive you several hundred miles to Chicago, to the Nord Seite (Northside) of the city, which comprises almost all German immigrants and their descendants. I have already arranged for all your needs, food, lodging, new identities, etc. Before you leave, you will pay me for the arrangements I have made. It is now Helmut's turn to interrupt," But how could you have arranged all of this so quickly with your people in America?" Wolfgang replies, "By coded message via shortwave radio. I know what I am doing. I had lived in Chicago for a time many years ago and I still have an extensive network of associates. Once you have had time to acclimate to your new home country, you will be sent on your way to stay with Uncle Otto."

Wolfgang explains that on Wednesday morning, Captain Peters will arrive early, before the rest of his crew. "I want him to meet you and see who he has to thank for getting him out of his gambling debt. He will personally oversee your training to be ready for next Monday's flight. I have a spare bedroom which you are going to rent, and you will drive with me to and from work. I need you to keep a low profile, so it's work, and then my house until the flight. Remember, you're supposed to be in Munich, so we can't risk you getting into trouble." Josef replies, "We understand. We will do as you ask." Wolfgang now turns to Gerhart and says, "My old friend, I don't have to remind you not to discuss this with anyone." Gerhart replies, "Of course not, this will all be kept between us, but what about Lena?" Wolfgang replies, "Now listen all of you, I know I can trust Lena, but I want to keep her out of this, anyway. The only thing I want you to tell her is that you are leaving for Munich on Tuesday, so you will have the next couple of days to say your goodbyes." Wolfgang turns to Josef and Helmut, "Alright then, I think we have covered everything you need to know so far. So, if all goes well, I will pick you up Tuesday night, as we discussed. Good luck boys!" As he leaves, he tells Gerhart that he will see him again in a few weeks, after they arrive safely in the United States, God willing. After Wolfgang leaves, Gerhart goes to the neighbors to bring Lena back home. While he is gone, Josef and Helmut finish Uncle Gerhart's last bottle of brandy. Helmut tells Josef that they will have to buy him a couple of new bottles to make up for all they drank. About an hour later, as they are resting in the parlor, Uncle Gerhart comes home with Aunt Lena. As she enters the room, she asks the boys how their meeting went with Wolfgang? Josef tells her, "We have enjoyed staying with you, but Wolfgang has told us of some excellent employment opportunities in Munich. As much as we will miss you both, we will be taking the Tuesday evening train to Munich." Aunt Lena replies, "I had a feeling that you would not be staying too long, but I totally understand." Aunt Lena laughs loudly and says, "Now that's settled, who wants some strudel?"

It's now Tuesday morning as they arrive at the train station. It is quite busy, but the ticket line is moving fast. Helmut asks for two tickets to Munich on the evening train. The ticket agent tells him it was good he came early as the train is almost sold out, just as Wolfgang had predicted. Josef tells Helmut he saw a liquor store next to the station. Josef says "Let's grab a couple of bottles of brandy for my uncle before we grab a taxi back to his house." They purchase two bottles of the most expensive brandy they find as a gift for Uncle Gerhart and Aunt Lena. Then they grab the taxi back to the house where they spend the day trying not to stress out. Aunt Lena tells them they will have an early dinner so they can get to the train station on time. Before dinner, they all share a glass of the new brandy and toast to their health and safe journey. Uncle Gerhart tells them, "Thank you boys for the brandy, this is the best I ever had." Josef replies, "No, it is Helmut and I that need to thank you both for the hospitality. We will never forget your kindness." As Aunt Lena leaves the room to finish dinner, Uncle Gerhart whispers to them, "I want you to get a message to Wolfgang, who will relay it to me when you arrive in Chicago. It should say simply, "We miss the Alps this time of year." When I receive that message, I can tell Aunt Lena that you are safe in your new country." After a quick dinner, Josef and Helmut say their goodbyes and head out to the train station. Aunt Lena is left sobbing softly in the kitchen, as Uncle Gerhart comes to comfort her.

They arrive at the station without incident and in plenty of time before the train is scheduled to leave. As they walk onto the train platform, they ask a porter if he knows where the dining car is. He replies, "two cars to the rear of this one." They think to themselves that it will work out perfectly. Hopefully, there are still some empty seats, and fortunately there are several. They are able to get seats in the last row, which is great as everyone else will be facing forward and they will be behind them all. After a few minutes, the conductor comes around and asks for their tickets, which he stamps. As expected, he asks for their papers and checks off their names on the travel manifest. Josef then asks Helmut, "My friend, did you remember to bring the rest of your money with you?" He replies, "Yes, of course, it's where I always keep it." The conductors have finished their car as they move forward to check the rest of the passengers. The train pulls out of the station and Helmut tells Josef to check his watch so they are ready an hour from now. It is now quite dark out and the cabin lights are extremely dim. They can feel the train speeding up as they begin their journey. They both sit quietly as they observe the watch slowly move minute by minute until finally an hour passes. As they try to peer out the window, they can see some rapidly approaching lights. That must be the town Wolfgang spoke of. As they quickly pass through the small town, they open the door behind them and make their way onto the landing between the cars. Josef tells Helmut, "I don't think anyone even bothered to turn around and see who was leaving the car. Now let's crouch down and get ready." Suddenly, they can feel the train begin to brake and decelerate. Josef whispers in Helmut's ear, "Be ready. Wait for it, Wait for it, Jump!!" As they both roll onto the ground into the brush, they see the train make the curve and disappear into the tunnel. Helmut asks Josef, "Are you alright, did you get hurt?" He replies, "Just a few scrapes, how about you?" Helmut says, "The same, but my ankle is slightly sore, but I think I can make it." Josef tells him he is lucky his foot is not broken. Wolfgang told them to walk up the hill to the top, but that was going to be easier said than done, as it was much steeper than described. After a little while, they make it to the top and stop to catch their breath. Helmut says, "I can't believe we made it." After resting briefly, they walk down the hill to the dirt road. Suddenly, they see what looks like car lights flashing just up the road. As they cautiously approach the car, the door opens, and to their relief, it's Wolfgang. He says, "I am so happy to see you made it. Are you all in one piece?" They reply, "Yes, Wolfgang, we are fine." He then takes and burns their identity papers by the side of the road. Wolfgang says, "Alright now listen carefully. Josef, your new name is Hans Becker. Helmut, you are now, Manfred Schmidt. You are both originally from Munich, from Barer Street, and as children, you attended church services at the Ludwigskirche. Here are your new papers which I had prepared for you. As I said before, these forgeries are perfect and will fool anyone who examines them. When we get to my office, I will give you a map of Munich and a short list of well-known landmarks and entertainment venues you need to become familiar with tonight. In case anyone asks you about Munich, you will have some general knowledge of the city." Wolfgang then instructs them to get in the back seat and to stay low during the ride to the factory. As they arrive, they are met at the gate by the night watchman. He asks why he is coming to work at such a late hour and who he has with him. Wolfgang replies, "We have a lot of preparations to make for next Monday's flight, and these two are new employees who are renting a room from me. By the way Ludwig, how is your daughter doing? Broken leg, wasn't it? Here is some money. I want you to buy her some chocolates to cheer her up." Ludwig is taken aback and so flustered by the gesture that he waves them through without checking their identities. Wolfgang pulls his car into the far end of the hangar. As they leave the car, Manfred-Helmut and Hans-Josef are in awe of the size of the Graf Zeppelin. Wolfgang tells them to follow him up the stairs to his office on the second level. As they enter his office, Wolfgang draws the drapes and locks the door for privacy. "All right, you two, have a seat on the couch and start memorizing this information," Wolfgang barked.

It's now nearly midnight and Manfred-Helmut and Hans-Josef have finished memorizing their identity and background information, along with the Munich maps. Wolfgang looks up from his desk and tells them, "Let's get some rest as Captain Peters will be here around 7:00 a.m.," but they are already sound asleep. The night goes quickly and Wolfgang is awakened by a knock on the office door. He opens it and finds that it is Captain Peters, right on time. As he lets him in, Wolfgang yells to the boys to wake up. As they jump to their feet Captain Peters tells them, "So you are the ones I owe a debt to. Come with me and I will give you a tour of the ship. But first I want to ask if either of you have flown in an airplane or airship before?" Both of them reply, "No, but we have been on boats before, and we didn't get seasick." Captain Peters says, "That is a good sign, as we don't need crew members getting airsick. Now I want you to spin around 10 times quickly and then walk in a straight line over to the desk." Both of them took the test and are not feeling dizzy at all. The captain says they are off to a good start, as they leave the office to begin the tour and training. Wolfgang tells the boys to meet him in his car at 5:00 p.m. when the factory closes for the day. Captain Peters looks back at Wolfgang and tells him not to worry. He will take good care of his newest crew members.

As they walk around the airship, Captain Peters points out the five reversible propeller Maybach engines that give the means of propulsion. He is proud of the fact that both the Zeppelin and the engines were built right here in Friedrichshafen. As they come to the gondola, Captain Peters explains it is approximately 30 meters long and contains the control room and passenger cabins. As they enter the gondola, they find at the very front the main control room. It is here that experienced operators control both the rudder and elevator control, which is what steers the ship and keeps it level. The elevator control station is the hardest on the ship and is usually kept to 4-hour shifts as it is so demanding. As you move aft thru the gondola, you pass through the chart room and then on either side a small radio room and a small kitchen. As no open flames are allowed because of the flammability of the hydrogen gas, they use a small electric oven and hot plate to prepare the food. Continuing further back, there is a small lounge area and then 10 passenger cabins, and men's and ladies' restrooms. The passenger cabins are very narrow and have bunk beds, and as is true with the rest of the ship, there is no heat. This was very problematic if the Graf Zeppelin was flying a route over northern Europe or the North Atlantic on a crossing. Passengers on these routes would be freezing and would wear layers of clothing and furs to keep warm.

As they moved back into the map room, Captain Peters pulled down a set of retractable stairs in the ceiling. They then ascended up into the superstructure of the airship. As they walked along the curved path, the captain pointed out the crew quarters and mess, water storage tanks, cargo storage, etc. They think to themselves, this really is a marvel of engineering and at that moment they felt pride in their country. The captain then summoned the head steward, Dietrich, and instructed him to train the newest crew members on their duties during the flight. As time was short before Monday's flight and they were not qualified for anything else, they would serve as waiters and janitors. The head steward instructed them in meticulous detail about how to set the table, serve the food and pour the wine, and make the beds, etc. They would also have to keep all areas of the ship clean and tidy at all times. So, the rest of the day was spent cleaning the kitchen and the dining/lounge. Oh, and what a joy it was to polish all the silverware, they thought, but they knew it was worth the effort for a chance to start a new life.

Well, it's quitting time, so they go to wait for Wolfgang in his car. They have to wait an extra 30 minutes before he arrives. Wolfgang greets them and asks, "Well, how did you enjoy your first day? The Graf Zeppelin really is quite remarkable, don't you think?" Hans-Josef replies, "Absolutely amazing. We can't wait to fly in it." Wolfgang asks them if they spoke with any of the crew other than the captain and head porter. Manfred-Helmut tells him no. They spent the day cleaning and polishing and everyone left them alone. They all pile into the car for the short drive to Wolfgang's house. As they arrive, he parks in the garage and closes the door. As they enter the house, he tells them they can share the spare bedroom at the end of the upstairs hallway on the right. Wolfgang says, "Get washed up while I go over to the tavern to get some sandwiches for dinner." As he returns, they are waiting for him in the kitchen. "I hope you like roast beef sandwiches as much as I do. Oh, and by the way, you owe me 5 Deutschmarks per day for food and lodging. Your uncle may be my friend, Hans-Josef, but I still have to make a living."

It's now Friday afternoon at the Zeppelin hangar. The boys have spent all their time cleaning, polishing, painting, and loading cargo. The captain said everything is ready to go except for the loading of the blau gas fuel which they will do Sunday night. They are taking a break sitting on a bench just outside of the hangar. They are enjoying a piece of bread and cheese. Suddenly, Dietrich comes over and joins them on the bench. They thought it strange that other than giving them orders; he did not say more than two words to them so far today. Dietrich asks if he can join them, and they move down to make room for him. Dietrich says, "So I understand you two guys are from Munich?" They both reply yes, that is where we grew up. He goes on quizzing them about Munich. They think to themselves it was good Wolfgang made them learn some facts about the city, but this feels more like an interrogation instead of friendly chatter. After this goes on for a while, Dietrich finally leaves and tells them they have been working hard and to rest up this weekend for Monday's flight. They finish out the shift and go back to Wolfgang's house, where they stay the rest of the weekend. It's now Sunday night around 7:00 p.m. and Wolfgang, Hans-Josef, and Manfred-Helmut are sitting in the kitchen enjoying a bottle of cherry schnapps. There is a knock on the door and Wolfgang rises to see who it is, as he wasn't expecting anyone. As he opens the door, he sees it is Dietrich, the steward of the Graf Zeppelin. He asks Wolfgang, "May I come in." Suddenly another man appears, and he pushes Dietrich into the kitchen and closes the door. Hans-Josef and Manfred-Helmut immediately recognize him. It's the Gestapo man from the square in Kelheim, who issued their papers. Wolfgang is now standing in front of the kitchen sink on the other side of the kitchen. The Gestapo man tells the boys to stay seated, and to keep their hands on the table as he stares at them. He says, "So, Dietrich tells me you grew up in Munich. I find that quite remarkable, as it just took me a minute to recognize your faces. You are from Kelheim." They are shocked that he remembers them, but they sit silently. The Gestapo man goes on, "Dietrich thought it very strange that you claim to have grown up in Munich, but gave him the wrong street name for the church you attended." Hans-Josef stammers and says, "Well, well, we were quite young. We must have been confused." He responds, "Confused! No, I am the one confused. What are two boys from Kelheim, doing working at the Zeppelin factory in Friedrichshafen, and telling people you are from Munich. Let me see your papers." After examining them, he says, "These papers are totally in order. If it were not for the fact that I recognize you, I would leave now and you could go on your flight tomorrow. Instead, we will all take a ride down to Gestapo headquarters so we can discuss this issue and find out what you two are really up to. I assure you that by the time that we are done with you, we will know everything." He then orders them to get up and move to the door. The Gestapo man and Dietrich are standing directly opposite from Wolfgang with the table between them. As the boys walk around the table, for a split second, the Gestapo man's vision of Wolfgang was obscured. That was all the time Wolfgang needed to reach behind himself and grab a gun he had hidden under the sink. Suddenly, both Dietrich and the Gestapo man fall to the floor. Wolfgang had shot them both in the head, and they died instantly. The gun had a silencer on it, so no one heard anything. They stood there in shock, shaking and terrified. They had never seen anyone killed like that before. Wolfgang yells at them, "Snap out of it, don't you realize I just saved your lives?" Manfred-Helmut looks at him and replies, "Yes, we do, but what are we going to do now?" He tells them to lock the door and close all the curtains. He then gets on the phone and makes a call to someone. Wolfgang tells them to sit back down and have some more schnapps while they wait as he peers out the window to the alley behind the garage. About 45-minutes pass and he sees a large white truck stop pull in. Wolfgang goes out to the garage before returning a few minutes later. He tells them "Drag those Schweinhund out to the garage." Once in the garage, they see two large metal drums that say medical waste on them. The truck driver is there, and he is dressed in a white orderly's uniform. Wolfgang instructs them to place the bodies in the drums. After they do, he gets his welding equipment and seals the drums. The garage door is then opened and they all help load the drums on the truck. Wolfgang says, "Get the bleach from under the sink and clean the kitchen thoroughly. Take any bloodied rags and burn them in the fireplace. Make sure no trace remains. I will help my associate dispose of these drums at the dump. I will be back in an hour or so." They do as he requested, and the kitchen is quickly cleaned. They add extra logs to the fireplace and really get a roaring fire going. As they place the blood-soaked rags into the fire, the room is filled with putrid odor. They rush to open all the windows in the house to get some cross ventilation. Luckily, there is a moderate but chilly breeze this evening and the foul odor dissipates quickly. Just as they finish closing up the house, Wolfgang returns and he inspects the kitchen. He remarks, "You have done well. You have left no trace, as I requested." Hans-Josef replies, "The only hard part was burning the rags, but the smell is gone and your house is back to normal." Wolfgang has them sit back down at the table to continue with the cherry schnapps. Wolfgang says, "Look. I know how scared you are feeling, but I can assure you as we speak, the barrels are being buried at the bottom of the landfill. They will never be found." Hans-Josef interjects, "But what of the Gestapo man, won't his disappearance cause trouble?" Wolfgang replies, "Now that he is gone, there is not another Gestapo agent in the city currently that we know of. They can have the soldiers search for him, and they will interrogate some people, but he will never be found. The local authorities will be of no help either. By the time Berlin sends a replacement, you will be long gone, and the only one left who knows anything will be me. As for Dietrich, I am glad I gave him what he deserved. There have been three people arrested at the Zeppelin factory over the last six months. We never knew why, but it has been made crystal clear here tonight. That traitor, Dietrich, was obviously spying on people and then ratting on them to the Gestapo. Good riddance to that lousy bastard."

As they finish the bottle of schnapps, Wolfgang exclaims, "Who's hungry? I'm starving." The boys both reply, "How can you think of food at a time like this?" Wolfgang replies, "It's quite stimulating to dispose of vermin, so I'm hungry. Please join me." He then gets out some bread, leftover strudel, and a few plums. After Wolfgang starts stuffing his face and drinking more schnapps, they join in as well. When they are done, Hans-Josef says, "Wolfgang was right, I feel much better now." Manfred-Helmut replies, "I think we all do." Wolfgang then asks them to join him in the parlor. He then goes over the route the Graf Zeppelin will take and reminds them what to do when they reach Chicago.

It's finally Monday morning, launching day for the Graf Zeppelin, for its latest trans-Atlantic flight. The captain has assembled the crew in the hangar for final preflight inspection and briefing. Captain Peters is perplexed at the absence of the head steward, Dietrich. He asks "Has anyone seen Dietrich or talked to him over the weekend?" The entire crew shake their heads no, except for Hans-Josef and Manfred-Helmut, who look down at the floor expressionless. The captain thinks to himself, what is going on now? Is Wolfgang involved? But it is too late to do anything about it as the ship is scheduled to leave as soon as it is taken out of the hangar and the first set of passengers gets on board. Captain Peters looks directly at Hans-Josef and Manfred-Helmut and tells them, "You two will have to pick up the slack as we are short-handed without Dietrich. Can you handle the extra responsibility?"

They reply, "Yes, Captain Peters, we have been trained in our duties. Everything will be taken care of." The captain responds, "Very well then, Attention Crew. Man your posts." All the ship's crew, and the ground crew, then go about the task of pulling the Zeppelin out of the hangar, and onto the adjacent field. Once that was accomplished, the flight crew assumed their assigned posts aboard the ship. The few passengers that boarded were shown to their cabins by Hans-Josef and Manfred (Helmut). After a few minutes, Captain Peters gets on the intercom and asks everyone to prepare for departure. The Graf Zeppelin slowly rises into the sunny clear sky. The weather is quite good and should make for some excellent sightseeing today as they depart Germany. Once the ship has reached some altitude above the field, the captain gives the order to start the engines. They use regular petrol to fire the engines, before switching over to the blau gas (similar to propane). This is because burning petrol would cause the ship to continually rise as opposed to the blau gas which does not. As the ship picks up speed, it continues to climb to cruising altitude. It heads north for the 250-mile trip to the city of Frankfort to pick up more passengers. As the ship normally cruises at a speed of 112 kilometers per hour (70mph), it only takes a few hours to reach Frankfurt. As they approach the landing field, the ground crew comes out to assist in the landing. Once safely on the ground, the remaining passengers are allowed to board, and Hans-Josef and Manfred-Helmut take them to their assigned cabins and help them with their luggage. The captain again announces their departure, and the Graf Zeppelin slowly rises into the sky. Many of the passengers have congregated in the small combination dining room/lounge and are peering out the observation window. The ship makes a turn to the west and will soon enter France on its flight to Rio de Janeiro. They think to themselves how smooth the flight is starting out and pray for pleasant weather. Well, it's late afternoon and time for dinner. As they are short-handed, the boys will really have to hustle to get everyone served. If all goes well, the trip should only take a little over three days, so it will be busy serving and cleaning, but nothing they can't handle. They are so excited to have crossed out of Germany and into France that their adrenaline is pumping and they make quick work of their duties. As luck would have it, the weather turned out great and the flight across Europe and the Atlantic Ocean went without incident. The passengers were, for the most part, quite jovial and respectful of the crew. They really enjoyed the phonograph that was kept in the lounge, and the evenings were filled with delightful music and singing. The captain announced they were on schedule and would arrive in Rio de Janeiro at dawn tomorrow. Hans-Josef and Manfred-Helmut were getting quite tired at this point, but they will get a slight break as the ship will lie over in Rio for a day before heading north to the United States.

It's early morning, and the sun has just risen. It is always quite a site for the locals, as the Zeppelin swoops in for a landing. The numerous ground crew are able to corral it as they normally do, and it makes a safe landing. As the passengers leave the ship, they thank the captain for the safe and smooth trip. It was definitely worth the price. The crew spends the rest of the day inspecting the ship, taking on provisions, and preparing for the next part of the flight. Hans-Josef and Manfred-Helmut are busy replacing the linens in the passenger cabins to prepare for the next set of passengers who will be picked up in the United States city of Akron, Ohio before non-stop service to Seville, Spain. Once that has been completed, they spend the rest of the day sweeping and cleaning the cabins and lounge areas. Now it's dinner time and the crew are happy to hear that, as usual, they will be able to leave the ship for some refreshment. There is a small building next to the landing area that has several sets of long tables in a common area and a couple of bedrooms in the back. As is customary when the Zeppelin makes its scheduled stop. One of the local German restaurants caters in some food for the crew. It's nothing fancy, some brats, schnitzel, bread, and cheese. Of course, they bring in a keg of beer to wash the food down with. Hans-Josef and Manfred-Helmut really enjoy the food and drink and when they are finished eating, they wander outside. As they light up a smoke, they remark on what a perfectly clear night it is and think to themselves what an adventure they have gone on. As they are just finishing their smoke, three cars pull up, full of some lovely local ladies of the night, as they would call them. Captain Peters comes out to greet them and invites them in. He sees the boys still standing outside and asks them, "What are you doing out here, don't you want to come in and have some fun. The girls here are certainly much cheaper than back home." After hearing that from the captain, Hans-Josef wastes no time and bolts into the cabin. He certainly never misses an opportunity to have some fun. Manfred-Helmut, on the other hand, is content to just enjoy the night air and the view of the city. When it gets a little later, he decides to call it a night and goes back into his sleeping quarters on the ship. The rest of the crew didn't arrive back onto the ship for several more hours, not until they have all had their fill of beer and women. As Hans-Josef staggers into his bunk next to Manfred-Helmut, he says, "Hey Manny, are you still awake? Where did you go? You don't know what you missed out on?" He replies, "I didn't miss out on anything. Come and sleep it off. We have to get up early in the morning." As soon as Hans-Josef's head hits the pillow, he is sound asleep and Manfred-Helmut thinks to himself, he is going to have a terrible hangover tomorrow.

Well morning comes quickly, and Captain Peters gets on the intercom and tells the crew to get to their stations. Manfred-Helmut is already awake, but Hans-Josef is slow to rouse from his sleep. He yells at Hans-Josef, "Get up, Get up." He can only reply sheepishly, "My head." Then he quickly smiles and says, "I should have listened to you last night, alright, alright, I'm awake." In a little while, the crew is at their stations and the Graf Zeppelin is ready to take flight again. There is no time to waste as there is the potential for poor weather as they leave South America. The ship rises quickly into the sky and the engines are again started. The Zeppelin turns to the northwest to begin its 2 ½ day trip to Miami, Florida where it will land outside the city for a day before continuing on. It will then leave for another day's flight, to the Century of Progress World's Fair in Chicago, where it will circle the exposition. When that is complete, it will travel to Akron, Ohio and temporary mooring at the Goodyear Zeppelin dock where it will pick up the next set of passengers. The captain radioed to the German Embassy in Washington D.C. to announce they have started the last leg of their journey to the United States. This information is relayed to the U.S. State Department for final approval. The flight is uneventful as it soars over South America. But unfortunately, as they feared, they hit rain and strong winds as they start the trek across the Caribbean Sea. The rudder operator struggles to maintain course as the ship is pushed around. The rain has caused the Zeppelin to take on extra weight and the captain orders the release of ballast to help them maintain altitude. The ship which normally has been kept level during flight begins to list, and throughout the ship you can hear items fall to the floor. Captain Peters has Manfred-Helmut come to assist the elevator control officer to maintain the ship at level. The officer barks at him, "Just do everything I tell you and we will get through the worst of this." He does as directed and after a couple of hours the weather clears and the stars finally become visible. The captain orders the navigation officer to manually use the sextant to get a fix on their position, as the high winds made it difficult to maintain a straight course. There is good news, and the navigator reports to the captain that they are only slightly off course. Captain Peters orders a course correction and they are soon back on track. The captain then orders some brandy to be served to the passengers as they were quite shaken up by the poor weather. The rest of the flight across the Caribbean to Miami goes smoothly and the passengers are again happy and relaxed. As the ship passed over Cuba, they received a radio message from the German Embassy that their request to enter American air space has been granted and they are cleared to make the predetermined stops while in the United States. The message also comes with a reminder that anyone leaving the ship without prior consent of the United States government would be subject to arrest.

All goes well, and the ship makes its scheduled stop in Miami, Florida, where it moors overnight. It's now early afternoon and the captain orders the ship to depart. The weather is warm, and the sky is again clear as they depart. The weather forecasts are for light winds and clear weather all the way to Chicago. They realize that by tomorrow, they will finally be free and be able to start a new life. Hans-Josef tells Manfred-Helmut, "Make sure you remember to wear your street clothes under your Zeppelin uniform tomorrow, as we must be ready to leave on a moment's notice." He replies, "I will be ready, but I am so excited I don't know if I will get any sleep tonight." Hans-Josef says, "I know what you are saying, but stay calm. Tomorrow is the day!"

It's now the next morning, Thursday, October 26, 1933, as the Graf Zeppelin approaches Chicago. The ship swoops in from over Lake Michigan, where it circles the World's Fair. The attendees of the fair look skyward and are very impressed with the size of the Graf Zeppelin. They can read the name of the ship and see the red and black markings painted on the hull. However, as Captain Peters knows the disdain for the Nazi's that the Americans have, he only circles the field counter clockwise so the people on the ground cannot see the swastikas that were painted on the opposite side of the fins. After spending some time circling the fair, the ship turns eastward for the approximately 5-hour flight to Akron, Ohio. As they approach Curtiss-Wright Airfield, the crew can see that a large crowd has gathered to observe the landing. An area around the landing zone has been roped off to keep the crowd away. As the ship makes its approach, the large number of ground crew helps moor the ship. As the stairs are lowered from the gondola, suddenly the crowd breaks through the rope barrier. Hundreds and hundreds of spectators surround the gondola, and some are trying to climb the stairs to get in. Hans-Josef and Manfred-Helmut see what's happening and quickly strip off their uniforms and bolt down the stairs. They are immediately lost in the sea of bodies surrounding the ship. Suddenly, the crowd is silenced after two loud shotgun blasts coming from the side of the field. The local police can be heard on bull horns, ordering the crowd to disperse. It doesn't take long for order to be restored. Captain Peters, in broken English, thanks the local police for their help and tells them once his passengers have been loaded, they will be departing.

They use their compass and run to the north end of the field, as Wolfgang had instructed. There are many cars parked there and quite a few spectators milling around. As they scan the lot, they finally see two men in white suits with the red handkerchiefs in their pockets. As they approach, Hans-Josef asks them, "Where can you get some good bratwurst?" They reply, "In Chicago, it's all good, man!" They then ask, "What are your names?" Hans-Josef replies, "My real name is Josef, and this is Helmut." The two men lead Josef and Helmut to the car and tell them to get in. It's different from the type of car that they were familiar with back in Germany. As they started driving, they were amazed at the power and acceleration they could feel. "What kind of car is this?" Helmut asks. The driver replies, "They call it an eight-cylinder Essex-Terraplane. It is produced in a place called Detroit, Michigan." He then laughs and says, "Yaa, a real gangster car." Josef asks what their benefactors' names are. They reply one at a time, "I am Hugo Aller, your driver." The other one says, "And I am Leo Wagner." Then Leo says, "We are happy to meet you. We weren't sure you would make it. We hear the Gestapo have been causing more trouble." Josef tells them they almost didn't make it, but that Wolfgang saved them. Helmut interjects, "It turned out to be quite an adventure. We have used up most of our money to get here." Hugo replies, "Do not worry, we will help you find a job and lodging, get you new identities, whatever you need, my friends." As they continue their drive, they wonder what is going on with the Graf Zeppelin.

As they speak, Captain Peters has finished boarding all his passengers. He wonders to himself how he is going to take care of the passengers now that he is down two more crew members. He realizes one passenger has two teenage boys on board. The captain discreetly approaches the boy's father and explains the situation. After some haggling back-and-forth Captain Peters agrees to pay them a daily wage for their services. The captain then asks one of his crew, who started out as a ship steward, to spend some time showing the teenagers what to do. Captain Peters hopes the passengers will not be angry as the level of service will be quite poor. But then he thinks his passengers are a bunch of uncultured Americans, so maybe they won't even notice. After the Graf Zeppelin departs, the captain radios the German Embassy in Washington and tells them to alert the American authorities of the two crew members that have jumped ship. He tells them their names, but changes the description of their appearance. In a big country like the United States, it is unlikely they would ever be found. The Zeppelin then continues on its journey back to Europe.

The Graf Zeppelin continued service for a few more years. A larger and more high-class Zeppelin was constructed in 1936 and was christened the Hindenburg. After its first flight across the Atlantic in 1937, as it came to land in Lakehurst, N.J., tragedy struck. The hydrogen in the airship ignited, and the ship burned, killing many passengers and crew. The era of the German Zeppelin airships had ended.

## Chapter 3
# Chicago

While their car has a top speed of 80 mph, it doesn't do them much good as much of the trip to Chicago is over dirt roads. As they traverse Ohio and Indiana, night has fallen, so there is little for Josef and Helmut to see on the trip. They spend most of the time either napping or learning a little about Chicago from Hugo and Leo. The drivers are hopeful that by traveling at night and watching their speed, they can reach Chicago without being pulled over by the police. The penalties for smuggling illegal immigrants are quite harsh and are considered a federal crime. As luck would have it, they do not run into any of the authorities. They make a couple of rest stops, get gas and food along the way, before arriving in Chicago after midnight. The car pulls into a large garage and the doors are quickly shut. Hugo and Leo tell them this is one of the properties that they work out of. There are a couple of couches along the back wall they will sleep on tonight. Hugo and Leo break out a bottle of bourbon whiskey and pour them all a drink. Hugo toasts them, "Welcome, my new American friends." They spend at least the next hour toasting each other and telling stories. There is no shortage of liquor as they can see cases of it stacked in the garage. While there is a lot of talk about prohibition being repealed, it is still the law of the land at this point. They could be in trouble for not consuming the liquor in their own home, and being in the possession of many cases of liquor. So, after being in the United States for a few hours, they have officially committed their second crime of the day. They are all exhausted from the long drive and the bottles of whisky they have just consumed, and decide to call it a night. Leo says, "Get some rest, my new friends. Tomorrow we will get you some new identities."

A new morning has come to Chicago, as Josef and Helmut arise from their sleep. As they walk around the garage, Josef asks Helmut, "Do you have any hangover this morning?" Helmut replies, "No, not at all. I feel good. How about you, Josef?" He replies, "Just a little, but considering I drank much more than you, I'm not surprised." Suddenly the door opens and Hugo and Leo enter. Leo greets them, "Good morning my friends, come have something to eat." They put on the table some wonderful warm crusty bread and German kuchen. Josef and Helmut are shocked to see what they have provided, and Josef asks where they have gotten such authentic bread and kuchen. Hugo goes over to the hotplate and brings over a pot of hot coffee. Leo explains that a sizable part of Chicago is made up of German immigrants, especially on the Northside of the city. Leo tells them, "Hugo and I were born in Chicago. Our parents emigrated to the states in the late 1880s, you will find many traditional German bakeries, restaurants, and shops in Chicago." He explains that is why this is the perfect place for them to start their new life, as it will be easy to blend in. Helmut asks, "But how do you know Wolfgang?" Leo replies, "Wolfgang lived here many years ago. We worked for him before he returned to Germany. His wife was not happy in Chicago as all the family was in the old country, so they went back." Hugo interjects, "Just so you are aware, what we do is not exactly legal. We have gambling interests and, of course, bootlegging." Josef and Helmut cannot believe that alcohol is illegal in the United States, as it is so common in Germany, even children get to drink beer. "So, Wolfgang was involved in all that stuff?" Helmut asks. Hugo replies, "Yes on the gambling, but Wolfgang also made a lot of money exchanging money for the new immigrants. He would take their German Marks and exchange them for U.S. dollars, after taking 30% off the top. He would then take the German Marks to the other side of Chicago, where there was a bank that he could exchange the currency at." When the first-year of prohibition started, Wolfgang set up the smuggling network out of Canada. If he had stayed, he would have become very wealthy. Josef explains, "My Uncle Gerhart was childhood friends with Wolfgang. It was my uncle who got us involved with him. We are so happy he did, otherwise I don't know if Helmut and I would have survived. We owe him an enormous debt of gratitude." Leo replies, "Yes, we liked Wolfgang as well. He was quite a character back in the day, and we also owe him. That is why he still makes a small percentage of our business dealings."

After they are finished, Hugo tells them it's time to go see their associate, Brenner, who will get them some new identification. Hugo then says to them, "He is not cheap for the service he renders. We will front you the money, as we know you are low on funds. But we are first going to stop on the way to get you guys a hot bath and some clean clothes." As they leave the garage and walk down the busy street, they are relieved at how many people are speaking German. They go into a small clothes shop and Leo greets the owner, "How are you today, Dirk? Can you fix my new friends up with a couple of sets of new clothes?" Dirk replies, "Of course, let me measure them and we will get them what they need." Josef and Helmut think to themselves that the shopkeeper, Dirk, reminds them of Uncle Gerhart, who they both miss. After they leave the shop, the next stop is to get them cleaned up. Just like back in Germany, they are taken to a bathhouse. Helmut exclaims, "Oh no, not another one of these places." After he explains to Hugo and Leo what happened to him, they tell him to relax. It's just for a bath. All the while, Josef laughs uncontrollably. Leo tells them to go get bathed, shaved, and get into their new clothes, and they will wait for them across the street in the coffee shop. After a little while, Josef and Helmut cross the street to join them. Hugo says, "You guys look like new men; I hope you disposed of your old disgusting clothes." Josef replies, "Yes, of course. We want to look our best in our new country." After they have finished their coffee, they leave to go meet up with Brenner at his basement apartment. They enter through the back alley and go down the steps to his place. Hugo raps loudly on the door, and they can see Brenner peering out the side window. Brenner opens the door and greets them. "I have been expecting you. Come in, all of you. So, you are my newest client. Welcome." He asks them their names? Josef replies, "Well, Wolfgang gave us new identities to get us out of Germany, but those obviously were not our names. I am really Josef Vogel, and my friend's real name is Helmut Lang". Brenner looks at them and says, "I think it would be better to Americanize your names, and that will help you assimilate easier. Josef and Helmut wonder to themselves how that would work. Brenner asks them, "What do you think about this? Instead of Helmut Lang, we change it to Harry Langer. Instead of Josef Vogel, we will make you, Joseph Vogler. At least that way they are derived from your real names." They both tell him yes, that sounds like an excellent compromise, as we never liked the names Wolfgang gave us. Brenner explains that people having any type of identification in the United States is not common. He thinks that less than a third of native-born Americans even have a birth certificate. He tells them, "Give me a couple of days and I will prepare you the documents. My niece just had twins, so I will use their footprints in the document. She lives in the town of Cicero, which lies just west of Chicago. That will be used as your birthplace." He continues, "Many years ago, I was able to buy a moderate amount of the paper that Cook County used for their documents. I will use a technique with some coffee to make the paper look older. As far as the ink goes, it is just a matter of mixing it with the right ingredients so it will appear slightly faded." Leo then asks Brenner, "I assume you want the usual fee for your services?" Brenner replies, "Yes, fifty dollars. Come back in a couple of days." As they leave Brenner's place, Harry and Joseph wonder what they will have to do to pay back the money Hugo and

Leo are giving them. They don't have to wait long to find out. Hugo and Leo explain to them that congress has passed a constitutional amendment that will repeal prohibition of alcohol. In order for it to be ratified, it must be approved by three-fourths of the states, and they only have three left to go. So, for now they have to supply their speakeasies (illegal drinking rooms) as they are known by, with bootlegged liquor from Canada and local hidden distilleries. The local police are not much of a problem as many have been paid off, but also as it is in the process of being repealed, nobody much cares anymore. Even the Feds have started to back off. Leo tells them a little of the history of prohibition in Chicago. Ever since prohibition was signed into law in 1920, there has been the illegal production and sale of illegal alcohol. What we can't import from Canada, we make in hidden distilleries and breweries. It has been quite a lucrative business. The only problem is there is always someone trying to muscle in on your territory, so you have to keep your guard up. He explains that the Italian Mafia runs the Southside of Chicago, and the Irish and Germans run the Northside of Chicago. For many years, the Italians and the Irish have been at war. A few years ago, things really hit the fan. Al Capone, the leader of the Italian Mafia on the south side, tried to kill Bugs Moran, the leader of the Irish gang on the Northside. They missed but killed seven people in what is known as "The St. Valentine's Day Massacre." After that happened, the Feds really cracked down. It took a couple of years, but they finally got Capone on tax evasion and put him in jail. Leaders and members of the more well- known mobs were arrested, or killed, and some even tried going legit. Our gang operates only in the German part of the Northside. We have an ongoing agreement with the Irish and we pay them a percentage of our profits to keep the peace. We leave them alone and they leave us alone. The police and politicians are paid off, so the only ones to watch out for are the Feds. But if it comes to pass that they repeal prohibition, then everything will change.

As they walk down the street, Joseph turns to Leo and says, "I just remembered something. Can you get a message to Wolfgang?" Leo replies, "That is not a problem. What do you want to tell him?" Joseph says, "Tell uncle, 'We miss the Alps this time of year.' It is most important that he gets the message." Joseph thinks to himself he knows Uncle Gerhart and Aunt Lena are worried about our safety, so this will set their minds at ease.

It's a couple of days later and Uncle Gerhart and Aunt Lena sit down for dinner at their home back in Friedrichshafen, Germany. Aunt Lena has done nothing but worry and pray for the safety of Josef and Helmut. Uncle Gerhart tells her to stay calm. He is sure everything will work out. You remember how devious Wolfgang can be. After dinner, they clean the kitchen and then sit in the parlor and have some more brandy. Gerhart tells Lena, "Ahh, that sure takes the chill out of my bones". Suddenly, there's a knock on the back door. Gerhart rises to see who is there. As he opens the door, he sees Wolfgang standing there with an ear-to-ear smile. Wolfgang greets Gerhart "My friend, please invite me in. I have news for you and Lena." As they enter the parlor, Lena gasps and says, "Wolfgang, have my prayers been answered?" He replies, "I have a message from the United States, from Chicago. It reads, "We miss the Alps this time of year." Uncle Gerhart jumps for joy and exclaims, "Lena, Lena, do you know what this means? They made it. Josef and Helmut are safe in the United States!" Aunt Lena can't control her emotions anymore, as she cries with relief. Gerhart exclaims, "More brandy, come let us toast to Wolfgang." Lena rises from her chair and hugs Wolfgang in a long embrace. "Thank you Wolfy, thank you," she says. They toast themselves into the wee hours of the morning and then pass out in their chairs. They sleep contently, knowing the boys are safe, and have started a new life.

Meanwhile, back on the Northside of Chicago, Hugo, and Leo take Harry and Joseph back over to Brenner's place to pick up their forged birth certificates. After he hands the documents over, Brenner asks for payment. "Here you go, fifty dollars, as we agreed," Hugo tells him.

They are told to keep the papers in a safe place in case they have to produce them. Unlike Germany, they do not have to carry identification at all times. As they leave Brenner's place, they instruct Harry and Joseph on what their new jobs will be. Leo tells them they will be paid well for their services. He estimates they can pay off their debt in just a couple of months. Then it's up to them if they want to stay in Chicago, or if they are ready to move on. That will be up to them to decide. Hugo asks them, "Do any of you know how to use a gun?" Harry responds, "I grew up on a farm so yes, I have fired guns and rifles." Joseph replies, "I have never even touched a gun." Hugo then hands Harry a handgun and tells him it may be needed to protect themselves when making the liquor deliveries. As I told you before, things have calmed down with the police and rival gangs, but one cannot be too careful. Leo explains that they will replace a couple of their drivers who ripped off some of the liquor deliveries for themselves. Needless to say, they won't be driving a truck, or even walking, for quite a while. Leo tells them they will be making the deliveries at night to their network of speakeasy clubs. The local police who patrol those areas have been well paid to look the other way, and we let them drink for free besides. So today you need to get some rest as your deliveries start tonight. I will be driving with you for a few nights until you learn the route. But first, I want to take you over to your new flat. No more sleeping in the warehouse for you. The flat Leo has rented for them is only a few blocks away and is located above a flower shop. They are both owned by Leo's sister.

They enter the flower shop and are greeted by a thin blonde-haired woman with quite a pale complexion. She says, "Leo, my brother, good to see you. Who do we have here?" Leo replies, "These are your new tenants for the flat upstairs. This is Harry, and this is Joseph. They don't speak a word of English yet." Leo's sister responds in German, "I am Chloris, it is very nice to meet you, you come and go as you please, but you make sure you keep things quiet, as I don't need any trouble." The entrance to the flat is just outside the front door of the flower shop. They all go upstairs to the flat, which turns out to have two small bedrooms, so Harry and Joseph will have a little privacy. Chloris tells them she will provide them fresh linens weekly, and there is a good diner a few doors down they can eat at. Leo tells them to go get something to eat and then get some rest. He will be back at 7:00 p.m. to pick them up to start the night's deliveries. Chloris turns out to be correct as the diners' food is quite good. Fortunately, because they are on the Northside, most of the people in this district speak German to various degrees, so communication is not a problem. As Leo had promised, he picked them up in the delivery truck precisely at 7:00 p.m. They drive back over to the warehouse and begin their tasks of loading the delivery truck with kegs of beer and cases of liquor. Business has been quite good lately, at the roughly dozen speakeasies that Leo and Hugo run on the Northside. They spend a good part of the night going from bar to bar, making their deliveries. Leo gives them a map of the Northside and tells them to get familiar with the street layout so they know where they are going. They are not to mark any locations on the map in case it falls into the hands of the federal agents. The next few nights go without incident and Harry and Joseph quickly learn what they have to do. It's Thursday night and Leo picks them up again. Harry asks, "Are we making deliveries again tonight?" Leo replies, "Not tonight. We are going now to the docks to pick up a shipment of Canadian liquor. Harry, do you have your gun with you?" He replies, "Yes," as they continue on to the docks. It is a cloudy night and quite dark on the water as the moon is obscured. As they are standing on one of the many docks, Leo tells them to duck. A police boat is making its once a night pass of the area. It is shining a spotlight on the docks, but not seeing anything, continues on its way. Leo says, "Alright, the coast is clear. They have a lot of territory to cover, so they should not be back. After waiting a few minutes, a medium-sized speed boat pulls up to the dock where they are waiting. Leo greets the driver of the boat and then they peel back the canvas cover to reveal 30 or 40 cases of hard liquor. Leo instructs Harry and Joseph to get it loaded quickly into the truck. As soon as the last case is removed, the driver speeds off across the lake and disappears into the darkness.

Joseph then asks who they deal with in order to get hard liquor across the border. Leo then explains that there are many criminal enterprises involved with bootlegging in the states. The Italian Mafia, for one, has connections out of Chicago, New York City, Cleveland Ohio, Auburn New York, and Detroit Michigan, which is across from Windsor Canada. They have connections throughout Canada and even down to an Island south of Florida called Cuba where they import rum from. Another one is rumored to be a rich Irishman who lives in Hyannis Port, Massachusetts. I am sure there are many others as well. It really happens all over the country with so many different groups involved. But at our level, they are all just rumors. We are too far down the food chain to be totally sure who is pulling the strings for the other gangs. In our case, we have people up in Toronto, Canada that we work with. Rest assured, Wolfgang did a lot in the old days to help set up our smuggling network, and the deliveries arrive like clockwork. You know, if we didn't smuggle our own booze in, we would never be able to buy any from the Italian or Irish gangs. They would be happy to see us go out of business and take over our territory. But no self-respecting German would ever set foot in one of their places. "Alright, let's go back to the warehouse and get the cargo unloaded," Leo tells them. They don't run into any trouble on the way back, and they are able to finish quickly for the night. Leo tells them to be up early tomorrow morning (Saturday) and be at the warehouse by 4:30 a.m.

When they arrive, they see Leo putting something on the doors of the truck. "What is that?" Joseph asks. He replies, "It's a sign that in English reads Fresh Produce. Joseph and Harry look at themselves and scratch their heads. Leo tells them, "This is our Saturday morning ritual. Now get in the truck and all will be explained when we get to the farm." They drive out into the countryside and arrive at a farm outside of Cicero, Illinois, which coincidentally is where their fake birth certificates say they were born. As they pull up to the barn, they park and go in. Just inside the door, they see cases and cases of fresh tomatoes stacked up. As they start walking to the rear of the large, oversized barn, Harry asks what the smell is. It seems very familiar, but with all the other farm odors, I can't quite make out what it is. Suddenly Harry exclaims, "What is this! You have a brewery in a barn?" They are amazed that they find themselves standing in front of what can only be described as a miniature version of the brewery, where Harry and Joseph worked previously. Leo tells them up until this past spring beer making was illegal, so it was hidden in this barn. Now we are allowed to make beer that is no more than 4% A/V, but we don't follow that law. We brew 5-6% alcohol to volume (A/V), so it's still illegal. Leo then introduces them to Gunther, who acts as Brewmaster. Gunther tells them he is happy to meet them and gives them a quick overview of how he makes beer. Leo then asks, "What have you made for us this time?" Gunther responds, "We made some good Hefeweizen (wheat beer). The barley malt shipment was delayed, so I brewed with the wheat." Gunther takes them all to another room attached to the back of the barn. As they enter, they are shocked at how cold it is. Gunther tells them how they used to pack the room with blocks of ice that were harvested from local lakes and rivers during the winter. The ice was then packed with sawdust to stay cold. A few years ago, they were able to convert over to mechanical refrigeration once the farm had been electrified. This was quite expensive to install but well worth the price, as beer is a valuable commodity during prohibition. Leo says, "Harry and Joseph, I want you to load the kegs into the back of the truck. When that is done, load the tomatoes so the kegs are not visible". We have been doing this every Saturday for years. We pick up and sell fresh tomatoes and other produce depending on the season. Otherwise, we use the trucks for delivery of dry goods to all the local restaurants. When they are done, Leo drives them back to the warehouse and has them unload the truck. The beer kegs are put onto an elevator and taken underground to another refrigerated room. The beer will be stored for later delivery to the speakeasies. He tells them to load the tomatoes back onto the truck. Joseph asks, "Why are we doing this?" Leo replies, "We are going to go down to the farmers' market and sell our produce. We have to keep up the appearance that what we are doing is a legitimate business."

It's Saturday evening and Harry and Joseph are back in their flat relaxing and sharing a bottle of bourbon whiskey. There is a knock on the door and Joseph goes over to answer it. To his surprise, it was Brenner. He asks if he can come in and they agree. Brenner tells them, "I want to talk to you guys. You know, fifty dollars was not nearly enough for my trouble. And besides, my niece deserves more money for letting us use her baby's feet to put on the birth certificate." Brenner is standing in front of Harry and tells him he wants another fifty dollars. Harry yells, "What do you mean, another fifty dollars? We don't have that kind of money, not yet anyway." Brenner yells back, "Not my problem. Get it or I go to the authorities." In that moment, Joseph loses his temper and strikes him over the head from behind with the whiskey bottle. Brenner falls to the ground, dead. Harry exclaims, "What have you done? See if he is breathing." After they check on him, they realize what a mess they are in. Harry asks, "What do we do now Joseph, you got us into this." Joseph tells him to make sure Brenner has no identification on him. Joseph says, "We will take him down the back stairs and into the alley, then throw his body down the manhole. Hopefully, it will not be discovered until long after they leave town. When it is done, we will never speak of this again." They get the body down the back stairs and out into the alley. Joseph tells Harry to search the car that is parked in the alley for a crowbar or something they can use to lift the manhole cover. He finds a car jack in the trunk and they use the lug wrench from that. Once the body is disposed of, they return the jack and head back upstairs. Harry tells Joseph, "Get some wet rags and try to clean the blood off the floor. When you finish, wrap the rags up and throw them in the trash cans back in the alley." Once the floor dries a little, Harry covers it with a throw rug from the bedroom. It can't be more than half an hour since they finished their dirty deed, and there is another knock on the door. Harry whispers "Polizei" to Joseph as they both stand there terrified. Someone knocks on the door and to their relief they hear Leo's voice, "Let me in, I know you are in there." As Leo enters the flat, he looks at them and asks, "What is all the commotion, you two? Chloris called me and said she heard arguing and a loud thud." Joseph thinking quickly replies, "Just hamming a litttttle fun with some whiskeeeeyy," he says slurring his words. Harry interjects, "Joseph has had too much to drink and stumbled and fell on the floor. We will try to be quieter." Leo tells them, "Very well, get Joseph to bed. I don't want any more phone calls from Chloris tonight." As Leo leaves, they close the door and breathe a sigh of relief.

Another day goes by and they are back at the warehouse, sweeping the place out. Leo and Hugo arrive with a beautiful young blond girl who looks to be around their age. Leo introduces her to them as his daughter Emma. Leo tells them, "My daughter was born in 1915, in this country. She is fluent in English and German and can read and write both languages. I have asked her to come here each day so you can start learning English." They tell her their names and that they appreciate her help. Emma replies, "Very glad to help you, as my father has requested. Now let's get started, as we have a lot to do. We will start with the English alphabet and some simple greetings." She is surprised to learn that Joseph knows some English. He confides that his mother taught him when he was very young. Emma spends a few hours with them and they are having an enjoyable time. Emma has a wonderful sense of humor and seems to be just a kind young lady. Harry seems so smitten by her he can barely keep his eyes off her. After she leaves, Joseph looks at Harry and laughingly says, "Could you be more obvious? You looked like you were going to pounce on her." Harry replies, "Oh my God, I cannot believe how beautiful and kind she is. I know I better not come on too strong." Joseph says, "Slow down and bide your time. You just met her. Give it a while before you dare ask her out. Oh, scratch what I just said. I meant to bide your time before you ask Leo's permission to go out with her!" The lesson continues for almost four hours every day. While Harry is progressing slowly, Joseph seems to have an innate ability to learn and speak other languages. The rest of the time they spend picking up and delivering alcohol to the speakeasy clubs. Leo also has them spending time acting as bouncers at some of them as well. Joseph seems to relish that job as he always seems ready for a fight. Almost a week goes by and Leo and Hugo enter the warehouse. Emma has just finished her daily lesson and goes up to hug her father. Leo asks, "How are your students doing?" She replies, "Great!" as she waves to Harry and Joseph. Leo and Hugo are happy to hear them say, "Good Afternoon" in English. Leo thanks his daughter and tells her he will be home on time for dinner tonight. Emma asks her father if she can invite Harry and Joseph to dinner. Leo replies, "Yes daughter, another night." After she leaves the warehouse, Hugo turns to the boys and asks them if either of them has seen Brenner? Harry quickly replies, "Not since we picked up the papers last week." Leo seems suspicious as Joseph keeps looking at the floor, avoiding eye contact. "Well, what about you, Joseph?" Hugo asks. He replies, "ah, ah, no, no." Hugo seems a little angry that he can't find Brenner, and he tells them he is going to go look for him again. After he leaves, Leo says, "Hugo and Brenner have been friends for over thirty years. I think he is a weasel, but Hugo does not agree." Leo then asks them to go over to speakeasy #4 and help them cleanup the place. They had quite a drunken brawl last night. It cost us a lot more money to pay off the Irish cops to look the other way.

The club Leo is sending them to is in the opposite direction of their flat. Leo is suspicious and gets the key to their place from his sister, Chloris. He enters the flat and searches the place. At first, he finds nothing unusual until he moves the couch. It looks like a piece of glass from a broken bottle, but with blood on it. Leo then realizes that when he was here last, there was no rug in that room. As he moves it out, he discovers the floor is discolored. He thinks to himself, "I knew they were lying. Something happened here." Leo then goes out into the alley and looks around and finds a drop of dried blood on the lid of the trash can. It all becomes crystal clear to Leo. "That bastard Brenner is known for shaking down his clients. He must have tried it with these two and they killed him." He wonders if he should share his suspicions with Hugo, as he knows he will go crazy. Leo puts everything back the way it was and returns home for dinner. As Leo and his wife Alice are enjoying their dinner, Emma drops a bombshell. "Father, I want you to know I am quite attracted to Harry," she says. Leo thinks to himself. "Oh boy, what do I do now?"

Leo tells Emma, "Alright, tomorrow when you are giving your English lesson, why don't you invite them over for dinner tomorrow night." Emma replies, "Father, do you really mean it?" "Yes Emma, it will be fine," Leo tells her. It is now the next night when Harry and Joseph arrive for dinner. After the family greets them, Leo tells Emma to help her mother finish dinner and get it on the table. He says he wants them to come into the basement with him to pick out some bottles of wine. They go down the stairs and Leo closes the large door behind them and clicks on the light switch. Harry asks where the wine is? Leo replies, "Along the back wall of the cellar, over there." Suddenly Leo comes up behind them and pulls his gun. He whispers to them, "Do not make a sound or I will kill you where you stand, Emma or no Emma." Leo tells Joseph to face the wall with his hands up. Harry is left facing Leo straight on. Leo reaches out with his left hand and constricts his hand around Harry's neck, while putting the gun to his head with his right hand. Leo exclaims, "I'll only ask this once, Harry, and you better not lie to me. If you want to live, if you want to see Emma, tell me the truth. What happened to Brenner?" Joseph sobs, "Tell him, tell him." Harry stammers and says, "Brenner came to the flat and threatened to turn us into the authorities if we did not pay him another fifty dollars. Joseph lost his temper and hit him over the head with the whiskey bottle. He did not mean to kill him." Leo says, "I figured as much, but where is the body? Joseph speaks, "We went to the alley behind the flat and threw the body into the manhole." Leo remarks, "An inglorious end to a total weasel." Leo lets go of Harry and he tells them both, "Relax, I am not going to hurt you. Brenner has been a thorn in my side for many years. I never trusted him and threatening to turn you in just proves what a rat he really was. However, he was a good friend of Hugo's, and he must never know what you have done. If Hugo asks about Brenner again, just play stupid. That should not be hard for you two idiots. Now hurry you two, get the wine and we will go upstairs to dinner."

Alice and Emma have provided quite a feast. They serve a large platter of schweinebraten (Bavarian pork roast with gravy), with sides of semmelknoedel (bread dumplings) and rotkohl (cooked red cabbage). They all enjoy the dinner and the wine and after a few minutes, Harry and Joseph start to relax. The more wine they drink, the more relaxed they become. Alice, wanting to get to know them better, asks if they were born in this country. Like a comedy movie, Harry says yes, and Joseph says no. Leo squirms in his seat and says, "They are from Cicero, Illinois, not far from Chicago." Alice looks incredulously at Joseph and asks, "Then why did you say you weren't born here?" Joseph looks at Alice and replies, "I think I have had too much wine; I must have misunderstood you." Alice glares at Leo, and without a word, Leo knows she has figured out they are hiding something. She knows her husband is always involved in many shady activities, but her primary concern is the well-being of Emma.

The rest of the dinner is uneventful. However, it is obvious that Emma is hanging on Harry's every word, and they can barely stop smiling at each other. Harry and Joseph retire to the other room to smoke a cigar with Leo while the ladies clean up from dinner. Leo tells them prohibition looks like it could end within a few months. It seems the tide of sentiment is against it in most of the country. Hugo and I are considering what to do if we lose that source of revenue. We are thinking of going legit and turning most of our speakeasies into legal bars, restaurants, and a nightclub, where it is feasible. We figure maybe 4-5 of them could be converted, and if they are run properly, they could be very lucrative. Leo asks, "What are you two guys planning on doing with your life? Do you want to keep working for Hugo and me, or did you have something else in mind?" Joseph then replies, "Once we pay our debt to you, we were planning to move to Wisconsin to be with my Uncle Otto. At least I am." Harry nods his head in agreement. "Yes, we will go stay with your Uncle Otto." Leo replies, "What part of Wisconsin?" Joseph says, "Some place called Sheboygan, but I don't have any idea where this Wisconsin is." Leo tells them, "You are in luck; Wisconsin is the state right above Illinois where we are now. Sheboygan is a few hours' drive north from here." Harry looks at Joseph and says, "Do you think it's time to send a telegram to your uncle and let him know we are in the United States, and we hope to be with him soon?" Joseph replies, "We will do that tomorrow, for now let's enjoy the cigar." After a few minutes, Harry looks at Leo and asks, "In the meantime, can I have your permission to date your daughter, Emma? Leo thinks for a minute and says, "You know I appreciate you being man enough to ask me to my face instead of running around behind my back. I will allow it, but if you ever try to take advantage of Emma, you will end up just like Brenner." Harry's sense of joy has quickly turned to fear. "Thank you, Leo, I would never hurt Emma," he says.

The ladies join them for some coffee and dessert before Harry and Joseph depart. Leo says, "Emma, now that they are gone, I want to ask you something. Do you like Harry? She replies, "Yes, Father, I do. He is quite handsome and very funny and kind." Leo looks at her lovingly. "I thought that's what you would say. I want you to know that I have given Harry permission to date you, if that is what your intentions are." Emma bolts across the room and hugs her father saying, "Thank you, thank you." After Emma has gone to bed, Alice asks Leo to join her on the back porch. As soon as they are out the back door, she pushes Leo against the brick wall of the house, and squeezes his genitals forcibly. "You know how much I love you, Leo, but you are pissing me off," she says. "Who the hell are these boys you have brought to my home?" Leo winces, "Calm yourself, please, I will tell you." Alice loosens her grip and Leo sighs in relief. He says, "We are doing a favor for Wolfgang; how can I turn down his request? Have you forgotten what he did for you?" Alice sobs, "I can never forget, Wolfgang saved me from being raped by those Irish scum. I still cannot believe he beat the heck out of all three of them." Leo hugs her. "Oh, you know how much Wolfgang enjoyed a good fight. Joseph is the nephew of Wolfgang's oldest friend back in Friedrichshafen, and Harry is Joseph's good friend. They got into some trouble with the Nazi soldiers and the Gestapo. Wolfgang helped them escape Germany, and asked for our help to get them new identities, clothes, a place to live, etc. Soon they will join Joseph's uncle up in Wisconsin, actually not too far from here." Alice then asks, "So you think it is alright for Emma to get involved with Harry?" Leo smirks "Thank God she likes Harry and not Joseph. I think Joseph will have nothing but trouble with his temper."

Harry and Joseph awaken early the next morning and begin walking over to the Western Union office to send a telegram to Uncle Otto. Joseph says to Harry, "We literally dodged a bullet last night. I am still shaking." Harry replies, "Why do you think Leo didn't kill us, then?" Joseph thinks briefly, "For two reasons. The first is he really seemed to dislike Brenner. The second and most important reason is he knows Emma has taken a liking to you." Harry confides, "We have only known her a short time, but I feel like I am falling in love with her more and more each day." Joseph says "Well keep it up, now that Leo knows the truth about what happened, we better stay in his good graces." "My friend, I intend to make Emma my wife," Harry explained.

They arrive at Western Union and go into the office. Josephs asks the attendant if he speaks German. "Yes, I do. You have to in this part of Chicago," he replied. Joseph tells him he wants to send a telegram to Mr. Otto Vogel, Eisner Ave. Sheboygan, Wisconsin. The message should read, "This is your nephew Josef, in Chicago, with a friend. Will arrive soon." They tell the attendant to send it and they will check back for a reply in a few days. As they continue their walk over to the warehouse for their daily English lesson, Harry thinks he would like to do something nice for Emma. Harry says, "Hey Joseph, do you think Emma would like some flowers or some chocolate?" He replies, "Flowers are always good. We live above a flower shop. Let's go see our landlady, Chloris." They enter the shop and are immediately struck with the heavy aroma of fresh flowers. Chloris approaches and says, "Make sure you boys keep things quiet. I don't want to be disturbed like the other night." Harry replies, "We will, but I really would like to buy some flowers for a beautiful young lady, your niece, Emma" Chloris smiles with a twinkle in her eye and says, "I see. What you want are some lovely red roses. Get them now because with winter approaching, they will be hard to get." Harry gets the bouquet of red roses and they continue their walk over to the warehouse. He is quite happy to give Emma a gift, and he hopes she likes it.

As they cross the street, they are only a block away from the warehouse. As soon as they step foot on the sidewalk, they are met by two police officers. The taller one says in English with a heavy Irish accent, "So you are the new krauts that are working for Leo and Hugo." Harry can barely understand them, but Joseph does. He replies, "Yes, we work for them." Suddenly, the police officer pushes them both up to the wall of the building. Each of them simultaneously gives Harry and Joseph a kidney punch. As they wince in pain, the police tell them, "Give a message to Leo and Hugo. We want twenty percent more for the protection we provide. Now get the hell out of here." As they both limp down the street, they both start thinking. This is like Kelheim all over again. The sooner we get to Uncle Otto's, the better. As they arrive at the warehouse, they find Emma, Leo, and Hugo waiting. She greets them, "Good morning, I came a little early. I hope you don't mind?" Harry rushes over to her. "Mind? Of course not! I am so happy to see you. Here, I bought these flowers for you." Emma's eyes open wide and she thanks Harry over and over for the lovely gift. Harry tells her, "Before we start our lesson, I need to speak to your father and Hugo in private." After she steps out of the room, they recant to Leo and Hugo their run in with the Irish police. Hugo was quite mad that they were attacked and says, "So the bastards want twenty percent more? We will see about that. Harry, did you or Joseph get their badge numbers?" Harry replies they did and he will write them down. Leo interjects, "The police captain is on our payroll. Those two Mic Irish bastards will be back walking a beat by tonight." Leo goes to the door and calls for Emma to come back in.

Harry tells Emma that he would like to take her on a date, and that her father has given his blessing. Emma and Harry bounce around a few ideas. Maybe a boat ride or a picnic? But being late November in Chicago, it is much too cold for that. Going out to dinner would always be fun, but what to do afterwards. Emma asks Harry, "Have you ever been to a motion picture? Harry replies, "No, I have heard of them but have never been." Emma says, "Then you are in luck. There is a new picture starting tonight at the Granada Theater." Harry responds, "I would like to take you to dinner and then to the picture show if that would be alright?" Emma replies, "It sounds wonderful. Pick me up at 6:00 p.m. for dinner. The picture starts at 8:00 p.m., so we have plenty of time." Harry, picks up Emma in a taxi for dinner that evening. Leo and Alice greet Harry and tell them to have fun, but to come straight home after the movie. Leo says, "The Granada Theater is exquisite; it reminds me of one I went to back east. When I was in Auburn, New York, we traveled to the nearby city of Syracuse. We went to a place I think was called the Lowes State Theater. Now that was a little smaller than the Granada, but very much more ornate. It truly was a Landmark for that city. As they set out, Harry asks Emma what she would like to eat. She replies, "I am tired of German food. Can we try Italian food for something different? There are many in Chicago to choose from." Harry says, "Why not, let's try it." Emma tells the driver to take them to a good Italian restaurant that's within a short drive. After a few minutes, they arrive at the Italian Garden Trattoria that opened in 1929. They are greeted by the owner, Mr. Scrovani. Emma asks him if they can be seated in a private booth, which he obliges. Harry tells Emma, "This place is beautiful. The murals on the wall remind me of Europe and look at the ceiling. It's painted to look like there are stars above us." As they gaze at each other lovingly, they have stars in their eyes. As Harry is still learning to speak and read English, she does the ordering. Emma tells the waiter, "We want to try the saltimbocca alla romana (which is sauteed veal cutlet with prosciutto and sage). We also want to try a sampler platter, which comprises pasta, eggplant parmigiana, and fettuccine alfredo. To drink, we would like a glass of red wine." She figures they will both find something they both like to eat. Their dinners come fairly quickly and they are both amazed at how delicious all the food is. Harry remarks, "The saltimbocca is delicious, and could have been easily served in any German restaurant." Emma tells Harry, "After this dinner, we should not be afraid to try new foods." He replies, "I agree Emma. Whatever you want."

Well, dinner is over and they are off to the movie theater. They arrive at the Granada Theater on North Sheridan Road and they buy a couple of tickets for the grand total of sixty cents. As they enter, Harry is amazed at the size of the theater. Emma tells him it seats 3400 patrons. The entire theater is covered in beautiful wall murals and carvings and is quite the sight. An usher comes right up to them and leads them to their seats. It doesn't take long for the theater to be filled. As they wait for the movie to start, various young ladies come to each row selling concessions to enjoy during the movie. Harry turns to Emma and asks, "What is this movie we are going to see?" She replies, "It is called The Invisible Man." Harry looks at her perplexed, but he figures he will find out what this is all about soon enough. And just like that, the lights go down and the curtain comes up, and the movie begins. Harry is dumbfounded by the size of the movie screen and how well the talking matches up to the mouths moving. Harry cannot understand all that is said, so he keeps whispering to Emma to explain. As the movie continues, he finds himself on the edge of his seat with his eyes transfixed on the screen. Harry is shocked when he sees the Invisible Man appear with no face or body, just a dancing shirt and things flying around the room. All the movie patrons are loving the movie, and when it is finished break out into a thunderous applause. Harry is so happy he leans over and kisses her on the cheek as the lights come back up. Emma blushes and gives Harry a quick hug before they leave their seats and stream out of the theater. They then go outside the theater and wait their turn for a taxi to take them back to Emma's house. Harry and Emma think to themselves, what a perfect evening it has been, as they arrive home.

As they enter the house, they are immediately met at the door by Leo and Alice, like all good doting parents that have been waiting for them to get home. Leo asks, "Well, did you have a good time?" Emma replies, "It was wonderful. I can't wait to do it again." Leo smiles and says, "That's fine. Maybe you can again next year!" Emma and Harry can only look at each other and shrug. Harry bows out gracefully and thanks Emma for the wonderful evening. Leo tells him, "Make sure you get to the warehouse early tomorrow, as we have a busy day planned." After Harry leaves, Alice says, "Alright, that's enough fun for one night Emma, time for bed." As Emma lies in bed, she can't get Harry out of her mind. Her heart is racing and her body feels warm all over. She reaches down and briefly touches herself between her legs before drifting off to a blissful sleep.

As Harry enters the warehouse, he finds Joseph, Leo, and Hugo are waiting for him. Harry says, "Good morning, all. What are we doing today?" Hugo replies "Well, Leo has canceled your English lesson with Emma for today. Go make sure the car has a full tank of gas, as we have a long ride ahead of us." As they get in the car Hugo tells them, "Harry, you drive, and Leo will be in the front to give you direction. Joseph and I will be in the back." Leo directs Harry to drive them north of Chicago to the town of Evanston. Along the way Hugo asks Joseph questions, "So, have you seen Brenner lately? Did you talk to him? Did you get into a fight with him?" Josef plays it cool and denies everything. After this goes on for a while, Leo finally says, "Hugo, would you please give it a break. The boys don't know anything or they would have told you before." Hugo thinks for a moment and replies, "Yes, you are right my friend. I will have to forget about it. I am sure he will turn up." They arrive on the outskirts of Evanston and park outside a lovely two-story home that sits alone at the end of the road. As they enter, Harry sees several beautiful ladies walking up the stairs holding hands with some unknown men. He thinks to himself, what is going on here? Joseph knows instantly what this place is. Harry asks "Leo! Hugo! Is this a whorehouse?" They smile and Hugo replies, "Yes, it is. We have several that we will visit today. Every four to six weeks we visit our houses of ill repute to get our cut of the proceeds. We provide security for the ladies and make sure the local cops are well paid to look the other way. Besides, we give the cops freebies all the time, so they are kept quite happy." As the day passes, they have made stops at four of their establishments. The last one they stop at is in Joliet, Illinois. After they collect their money, all of them were sitting in the car except for Harry, who went to relieve himself. They count the cash and are quite happy that it seems to be the best month ever. Suddenly, a gunshot rings out. Harry peers around the tree and can see two armed men firing at the car. Leo and Hugo return fire but are outgunned as the crooks have guns in each hand. Leo is able to take out the one that is standing in front of the car, but the other continues firing. Hugo, who is sitting on the side of the car closest to the other crook, is hit by gunfire and slumps over dead. Harry draws his weapon and comes up behind the other man and fires. He hits him, but the crook spins around and shoots Harry in the shoulder. At that moment, the whore's bouncer appears from the house and is able to get off a shot, and takes the last crook out, saving Harry. Harry falls to the ground panting heavily. Leo and Joseph rush to his aid. Leo yells out, "Good job. Where are you hit? As Harry winces in pain, he says, "Shoulder." Leo and Joseph help get him into the car and Leo drives with Harry and Joseph in the back. Leo pushes Hugo's body down and covers it with a blanket he had in the back. Hugo has no family, but Leo wants to give him a proper burial. As far as the dead crooks go, the bouncer will take care of burying their bodies. They know a local doctor who tends to the whores in case they get roughed up, so Leo drives there. Once Harry is examined, the doctor finds the shot went right thru without hitting an artery. He cleans the wounds, stitches him up and then bandages him. He then immobilizes his left arm. The doctor says, "I don't think you have lost too much blood, so that's a good thing. Change his dressings every couple of days and use this Sauvé on the wounds. You will be as good as new in a couple of weeks. For now, though, you must rest and take it slow, so you heal up properly." As they drive back to Chicago, Harry is in and out of consciousness. Leo says, "Harry, Harry, are you awake?" He replies, "Yes Leo, what is it?" Leo tells him "Try to remember, you were shot in an attempted robbery of our gambling assets, say nothing of the whorehouses. Emma and Alice are quite smart. They found out a long time ago about bootlegging and gambling. They do not care about either of those things, even though they are both illegal. But Emma and Alice must never know that we are involved in prostitution. That is something they cannot forgive. But that being said, I want you to stay at our house as you recuperate. Alice and Emma will be there to help get you back to health. How does that sound to you Harry?" He replies, "Yes, you are too kind. Thank you, Leo."

They switch drivers and Joseph drops them off at Leo's house, and then he drives back to the warehouse. Joseph puts Hugo's body in the basement refrigerated beer cooler where it will stay overnight. Leo plans on getting the undertaker to come over the next morning to pick up the body. Leo helps Harry into the house and calls out, "We are home. Can you come help please?" Alice rushes down the stairs, followed by Emma. Leo says, "Stay calm. Harry has been shot, but he is going to be alright." Emma immediately is reduced to tears as she hugs Harry. He smiles and moans, "Easy, Emma, easy, my shoulder!"

Leo has Harry sit with him in the parlor while Alice and Emma get his room ready upstairs. Leo offers Harry a glass of whiskey, which he downs rapidly. Harry asks, "May I have another?" Leo replies, "Have all you want; it should help with the pain." Alice calls down that the room is ready and Leo helps him up the stairs to bed. Harry is out as soon as his head hits the pillow. Emma leans over and she kisses him on the cheek. Now the three of them are back downstairs and the girls want to know what happened to Harry. Leo explains to them, "We had just collected the rest of the money from our numbers gambling operation and as we left the speakeasy, we got jumped by a couple of thugs. I was able to shoot and wound one of them, but not before Hugo was killed and Harry was shot. The other young punk who was not armed got scared and ran off, but the cops have the one that shot Harry and Hugo."

It's now the next morning and Harry is downstairs talking with Leo while Alice and Emma are preparing breakfast. Leo asks, "How are you feeling, my friend? Were you able to sleep?" He replies, "Some, my shoulder is quite painful and throbbing all night, but considering I could have been killed, I'll take the pain. But I must tell you Leo, the gunfight, Hugo getting killed, me being shot, it's all pretty terrible. All I can think about is not being able to see Emma. I appreciate what you are doing for Joseph and me, but this type of life is not for us. Please do not be offended," he says breathlessly as he winces.

Leo says, "I am not offended at all. I knew you had planned to go with Joseph to stay with his uncle up in Sheboygan, and that is what you both will do as soon as you have recuperated. So, for now, just take it easy and let Emma nurse you back to health. Besides, by the time you are feeling better, you will be speaking English as good as me. Emma will see to that!" After a leisurely breakfast, there was a knock on the door. Leo goes to check and finds it is Joseph. He says, "Good morning, Leo. I hope you don't mind me stopping by so early, but I was worried about Harry and I wanted to see how he is doing." Leo replies, "Not a problem, come in the kitchen with us. Alice and Emma made too much breakfast, so please join us." Harry is elated to see Joseph and they all visit while Joseph eats a hearty breakfast. Leo,

Harry, and Joseph go into the parlor after Joseph has finished eating. Harry says to Joseph "I was talking with Leo earlier and I told him we were not cut out for this kind of drama and that we wanted to go up to your Uncle Otto's place in Sheboygan, but I did not want to speak for you. So not to put you on the spot, but what are you thinking today about your future?" Joseph replies, "Nothing has changed, Harry. Even more so after what has happened, I want to go be with my uncle." Leo interjects, "As I told Harry earlier, that is fine with me. I will help make it happen. As of today, all debts are canceled. Once Harry is well, you can be on your way." Harry turns to Joseph, "Would you mind leaving Leo and I alone? I need to speak with Leo privately?" Joseph tells Harry he is going to the Western Union office to see if Uncle Otto has sent a reply to their message. He tells him he will drop in on him again tomorrow. After he leaves, Harry confides in Leo, "I hope you know by now how much I like Emma. I haven't been able to stop thinking about her. Please do not be angry, but what would you say if I told you I was in love with Emma, and would like to make her my wife, if she would have me, that is?" Leo stares at him and then smiles, "Harry, people would have to be blind to not see the way you look at Emma. But let me ask you, if you were to marry my daughter, where would you live?" Harry thinks for a moment and says, "I would still like to go up to Sheboygan. Joseph said his Uncle Otto, who works at a brewery, can find us a job. Joseph said they have been making ice cream, malt syrup, and yeast during prohibition." Like everyone else, they just recently have been allowed to make 4% A/V beer. This happened when President Roosevelt started making changes to prohibition, this past March 22, 1933. But maybe it will be totally repealed soon. Harry continues, "It is still my dream to work in a brewery. And Sheboygan is only a few hours from here, so we could visit anytime. Is that something you would consider?" Leo replies, "Let me talk to Alice about it and I will see what she thinks. I will let you know later." As Leo said, Alice and he go out on the back porch to speak about Harry. Leo says, "Well, Alice, it has finally happened. Someone has fallen in love with our daughter." She replies, "I know, and I spoke with Emma last night after all the excitement. She told me she is in love with Harry, so not a big surprise. Let's face it, Emma would make a good wife to anyone, and if we were back in the old country, Emma would have been married off several years ago." Leo tells her, "Harry has asked me for Emma's hand in marriage. He said it is still his intention to go to live in Sheboygan, where Joseph's Uncle Otto will help him get a job. I need to give him an answer. What do you want to do?" Alice thinks for a moment and says, "We should say yes. He seems to be a kind, respectful young man. And besides, we don't want them to run off together and elope. As far as living in Sheboygan, I guess we moved half a world away from our parents, so being a few hours away is not a big deal, but the final decision is up to Emma. We will not force her into anything she doesn't want to do. So, all that being said, tell him he has our permission to ask her."

Later that day, Leo calls Harry aside and gives him the good news. Harry is elated, but wonders to himself if Emma will accept his proposal. He asks Leo a favor. "I would like to propose to Emma today! Would you please go down to your sister, Chloris's, flower shop and buy me a dozen red roses? I know I just bought her some, but they are Emma's favorite, you know. Please also buy her some chocolates." Leo replies, "Yes, I will get them and will be right back." After a little while, Leo returns with a beautiful bouquet of roses and a box of the finest chocolates just as Harry had requested. Leo tells her Chloris was so happy to hear about the proposal, she sent two dozen instead of the one dozen you wanted. Leo calls upstairs to Emma, "Mom and I are going for a drive. Please keep an eye on Harry." As Emma comes down the stairs, she watches her parents leave. Leo turns and winks at Harry as they walk out the door. Harry tells Emma, "I got you some of your favorite flowers and some chocolates. I hope you like them?" Emma replies, "Like them, I love them." Harry responds, "But do you think you could love me as much as you love the flowers?" as he gazes into her eyes. Emma replies, "A thousand times more." Harry says, "I have something to tell you. Your parents have given their blessing for me to ask you something. Emma, will you marry me?" Emma is so elated she yells, "Yes, yes, my love, I will marry you." She hugs him so fast and hard Harry loses his balance and they fall onto the sofa, laughing hysterically. Emma is so happy she can't wait to tell everyone her good news. After an hour or so, Leo and Alice return. Emma runs up to them as soon as they step foot in the door, "Harry proposed, and I said yes!" Leo and Alice take turns hugging them and then Leo asks Harry, "If you feel up to it, I want to take us all out to dinner to celebrate!" Harry replies, "I feel much better. I am so happy, but can Emma pick where we are going?" Leo says to Emma, "What sounds good to you?" "That's an easy one, she replies. "Let's go to the Italian Garden Trattoria."

Leo, not wanting to disappoint Emma, agrees to her request. He says to Alice, "Well, Italian food will be something new for us." Harry interjects, "I was suspicious of it myself, but now that I've tried it, I find it to be quite delightful." As they are seated at the restaurant, Leo orders a bottle of their finest wine. He tells the waiter to bring several platters of their finest dishes for the table so they can all sample the cuisine. The waiter disappears into the kitchen and a few minutes later the owner comes to the table and says, "Welcome to my restaurant. I recognize the young couple from the other night. You have requested platters of our finest food, but we normally do not serve family style." Leo replies, "This is my wife's and my first time trying Italian cuisine. We are also celebrating my daughter's engagement tonight." Mr. Scrovani, upon hearing of the joyous occasion, is happy to oblige. He first delivers an order of hot crunchy garlic bread, along with an antipasti platter. It is full of salami, mortadella, prosciutto, roasted red peppers, marinated mushrooms and artichoke hearts. When they have finished that, the main course arrives. A platter of veal parmesan, with fettuccine alfredo on the side. Some ravioli in meat sauce, along with a platter of sauce meat, which consists of meatballs, sausage, and braciole. The dinner turns out to be as wonderful as Emma and Harry said it would be. They order some hot coffee and continue conversing while they wait for it to be served. The waiter comes over to the table and offers them some rainbow sherbet ice cream, compliments of the owner. This was the first of several desserts they would be sampling tonight. As soon as they had finished their scoop of sherbet, the waiter returned with a small platter of pastries to go with their coffee. Leo asks the waiter what they are, as they were unfamiliar with them. "The long-filled tubes are called cannoli, which is a fried pastry shell stuffed with a mixture of ricotta cheese and sugar. The round tarts are a baked pastry dough stuffed with a pastry cream filling, which is called pasti-ciotti. The third pastry is shaped like a lobster tail, which is also its name. It is flakey baked pastry stuffed with the cannoli cream filling." They waste no time wolfing down the pastries, even though they are already full from dinner. They all remark that these are the best pas-tries they have ever had. So different from the German pastries they grew up on. As they get up to leave, Mr. Scrovani, thanks them for their patronage and asks if everything was to their liking. Leo replies, "Everything was fantastic, especially the pastries." The owner tells them, "I love the pastries, too. The next time you come, I want you to try some pizza fritte, which is pizza dough that has been raised and then are cut into long strips. We then fry them in oil and, when done, we dip it in sugar to finish them off. Simple, but delicious!" Emma ex-claims, "I can't wait to try it. We will be back soon."

As they get into the car for the ride home, Harry thanks Leo and Alice again for the wonderful dinner. Alice replies, "It was our plea-sure, Harry. Soon you will be part of the family and we only want the best for our Emma." As they are driving, suddenly Harry starts slur-ring his words. His mouth appears crooked, and he is drooling slightly, and then he passes out. Emma begins screaming for someone to help Harry. Leo immediately floors the gas pedal and drives them to the nearby hospital. As the orderlies get him out of the car and on to a stretcher, Emma is besides herself. The doctor on duty at the emer-gency room quickly examines Harry, who has just become conscious. He is breathing well and has a strong pulse and normal heartbeat. He has stopped drooling and is able to speak slowly. In his broken English, Harry asks, "Where I am, what happened?" The doctor replies, "You are in the hospital. Just rest now while I talk with your family." He looks at Leo and Alice and asks if Harry is their son. They answer, "No, he is our daughter's fiancé. We were on our way home from dinner when he fell ill." After getting all the details of his symptoms, he believes Harry has had a mild epileptic seizure. The doctor tells them to go home and come back in the morning, as they want to keep him overnight for observation. Emma kisses Harry goodnight and tells him to get some rest. As they leave the hospital, Emma is sobbing, "Why did this happen? First, he was shot doing your illegal activities, Father, and now this. God help him get well." Leo is apologetic, "Calm yourself Emma, the doctors will take good care of him. I never wanted Harry to get hurt." She replies, "I know you say that, but let's face it, it's a dangerous world you live in. Harry and I don't want any part of it." As they arrive home, Emma bolts up the stairs to bed. Leo and Alice decide to get a glass of brandy to calm their nerves. Alice looks at Leo and says, "Well, not the way I thought the night was going to end. But I pray Harry will be alright." Leo replies, "We can only hope." When they are finished with their brandy, they retire for the night.

Morning comes quickly for Leo and Alice. But unfortunately, Emma did not sleep at all last night and she was totally exhausted and her eyes were red from crying. Alice yells up to her, "Emma, come join us for breakfast. Some coffee and food will make you feel better." As they sit at the table eating, Leo says, "We have not heard from the hospital, so I think no news is good news. As soon as we have eaten breakfast, everyone get changed, and we will head over to see Harry." About an hour later, they arrive at the hospital. They go into Harry's room and find him with a doctor. Emma rushes over to hug Harry. "How are you doing?" she asks. Harry replies, "I feel fine, but I still don't understand what happened." The doctor says he is having trouble communicating with Harry and asks if someone could help translate. Emma volunteers, "Yes, of course, I have been teaching him English." The doctor requests that she ask Harry if he had ever had any head injuries. Harry replies, "Yes, a few months ago, the German soldiers hit me in the head with the butt of their rifle and gave me a concussion." Emma is taken aback. She thinks to herself, what is he talking about. I thought he grew up in Cicero, Illinois, and his parents only taught him to speak German. Emma looks at Harry and then at Leo and speaks only in German so the doctor will not understand, "Father, where the heck did Harry grow up?" Leo responds, "Look, Emma, this is all a secret and no one can ever know. Our friend Wolfgang in Germany smuggled Harry and Joseph out of their country, as the soldiers and the Gestapo were giving the boy's trouble. I have given them new identities, clothes, a place to live, etc. Once they were on their feet, they were to go to Joseph's uncle's house up in Wisconsin. Please do not betray their trust." Emma replies, "Of course not. I love Harry, and Joseph is very dear to me. But Father, when will you start confiding in me? I am not a child nor am I stupid." Leo tells her, "I apologize for keeping that secret, but I did not think that you were going to fall in love with one of them." The doctor interjects, "Well, any head injuries?" Emma replies, "He said he had a concussion several months ago." The doctor says, "That is the answer. This confirms the diagnosis of my colleague last night. It was an epileptic seizure, which has to do with the brain being injured. We think it was a mild seizure, however, and we will prescribe a medicine called phenobarbital. It is quite inexpensive and should take care of his seizures. It is possible that he may never have another one. There are side effects of the medication, but we are starting him on a low dose, so hopefully he will tolerate it well. But it is important that he does not stop taking the medicine without checking with a doctor first. Now Harry, here is a prescription to get filled. You can get dressed. I am going to discharge you now. If you have another seizure, let us know, so we can adjust the medication."

On the way back to Leo's house, they stop off at the drugstore to get Harry's medicine. They don't want to wait to get him started on it, the sooner the better. Once they get home, Alice and Emma put together some breakfast for Harry. After he eats, he takes his first dose of medicine and relaxes for a bit. Emma asks, "How are you feeling now? Does your head hurt, or your shoulder?" Harry replies, "I actually feel much better. My head is clear and my shoulder only hurts when I move it." Leo interjects, "That is good to hear. You just take it easy, and give your body a chance to heal." There is a knock on the door, and it is Joseph checking in on Harry. Leo says, "Good morning, Joseph, come in. Harry will be happy to see you." Joseph looks at Harry and asks, "How are you, my friend? Better than yesterday, I hope?" Harry replies, "Good news and bad news. I spent the night in the hospital because of something called a brain seizure. They gave me medicine for it. But the good news is Emma, with Leo's blessing, has accepted my marriage proposal." Joseph says, "I am sorry you have more illness, but I am so happy for you and Emma. Oh, and I wanted to tell you, Uncle Otto sent a reply to our telegram. He sent his address and said to come anytime to Sheboygan, and he will help us find work." Harry is happy and relieved to hear that news.

Another week goes by and it's now the beginning of December. Harry has spent the last week convalescing and is doing much better. Joseph has kept busy making liquor deliveries, and working as a part-time bouncer/bartender. That night, December 5th, 1933, Emma and Harry are sitting in the parlor with Leo and Alice listening to the radio. Suddenly, the music is interrupted by a news flash. "Attention, The State of Utah has just voted to ratify the 21st Amendment to the Constitution. That means it has now been ratified by the required three-fourths majority of the states. It is now the law of the land. Prohibition has been officially repealed!" Just as soon as the announcement was made, they could hear cheering in the streets. Leo says, "Come on, everyone, let's go down to the bar and have our first legal drink to celebrate." As they drive, Leo thinks to himself that if he is lucky in converting some of the speakeasies, he will make even more money because he won't have to pay off the cops anymore. The cost of obtaining the alcohol should drop in price also, as it can be produced locally, and not have to be smuggled in. Obviously, the two speakeasies that are hidden underground will have to be closed, but that leaves a few above ground ones that can be modified to allow easy visibility and street access. He thinks short term I will use my gambling and prostitution money to fund the opening of the bars, restaurant, and nightclub. I will have to move fast to beat out the competition. Eventually, if all goes well, I can sell off my illegal operations and go legit. When they get to the bar, it is just mobbed with people. They are literally out on the sidewalk, and in the street, drinking and cheering.

As they enter the bar, Harry asks Emma, "Do you think it's alright for me to drink now that I have this seizure issue and have started medication?" She replies, "The doctor said you must be very careful and not drink too much alcohol, as it is dangerous for you. Maybe one regular glass of beer once in a while, but you must watch for side effects, especially seizures, breathing problems, drowsiness. So be extra careful. Remember you are recovering from a gunshot, and a brain seizure." Harry responds, "That sounds fine and even though I have been drunk before, in reality, that only happened a couple of times. But I do enjoy a good beer occasionally, and I can easily do without the hard liquor. So, I will be extremely careful." As Leo, Alice, and Emma each enjoy some cocktails, Harry slowly sips on a cold beer. He thinks to himself how lucky he really is to be here in a new country, and engaged to Emma. All the tragedy of the last few days seems to be so unimportant, as long as he has his Emma.

As they leave the bar, Alice says to Emma, "Your father has had too much to drink and Harry is in no condition to drive, either. Would you mind driving us home?" Emma replies, "Of course not, I love driving the Terraplane!" As they start the drive home, Alice is yelling at Emma, "Will you please slow down? We don't want to get pulled over by the cops." Emma seems exasperated. "Oh, alright, can't I have any fun?" she says. As soon as they get home, Alice helps Leo to bed. Emma and Harry stay downstairs so they can talk a little more before they call it a night. Harry asks Emma, "I hope I will be fully recovered in another week or so. How soon do you think we will be able to be married?" Emma replies, "The weather in Chicago now is getting pretty bad with winter setting in. I always wanted a spring wedding when all the flowers are in bloom." Harry responds, "I was hoping we would not have to wait that long, but I understand." She explains, "There is a lot to be done. We first have to line up a church and wedding hall, see who we will use to cater the wedding, and decide on the food. Wedding invitations have to be made and sent out. We need to make favors for the wedding. The most important thing I didn't mention is I have to find a wedding gown!" Harry smiles and says, "I didn't know it would be so complicated. But you deserve a beautiful wedding, so let's talk with your parents about it tomorrow morning." They then both go upstairs to their rooms and fall fast asleep. Emma dreams about her wedding, just as she has since she was a young girl. Harry finds it hard to sleep as he frets about how he will be able to support Emma after they are married. He will have to delay going to Wisconsin until after they are married in the spring.

The next day they are all awake, and having finished breakfast, Leo is about to leave. Emma asks Leo, "Are you feeling better Father, you were pretty wasted last night?" Leo responds, "Actually, I feel better than I thought I would, which is a good thing, because I want to start work on converting the speakeasy on Market Street into a bar and restaurant." Emma looks at him inquisitively, "What type of restaurant were you planning?" Leo explains, "A traditional German restaurant, of course. Why, what are you thinking?" She hesitates for a minute and says, "You know, Father, Chicago really has people from three different places in Europe; Germany, Ireland, and Italy. Remember how much we enjoyed the Italian restaurant we went to? Why not have a restaurant that caters to all three cuisines?" Leo looks at Alice and asks, "What do you think of that idea, my love?" Alice responds, "What would you have to lose, and besides, you could potentially get patrons of all the main ethnic groups. If the food is superb, we could draw customers from all over Chicago." Leo thought out loud, "But what do we call such a place?" Everyone throws out ideas until Emma hits on the perfect one. Emma suggests, "Why not call it Restaurant Europa? That way, you are not limited as to what you can serve." They all smile and look at each other, and Leo says, "Congratulations, Emma. Restaurant Europa, it shall be."

Just as Leo is about to leave, Joseph shows up. "How are you feeling today, Harry?" he asks. Harry responds, "I am feeling a little better each day, thankfully. I wanted to tell you, though, that I will have to delay going up to Sheboygan. Emma and I will be getting married in the spring. I hope you are not disappointed?" Josef looks at Emma and says, "How could I be? You are marrying such a wonderful person, beautiful inside and out. I am so happy for the both of you." Leo then asks Josef what his plans are as far as going to be with his uncle. Josef says to Leo, "I really want to leave as soon as possible. I have saved up a little money to put towards buying a car, but I don't know if I will have enough." Leo responds, "Don't worry about money. I will ask around and see if anyone has a cheap vehicle for sale. If you need some extra cash, I will help you with that. Just give me a couple of days, and we will get you on your way." Joseph shakes Leo's hand and thanks him over and over. Leo tells them, "I am glad to help. I have become quite fond of you and Harry. Now I am so glad Wolfgang asked me to help you guys out in the first place. Alright, I have to leave now. See you tonight for dinner." After Joseph leaves, Emma, Harry, and Alice spend some time talking about the wedding plans.

Alice tells them the first thing they need to do is to get the church reserved for the wedding. She looks at Harry and asks, "Are you Catholic like we are? That is very important to us." Harry responds, "Yes, of course, I was baptized as a Catholic, but because we lived on a farm, we usually only went to Sunday Mass once a month growing up. I have to admit, I haven't been in a couple of years." Alice tells them, "That is good to hear. I think we should go over to our parish, St. Joseph, over on Hill Street and talk with Father Weber." As the weather has turned quite cold, and snow has begun to fall, they call a taxi to take them over to church. As they arrive and enter the rectory, they are greeted by Father Weber, who says, "Alice Wagner, it is so good to see you. What has brought you here today?" Alice responds, "You remember my daughter Emma, and this is Harry, her fiancé." The priest responds, "Of course I know Emma. I baptized her and see her at Mass every Sunday. Very nice to meet you, Harry. I don't think I've seen you before?" Harry, not wanting to lie to the priest, says, "I recently moved to Chicago and have been lucky to find the love of my life." Alice interjects, "Emma and Harry want to be married in the spring, and we wanted to reserve a date." Father Weber asks Harry if he has been baptized, to which he replies yes. He goes on to say, "We only have a couple of requirements. The first is you would need to join the parish and attend weekly Mass, along with making whatever contribution you feel you can afford. The second is I would like you to attend a class we put on. It's weekly, for three months. It is basically a review of our Catholic faith, as well as a few tips on what makes a happy marriage. I will handle the religious part of the class, and we have a couple of married parishioners that will handle that part of your relationship. Well, how does that sound to you?" Emma and Harry both say yes, and that they are looking forward to it. Father Weber responds, "That is wonderful. Now let's go check the marriage book and see what dates we have available in the spring." As they look through, Father Weber suggests May 26, 1934. That date is open, and by then the weather should be warm and the flowers should be in bloom. They all agree on that date, and they reserve it. Father Weber tells them, "Alright, I expect to see you at Mass this Sunday, and you start classes next Wednesday at 7:00 p.m. We will see you then. Please have a safe and blessed week."

A few days go by and Leo, true to his word, has found a car for Joseph. It's a 1930 Nash 400 with an 8-cylinder engine. Joseph asks Leo if he can afford that type of car. Leo replies, "I have lots of people that owe me money on their gambling debts. The guy I got this from runs a used car lot, so we made a deal for this car and he is happy to have me off his back. How much money have you saved up?" Joseph replies, "Only $150.00, Will that be enough?" Leo replies, "Not a problem, as I have been in contact with Wolfgang. He said I was to help you out financially, and he would reimburse me for expenses, if needed. Here is the bill of sale. This afternoon we will register the vehicle in your name. Go find your birth certificate, as you will need it for identification." Everything ends up going well at the motor vehicle department. For some reason, it cost an extra $20.00, but he doesn't care. The car is registered to Joseph, and they issue him something new, a Photo Identification card, which he can pick up tomorrow. Joseph is happy to have the car but also, he will now have what appears to be a legal identity card. Joseph asks Leo if it would be alright for him to leave for his uncle's house tomorrow after picking up his new driver's license. Leo replies, "Of course, it's alright. But I want you to come over for dinner tonight to say goodbye." Joseph says, "That sounds good. I'll see you tonight."

Joseph gets some flowers at the shop downstairs from where he lives, from Leo's sister. Alice and Emma are happy to see him, and appreciate the thoughtful gift. During dinner, the topic turns to cars. Leo tells them, "I got a used car for Joseph today so he will have transportation to use in Sheboygan. I was also thinking of getting a new car for Alice and me, maybe a Cadillac or a Lincoln." Emma then asks, "But what are you going to do with the Terraplane, Father?" He replies, "That, my dear, will be my wedding present to you and Harry." Emma leaps from the table, hugs her father and exclaims, "Thank you so much. You know how much I love that car." Alice responds to the news and sarcastically says, "Great idea Leo, do you think you can have a mechanic put a governor on the engine so she has to stay under 100 mph." Emma looks at her mother and rolls her eyes. Joseph interrupts and says, "I want to thank you all for the hospitality. I want you to know I am leaving for Sheboygan tomorrow." Emma asks, "But are you planning on coming back in the spring for our wedding?" He replies, "Of course, I wouldn't miss it. Do you think I could bring Uncle Otto as well?" Leo and Alice answer together, "Absolutely! We can't wait to meet him." After dinner, Joseph says his goodbye to his old friend Harry, and the rest of them. Harry says, "Keep in touch, Joseph, and good luck on everything. Hopefully, once the wedding is over, we will be able to join you in Sheboygan. As he leaves the house, they all hug him goodbye, and wish him good luck in his new life.

The next day, Joseph has no problem picking up his new license. He still has a little food and gas money for the brief trip to his uncle's. He buys a road map, and he is on his way. The weather is not very good, and snow is falling, but he makes it safely to Sheboygan. Joseph is impressed at the very nice neighborhood his uncle lives in. As he walks up to the door, he wonders if his uncle will recognize him. He knocks, and after a couple of minutes, the door opens. Uncle Otto looks at him head to toe and says "Joseph, my dear boy, you made it." Otto sheds a few tears as he hugs Joseph, "Come in, please, we have much to talk about." Joseph thinks to himself I'm finally home!

Back in Chicago, Leo has been very busy the last couple of months getting his speakeasies converted over. The bar over on Chestnut Street has already opened for business and is doing well. There is so much pent-up demand for alcohol they can barely keep up. For now, he is putting his plans for a nightclub on hold until he gets the restaurant up and running. The exterior renovations have been completed, and new kitchen equipment has been installed. Harry has been put in charge of the bar operation and has just completed getting the bar stocked and everything in working order. Leo is outside the restaurant when a taxi pulls up. Alice and Emma come to see how the renovations are coming. Leo says, "I am glad you took time off from wedding gown shopping to stop by. Look Emma, the new neon sign has been installed above the window, Restaurant Europa." Emma replies, "That sign looks fantastic, and the exterior looks good as well. Leo takes them inside for a tour of the restaurant. Emma spots Harry at the bar and is happy to see him looking so good. He really has recovered from his injuries well. After checking out the main floor, Leo takes them all upstairs. It's a sizeable room that lays above the bar and restaurant, but also extends over the business next door. Leo asks, "How many people do you think this room could hold?" Alice answers, "I would think, depending on the size of the tables, at least 200 people. But why do you ask?" Leo explains, "I was thinking of making this into a catering hall. We could have weddings, parties, religious events, just about anything, really. If we can get it fixed up properly, what do you think about having your wedding reception here, Emma?" She replies, "That's a good idea. I'm all for it. Maybe you can let Mother and me be involved in planning how to decorate the room?" Leo says, "Absolutely, you can help. I was thinking of putting the tables this way, so they surround the dance floor in the middle of the room. The band can go on that wall, with a wet bar in that corner. And over here, we can install a series of dumbwaiters to bring the food up from the kitchen. I will have to install a water closet in the opposite corner of the room to make it convenient for the guests. But that should all be easy to do, as we will plan it, so it overlays the plumbing and layout downstairs, and we can tie it in easily." Leo stops and thinks for a moment and says, "Do you all remember when we went to the Italian restaurant and we got platters of food? Why don't we serve all the food family style for any of the banquets we put on up here?" Everyone loves the idea and nods in agreement. After they spend some time brainstorming as to the type of lighting, paint color, decorations, etc., they decide to all go shopping together at the various supply houses to get everything picked out.

As another month passed, the renovations to Restaurant Europa, which is located near Lincoln Square, are completed. The staff has been hired and trained, and the menus have been printed. Leo hired a chef who had worked in restaurants all over Europe, so he was well versed in many different types of food. As Leo had discussed with his family, they are offering a limited menu of the three main cuisines served in Chicago. For the Irish dishes, they have Irish stew, boiled bacon and cabbage, smoked salmon, Guinness pie, and gammon (cured pork leg). For the Italian, they offer lasagna, veal parmesan, spaghetti, and meatballs, arancini (stuffed rice balls), and something not very common in the states, pizza. Last but not least, for the German, roulade (bacon and onions rolled in thinly sliced beef), wiener schnitzel (breaded veal cutlet), sauerbraten (vinegar marinated beef roast), kaesespaetzle (sauteed dumplings with fried onions and cheese), and bratwurst (sausage).

It's finally opening night at the restaurant. Leo has reached out to his contacts all over Chicago. The restaurant is fully booked for the night. He has invited an eclectic mix of gangsters, police, politicians, and business owners. Leo greets every guest who has come in and offers each a free glass of wine to celebrate the restaurant opening. The food is a little slow coming out, but as the night progresses, things smooth out nicely. As Leo goes from table to table asking how their food is, he is elated to hear all the compliments. He even sees some patrons trying dishes they are not familiar with. Harry is busy at the bar and is doing a brisk business. Many people have come in just to drink and munch on the pickled eggs and pickled sausage that are kept in jars atop the bar. Emma and Alice are seated at a small table in the corner of the room, and are taking great pleasure in trying to figure out who some of the politicians are and watching their reaction as they eat their food. At the end of the evening, the restaurant has closed for the night. Leo, Alice, Harry, and Emma are seated at the large booth on the back wall. They are quite pleased at how much money they took in tonight as they sort and count the proceeds. Leo says to Alice, "This is a fantastic start to our new business venture. I even had a couple of people inquire about booking a banquet." Alice replies, "That is fantastic news. Congratulations, my love." Emma interjects, "You know, Father, when you have banquets, there could be up to a couple hundred people at one time. As a way to increase business in the restaurant itself, why not give each banquet guest a coupon for 10% off their next meal in the restaurant." Leo and Alice both shake their heads with approval and say, "Great idea, Emma. Thank you for the suggestion."

Leo says, "Well, let's head home for the night. The staff will finish the cleanup."

The next day, after sleeping late, Alice and Emma are out gown shopping again. They have visited almost every wedding gown shop in Chicago. Alice says, "Emma, it's time to decide. You have it narrowed down to three gowns at this shop. That is great, but no more shopping. This is it; my feet are killing me." Emma smiles, "I get it. I assure you we will leave with a gown today." Emma goes through trying on the three gowns. It is the second one that she spends the most time in, observing how she looks in the mirror from every angle. Alice tells her she thinks number two is the best choice, as she looks stunning in it. Emma looks at Alice and says, "You are right, Mother, this is the one. I am saying YES to this dress!" Alice is so happy she yells "Hallelujah!" Alice thinks to herself, this is a major headache out of the way. "So, we have the church booked, we have the gown, we have the restaurant, but we need to decide on a menu. That also leaves the invitations and wedding favors to be completed. So much still to do, but we will get it done."

Later that afternoon, Leo is home and has some time before going to check on the restaurant. Alice says, "Leo, did I tell you the good news? Emma bought a gown." Leo laughs, "God in heaven, can it be true?" Alice responds, "Yes, it is, but we also have other matters to discuss if we are going to have the wedding in May. Let me call Emma and Harry so we can talk about it." After the four of them are together at the kitchen table, Alice starts off, saying, "There are many things left to plan for the wedding. The first and easiest item is the flowers. Now Leo, I assume we will have your sister Chloris do that for us, correct?" Leo replies, "I already mentioned it to her, and she can't wait. She said leave everything to her." Emma says, "I can't wait to see what she comes up with. I know they will be beautiful." Alice asks, "Does anyone have an idea for wedding favors?" Leo speaks up immediately, "Harry, do you remember all of those cases of very small empty liquor bottles we have stacked at the warehouse?" Harry says, "Yes, I know just where they are." Leo continues, "Why don't we fill each one with liquor, vodka, or whiskey maybe, and each guest gets a bottle and a shot glass." Everyone seems to like that idea, so on to the next item. Emma asks, "How many people can I have in my wedding party? Do you think 6 or 7 bridesmaids would be alright? I was thinking, "I don't have a sister, but I have a couple of friends and five cousins." Alice tells her, "Emma, have as many as you like." Then Leo asks Alice, "Can you check with your sister and ask her the name and phone number of the person who did the pictures for her daughter's wedding?" Alice responds, "Great idea. Those were the best wedding pictures I have ever seen. I know she said they were very expensive." Leo smiles, "That's fine. I will make him an offer he can't refuse! Well, that's enough for now. I have to get to the restaurant. Let's talk about the wedding dinner tomorrow."

Alice and Emma spend the evening talking about the wedding banquet and which friends and family they should invite. Alice knows Leo will be inviting many business associates, but the Restaurant Europa Hall should fit everyone nicely. The next morning comes, and after breakfast, the family is gathered in the parlor to discuss the wedding banquet. Leo starts by asking, "Has anyone come up with any ideas?" Harry responds, "Whatever Emma wants is fine with me." Emma smiles and says, "Yes, Father, Mother and I talked about it last evening. Do you remember how we all enjoyed that antipasti platter when we went to the Italian restaurant?" Leo smiles and says, "It was very good, but not something I have seen served at any German wedding I have been to. But you are right, it was delicious. Alice, what do you think about Emma's idea? Maybe we could serve it with some fresh baked crusty bread?" Alice thinks for a moment and replies, "Why not try something different? I know I get bored with the same food all the time. Besides, isn't that the whole point of our restaurant, having multiple cuisines available for our guests?" Leo nods in agreement and replies, "Let's try it. Alright, what's next?" Alice says, "Even though I agree with Emma on trying some different things, Emma and I both thought a bowl of hochzeitssuppe (beef-based wedding soup) would be nice." Everyone nods in agreement on that item. Alice says, "Now, for the main course, we have had a lot of discussion about what that should be. We were thinking of two entrees, one German, and one Italian. For the German entrée, how about some good pork schnitzel, with jaeger sauce (mushroom sauce) served with spaetzle? For the Italian, let's do platters of Italian meats like we had before: meatballs, sausage, beef meat, braciole, all cooked in a rich red tomato sauce served with ravioli pasta. I know we all enjoyed it before, and I think the guests will as well." Leo responds, "I can't argue with the fact that we enjoyed all the foods you described, so let's go with that." Emma says, "Fantastic! I'm so happy we all agree." Alice turns the discussion to the cake. "I spoke with Her Klug over at his bakery last week. He is known for making some of the best wedding cakes in town, you know. I asked him if he could bake us something unique for the wedding. While you were all sleeping, I drove over to the bakery and picked up a sample cake he had made. Come into the kitchen and let's try it." Leo asks, "Did he give you an idea of what he has made?" Alice responds, "Something he calls carrot cake with cream cheese frosting. I will cut you all a slice to try." Emma takes one bite and is amazed, saying, "This is the best cake ever! We need to have this, please Mother, Father!" They are all in agreement that this is a unique and delicious cake. It's so good, Harry has a second piece. Alice says, "Emma and I will talk with Her Klug, and order the wedding cake. I will also ask him to provide trays of assorted cookies that you and Harry will pass at the wedding."

Alice looks at Leo and says, "I am going to take Emma over to the printers so we can design a wedding invitation. Is there anything special that you want?" Leo responds, "I don't think so. Whatever you come up with will be fine. I have also been thinking about which of my friends and associates to invite, so we can put a list together in the next few days. See you all for dinner tonight."

The next few months go by uneventfully. Leo's restaurant is doing a substantial business. Everyone loves the chef's food and there are few, if any, nights. The place is not packed. Harry has been thrilled tending bar and helping in the restaurant as needed. He thinks to himself, this is better than being shot at. He still dreams of working in a brewery and can't wait to move to Wisconsin after they get married. The wedding is next week, and the weather has warmed nicely. The flowers were starting to bloom, and Emma couldn't be happier. Tomorrow, Emma and Harry are going to the County building to register the Terraplane. While they are there, they will also apply for their driver's license. They thought it would be a simple process to get all their paperwork done for the car and license. But the next day, the clerk seems to not be accepting Harry's birth certificate and starts quizzing him on growing up in Cicero. Question after question is asked and answered. Harry has really improved his English language skills, as Emma still teaches him daily. The clerk tells Harry, "Well, I think these papers are suspicious, and I don't believe you are from here." Harry replies, "Yes, I am from Cicero. I grew up there, and work at Restaurant Europa." Then the clerk's true motivation comes to light. "I would be willing to fix and approve all your applications, but it will cost you an extra $20.00." Emma is steaming mad and says, "This is a shakedown." The clerk shoots back with, "I am offended that you would criticize me. If you don't want my help, then move on." Emma looks at Harry and says in German, "Pay this Schweinhund the money he asks, and let's get the hell out of here." It turns out to be a common occurrence in Chicago, shaking down immigrants and people not knowing what is really going on, especially with the language barrier. Well, they leave the building with everything approved, totally aggravated, but at least it's done and legal. They can pick up the licenses in the morning. Harry remembers what Leo taught him, stay calm, think, learn to play the game, but most of all, don't pick a battle you can't win. Harry smiles as he realizes that he now has been issued an authentic driver's license, which means his new identity is secure. He says to Emma as he holds her hand, "Farewell to Helmut Lang. I am now officially Harry Langer, soon to be Mr. & Mrs. Harry Langer!" he says.

The wedding day has finally arrived, and it's a lovely Saturday afternoon. The sun is shining, and it's about 70 degrees Fahrenheit. Emma and the bridesmaids have just finished their hair, and each one looks stunning in their gowns. The bride is in white, of course, and the maid of honor and the flower girl are in light green gowns. The other five bridesmaids are wearing light pink gowns. The photographer has arrived, and is lining them all up in front of the house for a picture. After that, he takes one of Emma being flanked by Alice and Leo. The photographer finishes and tells them he will leave and get set up at the church and await their arrival. After a few minutes, a couple of navy blue eight door stretched Checker cabs arrive to take the wedding party and Emma's parents to the church. As they arrive, they see a few people milling around on the outside steps of the church smoking, but they quickly put out their cigarettes and enter. As the wedding party goes in, they are greeted by Father Weber, who asks them for a favor. "We are running behind today because of the earlier wedding, and Saturday Mass will start at four o'clock. Would you mind processing out the side door of the church, into the parking lot, instead of up the main aisle?" Emma hesitantly replies, "Sure Father Weber," At this point Emma 's blood is boiling. She thinks, "I have waited all my life to get married, and he wants me to sneak out the side door? No freaking way." As Emma processes down the aisle with Leo, she is so excited to see Harry standing with the ushers in front of the altar. The Mass and wedding ceremony go off without a hitch. Father Weber really does a good job, and everyone feels happy and uplifted. The church choir was right on key, and the soloist belted out a fantastic rendition of Ave Maria. As the ceremony is finished, Emma and Harry are standing in front of the altar, ready to process out. Father Weber looks at Emma as if to say remember what I asked you. Emma smiles, grabs Harry's arm, and leads the procession right up the main aisle and outside to the front of the church. Father Weber can do nothing to stop the crowd, and just stands there shaking his head. The wedding party, including best man Joseph, lines up at the entrance to the church and greets each guest as they leave. Joseph's Uncle Otto has come down from Sheboygan and he warmly embraces and congratulates the bride and groom. Harry says, "Thank you for coming. We will talk with you later at the reception. The bride and groom are ready to leave, and as they exit, they are pelted with rice. It is said the number of grains of rice that stick to the bride's hair is the number of children they shall have. Once outside, the photographer again starts lining the wedding party up for a few pictures. As Leo is shaking hands with everyone, he happens to glance across the street. He is surprised to see men with cameras apparently taking pictures of the wedding. He grabs police Captain O'Brien, who is in attendance, and asks, "Hey, Sean, what gives with the suits with cameras across the street?" The captain doesn't even have to look, and replies, "That's Hoovers G-Men." Leo sighs, "I guess I should not be surprised."

Once the pictures at church are complete, they all gather into the Checker cabs for the drive to their next stop. The bulk of the pictures are going to be taken at a lakefront park before heading over to the reception. As they get over to the park, the photographer remarks how lucky they are today because the winds are quite calm, which is unusual. Alice asks Leo, "What is going to happen if we get delayed with the pictures, and our guests are waiting at the restaurant?" He replies, "I thought of that before, and the chef has arranged for coffee and donuts to be served while they wait for us to arrive. It does take a little while to complete the pictures, and the photographer seems confident they will be of good quality. As they arrive at the restaurant and get out of the cars to enter, Leo sees a couple of his guests leaving. "Where are you going?" he asks. The couple replies, "We enjoyed the coffee and donuts, thanks for inviting us." Leo laughs, "No, no, you are not going anywhere, that wasn't the dinner. Please go back to your table. We will be eating a large meal shortly."

As the wedding party enters the upstairs banquet hall, they are greeted by much applause. The band leader announces each couple, saving the bride and groom for last. Finally, it's their turn to enter, and they hear, "Introducing Mr. & Mrs. Harry Langer." Everyone is clapping for them, as they make their way to the dance floor for the traditional first dance. As is tradition, they dance to a Viennese Waltz, and are soon joined by Emma's parents, Leo and Alice. They then do one more dance, where the entire wedding party is on the dance floor together. As the four of them are returning to their seats, Joseph and Uncle Otto approach. Joseph says, "Leo and Alice, I want you to meet my Uncle Otto." They greet him and thank him for helping Joseph and Harry. Uncle Otto says, "It is my pleasure, Joseph is my favorite and only nephew," as he winks at Joseph. "Any friend of his is a friend of mine." Otto asks Leo, "So I understand you and my old friend Wolfgang go way back" Leo responds, "Yes, Wolfgang laid the groundwork for my business interests. I owe him much, so when he asked for my help in getting Joseph and Harry settled, I was happy to oblige." Otto continues, "Once the newlyweds get settled, I want you and Alice to be my guests at my home in Sheboygan." Leo and Alice agree and tell Otto to enjoy the reception, and they look forward to visiting.

Soon, they are all seated and ready for the banquet to begin. Just as they had planned, the chef has his waiters deliver the most delicious platters of food Emma has ever tasted. As she gazes around, it seems everyone is enjoying themselves. Leo takes the opportunity to go to each table and check if his guests are enjoying themselves. Everyone is happy with the food, and are trying new things. As Leo expected, his associates are questioning why the police are guests at the wedding, and vice versa. The police are paid well to look the other way, but that doesn't mean either side likes each other. He tells all of them, "Put everything else aside. Today is a celebration of my daughter's wedding." Leo orders more wine for their tables, and soon everyone has drunk their fill, and has mellowed out and enjoyed the evening.

After dinner has ended and they have relaxed for a few minutes, Emma and Harry go around to each table and pass the wedding cookies. As is tradition, as each guest or couple takes cookies from the tray Harry is holding, they each give Emma their wedding gift. She puts each card into a large white silk sack, which she later gives to Leo for safe keeping. Emma and Harry don't know it yet, but the gifts total almost $3500.00, enough to buy their first house outright. At this point in time, you could buy a house kit from the Sears & Roebuck catalog for $2800.00, so that's an option.

The evening is coming to an end. Emma and Harry are so happy with the way the wedding and reception has taken place. Emma asks her mother and father to safeguard her wedding gifts until the money can be deposited in a bank. She takes out a hundred dollars to use on their honeymoon. They have decided to stay in Chicago, because today is the re-opening of the Century of Progress World Exposition that they plan on attending. After saying their goodbyes to Leo and Alice, the happy couple leaves for a week's stay at the Palmer House Hotel in downtown Chicago. As they arrive at the hotel, they are directed to the attached parking garage. This is unlike anything they had ever seen. They park the car into a huge lift, and as they walk away, they can see it being lifted by machine to a different floor for storage. As they enter the lobby of the hotel, they are in awe of the grandeur in front of them. The ceiling has elaborate murals on them, and the chandeliers appear to be made of gold. The furnishings are so plush you hardly want to sit on them. They check in at the front desk, and tell the clerk they had reserved the honeymoon suite under the name of Lang. The clerk responds, "Congratulations on your wedding. Your room is ready and the bellman will help with your bags." As they enter the suite, they are blown away at how large it is. It has a large bedroom, with a king-size canopy bed, a private bath, and a sitting room. As soon as the bellman leaves, there is a knock on the door. It's room service, with a silver bucket filled with ice and a bottle of champagne. The first thing they do is take turns taking a shower. After the long day, and dancing at the reception, they were both feeling overheated and sweaty. As they finish their showers, they each put on robes that the hotel has provided. As they go to relax in the sitting room, they embrace each other and kiss passionately. Harry says, "I love you, Emma.

Let me pour you a glass of champagne." Emma replies, "I would love some. Fill the glass to the top." After a couple of glasses, Emma is feeling especially amorous. She kisses Harry again and lets her robe fall to the floor. Within seconds, Harry is totally aroused. He picks her up and carries her to the bedroom, and puts her on the bed. As he reaches to turn off the light, Emma says, "No, leave it on. I want to see you, my love. I am not ashamed of our bodies." Harry quickly lies on top of her and their marriage is consummated. Soon afterward, they crawl under the covers and fall fast asleep in each other's arms. Emma is the first to awake in the morning, and she waits patiently for Harry to awake. After a little while, she begins kissing him and he starts to get excited. "Emma? Again?" he asks. She puts her fingers over his mouth, and tells him to shush, and then they make love again.

After holding each other for a while, they both look at each other, and Harry asks, "Are you hungry, Emma? Should we get dressed for breakfast?" Emma replies, "I'm starved, let's shower and get dressed." They go down to the dining room and have a truly scrumptious breakfast. When they are finished, they decide to take a taxi over to the Exposition. They are surprised at how busy the fair is. They wander around trying all manner of treats; an ice cream cone, some taffy, and some delicious fried dough dipped in cinnamon and sugar. Their favorite area of the fair is the World Village section. They stop at the German Village, and get a brat at the Heidelberg Inn. The next stop is the Swiss Village, for some delicious chocolates, and on to the Shanghai Village, for some hot noodles in broth. They also spend time on some rides, like the roller coaster. It's now early evening, and they decide to go see a performer who is all the talk of Chicago. It is a lady called Sally Rand, who is famous for doing a fan dance. The audience gasps as she performs. She appears to be totally naked, although it is rumored that she wears a bodysuit. It sure seems that she has nothing on, and most of the crowd is quite enthralled with the performance. However, a few ladies slap their husbands in the face and make them leave. Emma just laughs and enjoys the show.

The week's honeymoon seems like a whirlwind. They go back to the Exposition a couple more times during the week. Much of the time, when they are not at the fair, they are found swimming in the hotel pool and sunning themselves on the terrace. Emma was quite happy with the amenities at the hotel. She can get not only her hair done but also a manicure and pedicure. The spa is comfortable, and staffed by a wonderful female masseuse. Emma gets two or three massages during the week. Harry still has not forgotten his happy ending massage in Germany, so he stays far away, although he hopes nobody is getting funny with his new bride. Harry goes to the hotel barbershop for a shave and haircut. Once finished, the barber asks, "Would you like a complimentary cigar?" Harry responds, "If it's on the hotel dime, I'll take it." One of their favorite features is the nightclub they have in the hotel. It's called the Empire Room, and it's all the rage in Chicago. As they are preferred guests staying in the honeymoon suite, they get first priority for each show. The performers are there for only a night or two at a time, so they are able to see a variety of acts. A dancing couple, a comedian, and a singing group all put on lovely shows. The cocktails are top-notch, and Emma has several each night. Because of Harry's seizure medicine, all he can do is nurse one beer per night, but he couldn't care less about the drinks. It's being with Emma that he cares about. After tonight's show, they take a walk around the block from the hotel. It's a nice evening and the stars are out. As they pass a stand on the corner, Harry buys Emma a beautiful bouquet of roses. As they turn the corner, they see a couple of Irish cops harassing someone he recognizes. It is a gentleman who frequents the Restaurant Europa bar, who Harry has served many times. Harry looks at Emma and says, "Turn around and we will go back to the hotel. I don't want to be around any trouble." Emma replies, "I agree, and besides, I want to make love to you again." Harry smiles and holds her hand tight as they walk back to the hotel. It is sure to be a wonderful night.

The end of their honeymoon has come today, and they check out of the hotel. They retrieve the Terraplane from the mechanical lift and are on their way for the short drive back to her parent's house. Joseph had previously sent Harry the information on where he is staying with Uncle Otto. Joseph told him they can stay in a spare bedroom his uncle has until they get settled. They plan on spending the night with Alice and Leo, and drive on to Sheboygan, Wisconsin, the next morning, to start their new life together. As they arrive home, Alice is there alone, as Leo won't return until dinner. As soon as they ring the bell, Alice bolts to the door and embraces the newlyweds, and says, "Emma, I can tell you had a wonderful honeymoon, as your face is glowing." Emma replies, "We had such a good time in everything we did. I could not be happier! I know father is not home, but is he going to be here for dinner?" Alice says, "Yes, he wants to see you before you move tomorrow. Now Harry, why don't you sit down and relax while I talk with Emma in the kitchen." As Harry sits there in the parlor, he cannot hear their conversation, but Emma is giggling away. Harry just smiles and dozes off for a couple of hours. After he awakens, Alice says, "It's lunchtime. Let's drive down to the waterfront. There is a lovely French cafe that everyone seems to love." Emma and Harry think that's a good idea. As they sit outside, the weather is sunny and warm. They love the way the light reflects off the lake. As they eat their croissant sandwiches, Alice tells them she is happy for them, but they will be missed. Emma smiles, "Mama, it is only a few hours' drive. I am sure we will see each other on weekends as much as we want." Alice seems relieved and says, "I am so glad you feel that way, and what do you think, Harry?" He replies, "Absolutely. We will see each other as much as circumstances allow." After lunch is over, they stroll along the waterfront, window shopping, and talking. Finally, Alice says "This has been fun, but we better get back so I can start dinner." After spending the next couple of hours cooking, Leo arrives home around 6:00 p.m.

As he enters, he says, "Emma, Harry, it is so good to see you. I am so happy that you could stay over tonight." Emma hugs her father and says, "We would never leave without saying goodbye." Alice calls from the kitchen for everyone to sit down for dinner. As this is a special occasion, she has prepared quite a feast; wiener schnitzel, brats, spaetzle, sauerkraut, and for dessert, a luscious black forest cake. After finishing the meal, Leo says, "Alice, my love, you have outdone yourself. Everything was delicious." Alice thanks him, and looking at Emma says, "I hope you remember how I taught you to cook. That's the secret of a happy marriage." Emma laughs, "Oh, Mother, I know how to keep my man happy, and it isn't cooking." Harry blushes and sinks down in his chair, as the rest of them roar in laughter. After dinner, they sit in the parlor and enjoy a cocktail. Leo tells them he has to run down to the restaurant for a few hours to help out. He says, "I will see you all in the morning. If you get up early, please do not leave before your mother and I see you." Emma replies, "Of course not. See you in the morning." Leo leaves, and they spend some time reminiscing about the past, and making plans for the future. Then they all retire for the night. Emma lies beside Harry in bed and snuggles with him. She whispers in his ear, "Sleep well, my love. Tomorrow starts our new life together." As they fall asleep, they think about how happy they are, although they both are apprehensive about what the future will bring.

Morning comes quickly for the married couple. Leo got home from the restaurant much later than he would have liked to last night, so he was still sleeping. So, Emma and Harry shower and get dressed. They get the rest of their things packed. Alice is now awake and asks Harry for a favor, "Would you mind going over to the bakery and get some pastries for breakfast?" Harry smiles and says, "Nothing I like better than pastries for breakfast. I'll be right back." As he drives to the bakery, he remembers, with fondness, all the times he would go to Herr Meyers shop in Kelheim, and he is saddened by what tragedy befell him. He again thinks about how blessed he truly is. By the time Harry returns to the house, Leo is awake. They all enjoy the pastries, with some hot coffee, as they sit around the kitchen table. Leo says, "Now remember, please call us tonight and let us know you are safe at Joseph's uncle's house." Emma replies, "We will be fine, and will call you tonight." Harry says, "I think we better pack up the car and get on the road, as they will be expecting us." After everything is ready, the happy couple hugs and kisses Alice and Leo goodbye and thanks them for everything. As they drive down the road waving goodbye, Alice sheds a tear as Leo holds her tight. She says to Leo, "Where has the time gone? Little Emma is all grown up and married. Leo replies, "Do you remember when we got married and went on our own? It is the way of life." Alice smiles and says, "Oh, and you know what this means? Someday soon, we will be grandparents. Talk about getting old!" They laugh, and go back in the house, thinking all they want is for Emma to be happy, and to have at least five or six babies!

## Chapter 4
# Brew Heaven

It's a lovely Sunday morning as they leave Illinois and enter Wisconsin. Emma and Harry spend their time talking about their future life together. They both have the same ambitions; to live in a nice home, in a safe neighborhood, and to have children. Most of all, they want the same thing most other people want, to live the American dream. They are about halfway through the drive to Sheboygan, and Harry asks, "Do you want me to take a turn driving? Are you getting tired?" Emma smiles and replies, "No way, my love. I never want to stop driving." She then laughs and steps on the accelerator a little more. They have the windows open, and Harry thinks how beautiful she is with her hair blowing in the wind. As they enter Sheboygan, they pass a gas station, and decide to top off the tank and ask for directions. The clerk directs them to where they want to go, and tells them, "If you are hungry for lunch, there are some good German restaurants up the street." Sheboygan had a large influx of German and Dutch immigrants in the last century. The city of Sheboygan, as is the city of Milwaukee, is known for their breweries and their brats. After they stop for lunch, they drive by the lakeshore and pass a large brewery and malt house. This was the largest brewery at the time in Sheboygan, the

Miesbach Brewing Company. The brewery's owner and Brewmaster is Frederick Gambrus, who is the son of the breweries founder. It is named after the town in Bavaria, where Frederick Gambrus's grandparents are from. Harry doesn't realize that this is the brewery where Joseph's uncle Otto is a general foreman. Maybe his dream is closer to reality than he thinks.

As they drive down Eisner Street where Joseph's uncle Otto lives, Emma remarks what a beautiful neighborhood it is. Harry, while gazing out the window, tells Emma, "This is very nice, but there must be 5 or 6 houses on this block that have foreclosure signs on them." Emma replies, "You are right about that, but I wonder if we could get one for a substantially discounted price?" Emma has obviously learned some good business sense from her father, Leo. Then they pull up to the house and start removing their bags from the car. Suddenly, Joseph appears on the front porch and says, "I thought I heard a car door close and I was hoping it was you. Come right in. The door is open and let me help you with your luggage." Once in the house, Joseph takes them straight upstairs and shows them to their room. He says, "Why don't you get unpacked, and then come downstairs to the parlor. Uncle Otto and I will be waiting for you." Once they are done, they join them in the parlor as requested. Uncle Otto embraces them saying, "Welcome, welcome, so how are the newlyweds?" Harry responds, "We couldn't be better. Thank you for inviting us into your home." Otto tells them, "You are welcome, and please stay as long as you like." Emma says "Only long enough to find a house, but can you tell me about this neighborhood?" Otto explains, "This is a mixed neighborhood of German, Dutch, and English residents. Even though there are more foreclosures than I would like to see, considering the depression we are in, things could be worse. The neighborhood is still safe, and a good place to live. There are a couple of young couples who have inherited the properties from their parents, who live on the street now." Emma then asks, "I may be getting ahead of myself, but do you know which bank owns these properties?" Otto replies, "Yes, Sheboygan National Bank on Superior Ave." Emma thinks for a minute and asks, "Otto, do you think there will be some employment opportunities for Harry?" Harry is surprised she was so vocal and says, "Emma, I can speak for myself!" Otto interjects, "Don't worry about it, you two. Joseph has been working at the brewery. He is working in the packaging department, helping to ramp up production on the keg line. I have been working on getting Harry a job, and I have good news. I have procured a position for him in the malt house. Tomorrow, Harry will come to work with me, and I will introduce him to the Brewmaster. If he likes him, he can start immediately."

The next morning, they all get up early for work. Emma has made breakfast for them with the supplies on hand. After a quick breakfast, they are off to the brewery. Emma hugs Harry goodbye and says, "Good luck today. I know you will do fine." He replies, "If the Brewmaster likes me a tenth as much as you do, I will have a job today!" As Otto and Harry arrive at the brewery, Harry remarks at the smell of malt in the air. Otto says, "We are brewing today, but it has been hard to ramp up production. The demand for our beers is there, but we are having problems getting consistent deliveries of malt and hops. With prohibition ending abruptly last year, the farmers did not want to over plant and take a big loss." Harry asks, "What are you going to do? Is there a solution?" Otto replies, "Yes, there is. Miesbach Brewing has signed contracts with the farmers to ensure a consistent supply of malt and hops. It just takes time for the crops to be planted, harvested, and shipped to us." Otto leads Harry up the stairs to the upper level where the Brewmaster's office is located. As they enter, they are greeted by Herr Gambrus, and he says, "Otto, is this the man you told me about?" He replies, "Yes, I would like you to meet Harry Langer." Herr Gambrus, who towers 6 ft 6 inches tall, and dwarves Otto and Harry, looks down on him and asks him in German, "Where are you from?" Harry answers, "I am from Cicero, Illinois." Herr Gambrus scowls. "No, where in Germany is your family from?" Harry responds, "Oh, I misunderstood you. My family is from Kelheim, in Bavaria."

Herr Gambrus is taken aback and says, "You could not know this, but my father interned as a young man at various breweries throughout Bavaria. One of those was in Kelheim, the Baumer Brewery, I believe. Does your family know of it?" Harry responds to the question, "My parents recently passed, but I have received letters from other family members still living in Kelheim. They wrote of a devastating flood that destroyed part of the city, and destroyed the Baumer Brewery." Herr Gambrus seemed genuinely sad at that news, and went to sit back at his desk. He then asks, "Well, what are your intentions, Harry?" He looks directly at Herr Gambrus and says, "My dream is to someday be a Brewmaster, just like you!" Herr Gambrus replies, "I like your initiative, and the fact you speak fluent German. We only allow German speakers to work in the brewing and malting departments. Otto, show him around, and he can start today." Harry shakes his hand, and thanks him multiple times. As Otto and Harry leave the office, Herr Gambrus says, "I will have my eyes on you, Herr Langer, please do not disappoint me!"

As Otto and Harry tour the brewery grounds, the topic of discussion is how did the brewery survive the last 13 years during prohibition. Otto says, "Unfortunately, thousands of small breweries have gone out of business. We are fortunate to still be in operation. We have made a variety of products to keep us in business over the years. We used to make a non-alcoholic malt beverage that sold well to some limited extent, but it was nowhere near as popular as our cold alcoholic beer. What people really wanted, and we can now give them, is real beer. There are several other items that we will continue to make. One of these is a malt syrup, which is made from extracting sugars from the germinated barley grains, and then concentrating the liquid. They use it in different bakeries, and also for malted milk shakes. The other beer related business is the production and sale of yeast cake. If you stand here and look at the brewery, you will see the yeast cake operation is in a separate building to the right of the main brewery. We do this because the yeast we brew lager beer with is different from the yeast you make bread or ales with. So, we have segregated them into different buildings, as they cannot be allowed to cross contaminate. The dried yeast cake is sold in bakeries and grocery stores throughout the region. The last item I must say is one of my favorites. Because Wisconsin has an abundance of dairy cows, we have been in the ice cream business. Our brand is called Miesbach Darling Ice Cream. We decided to focus on ice cream because our largest competitors in the brewing industry are located down in Milwaukee. One in particular is in the cheese business, which has been quite lucrative for them. But I must say, our ice cream is quite popular in Sheboygan, and all over Wisconsin, for that matter. We are not the largest, but we make a high-quality product." Harry is fascinated with all the different business sectors they have. He thinks to himself and chuckles, "While I may never be able to drink too much beer because of my medication, I would sure like to taste ice cream for a living."

As they walk around the side of the brewery, they see a large truck with a long rectangular bed stopped at the side gate. A guard is having words with the driver, and then the guard walks around to the back of the truck. Suddenly Otto sprints towards the truck, yelling, "Don't open that truck gate." But the guard doesn't hear him, and it's now too late. As the guard unlatches the gate, a ton of grain comes cascading down on him and piles onto the ground. Otto helps pick him up and yells at him, "Dummkopf, what are you doing, don't you know any better?" The guard with a red face replies, "But Sir, I just started today, and the head of security told me to search all vehicles leaving the plant." Otto laughs and says, "He didn't mean that for a wet, spent grain truck. Now get a shovel and clean this mess up!" Harry asks, "What is that stuff, Otto?" He replies, "That is the remnants of the malt that is left after the brewing process. We collect it, and ship it out to the dairy farmers to feed to the cows. The farmers love it because it is free for them, and it helps the brewery have a place to dispose of a waste product. Now come with me, and I will introduce you to the foreman of the malt house." Otto takes Harry over to the foreman's office. As they enter, Otto says, "Klaus, I want you to meet Harry Langer. Frederick has assigned him to the malt house." Klaus gets up and shakes hands with Harry, and starts conversing with him in German. Harry feels at ease speaking German with him. While he has learned to hold his own when speaking English, German is his first language. Klaus tells him, "Come with me, and I will get you started. As we will be ramping up beer production this fall, after we malt the next crop, we need to get all the unused equipment back in good condition. Do you have any mechanical ability?" Harry replies, "I have done some truck repairs, and stuff like that." Klaus replies, "Good then, I will have you work with our head mechanic as his assistant. We need to get the malt blenders ready to use. When you are not doing that, we have a tremendous amount of cleaning that needs to be done before we bring more barley into the malt house." Harry spends the rest of the day with the head mechanic, as they start tearing down the malt blenders. Harry can't wait to get home to Otto's house to give Emma the good news.

While Harry is finishing his first day, Emma decides to make a celebration dinner, as she is confident Harry got the job. She takes a taxi down to the meat market and then stops at the produce market next door. She returns home and starts preparing dinner. It's about 5:15 p.m. when Harry and Otto walk in the door. Joseph gets home a minute later. Otto exclaims, "What smells so good, Emma? What have you made?" Emma greets them, smiling and says, "Before I tell you, please give me some good news. Harry, did you get the job?" Harry embraces her. "Yes, my love, I got the job, thanks to Otto. I am working in the malt house." Emma is so happy. After hugging Harry, she does the same to Joseph and Uncle Otto. She says, "Thank you, Uncle Otto, for helping us. Please come sit down. Everything is ready. I hope you all will like it" As it turns out, Emma is as good a cook as her mother Alice. She prepared some wonderfully tender wiener schnitzel (veal cutlet), roasted potatoes with onions and carrots, some pickled beets on the side, all washed down with some steins of Miesbach Lager.

After they finish dinner and clean up, Harry and Emma go for a stroll through the neighborhood. As they walk, they check out each of the foreclosed houses on the block. Some are boarded up. Some have broken fences, broken windows, and one has a tree limb through the roof. Emma looks at Harry and says, "Let's see if we can figure out which one of these houses would need the least work if we were to buy it. I think it would be good to live near Otto and Joseph, as I am sure we will be spending a lot of time together." Harry says, "Absolutely, I would like that also, and besides, it's close to work." They spend the rest of the evening until it got dark checking the exteriors, and peering in through the windows. When they get home, they tell Otto and Joseph, "We found a couple of houses we really like on the street. Uncle Otto, would you mind having us as neighbors?" Otto replies, "I welcome it, and if you need help at the bank, let me know." Emma and Harry thank him. Emma says, "While all of you are at work tomorrow, I will go down to the bank and see what I can find out.

It's the next morning and Harry, Joseph, and Uncle Otto have finished their breakfast, and leave for work. Emma kisses Harry goodbye. Harry says, "Good luck at the bank today. I'll see you tonight." Emma replies, "Hopefully it will go well. I will see you for dinner." After they leave, Emma calls a taxi and goes over to Sheboygan National. As she enters, she asks a teller who she can speak with concerning purchasing a foreclosed property. She is told to see Mr. Westhoven, in the corner office. "Please wait on the bench outside his office and I will call him. I am not sure if he can fit you in, but I will try," said the teller. After sitting and waiting for a couple of hours, Mr. Westhoven calls her in. He greets her and asks her name. Emma responds, "I am Mrs. Harry Langer." He replies, "Well, Mrs. Langer, do you mind me asking your maiden name?" She replies, "It is Emma Wagner. My father is Leo Wagner." He says, "Thank you. What brings you in today?" Emma says, "I am recently married, and my husband and I are interested in purchasing a foreclosed property." He replies, "May I ask if you are from Sheboygan? Emma says, "My husband and I are from Chicago. We are staying with our good friend's uncle, Mr. Otto Vogel, at his home on Eisner Ave." Mr. Westhoven thinks for a second and says "Eisner Ave, yes, we have at least six homes on that street in foreclosure. The economy is slowly improving, but I am afraid we will have many more foreclosures. Now, please tell me where your husband works?" Emma smiles, "He started yesterday at the Miesbach Brewery." Mr. Westhoven is impressed that Harry is working at the brewery. He asks, "Which house are you interested in?" Emma replies, "It's number 403 Eisner Ave, directly across from Otto Vogel's home at 400 Eisner Ave." Mr. Westhoven goes over to the file cabinet and starts searching through it. Finally, he finds the file on that property and says, "Well, Mrs. Langer, that property has a balance of $3750 on the mortgage. We would consider selling it to you and your husband at that price, if you can afford it." Emma thinks for a minute, and blurts out, "That is outrageous, what you want. That house, while better than some on the street, needs much work, and you have to take that into account. I would not offer you more than $2500.00." Mr. Westhoven chuckles and says, "That is not a serious offer. Do you take us for fools?" Emma gets that fire in her eye and says, "No sir, but do not treat me like I am one either." Mr. Westhoven is taken aback and says, "How dare you talk to me that way." Emma says, "Look, you know as well as I, every month that house sits in foreclosure, you lose money. Once it falls into disrepair, you will never recoup your investment." He looks at her and asks, "What is your offer again? I am willing to take it to the lending committee. But please, don't waste our time." Emma restates her offer. "I said $2500.00, and that's an all-cash offer." Mr. Westhoven sits up in his chair with his mouth open, and says, "What's that, cash you say?" Emma shoots back, "You heard me. Here is the phone number where I can be reached. I hope to hear from you soon." Emma leaves the bank visibly perturbed, but still has hope they will take the offer. She remembers what her father Leo taught her, that, "Cash is King."

Later that evening, Emma and the rest of them are relaxing and having an after dinner drink. Harry is so excited about his new job he hasn't stopped talking since he got home. Emma could not get a word into the conversation during dinner. Finally, Harry calms down and Emma says, "I went to the bank today, and put an offer on the house directly across the street from here." Otto smiles, "How did that work out for you?" Unfortunately, they dislike talking to a woman without her husband." Emma replies, "The banker was a Schweinhund, and he tried to make me feel like a fool because he didn't like the offer, although, at the end of the conversation, he seemed to perk up when I said it was an all-cash offer." Harry says, "Did you offer all of our money, Emma?" She replies, "No, I did not. If he takes it, we will have some left over. I really think it is better to buy a house outright, as we have the cash now. You never know what the future will bring. So, let's see what happens over the next few days. See you all in the morning." Emma retires for the night, while the men enjoy their drinks and a good cigar.

The next day, Mr. Westhoven, at the bank, is preparing for the weekly meeting with the lending committee. He decides to check out Emma's background before presenting her offer. He is suspicious of why such a young lady would have so much cash. He makes a call to a private detective that the bank employs to do background checks on potential clients. He gives the detective the names Emma gave him, along with the fact they were recently married in Chicago. The detective's first thought was to call the Chicago Tribune and see if they had a recent wedding announcement for Mr. and Mrs. Harry Langer. He is happy to hear that the paper confirms they were just married in Chicago. He is shocked when the newspaper tells him they have an article having to do with local gangsters that pertain to that wedding. As they read from the paper, he quickly realizes that Mrs. Langer is Emma Wagner, daughter of the gangster Leo Wagner. He thinks, "Oh boy, the bank will love to hear this one!" Mr. Westhoven is surprised that the detective called back so fast. After the situation is explained to him, he decides he better present the offer to the committee today. As he walks into the conference room, he looks at the other four members and asks, "Has anyone heard of a gangster down in Chicago named Leo Wagner?" Two of the members raise their hands and one of them says, "He is reputed to be involved with bootlegging, prostitution, loan sharking, you name it. But why do you ask?" Mr. Westhoven continues, "We have a situation to deal with. Evidently, his daughter just got married and has moved to Sheboygan, and she wants to buy a foreclosed property from the bank. But I think she has made us a lowball offer." After he details the property and the amount owed on the property, he presents the offer to them. "She has offered us $2500.00, which I think is low, however, it is an all-cash offer." The head of the committee says, "We cannot afford to pass up an all-cash offer, but I agree with you on price. Let's see if she will accept a counteroffer. We do not want to have to deal with Leo Wagner. I suggest we cut the best deal possible and move on safely, if you get my meaning. Let me have her phone number and call her right now." He dials, and Emma picks up after a few rings. "Is this Mrs. Langer I am speaking with?" Emma replies, "It is. What can I do for you?" The voice on the phone says, "My name is Henry Beek, I am the head of the lending committee at the Sheboygan National Bank. Mr. Westhoven has presented us with your offer, but we feel it is a little low, so we would like to counter." Emma says, "I will listen to it, so what is your counter offer? Mr. Beek says, "How does $2750.00 sound to you? But it must be in cash." They can't see her, but Emma is jumping up and down while holding the phone. She thinks for a second and says, "I appreciate that you have made a reasonable counteroffer. I accept it!" Mr. Beek says come to the bank anytime tomorrow, and Mr. Westhoven will complete the transaction. Please bring Mr. Langer, too, as his name should also go on the deed." Emma tells them, "We will both be there. Thank you so much!"

After Emma hangs the phone up with the bank, she puts a call into the brewery and asks to speak to Uncle Otto. Fortunately, he is in his office when the call comes through. Emma is ecstatic on the phone and tells Otto, "It's Emma. The bank came back with a counter offer and I accepted. We got the house! Harry and I will need to go to the bank tomorrow to sign the papers. Can Harry get off work for a couple of hours?" Otto replies, "I will make the arrangements for Harry. Congratulations Emma! I am so happy for you both. Tonight, we will go out to a restaurant to celebrate."

At the same time Emma was on the phone call with Otto, Harry had been learning more about the malting process from Klaus, his boss. Harry says, "Herr Klaus, I am confused about this malt process. I have been working on getting all the equipment running, and I understand how the machines work, but what does malt have to do with making beer?" Klaus replies, "This is a common question. Let me try to explain." Taking a handful of barley, he points out the various parts of the seed. He explains, "The outer coating is termed the husk. If we peel that off, you can see a brown layer covering the inner part of the seed. They call that the pericarp. The plump white material in the center is technically called endosperm, and is almost entirely made up of starch, and some protein. At the bottom of the seed is the germ, or embryo. This is where the shoots emerge from. We get most of our barley from farmers in North Dakota, Wyoming, and to a lesser degree, from Wisconsin. Their crop is planted in the spring, April to May, and harvested in August to the beginning of September, for the most part. There are two main types of barley. The first is a 2-row variety, this means there are two rows of kernels on each stalk. This type is more expensive because the yield per acre is less, but produces more sugar extract during mashing. The second type is called the 6-row variety. As you can guess, this means there are six rows of kernels on each stalk. This is the more common variety. It's cheaper than 2-row because of the higher yield per acre, but it produces less extract in mashing than a 2-row variety would. The barley is shipped to us by railcar and stored in the large silos attached to this building." Now let me ask you a question, "Where does a plant get its food in order to grow?" Harry looks perplexed, and says, "I don't know of such things, plants need the sun I guess." Klaus continues, "When a seed puts up shoots that become leaves, the leaves catch the sunlight and use that to convert carbon dioxide gas in the atmosphere into sugars. They call this photosynthesis. This is how all plants live. But what does the plant embryo live on while it is developing, since it has no green leaves yet?" Harry just shrugs his shoulders. Klaus says, "Now we get to the good part. The plant embryo lives on the starchy endosperm. When the seed stops being dormant, enzymes produced in the seed will convert starch into sugar and that is what the plant uses for food until photosynthesis starts. Remember, in order to make beer, or wine, or bread the yeast needs sugar to ferment. It cannot ferment starch, only sugar. The purpose of malting is to get the seed to germinate, which will activate the enzymes so they are ready to convert the starchy endosperm into sugar during the mashing process in the brewhouse. In order to do that, it takes a three-step process, which is, Steeping, Germination, and Kilning."

Klaus continues, "In steeping, there is a wet and a dry phase. In the wet phase, we put the barley into the steeping tanks with lukewarm water. The seeds will take up the water, which is needed for the seed to germinate. We also blow clean air up through the tank water as the barley embryo needs oxygen to live. Once the seed begins to actively respire, we enter the dry phase. The water is drained, and the grain is allowed to sit. Now the grain is really active, and more CO2 builds up in the tank. A fan will pull room air down through the grain and exhaust the CO2, as too much of it is toxic. The entire steeping process will take about a day and a half, and the rootlet will start to appear. Then, the soaked barley is sent down to the germination beds.

In germination, over about a 4-day period, the barley will develop the enzymes we want. The seed will continue to germinate, and the rootlets will grow longer. We can add some more water, if needed, and we also blow air up from the bottom of the germination bed through a slotted false bottom, so the embryo has oxygen. The turning machine will move back-and-forth down the beds to level the malt initially, but will continuously turn the beds from bottom to top so the barley is malted evenly, with release of heat and uptake of oxygen. When this stage is finished, we call the product green malt. The enzyme activity will be at its peak. It will now be moved to the kiln for the last step.

In kilning, the green malt is subjected to heat, in order to dry the malted kernel which will deactivate the enzymes. We can activate them again during mashing in the brewhouse, when we really need them to convert starch to sugars. The kilning process will also develop flavor and color in the malt. Depending on the kiln temperature, humidity, and drying time, we can make malts that are light or dark in color, each with unique flavor characteristics, like pale malt, caramel malt, and chocolate malt. Once the kilning is done, the malt will go through machines that will abrade off the rootlets, and further clean the malted kernel. We then store it until we are ready to mash."

Harry looks at Klaus and says, "Thank you for explaining that, but my head is spinning. I hope I can remember what you have told me." Klaus replies, "The malting and brewing process is quite complex. If you want a good finished product, it's attention to detail that makes the difference. In time, you will learn. Just keep asking questions. Think about it tonight, and I would be happy to go over it again with you tomorrow." It's now quitting time, so Harry leaves to go home. He can't wait to see Emma and find out what happened at the bank.

As Harry pulls up to the house, he finds Emma, Otto, and Joseph on the front porch waiting for him. Harry says "What is going on?" Emma runs to him and hugs him and says, "We got the house, my love, and for a very good price. Otto has arranged for you to get a couple of hours off tomorrow so we can go to the bank and sign the papers." Harry sees how excited Emma is, and he embraces her, and starts to dance with her on the sidewalk. Otto and Joseph are watching them dance, and can't contain their laughter. Otto says, "Alright, you two, give it a rest. Let's go now, as I am treating you to dinner to celebrate." As is Otto's custom, they head over to his favorite German restaurant. On the way, Emma asks Otto, "Do you know if there are any Italian restaurants in Sheboygan?" He replies, "You know, Emma, I don't think I have ever even looked for one, so I don't know. I will ask around for you, but for tonight, I am in the mood for some sauerbraten. Like I said, it is my treat."

While at dinner celebrating their good fortune, Harry tells Otto all he has learned about the malting process from his boss. Otto replies, "I am happy to hear you are asking questions and starting to learn. The Brewmaster, Frederick, likes his employees to take some initiative. Too many people just perform the task and never ask why they are doing the task. Emma enters the conversation, "Harry, once we sign the papers tomorrow, we will need to work on getting the house fixed up." Harry nods his head and replies, "I think the first thing we should do is get the house painted and fix the railing on the front steps." Emma says, "That would be great, and don't forget the front picket fence needs to be repaired and painted as well." Harry replies, "Not a problem. Joseph, would you be willing to help me paint?" He answers, "Of course I will. I was hoping you would ask." Then Uncle Otto interjects and starts organizing, saying, "This is what we will do. Harry and Joseph are in charge of painting. Emma, you clean the interior of the house, and I will repair the railing and the picket fence. Harry and Emma, on your way back from the bank tomorrow, stop at the store and buy the white paint, brushes, and whatever else you need." Harry says, "That will work out good. I just hope there are no problems at the bank, so we don't get delayed." Otto says, "I doubt there will be any problems, and if there is, just call me, and I will come over."

It's the next morning, and Harry leaves work to pick Emma up and get to the bank when they open at 10:00 a.m. As they drive, they talk about having their own house and starting a family. As they enter the bank, the guard escorts them directly to Mr. Westhoven's office. He greets them and says, "Welcome. It's nice to meet you, Mr. Langer. How are you Mrs. Langer?" They reply they were doing fine and excited to be purchasing the house. Before they go through the process of signing the deed, the banker asks, "Do you have the agreed upon price, in cash?" Emma opens her purse and counts out the $2750.00. Mr. Westhoven can't keep his mouth shut and says, "It's unusual for a young couple to have so much money." Emma explains, "We just got married, and my father's business associates were quite generous. Would you like to meet my father when he comes to visit?" Mr. Westhoven gulps, "No, no, that won't be necessary. Here is the deed. Sign this, and the transaction is complete." As they leave the bank, Emma thinks to herself maybe being a gangster's daughter does have some advantages. Once they leave the bank, they drive up the main street to the hardware store and purchase the supplies. On the way back to the house, Emma tells Harry, "I want to call my parents tonight and tell them the good news. Can I invite them up to visit in a few weeks when the house is ready?" Harry says, "Yes, let's get the house looking good and buy the furniture and appliances. We also need to furnish a spare bedroom for your parents to stay in as well. If the weather holds out, I will start painting tonight after work."

After dinner, Emma, Harry, and Joseph walk across the street to start work on the house. Emma remarks, "I didn't realize it, but that maple tree in the front yard looks mostly dead. We will have to have that removed." As they stand on the sidewalk discussing the tree, the neighbor next door comes out to greet them. She says "My name is Carol. I see you have painting supplies. Have you purchased the house?" Emma replies, "Yes, we did. I am Emma. This is my husband Harry, and our good friend Joseph." Carol says "Pleased to meet you. You know, everyone in the neighborhood calls this the dead tree house." Harry laughs. "Yah, we noticed that. Don't worry, the tree will be gone soon. Now if you will excuse us, we have a lot of painting to do. Pleased to meet you." Carol replies, "Same here. Welcome to the neighborhood. You will have a nice house when you are finished, although I think mine is bigger." Fortunately, there was a strong rain storm the other day, which has done a good job of scouring the dirt off the house. Harry and Joseph can get right to painting. There is very little scraping to do before painting, so the task should move along quickly. While Harry and Joseph work on the paint, Emma sets to work cleaning the interior of the house. Fortunately, just dust and cobwebs. The roof does not have any leaks, and the ceilings and hardwood floors are in excellent condition. As Emma moves through the house, she is taking notes on what they need; light bulbs, door stoppers, new screen for back door, new drapes for the window. She thinks to herself that she is glad they have some money left over after purchasing the house. They will be able to afford everything they need now, without having to save up for it. As she cleans the living room, she goes over to the fireplace and looks into the hearth. There seems to be quite a bit of soot that has fallen down. Emma thinks they better get a chimney sweep in right away to get the stack cleaned out. They don't need to burn down their new house. It's getting dark out, so Harry and Joseph call it quits on exterior painting. Harry says, "Come on Emma, let's go home and get some rest. Joseph and I have to get up early for work tomorrow." Emma replies, "Sounds good. Tomorrow I will take a taxi down to the hardware store for more supplies and keep cleaning and fixing what I can while you are at work."

The next week goes by like a whirlwind for Harry and Joseph, with long days at work, giving way to long evenings at home working on the house. But finally, everything is complete, and the house is looking great. Emma has gotten the chimney cleaned, so it is ready for use. The new appliances, which Emma picked out, have been delivered, a Kelvinator refrigerator and a Hotpoint electric range. All the furniture was delivered and set up earlier today. Emma is going to surprise everyone by cooking dinner in her new home tonight.

Harry is quite busy at work today in the malt house. His boss Klaus is instructing him on how to monitor the germination process. It takes approximately 4 days for the barley to germinate to the point the green malt can be sent to the kiln. Klaus tells Harry, "You can measure the growth of the rootlet each day, and you will see if everything is done properly. The growth will be predictable." Harry picks up some grain from two side-by-side germination beds. As he analyzes them, he looks perplexed, and asks Klaus, "Why does the rootlet growth on a 2-day-old bed look longer than the growth on a 3-day-old bed?" Klaus replies, "This is a good observation. I was hoping you could see that there is a problem. To answer your question, it should not be. Each day of germination, they should get longer. I want you to go get the mechanic and you both check out the air compressors and the vacuum pumps on the steep tanks, and the air compressors for the germination beds." Harry and the mechanic can see pretty quickly that everything looks good on the air delivery system in the germination beds. Pressure and airflow rates are all consistent between beds. They find the same situations at the steep tanks. The air delivery system looks fine. The mechanic says "Harry, climb up on the catwalk and check the CO2 vacuum pumps for the steep tanks." After checking them, he calls down, "Number 2 vacuum pump seems to be running hot." As the mechanic joins Harry, they witness the pump stop. After a few minutes, it starts up again. The mechanic says, "This is the problem. The pump is overheating and tripping out. If it can't pull off the CO2 from the dry steep phase, the grain can get poisoned from the CO2. Let's go over to the storeroom and get another vacuum pump, and we will get this bad one changed out." Once they made the repairs, they reported the problem was corrected to Klaus. He asks the mechanic, "Was that an old vacuum pump?" The mechanic replies, "Not really, the pump must have been defective to fail this soon." Klaus replies, "Very well, but I want you to start monitoring the pump temperatures on a more frequent basis so we can catch a problem before it starts." Klaus turns to Harry and says, "Good job today, Harry. Have a good weekend, and I will see you on Monday." Harry replies, "Thank you Klaus, see you then." Harry leaves work and thinks to himself how much he is enjoying working at the brewery. So far, as long as you do your job, none of the bosses seem to bother you, and of course, it helps to have Joseph's Uncle Otto as your benefactor.

Harry and Joseph arrive at Uncle Otto's house at the same time as they normally do. Joseph tells Harry, "Uncle Otto said to tell you he will be an hour late tonight, as he is dealing with a problem at the brewery." Harry responds, "Thanks for telling me. I will run over to the new house and have Emma hold dinner." Harry goes into the new house and finds Emma in the kitchen. They embrace and Harry tells her Otto will be late. Emma says, "Not a problem, as I haven't cooked the brats yet, and the potato salad, sauerkraut, and tomato cucumber salad will go back in the fridge." Emma says, "Hey Harry, check out the new stove and refrigerator." Harry opens the refrigerator and says, "I can't believe how cold it is! Something to be said for buying new. The electric range has four burners and an oven, fantastic." Emma says, "I am happy you are pleased. Come and look at the furniture I bought while we are waiting for our guests." They go room to room, and Harry is ecstatic at how well everything looks in the house. Most of the furniture has a darker wood frame which compliments the dark woodwork that runs through the house. They painted the interior of the house a nice bright beige color so the rooms do not look too dark, especially with the dark furniture.

Uncle Otto finally arrives at the new house and says, "My apologies for being late, but we had a problem in the brewhouse." Harry and Joseph ask, "What happened?" Otto replies, "Frederick the Brewmaster said the last brew we made seemed to have a very slight saltiness to it, which is unusual. He was very concerned that the hot caustic that is used to clean the vessels and lines was not rinsed out sufficiently. We checked that out and we don't think that was the problem. I also checked to see if there was anything different with the grain bill. I called Klaus over in the malt house, and we found out something interesting. Klaus said we just started using barley from a new group of farms in Wyoming. Their cooperative is named Fleichstag Barley. It seems the soil in that region naturally has a high sodium content, therefore, the barley has a higher sodium level. So, in the future, Frederick told Klaus to make sure he blends the Fleichstag barley with the other ones, so the sodium level is moderated."

Emma says, "Alright, that's enough work talk. Let's sit down and have dinner. I just finished frying the brats and sauerkraut, and on the side, we have some potato salad, and some tomato/cucumber salad.

Uncle Otto says, "Sounds good, Joseph, would you get some bottles of cold Miesbach Lager?" Joseph replies, "Yah, several bottles each. It was a long day." Emma asks Uncle Otto, "What do you think of the house? Do you like it?" Otto replies, "Yes, I do. It really looks good inside and out. To be completely frank with you, it's nice to see at least one eyesore gone on the street." Emma smiles and says, "I think we will be very happy here." Harry then looks at Joseph and asks, "What about you, Joseph? Do you think you would like to get your own house someday?" Joseph replies, "I was thinking of it when I was helping paint this house. Maybe someday, but for now, I am happy staying with Uncle Otto. Hopefully, I will not wear out my welcome." Uncle Otto laughs and touches Joseph on the shoulder. "My brother's son is welcome to stay as long as he wants. Family first!" Joseph replies, "Thank you, Uncle Otto. I was wondering if we could send a cable to Uncle Gerhart and Aunt Lena back in Friedrichshafen, and you can ask how they are doing. Remember not to mention us." Otto says "I have not forgotten that you are not here. I miss Gerhart and Lena as much as you do. I wish all those years ago, they had moved to America with me. I worry about their safety. Tomorrow I will send the cable, so we should get a reply in a few days."

Dinner is done, and Emma asks Harry, "Now that the house is ready, do you mind if I call my parents and invite them for the weekend?" Harry replies, "That's an awesome idea. I hope they are free on such short notice." Emma replies, "I really hope they can come, so let me call, and I will let you know. Why don't you serve dessert to Otto and Joseph in the parlor, and I will be right in." Emma makes the call to her parents, and catches them both at home. After hanging up with them, Emma goes into the parlor and says, "Great news. My parents are coming for a visit Saturday and Sunday, and should be here by lunchtime tomorrow. Otto and Joseph, I hope you can join us for lunch?" Otto replies, "Yes, thank you. Joseph and I will be there."

The next day, her parents arrive at the house around lunchtime. As they exit their car, they are quite happy to see Emma's new house is in such good condition. Suddenly Emma opens the door and rushes out to greet them and says "Father, Mother, how do you like my house?" Leo replies, "You have done well, but do you mind if I ask what you paid for it? Emma says, "Don't worry, we bought it out of foreclosure, and we paid cash for it. We got it for only $2750.00." Leo and Alice look at each other and say, "That is a fabulous price. How did you negotiate that deal?" Emma replies, "You taught me cash is king, and besides, they found out I am your daughter. Your reputation precedes you." Leo throws up his hands and smiles, "Whatever works, as long as you are happy." Emma replies, "I couldn't be happier. Now come inside so I can show you the interior." As they enter the house, they are greeted by Harry. After exchanging pleasantries, he joins them in touring the house. As they look around the kitchen, Alice opens the refrigerator and remarks, "It's so cold!" Harry laughs and says, "I thought the same thing, it's pretty awesome." Alice looks at Leo and says, "Monday you are buying me one of these." Leo smirks and says, "Yes, dear, whatever you would like." Just then, Joseph and Uncle Otto arrive for lunch. Leo shakes hands with them both and says to Otto, "So nice to see you again. I wanted to thank you for helping Harry and Joseph get a job at the brewery." Otto replies, "Anything for family and as I told you before, any friend of Joseph's is a friend of mine. Harry and Emma are a wonderful couple, and it is my pleasure to help them anyway I can." It turns out to be a wonderful weekend. Otto and Leo really seem to hit it off, and spend much time together talking about the old country, and telling stories about Wolfgang. The weekend flies by and it's now Monday morning, and the men have left for work. Leo and Alice are sitting at the kitchen table having some more coffee before they leave to go back to Chicago. Alice says, "Your father and I are so happy that you and Harry are married, and what can we say about this house? You have done well for yourselves." Emma replies, "Thank you. Harry is feeling better. He has a new job, we have a new house, what else could we ask for?" Alice looks at Leo and smiles, then she replies to Emma, "Children for you, and grandchildren for us." Emma blushes, "Oh, we will get to that soon enough." Soon after, Leo and Alice are on their way back home, and Emma spends the rest of the day straightening up the house and doing laundry, waiting for Harry to come home.

Over at the brewery, Joseph is hard at work on the keg line. The brewery makes bottled beer and keg (draught) beer. The bottles are a heavy, tall amber colored glass with a long neck. These are returnable bottles and will be sent back from the bars or individual customers, cleaned with hot caustic, and reused at the brewery. Joseph and two other men spend the day filling and bunging (sealing) the wooden kegs. The unit of measure of these kegs is 15.5-gallon capacity, and is termed a half barrel. It is quite a physically demanding job. Moving the wooden kegs into the filling station is not too much of a problem, but once they are filled with beer, the operator must then hammer a seal into the filling hole, called a bung hole. Then, the filled kegs must be lifted off the filling station and moved so other workers can roll them into the keg storage room. At this time, mechanical refrigeration is still not available in all bars and venues. Some have it, some still use ice, and some have none at all. Because of this, Miesbach Brewing pasteurized its draught beer. The other problem is transportation. If the beer was not pasteurized, it could only be sold in areas close to the breweries because it would spoil quickly.

Some of the very largest brewers use rail cars packed with ice to ship their beer unpasteurized. Miesbach Brewing so far has not been able to use the iced railcars because of logistical challenges. Unfortunately, a pasteurized product, which involves heating the beer to over 140 degrees Fahrenheit, causes the beer to taste slightly different. Still very good, but maybe slightly less fresh tasting. In the future, mechanical refrigeration will become more common in all types of bars and restaurants, as well as in shipping containers.

One of the other problems many brewers are facing is a shortage of wood kegs. With prohibition totally over, the demand for kegs has skyrocketed. Miesbach, on the other hand, has its own barrel making operation and can supply itself with all the wood kegs it needs. They also have a good relationship with its customers, and find a very high percentage of used kegs are returned. Because of the wooden keg shortage, some brewers are experimenting with metal kegs. There can be many advantages to a metal keg. They are stronger, can hold a higher pressure, and are easily cleaned. At some time in the future, Miesbach will look at changing to metal kegs, but for now they will stick with what's working.

Joseph and his co-workers are on lunch break when Lar's the keg line foreman stops by. He says, "When lunch is over, you better get moving and pick up the pace this afternoon. Yesterday you were short ten kegs from your production target." Joseph is visibly upset and says, "Lar's, with all due respect, I think you are forgetting the fact that Paul got hurt yesterday. We were short-handed for a couple of hours." Lar's replies, "I don't care, make you production targets, or we will find someone else that can." Lar's turns his back and starts walking away. Suddenly, Joseph mutters under his breath, "You stupid son of a bitch." Joseph gets up and lunges at Lar's. Luckily, his co-workers grab him and wrestle him to the ground. Joseph tries to shout and swear at Lar's, but they keep his mouth covered. Fortunately, with all the noises in the packaging area, Lars does not see or hear what Joseph has done. Finally, Joseph calms himself and they let him up. Paul says to him, "Joe, you got to keep it together. Don't let Lar's get to you. He pulls that crap all the time. He is just a loud, bellicose pain in the ass. But as much as he yells and threatens, no one ever gets fired." Joseph replies, "I'm sorry I lost my temper. He was totally wrong for yelling at us. I don't enjoy getting yelled at, especially when everyone is busting their asses." Paul replies, "You know the company talks a good game about being family, and we are all in this together, yada, yada, yada, but when push comes to shove, they will throw you under the bus." Joseph asks what that saying means. Paul tells him, "Throwing you under the bus means sticking it to you." Joseph nods his head and says, "Yah, I get it now."

Over in the malt house, Klaus has called a meeting with Harry and the maltsters. Klaus begins, "I wanted to let you know that Frederick the Brewmaster has notified me that we are going to start producing a new product. He said it will be called Miesbach Dark Lager. Some of you may be familiar with a traditional German dunkel style beer. It will be similar to that. In order to brew that style of beer, we will have to produce some caramel malt, which will impart a dark color to the beer as well as some different flavors. Approximately 10% of the grain bill will be made up of caramel malt, the rest of the grain will be our regular pale malt. In order to make the caramel malt, we will leave the green malt wet, and in the kiln, we will raise the temperature to a typical mashing temperature, and hold for a couple of hours. Between the moisture and the warm temperature, we will convert the grain starches into sugar within the kernel. We will then raise the kiln temperature to first caramelize the sugars, which will produce the dark coloration we are looking for, and then further dry the malt."

Over the next year, the lives of Harry, Emma, and Joseph are filled with hard work and joy, by all of them. Emma loves taking care of the household as a traditional German wife was expected to do. Emma and Harry have been trying hard to have a family, but so far, Emma has not become pregnant. She promised Harry he would not be getting much sleep until that happy day finally arrived. Emma's parents, Leo and Alice, make the drive up from Chicago every few months to visit. On the other hand, Emma and Harry drive down to Chicago a couple times a month to see them. They enjoy this because besides visiting, they can take advantage of the vast number of restaurants and nightclubs Chicago has to offer. And they always stop at her father's restaurant Cafe Europa, even if only to get a cup of coffee and dessert. Harry has really found his niche in the malting department, but he still longs to move into the brewhouse. He knows if he bides his time, he will get the opportunity to make his dream come true. They are still producing the new caramel malt, and sales of the Miesbach Dark Lager have been strong.

Joseph has been quite busy in the packaging department. It's now June 1935, and the company has been installing a packaging line to put beer into metal cans. This is a recent phenomenon that had started back east, but is now being adopted by many breweries, large and small. The advantage of the metal cans over glass bottles is they are much lighter to transport and carry, don't break, are cheaper, get cold quicker, and are disposable. Another enormous advantage is the cans come with pre-printed labels on the can, unlike bottles that have to have a separate paper label glued on them. At this time, there are a couple of competing beer can products on the market, one of which is a metal can that has a top that looks like the top of a bottle. This can is made to be filled and then capped with a bottle crown on an existing bottle line. Miesbach Brewing has instead invested in a totally new canning line which uses a different type of can. All beer cans are made at this time with tin plated steel. The can Miesbach is using is produced by National Can and consists of 3 parts: a can body, to which a can bottom has been soldered on to, and a flat can lid that is seamed (crimped) to the top of the can after filling. These cans also have an interior coating made of various materials that will keep the beer from contacting the metal can and altering its flavor. Because the top of the filled can is flat metal, a method had to be devised to open this type of beer can. What somebody invented was a short strip of heavy metal that had a triangular shaped curved end. This was used to pierce the can lid on opposite sides of the lid to allow the beer to flow. These openers were very common and are known as "churchkeys"

The initial test run of the can line went well. The cans per minute that could be produced are within target. The seam integrity appears to be good, so there should not be any flat beer or leakers. The only issue is the oxygen content in the packaged cans is too high. This was determined by the Brewmaster after tasting the test cans, which were stored at a warm temperature for a week to try to prematurely age the beer, which is called punishing the beer. When beer is exposed to oxygen, the flavor will rapidly deteriorate. Typically, the beer will develop a paper or cardboard like flavor note, and worse case, stale tasting. The beer will also not be smooth in mouthfeel, and can taste harsh as you swallow. The more oxygen in the package means, the faster the beer will age, which is detrimental to the product.

Several adjustments were made to the filling operation to reduce the oxygen content in the can headspace. The first was to increase the carbon dioxide that is blown into the empty can when it is on the filler valve, which will purge out oxygen from the headspace of the can, as it is filled from bottom to top. The second was to increase the carbon dioxide pressure on what is termed the bubble breakers. As the can is filled, air is trapped in bubbles on top of the foam. By spraying the top of the can with carbon dioxide, the bubbles break and release the trapped oxygen to the atmosphere. The third adjustment was to increase the carbon dioxide pressure on what is termed the undercover gasser. Just before the lid is dropped onto the top of the can, prior to seaming, a jet of carbon dioxide is sprayed across the surface of the can liquid, which again removes oxygen from the headspace of the can. Once these adjustments were made, the Brewmaster was pleased with the taste of the canned beer after it was again punished.

Joseph has been selected to become what they call the filler operator on the new can line. His job is to ensure the packages are filled properly and efficiently, and to continuously feed can lids into the seamer so the filled cans are sealed properly. Today he is training with the packaging and construction manager. As they survey the can line, Joseph learns the steps the cans go through before the finished product is shipped out of the brewery. In this case, the empty cans will be delivered to the brewery on pallets. The cans will be taken off the pallets and fed onto the packaging line, where they will be inverted and sprayed with water to clean them. After the water drains, they are then inverted again to return to being right side up, and continue into the filler. The cans are then filled and seamed and continue down the line to be pasteurized. The next step as the cans enter the pasteurizer is to spray warm water over them until the internal beer temperature is above 140 degrees Fahrenheit, in this way, any residual yeast or beer spoilage bacteria will be neutralized. This pasteurizer consists of seven temperature zones. The first three zones gradually and sequentially increase the beer temperature. They call the fourth zone the hold zone, which is where the pasteurization takes place. The remaining three zones gradually and sequentially decrease the beer temperature back down. After the cans exit the pasteurizer, they move down the line to be packaged in cardboard crates and are stacked on pallets. Joseph and the rest of the can line crew spend the rest of the next week training and running test runs. Finally, everything is in order and production has officially started. At first, they were only running a couple of days a week in order to fill the pipeline with products. As this is a new type of packaging, and the consumer is not familiar with it, and it's unknown how well it will sell. It is becoming quite popular back east, so they expect sales to be good in Wisconsin as well.

It's Monday morning as Uncle Otto arrives at the plant. As soon as he sits down at his desk, he receives a call from the Brewmaster to come up to his office. As he enters, Frederick says, "Otto, good morning. Come sit down. I have some news I think you will be excited about." Otto replies, "What is going on Frederick? You seem uncharacteristically happy, may I say, almost giddy." Frederick tells him, "I am happy in this sense; I have decided to change the organizational structure of the brewery. Things have become too complex for me to keep track of everything properly. Being the owner, the Brewmaster, and juggling all the finances has been hard enough. But the way things are now with making new products, new types of packages such as the cans, and ancillary products, is getting too much to keep track of, so I have decided to promote you to the newly made position of Plant Manager. You will be responsible for everything except for the brewing department, which will stay under my control. As far as the financial stuff goes, I am going to have you assist me in that area. As sales and profitability are going very well, I want to create a few more positions who will all report to you, and you in turn will report to me, as the owner of Miesbach Brewing. I want to create the new position of Manager of Ancillary Products. This will cover the ice cream, malt syrup, yeast cake, and barrel making. The next new position will be titled Packaging Manager to oversee the combined areas of keg line, bottling line, can line, warehouse and shipping. Each of the line foreman and warehouse foreman will report to the Packaging Manager. There will also be a new Maintenance Manager for the plant who will be responsible for all areas except the brewing department. I will have a separate Maintenance Manager for the brewing department who will report to me. As you know, we currently have a Sales Manager who will continue to report to me, and I have decided to give him an assistant. I think it is very important that we really aggressively push sales and promotions. The competition from down in Milwaukee is getting fierce with the large brewers down there, not to mention the one in St Louis who is trying to ship products nationally. Otto, your most important task as Plant Manager is to make sure the plant runs efficiently and on budget. I know this is more responsibility to throw on your back, but I know you are up to it." Otto replies, "I accept the position and am overwhelmed by your confidence in me."

Otto says to Frederick, "The first order of business is to determine who fills the newly created positions. As far as the position of Manager of Ancillary products, I think the only choice is Wilhelm Adler. As one of our best and oldest employees, he has experience in most, if not all, of those product areas." Frederick replies. "I agree with you. Wilhelm will do great in that position. He was a loyal employee through prohibition and really helped us produce all the products that kept the doors open when we couldn't brew beer." Otto says, "I will give some thought to the other positions and will get back to you tomorrow to discuss it further."

Later that day, Otto puts in a call to Emma and tells her not to cook because he is taking her and Harry, along with Joseph, out to celebrate. Emma asks, "What are we celebrating?" Otto responds, "I will tell you at dinner, but be assured it is something that will help Harry and

Joseph in their careers." Emma replies, "That is good to hear. I also have some news to share. See you tonight and thanks again." Harry and Joseph arrive home about an hour before Uncle Otto and quickly get washed up and changed. They are filled with anticipation and wonder what his good news could be. Emma purposefully does not let on that she also has some good news to share with them. Finally, around 6:00 p.m. Uncle Otto arrives and finds the three of them waiting on his front porch. Joseph cannot contain himself, saying, "Uncle, please tell us what the good news is." Otto laughs and replies, "You will have to wait. What I have to tell you has to be shared over a wonderful dinner and a glass of schnapps. Let me get cleaned up and I will be right back. I hope you are hungry, because tonight we feast."

As they are now all ready to go, they all drive in Otto's car to the best steakhouse in Sheboygan. They are seated, and the waiter brings them each a menu to look at. The waiter recognizes Otto from when he used to work in a different restaurant that Otto used to go to frequently. He says "Otto, is that you? It's so nice to see you again." Otto replies, "Charles, I didn't know you were working here now." Charles replies, "It's been about a year and a half and things are going very well, thank you for coming in tonight," Emma and Harry are amazed at how high the prices are and try to find the cheapest thing on the menu. They appreciate Otto taking them out, but they don't want to take advantage of him. Otto then says, "Come everyone, put your menus down. I am ordering for the table." He then calls Charles, "We are ready to order." Charles asks, "What can I get for you tonight?" Otto replies, "I want your best steak for each of us, along with a baked potato and sauteed mushrooms. We will also have a bowl of your French onion soup along with some crusty hot bread. Oh, and also for an appetizer, bring us each a shrimp cocktail." Charles replies, "Right away, this must be a special evening indeed."

Joseph speaks up, "Uncle Otto, thank you for taking us out, but this is too extravagant." Otto replies, "Nothing is too good for my nephew and his friends. Now listen all of you. I want to share my good news. Today, I got called into Frederick's office, and he offered me a promotion, which I accepted. I am now the Plant Manager for Miesbach Brewing Company. I am in charge of everything except the Brewing department." Joseph, Emma, and Harry all get up to shake his hand and congratulate him. Otto says, "I appreciated your well wishes. It is going to be a challenge, but the opportunity is quite exciting. I will also be in a position to help you in your careers at the brewery." Otto calls to the waiter Charles, "A glass of blackberry schnapps all around, except for Harry." Emma looks at them all and says, "None for me either, thanks." Harry asks, "Are you alright, are you feeling sick?" Emma replies with a beaming smile, "Not at all. I am feeling just fine. But the schnapps is probably not good for the baby!" The men sit there stunned at what she has just said. Finally, Harry asks, "Baby, you said baby, can it be true?" Emma kisses Harry and says, "It's true, my love, we are having a baby next year." Harry gets up and is literally jumping for joy as they are all laughing. Otto says, "This is truly a special evening. Let's raise our glasses. Here's to much success for all of us at the brewery and many congratulations to Emma and Harry on the baby. Viel Gluck (Good Luck)!"

Later that evening, after arriving home, Emma and Harry call Emma's parents to give them the good news. Leo and Alice are ecstatic about the news and ask if they can drive up this weekend so they can celebrate. Emma says, "Of course you can. I will prepare a celebration dinner for us." Leo replies, "Nein, Nein, we will go out to celebrate our treat. We will also bring you some of your favorite German pastries. Your mother and I are so happy for you!" Emma says, "Great, see you on Saturday, Grandma & Grandpa," as she smiles lovingly. Harry is happy to hear that his in-laws are coming for a visit. Harry looks at Emma and thinks for a moment before saying, "What do you think about taking the small spare bedroom upstairs and turning it into a nursery?" Emma replies, "That is just what I was thinking. We should go downtown some evening and look for a crib and a small dresser." Harry smiles and says, "Absolutely, let's do that. Do you think you would like a rocking chair, also?" Emma replies, "I think that would be great. I remember my mother telling me how much she enjoyed rocking me to sleep when I was a baby." Harry says to Emma, "Have you given any thought to whether you want a boy or girl baby?" She replies, "Whatever God wants is fine with me, as long as the baby is healthy. What about you Harry?" He says, "I bet you think I am going to say I want a little boy. Would it surprise you to know that I would love a little girl?" Emma smiles. "It surprises me a little, but time will tell. The other big thing is we need to start thinking of what to call the baby." Harry thinks for a while and says, "Well tradition says if it's a boy, he gets named after my father, and if a girl, she is named after my mother." Emma inquires, "Remind me, what were their names, Harry?" He replies, "My father's name was Peter, and my mother's name was Jana." Emma replies, "Those are good names. What do you think of Peter Harry Langer if it's a boy, and Jana Emma Langer if it's a girl?" Harry says, "Wonderful, then it's decided. I hope your parents won't be disappointed." Emma says, "They are very traditional in such matters, so they will not care, as it is to be expected." Emma then hugs Harry and whispers in his ear, "And besides, who said we are going to stop at one baby?" As life would have it, Emma and Harry are destined to have only one child after all.

The next day, Harry is hard at work in the malt house. His friend Joseph is running the can line filler over in packaging, or at least attempting to run it. It seems like one minor problem after another, lids not feeding constantly, stuck filler valve and short fills, cans falling after the seamer, etc. Just as Joseph is starting to let his frustrations show on his facial expression, his old supervisor from the keg line walks by the can filler. As always, Lars is loud and bellicose as ever and says, "Hey Joseph, your line is down more than it is up. Do you know what you are doing, dummkopf?" Joseph turns in a rage and yells back at Lars, "Yes, I know what I am doing, go back to the keg line where you belong. You are not my boss." Lars replies, "You cannot talk to me that way. I will report you." Joseph shoots back, "Go ahead, report me, everyone knows what you are." Lars walks away fuming, and he can't wait to make trouble for Joseph. However, he is unaware that Joseph's uncle Otto has just become the Plant Manager. Finally, after lunch, things smooth out on the filler and run very well the rest of the day. It certainly is turning out to be a large learning experience for both Joseph and the mechanic to keep the filler running properly. Attention to detail proves to be quite important, especially at the speeds the can line runs at. After a long day, Joseph decides to stop by the tavern across from the brewery to have a drink and wind down. He is joined by many of his friends from the packaging department. After a couple of shots of schnapps and a couple of beers, Joseph is feeling pretty mellow. Unfortunately, as he downs another beer, he hears Lars loud mouth as he addresses the other foreman in the bar, saying, "That can line was running like shit today. Why don't they get someone who knows what they are doing?" On hearing this, Joseph stands up and goes over to Lars, but keeps his hands behind his back and says, "Lars, if you have a problem with me, say it to my face." Lars is incensed. "You are a lazy dummkopf. A monkey could run the line better than you." Joseph replies, "And you are a loud, obnoxious bastard." At that moment, Lars loses control and pushes Joseph back. That's all it took, and in a flash, Joseph pummels Lars with a series of jabs to the face and body and then a right cross. As Lars looks up at Joseph from the floor, Joseph tells him, "If you ever touch me again, I will kill you, if you ever call me a dummkopf again, I will kill you." Fearing for Lars' safety, his fellow foreman pull him off the floor and whisk him out the door. Joseph's fellow employees let out a cheer after Lars left, telling Joseph you don't know how many times we wanted to do that. Thank you for giving him what he deserves. Joseph replies, "That probably cost me my job, but I don't care. I will not be pushed around by him or anybody."

The next morning bright and early, Lars is in the Brewmaster's office. "Frederick, I need to speak with you." Frederick looks up and says, "It looks like you have been in a fight." Lars says, "That can filler operator Joseph beat me up at the tavern after work last night." Frederick, knowing Lars' reputation too well, says to him, "And what did you do to provoke him?" Lars says, "Me, what did I do? I was minding my own business, and he hit me." Frederick grows angry and says, "Don't give me that bullshit Lars, I am only going to ask you once more, what did you do?" Lars looks down at the floor avoiding eye contact, "Well, we were arguing, and I guess I pushed him" Frederick says, "So you pushed him and he kicked your ass. What's wrong with that? I would have kicked your ass, too." Lars is dumbfounded and then Frederick says, "Look Lars, what happens outside of work is not my concern. You picked on the wrong guy, so suck it up and stop your whining. Now get out of my office and get to work." Lars turns and, looking down, walks towards the door. Frederick says, "Oh Lars, by the way, just so you know I have promoted Otto to the position of Plant Manager and he is now in charge of everything except the brewing department." Lars replies, "Otto is a good man for the job." The Brewmaster says "I am glad you agree with my choice, and by the way, that Joseph you came in here to complain about, he's Otto's nephew!" Lars stands their terror-stricken and thinks to himself, "Oh shit, this was a mistake, now I am going to get fired." As Lars leaves and closes the door, Frederick sits back in his chair and has a good laugh.

Later that morning, Otto and Frederick are discussing the unfilled positions Frederick has authorized. "Have you come up with any ideas, Otto?" Frederick asks. Otto replies, "I would like to propose Hanno Berg for maintenance manager and Kurt Hoffman for packaging manager." Frederick thinks for a minute, "Hanno will be an excellent choice; he is very well versed in just about all the trades. I would like to know how you came up with Kurt Hoffman. He is not one of the senior employees." Otto replies, "Admittedly, he is one of the less senior people, but he is very smart and has experience with everything except the new can line. He worked for a time down in Milwaukee at one of our competitors when he first entered the brewing industry. He has been a model employee for us and I think he is well respected. What I like about him is he is very articulate and driven to succeed. I would prefer a younger man for this position, as I expect it to be quite demanding." Frederick says, "Otto, I trust your opinion, and since they will be reporting to you, the choice is yours to make." Otto replies, "Thank you, Frederick, for your confidence. I will do everything possible to make them succeed in their positions. I will offer them both the promotions today, and if they accept, we will get to work on replacements for their current positions."

About a month goes by and finally all the new positions are in place and their old jobs have been backfilled. Otto notifies Hanno, Kurt, and Wilhelm to meet him in the office down the hall from the Brewmaster's and Plant Manager's office, which are now side-by-side. As they enter, it surprised them to see an ornate long wood table with eight leather clad chairs. Otto says, "Good morning, everyone. Please take a seat. I have called you here to tell you what my plans are. The Brewmaster and I have decided to make this our conference room. We still have some redecorating to do, but at least the table and chairs have arrived. What I would like to propose is we have a meeting in this room each morning at 9:00 a.m. At that time, we can go over the previous day's production numbers, maintenance issues, and personnel issues. Our shared goal is to produce the best products we can, for the lowest cost. Also, my hope is long-term we can move from being reactive in dealing with issues to being more proactive. Now Kurt, have you been able to get up to speed on the new can line?" Kurt replies, "Yes Otto, I have spent a lot of time over there the last couple of weeks and I now feel comfortable with its operation." Otto replies, "Very good, Kurt. Now I would like you all to spend the rest of the day getting organized, so you are ready for our first 9:00 a.m. meeting tomorrow. I would like you to come up with a standard template from which to discuss your areas, so we are consistent each day in discussing the most important items." Wilhelm raises his hand to ask a question. Otto acknowledges him, "What's that on the wall, MWOTHW?" Otto laughs and replies, "We are sharing this conference room with

Brewing, who will have their daily meeting in the afternoon at 3:00 p.m., right after the taste panel. For those of you who do not know, that is Frederick the Brewmaster's favorite saying in managing his brewers and foreman. MWOTHW means, My Way Or The Highway." Wilhelm bursts into laughter, along with the rest of them and says, "OMG, I'm sorry I asked." Otto says, "The one thing to know about Frederick, he knows what he wants, and he is going to get it, one way or another. Ok, see you all in the morning meeting, unless something comes up in the meantime."

The next morning comes and Otto, Hanno, Kurt, and Wilhelm are gathered in the conference room. Otto says, "Good morning, gentleman. After we conduct our daily production and maintenance review, I have some exciting news to share with you. Now Wilhelm, what information do you have for us on Ancillary products?" Wilhelm responds and gives the rundown on each of the product lines he is responsible for, and they are only having one major issue. Wilhelm explains, "We currently have a shortage of cream and may have to shut down the ice cream plant." Otto replies, "That is strange, what is going on?" Wilhelm responds, "The dairies are complaining that they haven't been paid in a timely fashion and they are threatening to stop all shipments of cream. I checked with accounting and they are waiting on Frederick to approve the payments." Otto responds, "As soon as this meeting is over, we will go see Frederick and get this ironed out. Once we get the approvals and the checks cut, I want you to take a road trip and personally deliver the checks to each of the dairies, and smooth things over with them. Please do everything you can to get the cream delivered on time. Remember, if we can't supply the product to our customers, our competitors will."

After Hanno and Kurt finish reviewing maintenance and production, Otto tells them he is pleased with how the plant is running. Otto says, "It is going to be more and more important that we keep a close eye on our operation, as it is about to become even more complex." They all look at each other and then Otto tells them that the plant will be installing a new bottle line. Otto says, "I spoke with Frederick last night and he said he just got approval from the bank to add another production line. We thought we were doing good with the addition of the can line. Now, there is another new fad back east that Frederick wants to be in on. As you know, all the bottled beer we produce is the heavy longneck returnable bottle. After they are consumed, they are returned to the brewery for cleaning and refilling. The new line that we will install is to produce a non-returnable bottle." Kurt interjects, "What is that you say, non-returnable bottles? People just throw them out when empty? I have never heard of such a thing." Otto says, "That's exactly right, the bottles are much lighter than the returnables. The consumers back east like the fact they are easier to carry, and they don't have to be stored and brought back to the store." Kurt replies, "Otto, I have another question you may know the answer to. Why do we only make beer in brown glass bottles? When I go to the store, I see different products in clear glass, or green glass?" Otto replies, "I really don't know the answer, other than it has something to do with sunlight. Oh, wait, there's Frederick now. Let me ask him." Otto opens the door and catches Frederick as he is leaving his office and says "Frederick, do you have a minute to answer a question for us?" Frederick nods yes and enters the conference room, and says, "What can I do for you, come, come, I am a busy man." Kurt asks, "I was wondering why we only make beer in brown glass bottles, and not in clear or green?" Frederick explains, "Sunlight will make the beer smell like the skunk. This is called light-struck. The brown bottles keep the light out." Frederick's face, slightly red, exclaims emphatically, "Just so you know, Miesbach Brewing will never put beer in clear or green bottles. Nein, Nein, so don't ask again!" As Frederick turns to leave, Otto says, "Frederick, Wilhelm and I need to talk with you. There is a problem with the cream deliveries." Frederick replies, "Alright, come to my office and we will get the problem taken care of." After Frederick leaves, Kurt smiles and says, "Well, that went well. Hanno, let's go down to the production floor and see if we can get a preliminary idea of where to place the new line. Otto said Frederick wants to hurry and get the new equipment ordered as soon as possible."

Later that day, over in the malt house, Harry and the rest of the crew have just completed transferring the most recent batch of malt out of the kiln and over to the brewhouse. Suddenly, Frederick the Brewmaster enters the kiln area and asks Harry how things are going. Harry replies, "Very well indeed, everything is running according to schedule with no major equipment problems." Frederick smiles slightly. "No, I meant how are you doing Harry?" He replies, "Very well, thank you for asking." Harry takes the opportunity to ask Frederick about his future. "Frederick, I wanted to ask you about the possibility of transferring out of the malt house, and into the brewhouse." Frederick replies, "Are you not happy here?" Harry stammers, "No, no, it's not that at all. It has been my dream to become a brewer. I am fascinated by it, although I know little about it." Frederick nods his head. "When Otto brought you to me to see if I would hire you, I recall you said your ambition was to become a Brewmaster someday. I can assure you it takes many, many years to learn how to brew beer. That being said, I appreciate your enthusiasm and your supervisor Klaus has told me about your fine work ethic. Alright Harry, I will give you a chance. We will have an opening within a year, as we have someone retiring." Harry is overjoyed and says, "Thank you, Herr Gambrus, thank you!" Frederick replies, "Don't thank me yet, as I will expect a lot from you." Harry tells him, "You will not be disappointed, I promise!"

## Chapter 5
# Birth & Rebirth

Emma has been patiently counting down the months and days until their baby arrives. Emma prays that it will be a little girl, but a little boy will be loved just as much. The spare bedroom has been turned into a nursery and Emma has it all furnished as she patiently awaits the happy day. A lovely wooden crib sits on one side of the room, a small dresser on the other side of the room. In the middle of the room is Emma's wooden rocking chair. Next to the nursery is the other very large spare bedroom that Emma has converted into a knitting room. It's full of all types and colors of yarn and miscellaneous fabrics. Almost every day, once she has completed her household chores, she is in that room knitting the baby a complete wardrobe of clothes, shirts, hats, socks, and baby mittens. As she doesn't know yet whether it will be a boy or girl, she knits everything in white. Once the baby is delivered, she will knit on to each piece of clothing a few strands of pink or blue yarn, depending on if it is a girl or a boy. This will get the baby started, and as she grows, Emma will knit using the appropriate color. Up until the last month of her pregnancy, she has been feeling fine and hasn't lost a step. One night, as Harry and Emma are having dinner, they talk excitedly about the upcoming birth. Harry is also excited because Frederick the Brewmaster told him today that starting in a couple of months, he will be transferred into the brewhouse. Emma and Harry are both so happy that Harry will soon achieve his dream of being a brewer. As they finish dinner, Emma rises to start cleaning the kitchen with Harry's help. As she smiles broadly at Harry, she suddenly collapses on the floor. Harry calls to her, "Emma, Emma, what's wrong?" Trying to keep his wits about himself he manages to first call for an ambulance, and then he calls Uncle Otto across the street. In a flash, Otto and Joseph bolt across the street. They find Emma on the floor and Otto immediately checks her breathing and pulse. Otto says, "She is breathing fine. Let's hope the ambulance arrives quickly." Fortunately, there is a hospital nearby and the medics quickly transport her for treatment.

Emma opens her eyes and looks around, but doesn't know where she is. She turns her head to see who she thinks is Harry, Joseph, and Otto in the hallway outside the room. Just as she can focus her eyes, the doctor enters the room and says, "Well, Mrs. Langer, you have had quite a scare." Emma replies, "What happened? Harry and I had just finished dinner, and that's all I remember." The doctor says, "You fainted, Mrs. Langer. You are a little dehydrated, and I suspect you are suffering from exhaustion. We will keep you here tonight for observation. I will speak with your family doctor in the morning and insist that you are to be on bed rest until you deliver the baby next month. Do you have someone that can help you at home?" Emma replies, "I am sure my mother can come up from Chicago to help." The doctor then let the men into the room to see Emma.

Harry immediately embraces his beloved Emma. "What is wrong with you? What did the doctor say?" Emma replies, "Just exhaustion and dehydration, nothing that can't be fixed. Please do not worry about me. I will be fine." Harry says, "Of course I worry about you. What did the doctor say we need to do to keep you and the baby safe and healthy?" Emma tells him, "I am to be on bed rest until the baby arrives next month. When you get home, please call my parents and tell them what has happened. Ask my mother if she would come and stay with us, as I will need a lot of help." Just then the nurse arrives and says, "Visiting hours are over so I will have to ask you gentleman to leave. Our patient needs to get some rest, so move along." They give Emma a kiss goodnight and tell her they will be back in the morning, which is a Saturday, so they will be free to visit.

As they drive back to the house, Harry begins to weep. Otto says, "Get ahold of yourself. She will be fine. This is just a little warning that she needs some extra rest." Harry replies, "I hope so. I could not bear it if anything happens to her or the baby." Joseph says, "Harry, everything will be fine. And remember, Otto and I are here for you." Harry responds, "Thank you, my friend. I know you are. We have been through a lot together to make it to our new life. I guess this is just another bump along the way." Joseph smiles and says, "That's the attitude Harry, heads up and keep moving forward." As they pull up to Harry's house, Otto says, "Now go call Emma's parents and then get some sleep. We will see you in the morning. Remember, Harry, Emma is going to be fine." Harry enters the house and immediately has a large glass of schnapps, which he is not supposed to have, to calm his nerves. After a few minutes, he gets on the phone to call Leo and Alice. The line rings five or six times until finally Leo picks up. Harry says, "I hope I did not wake you, but I need to speak with you." Leo replies, "We had just turned in early for the night, but we were still awake. Why are you calling so late? Is everything alright?" Harry responds, "I don't want you to worry, but Emma fainted tonight. We called an ambulance and took her to the hospital. She is fine, nothing serious to worry about. The doctor said it was just exhaustion and dehydration." Leo, who is visibly upset, yells up the stairs for Alice to come down. Alice runs down the stairs and exclaims, "Oh my God, what is wrong?" Leo tells her what happened, and she then grabs the phone from him. Alice says "Harry, is my Emma going to be alright?" He replies, "Yes, the doctor said she will be just fine. We need your help, as the doctor wants Emma on bed rest until she delivers the baby.

Is there any way you could come stay with us for the next month?" Alice tells Leo what needs to be done and they both agree. Alice gets back on the phone. "Harry, of course I can stay and help. It's not a problem. We will see you tomorrow." Harry is so relieved and appreciative, "Thank you both so much. See you on Saturday. Goodnight now, and have a safe trip up."

Harry is relieved the cavalry will be arriving tomorrow. He sits in his favorite chair, puts a record on the machine, and has many, many shots of schnapps until he finally relaxes and dozes off in his chair. Suddenly he awakes to the doorbell ringing and someone knocking on the door. The record is still spinning with no sound on the player, as the needle has run out of grooves. He tries to focus on the clock and it says it's two o'clock in the morning. Who would be coming over at this hour he thinks? Harry strides over to the door, visibly still feeling the effects of the schnapps, and opens it. He looks and says, "Alice, Leo, what are you doing here? I thought you were not driving up until tomorrow?" Leo replies, "We were both too nervous to sleep, so we thought we would come up now." Harry embraces them, saying, "Thank you for coming. It is such a relief that you are here." Leo looks at Alice and they smile at each other, and then he says, "Hey, Harry, I have a question. Did you leave any schnapps for us?"

It's Saturday morning around 10:00 a.m., and everyone has just woken up. Harry sees his in-laws in the upstairs hallway and asks them if they had gotten any sleep. Alice replies, "Yes, we slept fine once we got to bed, but it took a little while to clear all of Emma's yarn and fabrics off the bed." Just as they all come downstairs, they receive a call from the hospital. They tell Harry that Emma is doing fine and will be discharged later this afternoon. Harry replies, "That is wonderful news. What time should we be there?" The nurse on the phone tells him Emma will be ready to be picked up at 3:00 p.m. Harry tells Alice and Leo the good news and both are so relieved. Leo says, "Let's go out and get a big breakfast. I don't know about you, but with all the excitement, I am quite hungry."

Later that afternoon, they all arrive at the hospital to pick up Emma. As they enter her room, Emma is ecstatic to see her parents and says, "I am so relieved to see you. Thank you for coming." Alice replies, "Of course we came. All you had to do was ask. Now don't you worry about anything. Mother will take good care of you. How are you feeling now? Have you eaten?" Emma replies, "Much better than last night, I have to say. I had a small breakfast and lunch, but I am starving, and I want some ice cream." Alice laughs saying, "My dear, you can have all the ice cream you want." Alice turns to Leo and Harry and says, "What do you guys think? Why don't we go for an early dinner on the way back to the house?" Leo says, "Of course, if Emma feels up to it," Just then, an orderly arrives with a wheelchair to take Emma downstairs. They get Emma into the Terraplane and off they go to dinner. They arrive at Gruen's Restaurant, which is their favorite German restaurant, and because it is early, they are the only ones there. The waiter comes over to take their orders and get them some beverages. Emma can't contain herself, and is the first to order. She says, "Bring me some bratwurst with sauerkraut, pickled eggs, some bread with honey, and a triple scoop of vanilla ice cream." The waiter smiles and says, "Let me guess, you are expecting a child, aren't you?" Emma smiles and nods her head yes. The waiter then asks the rest of them what they would like. Leo says, "Alice, if you and Harry agree with me, I will order for all of us." They both nod in agreement, so Leo goes on to order, "We will have the bratwurst, sauerkraut, German potato salad, tomato cucumber salad, and a plate of spaetzle." The waiter replies, "Coming right up, and what would you like to drink?" Leo replies, "Harry and Emma will have water. Alice and I will have a glass of that Miesbach Dark Lager, that Harry has told us so much about." Leo tells his family, "I have decided to stick around for a few days before returning to Chicago, but your mother will be staying the whole time." After they are done eating, they leave the restaurant and head straight home so Emma can get to bed.

The last month of Emma's pregnancy has thankfully been uneventful. Emma does as the doctor ordered and has been on bed rest. As she has been confined to bed, time passes slower and slower with each passing day. She tries to keep busy knitting and reading, as Alice keeps her supplied with a steady supply of books from the library. Harry has moved his record player from the living room into Emma's room so she can listen to some music to help pass the time. As her physical activity has been curtailed and her appetite has increased, Emma has gained a good twenty pounds in the last month. It's really not an issue because she was very thin to begin with. The family doctor made a house call yesterday and said both she and the baby were doing fine. Emma is due to deliver any day now and can't wait for the blessed day. Alice is having the time of her life cooking and baking all of their favorite pastries. Her cooking is so good, Otto and Joseph join them all for dinner several days a week. Otto really enjoys the company of Alice and they have become close friends over the last month. While they get along very well, Otto knows not to discuss Leo's shady business dealings with her.

It's Friday, March 20, 1936, and Harry has just arrived home from work. A few minutes later, he is joined by Otto and Joseph, who have come over for another one of Alice's delicious dinners. Harry has delivered Emma's dinner to her room and tells her they will all be up to visit her as soon as dinner is done. The family sits down for dinner in the dining room. Alice brings out large plates of wiener schnitzel, noodles, and gravy, and pickled red cabbage, which Emma is already devouring hers upstairs. Halfway through dinner, they hear Emma calling, "Harry, Harry, I need you!" He runs up the stairs and enters the bedroom, "What do you need?" Emma replies, "I think my water just broke, and I just felt a contraction. The baby is coming!" Harry runs out of the room and yells from the top of the stairs, "The baby is coming, what do we do?" Alice takes charge and says, "Otto, grab her suitcase and pull your car around front, and keep the engine running. Harry, Joseph, you help Emma down the stairs and into the car. I will get the doctor's name and phone number from the wall next to the phone and let him know Emma's water broke, and she has started contractions, and we are taking her to the hospital."

As soon as they get Emma into the car, Alice says, "Joseph, thank you for helping. Would you please clean up from dinner and lock the door when you leave? No telling how long we will be at the hospital." Before Joseph can utter a reply, the car zooms off down the street. As soon as they arrive at the hospital, they get Emma inside, and then Otto drives back to his house. The nurse and orderly wheel Emma up to the third-floor maternity ward. The nurse tells Harry and Alice they can use the maternity waiting room if they wish to stay. She also says that the cafeteria is down on the second floor if they need anything. As they wait, Alice makes a phone call down to Chicago to tell Leo the news. In a flash, Leo finishes his business and drives back to their house to pack a bag. Shortly thereafter, he is in the car and on his way up to Sheboygan. After a few hours of waiting Alice says, "I am going downstairs and get some coffee and a snack. When I get back, you can take a turn, and I will keep watch. Harry, can I bring you back something?" Harry smiles and replies, "Thank you, no, I am too nervous to eat or drink. You go down and get something." Just then Leo arrives. "Any news yet?" he asks. Alice hugs him and says, "You made good time getting here. Nothing new yet, just waiting. I was just going down to the cafeteria. Why don't you come with me and get some coffee? You must be tired from your drive." Harry says, "Take your time because we may be here all night." Well, truer words were never spoken as they patiently wait hour after hour. It's 5:15 a.m. and Harry, Leo, and Alice have been sound asleep in their chairs for the last couple of hours. Suddenly, they are awakened by a nurse who says, "Harry Langer, wake up, are you Harry Langer?" Harry opens his eyes and jumps out of his chair, "Is Emma alright, did she deliver the baby?" The nurse replies as Leo and Alice also awake, "Congratulations Dad, you are the father of a lovely baby girl, 6lbs, 4 oz, born at 4:45 a.m., Saturday March 21, 1936. Both the mother and baby are doing fine, and resting now. Give it an hour or so and we will bring you all up to see Emma and the baby." Harry is so happy he cannot contain his joy and says, "Did you hear that Leo, Alice? She had a baby girl!" As they all hug and kiss each other, Alice says, "We are so happy for you both. I know how much you were both hoping for a baby girl. Your prayers have been answered. And you know what is so funny? I remember when Emma was born, she weighed 6 lbs., 3 oz., almost exactly the same weight." Harry replies, "That is interesting. I wonder if she will be blonde-haired and blue-eyed like Emma?" Alice smiles and says, "I wouldn't be a bit surprised."

After an hour has passed, the family goes to visit Emma and the baby. Emma is resting comfortably and is so happy to see her Harry. Harry embraces Emma and says, "I love you, Mom." Emma laughs and winces in pain, "I love you, Dad." Leo and Alice take turns kissing her and giving their congratulations. Leo smiles and then says, "Emma, where's my granddaughter?" Emma replies, "She is in the nursery. The nurse said she will be right back, and then she will take you to see the baby." After a few minutes go by the family is gathered outside the nursery window peering in. The maternity nurse wheels one of the baby carts in front of the window. As they look, they see the name tag says, "Langer." As the nurse moves the blanket from the baby's head, they can see Harry was right. Blonde hair and blue-eyed, just like Emma! Leo remarks how beautiful the baby is and asks Harry if they decided on a name yet. Harry replies, "Emma will want to tell you when we get back to the room." After the nurse takes the baby away, they return to Emma's room. Harry exclaims, "Emma, the baby looks just like you." She replies, "I know. She is just so darn cute." Alice says, "Emma, we were asking Harry for the baby's name. Is it going to be what you told me earlier?" Emma replies, "Yes, we are calling the baby Jana Emma Langer," after Harry's mother. Alice and Leo both love the name and say, "Wonderful, that is a fine name!"

It's now been an entire week since the delivery and Emma is finally going to be discharged from the hospital. Leo and Alice had gone back to Chicago the day after the birth, but have just returned. They are at Harry and Emma's house cooking and getting everything ready for when Emma and the baby arrive. Fortunately, Harry is off from work, as there was no overtime this weekend. It's late Saturday morning and Harry is just pulling up to the hospital to get his Emma and baby Jana. As he arrives at her room, he finds Emma fully dressed and in a chair, holding the baby. Harry says, as he kisses her hello, "Emma, you look radiant. Are you ready to go home?" She replies, "Yes, my love, I feel fine and can't wait to get home." Harry replies, "I can't wait either. I missed you so much. Oh, and you will be happy to know that your parents have come back from Chicago and are at the house as we speak." Emma smiles, "I am so happy to hear they could come back. Hopefully, Mother won't mind staying a little longer." Harry says, "She said to tell you she will stay as long as you need her." Just then, an orderly arrives with a wheelchair to transport Emma and the baby downstairs. They make their way to the main entrance and Harry leaves them to go fetch the car, which is parked a short distance away. Emma is holding Jana tight to her when the baby starts to stir. Emma repositions the pacifier in her mouth and Jana falls back asleep. The baby was just fed a little while ago, so she should be good until they get home. Harry pulls up in his car and gets Emma and the baby inside. As they drive off, Emma says, "Harry, get us home safe, and no speeding!" Harry bursts out into laughter and says, "Emma, what are you saying? You are the speed demon, not me!" Emma smiles and replies, "I know, I know, but go slow anyway." The ride is uneventful and they return home safely. As they enter the house, Emma is startled as she sees her mother and father, Otto, and Joseph, standing in the dining room cheering loudly at their arrival. They all come out to greet her and see baby Jana, and get to take turns holding her. After a little while, Alice says, "Come, let's go into the dining room. I have prepared something to celebrate the joyous occasion." As they gather around the dining room table, they find a two-tiered cake with pink frosting, decorated with a balloon design. There is writing on it which says, "Happy One Week Birthday Jana." Leo takes a match and lights the single candle on the cake. Alice says, "Join me in singing, all of you." With that they break out into song, "Happy Birthday to you,

Happy Birthday to you, Happy Birthday dear Jana, Happy Birthday to you." But it doesn't stop there. "Many Birthdays to you, Many Birthdays to you, Many Birthdays dear Jana, Many Birthdays to you." And more "How old are you, How old are you, How old are you, How old are you?" Emma laughs and sings, "She's One Week Old, She's One Week Old, She's One Week Old, She's One Week Old." At that, everyone claps and yells Hooray! Then Leo says "Alice, you cut the cake, and I will get the schnapps."

Emma was so happy to finally be home from the hospital. She can't thank her mother enough for all the help she has given them over the last month. After Otto and Joseph leave to go back to their house, the rest of them are relaxing in the parlor. Emma asks her parents, "Mother, Father, when do you have to leave to go back to Chicago?" Leo replies, "I am leaving tomorrow morning, as business awaits. I can't speak for your mother." Alice replies with a question. "Emma, Harry, would you like me to stay a couple more weeks to help? I would be happy too." Emma and Harry speak at the same time, "Yes, please, that would be great!" Alice smiles and replies, "I would love to and will plan on staying as long as you need me. Now Leo and Harry, why don't you turn in for the night. Emma will give Jana another feeding and then put her to bed. Harry and Emma, remember to leave your bedroom door open so you can hear if Jana wakes up during the night." Harry and Leo both get up and kiss their wife's goodnight and then head upstairs. Once they leave, Emma breast feeds the baby. After a few minutes, Emma remarks how hungry the baby is. When the feeding is finished, they bring the baby upstairs and put her in the crib. Jana is fast asleep as soon as she is laid in the crib. Emma and Alice then retire for the night. As Emma lays in bed, she stares at the ceiling with her eyes wide open. Harry looks at her and says, "You need to get some sleep. Try to relax." Emma, without blinking replies, "I have to listen in case Jana needs me. Don't worry Harry, you go to sleep." Harry dozes off after a few minutes, and then Emma's eyes grow tired. After a half hour of listening and fighting to stay awake, she drifts off into a sound sleep. Emma will soon learn the first lesson on having given birth to a baby. When the baby sleeps, the parents sleep!

Everything over the next month has gone very well with baby Jana. Fortunately for Emma and Harry, the baby has been sleeping through the night. Emma's mother, Alice, has returned to Chicago for a well-deserved rest after taking care of Emma and the baby the last couple of months. Alice told Emma to expect to see her a couple of times a month, depending on when Leo can get away from his various legal and illegal enterprises. Emma is back to knitting and sewing in her spare time. Besides making the baby clothes, she has learned to sew her own clothes. Turns out she has a real knack for clothes making and thinks maybe that is something she could do to earn some spare money. But that will probably have to wait until baby Jana gets a little older, and she has more time to devote to it. Things are going good for Harry at the brewery. The Brewmaster has informed Harry that he will start his new position in the brewhouse next Monday. Harry makes a call to Emma from the phone booth outside the brewery, saying, "Emma, it's Harry. I am going to stop off at the bakery and get some pastries, so we can celebrate tonight. I wanted to let you know I will be a few minutes late getting home." Emma replies, "Celebrating? Did you get good news at work?" Harry replies, "Yes, Emma, I start Monday in the brewhouse. My dreams are all coming true. I don't know why I am so blessed. I feel like I have been reborn. Alright, I am hanging up now. See you in a little while. Love you!"

Just as the Brewmaster had promised, it is now Monday morning and Harry has received his transfer to the brewhouse. As he enters the brewhouse, he walks over to the large copper brew kettle and peers inside. The kettle is full to the top and is boiling vigorously. The aroma of the malt and hops hangs in the air and is almost overpowering. Just then Harry hears a voice saying, "Not too close to that kettle, you dummkopf." Harry whirls around and sees a man standing behind him and says, "I am sorry if I did something wrong. Frederick told me to report working here this morning." The man smiles and says, "I know who you are. Welcome, Harry, Frederick has told me much about you." Harry chuckles and says "Oh no, is that good or bad?" The man says, "If it wasn't good, you wouldn't be here. Let me introduce myself. I am Max Engle, the brewhouse foreman." Harry shakes hands with him and says, "I am very pleased to meet you, and even happier to be here. This has been a dream of mine for a long time." Max says, "I am aware of that, so come with me and let me show you around." They then leave the brewhouse floor and walk up multiple levels of stairs until they reach the top of the silos. Max says to Harry, "I know you worked in the malt plant so you are familiar with the grain storage and handling. The only difference is these silos hold the finished malt that you have provided. As is the case with all the silos, the air must be kept free of grain dust as it is highly explosive, so no smoking or having anything that can make a spark is allowed anywhere near the silos. Now let's go down a couple of levels and I will show you the malt mills." As they enter the mill room, Max says to Harry, "If you look up, you will see the scales on the floor just above us. As we prepare the next brew, the malt is transferred from the silos and weighed in the scales. The malt is then discharged from the scale, down the chute, and into the twin mills." Harry looks and says, "I have never seen this device. What is its purpose?" Max says, "Do you remember the parts of the barley seed? I assume you do, after working in the malt house." Harry replies, "Yes, I remember the parts." Max smiles and says, "Good, now in order to make the mash, we need to first grind the malt kernels into smaller pieces. These mills have a series of three paired rollers that the malt is passed between in order to break it down into the proper size, before moving it to the mash tun.

We are trying to accomplish three tasks in malt milling. The first is to crack the kernel open, the second is to separate the husk from the endosperm, the third is to grind the endosperm into smaller pieces. We want the husks retained at a certain size, as they will be used to form a natural filter bed later in the process. As far as the grind goes, if we grind it too little, then all the starchy endosperm will not be converted to sugar and the mashing time is long. If we grind it too much, the particles will be too small, and will cause very slow runoffs out of the mash tun. In addition, too fine a grind of the husks will make for poor filtration, and will adversely affect the taste of the beer."

Max says to Harry, "I want to point out the various sample ports on each mill so you know where they are. Each port will sample a different fraction of the grind. The problem with this type of sampling is it is very inconsistent from brewer to brewer, so we don't use it much anymore. Instead, we will fill a sample bag of the milled malt that is actually going into the mash tun so it is all the fractions combined. Now take the sample over to the desk in the far corner. This device is just a stack of six sieves and a bottom pan. Stack them on the shaker, with the largest sieve on top, in order to the finest sieve on the bottom. Empty the grain sample onto the top sieve and place the cover on it. Now, set your watch and shake it for five minutes. Once that is done, we will weigh the contents of each sieve and I will show you how to calculate the percent of milled malt that ended up in each sieve. We can then compare those numbers to what our targets are to make sure we are milling properly. We will do this at least weekly, or more, if we suspect a problem. If you don't have any questions, let's begin." Harry was a little nervous at first, but as it turns out, it is quite a simple procedure. Max says to Harry, "Now, record the information on this form and complete the calculation. As soon as Harry finishes the first mill, he quickly repeats the procedure on the second mill. Max says, "Very good, Harry. You are to perform sieve analysis and report the results to me each Monday. If we need it more frequently, I will let you know."

Max says, "Let's continue the tour and go down to the mash tun." Harry replies, "What is a mash tun?" Max explains, "It's a circular tank that we add warm water and the milled malt into. Come now, I will show you." They walk down to the next level and peer into the mash tun. Max says, "There you can see the malt and water is mixed together in the tank, which we call the mash. We also have a paddle agitator that keeps the mash well mixed to aid in conversion." Harry looks puzzled and asks, "What is conversion?" Max replies, "In making beer, or any kind of alcoholic beverage, the yeast converts sugars into alcohol. The yeast cannot convert starch into alcohol, so first we have to convert the starch into sugars. That is the purpose of mashing. As I am sure you learned from your time in the malt house, you were taking the barley and turning it into malt. The malt has an enzyme system that was developed in steeping and germination, then made dormant in kilning. The enzymes are located in the layer that surrounds the starchy endosperm. This enzyme layer has a name and is called the Aleurone. The domestic barley that we use in our brewery has a white colored layer, but Canadian barley has a blue colored layer. Once the malt is mixed with warm water, we use a steam jacket that surrounds the tank to maintain a constant temperature. The warm water re-activates the enzymes, which then go about their work of converting starch into sugars. The solution of sugars that results is called Wort. It is very important to remember that the enzymes are temperature dependent, so we need to monitor the mash temperature closely so we can achieve maximum conversion of the starch into the types of sugars we desire. It's all a function of time and temperature and ph." Harry says to Max, "I think I am finally understanding how this whole malting and mashing process is needed to make beer." Max replies, "As you will learn, making beer is truly an art and a science. Now, I rarely go into this much detail with our regular brewers, but I think you may be able to understand. There are three main enzymes present in the mash. The first is called alpha-amylase, which will break up the starch molecule into long chains that are not fermentable. These long chains are called dextrins, and contribute to the mouthfeel of the beer, making it taste fuller bodied. Then Beta-amylase and maltase come in and break the dextrin's up into smaller fermentable pieces. However, they are deactivated at higher mashing temperatures, which leads to less fermentable sugars. As I said before, depending on the mash temperature, pH, and time of conversion, you can make the sugars more or less fermentable. We can monitor the ratio of fermentable to unfermentable sugars by adding yeast to a finished brew of known sugar content, and mixing it for a specified period of time, and then testing it for residual sugar content. This test is called an Attenuation and is something we monitor routinely. Harry says, "I know you have worked here for many years, but you seem extremely knowledgeable about the process." Max chuckles, "That's true, but many years ago, Frederick the Brewmaster sent me to brewing school. I took a course on all things brewing at the Siebel Institute down in Chicago. Maybe someday you will be fortunate enough to attend. Now, if you are interested, I can get a copy of a book called "The Master Brewer" which is put out by the Master Brewers Association. This book contains a wealth of knowledge concerning brewing beer, and I highly recommend it." Harry replies, "Absolutely, please buy me a copy, and let me know what I owe you." Max says, "Ok, so let's move onto the next step, the lauter tun."

Harry says to Max as they walk down to the lauter tun, "Correct me if I am wrong. In order to brew beer, we are using water, malt, yeast, and hops." Max nods and says, "That is correct. Those are the four principal ingredients. Back in the old country, German law only allowed for those four ingredients to be used to brew beer. Here in the states, you may use other cereal grains also, which we call adjuncts. There are many domestic breweries that use rice and/or corn to brew their beers. The advantage of these adjuncts is they are much cheaper than malt, which helps profitability. But they also can provide for a lighter tasting product and/or a slightly sweeter flavor. Frederick is quite traditional and has vowed never to use adjuncts."

Harry replies, "That is all good information. I never knew you could brew beer with anything other than malt. If you have time, could I ask you about the water that we use?" Max replies, "Yes, what do you want to know?" Harry relates a story saying, "My friend, Joseph, and I were at a bar one time and the barmaid, whose father owned the place, was trying to teach us about various beer styles. She said her father told her that a dark Munich style beer differed from a pale colored pilsner beer, solely because of the water. Was she correct in what she was telling us?" Max says, "Yes, to a point she is correct, aside from the fact that you can use dark roasted malt to make dark beer. It's all in the water. We use the term pH to tell us if something is acid (below 7.0), or basic (above 7.0). This is important because the pH that we mash at will affect the enzyme activity, the color of the wort, and the taste of the wort. We target our wort pH at approximately 5.50."

Max continues saying, "There is another term that we use in describing water, and that's called alkalinity. In other words, alkalinity tells you how much the water can resist changes to its pH. During mashing and wort boiling, minerals in the water will react with components of the malt and cause the pH to lower. In our brewery, we add some gypsum, which is calcium sulfate, to the brew in order to raise the mineral concentration. The calcium will aid in lowering the mash pH, stabilizing the enzymes, precipitating proteins, and in fermentation it will help the yeast flocculate.

Now, the pilsner style beer is a pale-yellow colored beer, which was first brewed in Pilsen, Czechoslovakia. This is a radical departure from the darker beers brewed in Munich and Bavaria. The Pilsen water has a much lower alkalinity and mineral content than the water found in Bavaria. Brewing with this water results in wort with a final pH of around 5.5, which leads to a lighter beer color. The Bavarian water has a much higher alkalinity and mineral content. Brewing with this water results in wort with a final pH around 5.9, which leads to a darker beer color. Let me show you the lauter tun before I have to leave for a meeting with the Brewmaster."

Again, they walk down to the next level to where the vessel is located. They constructed the Miesbach Brewery brewhouse in this manner, so at each step, gravity would move the product to the next step, reducing the need for pumps. As they arrive at the lauter tun, Max says, "Harry, I told you earlier that in milling we did not want to grind the husks too much because we would use them to filter the wort. If you look now, the vessel is empty. There, you can see the false bottom which is slotted to allow the wort to drain thru on its way to the brew kettle. The malt husks will fall to the bottom, and make a filter bed, which will allow the mash to be clarified. There are also a series of mechanical rakes that are used to gently break up the filter bed if it becomes too tight for the wort to flow easily. I forgot to mention that at the end of the mashing cycle, the temperature in the mash tun is raised to what we call the mash off temperature. The purpose of this is to start deactivating the enzymes so the fermentable/unfermentable sugar ratio does not change. It also makes the wort less viscous, so it will flow easily thru the filter bed. The first wort that arrives at the brew kettle will not be clear. There is a very small open vessel next to the kettle called the Grant. As the wort flows through it, the brewer can observe its clarity as there will be a lot of particulates left in the wort. Until the wort runs clear, the brewer will use a pump to recycle the wort back up to the lauter tun. This is what we call Vorloff. Once the wort runs clear, it will then fill the brew kettle. Even though we drew off all the liquid wort, there is still a considerable number of sugars tied up in the grain bed. In order to get those sugars, we spray the grain bed with hot water, in a procedure we call sparging. It is important that the sparge water has the proper pH, so we add some acid to it before we use it. If we didn't, we have found that as we sparge, the pH of the bed would increase, and extract a lot of astringent compounds. These compounds are detrimental to beer flavor. By keeping the sparge water pH low, this does not happen. Once sparging is complete and all the sugars have been removed from the grain bed, a hatch is opened and the grain bed is removed. We call this wet spent grain, and it is collected and trucked out and sold to farmers, as animal feed." Harry remarks, "I have seen those grain trucks leaving the brewery every week. Now it makes sense." Max replies, "I am going to take you over to meet Gottlieb. He will be training you for the rest of your duties. We did not have time to discuss the brew kettle yet, so come see me later in the week, when I should have some free time to discuss it with you. Alright, good luck Harry." He replies, "Thank you Max, it's my first day, and I have learned so much already."

The week goes by in a flash and Harry has been rapidly learning his duties. It's now Friday afternoon, and Max stops by to see Harry and says, "I just spoke with Gottlieb, and he has told me you are doing a fine job." Harry replies, "Thank you, Max, I am trying as hard as I can." Max smiles and says, "That is quite evident. Keep up the good work. I am sorry we didn't have a chance to talk again, as I promised. Would you like to stop for a beer after work, and I can answer more of your questions?" Harry says, "That would be great. I will run over to the bar as soon as the shift ends and grab a table in the back." Max replies, "Sounds good. I will be there as soon as I can." Harry makes a quick phone call to Emma, telling her he will be a little late. He then goes to the bar and finds a table and waits patiently for Max. About fifteen minutes later, Max arrives and says, "I hope I didn't keep you waiting too long. I had to wrap up a few things before I left." Harry replies, "No problem at all. Thanks for the invite." Max turns and shouts to the bartender. "Bring two bottles of Miesbach Dark beer." Harry interjects, "Just one beer and one Coca-Cola." Max looks surprised and says, "A brewer who doesn't drink, what's up with that?" Harry confides in him,

"I am on medication for epileptic brain seizures. I am not supposed to drink, although I do cheat on special occasions. There would be hell to pay if my wife Emma found out I was drinking alcohol today." Max, looking concerned, says, "But Harry, are you alright?" He replies, "Yes, I have only had one seizure. The medicine does a wonderful job of keeping me under control." Max replies, "The brewhouse can be a dangerous place, so I want you to be extra careful. If you do not feel good, please say something so we can get you help." Harry says, "I will. The doctor said as long as I take my medicine daily, I should be just fine." Max then asks him, "So Harry, are you married?" Harry says, "Yes, my wife's name is Emma, and we just had a baby girl named Jana." Max smiles and lifts his glass, "A toast then, to your new baby.

Here's to Jana!" Harry then asks Max, "What about you? Do you have a family?" Max replies, "A wife, Adelina, and a 10-year-old daughter, Brigitta." Harry raises his glass of Coca-Cola and speaks. "A toast! Here's to Brigitta."

Harry says, "Max, I wanted to ask you two questions. The first is about wort boiling in the brew kettle. Can you please explain what is happening to the wort as we boil it? The second question, I would like you to explain what the 'kettle break' is, and why it's important?" Max replies, "The most obvious reason we boil the wort is to hit our target sugar content, which is 11.0%. In the brewing industry, we use an instrument called a hydrometer to measure the sugar content. This device has been calibrated against the specific gravity of a wort sample, which corresponds to the percent sugar it contains. We call the hydrometer a "Balling Spindle" and the results are read as degrees of balling (plato). So, one degree of balling (plato) equals one percent sugar, and so on."

He continues, "You asked about the kettle break, and yes, it is very important. At that stage of the boil, compounds react with proteins in the wort to form a precipitate." The precipitate is called "trub," which is pronounced "trube." This material then falls out of solution in large flakes. This precipitate will be removed as we transfer the contents of the brew kettle through the next steps. First the wort goes through a tank called a hop jack, which removes the hops. Then to a Hot Wort Settling tank, where the "hot trub" as we call it, will settle out. If we did not remove the "trub," it would make for a cloudy product and affect the flavor. Once this step is completed, we send the hot wort down to the starting cellars, where it is cooled by ammonia chillers, and then placed in a tank in a refrigerated room. Then additional precipitate, which forms at cold temperatures, which we call "cold trub," will settle out. But there are many, many reasons besides that. For example, boiling the wort deactivates all the enzymes that produced sugars from starch. Once deactivated, the ratio of fermentable to unfermentable sugars is fixed. Through wort boiling, we also help to sterilize the solution, which will retard bacteria growth later. Boiling also develops color and flavor, which is obviously important." Harry asks, "Gottlieb told me a good rolling boil for a prolonged period helped drive off sulfur and other compounds. What is that?" Max tells him, "That is an excellent question. Sulfur, for example, is an element that, under the right conditions, can form some very unpleasant compounds. At a very low pH, sulfur will react to form a rotten egg smell. While our wort pH is not anywhere low enough to form that, there are many other ones produced. An example would be dimethyl sulfide, which smells like creamed corn. So, boiling the wort properly helps remove many unwanted compounds that can cause aroma problems in the product." After finishing their drinks, they both head home for the weekend.

Harry gets home a few minutes later and Emma is just getting ready to put the dinner on the table. Baby Jana is dozing in the extra crib they keep downstairs, which Emma put in the dining room so they could watch her while they eat. Emma says, "So, how did things go with your boss, Max?" Harry replies, "It was wonderful. Max is so knowledgeable I can't tell you how much I learned." Emma smiles, saying, "That is good. The more you know, the more valuable you will be to the brewery." Harry changes the subject and asks, "Well, that's enough about me. How was your day?" Emma says, "It was very good. Baby Jana is such a contented baby. Ever since she was born, she hasn't cried or fussed unless there was a reason. She is just wonderful, and did you know she loves listening to your classical records? I put the record player on almost every afternoon, and after listening for a while, she quietly takes her nap." Harry replies, "I am so happy to hear that. I know you have your hands full with everything around here while I am at work." Emma says, "Right now, we have a pretty good routine going, so I will be fine. I wanted to remind you that my parents are coming into town on Saturday, so they can be here for Jana's Baptism on Sunday." Harry says, "I did not forget, it's going to be Sunday after the 11:00 a.m. Mass." Emma replies, "That's right, and then we will all be going out to dinner to celebrate." Harry says, "Joseph was so happy we asked him to be Jana's godfather. Unfortunately, the priest was giving him a hard time about his paperwork and proving that he was baptized in the church and had completed his sacraments." Emma puts her fingers up to her mouth and smiles as she whispers to him, "I talked to my father and it's all been taken care of." Harry smiles and says, "OK, say no more. Let's eat. It smells wonderful!"

Emma's parents, Leo and Alice, drive in from Chicago the next day and arrive just after 12:00 p.m. as planned. As they enter, Emma greets them and says, "It's so good to see you," as she kisses them hello. "Come and sit down. I have lunch ready." Alice replies, "Lunch? Who wants lunch? I want to hold baby Jana." Emma says, "Alright, first things first, Harry will be down with her in a minute." Just then, Harry comes down the steps with the baby and hands her off to Alice. She is so excited she dances around the room with Jana close to her. After Alice and Leo are done holding her and playing with her, they lay her in the crib so they can have lunch. Emma has prepared a simple lunch of various dried sausages, cheeses, and crusty bread. As they eat, Leo says, "What is new with you, Harry? How are things at the brewery?" Harry responds, "It could not be better. I was granted a transfer out of the malt house. This past Monday, I started in the brew house, which is something I have always wanted to do." Leo replies, "Alice and I are happy for you both. A beautiful new baby, and a new job. You truly are blessed." Emma interjects, "We definitely are, and tomorrow Jana will have her Baptism."

It's Sunday now and they are all gathered at the 11:00 a.m. Mass. Emma, Harry, Leo, and Alice are in the front row. Uncle Otto and Joseph are seated behind them. Baby Jana was just fed and changed prior to the Mass starting, so she was very content and quiet until the Mass ended. After the congregation has exited, the family is brought up on the altar to stand around the Baptismal Font. The priest asks, "Who is the Godfather of this baby?" Joseph replies, "I am." The priest then asks, Emma and Leo, "What name do you give your daughter?" They reply, "Jana Emma." The priest continues, "What do you ask from God's church? They reply, "Baptism." After many Invocations by the priest, the family's and Godparents' Profession of Faith, the priest performs the Baptism. As he pours holy water across baby Jana's forehead, he says. "I Baptize you in the name of the Father, and of the Son, and of the Holy Spirit, Amen." As expected, baby Jana cries a little, as the water has startled her, but Emma is able to quiet her. As they all gather around, Jana opens her eyes and smiles at them. Before they leave the church, Leo extends an invitation to the priest to join them for a celebration lunch. He replies, "It would be my honor. I will meet you at the restaurant in a few minutes." A wonderful time is had by all, with much eating and drinking, and laughter. After lunch is concluded, they head back to the house. As they are all gathered in the parlor, Leo says, "Harry, please go upstairs to my bedroom and in my suitcase, you will find a couple of bottles of schnapps. Please bring them down for us." They put baby Jana in the crib and turn on some soft classical music, and soon she drifts off into sleep. The family spends the next couple of hours telling stories and toasting their good fortune.

Come Monday morning back at work, Harry asks Max, "What about the hops that we add to the kettle? That's just for flavor, right?" Max replies, "Of course, flavor is an important part of adding hops to the wort. But besides that, the hops give the beer a wonderful aroma. Come with me to the hops room." As they enter, Harry realizes that it is a refrigerated room. Max explains that the hops plants are grown on a tall trellis. After they are picked, the hops are dried and baled, and shipped to the brewery, where they are stored cold. Max shows him the 200 lb. compressed bales of hops that are wrapped in burlap. If you touch them, you will see they are whole hops leaves. That is the only type we will ever use. He explains that we use a combination of imported and domestic hops. Some are added just to get the proper bitter content in the beer, while other hops are added primarily for the aroma that they impart to the product. It also makes a difference when they are added to the kettle, and in what sequence. One of the most important jobs a Brewmaster has is to adjust the hops bill to take into account the various kinds of hops to get the desired finished product. Miesbach uses types of hops such as imported Hallertauer and Fuggle, and domestic Cluster, just to name a few. Different types of hops can give you more or less bitter, more or less aroma. The aromas can be hoppy, or floral, or citrus, etc. There is also crop year variation in the hops, or availability and price, how long they have been stored, etc. In the end, the Brewmaster is trying to produce a consistent product year after year. The consumer can be very fickle, and once you lose a customer because the beer tastes a little different, it's impossible to get them back. So, Harry, the next time you are in the hops room, take some hops and examine them. You will find on the underside of the leaves some yellowish beads. These are the lupulin glands that produce the bittering compound called Humulone, and the aroma compound called Humulene. In wort boiling, these glands break open, and the bittering and aroma compounds are released and solubilized. One interesting phenomenon is that the compounds become less bitter, but we say it is a better bitter flavor. That is to say, that it is not a lingering bitter that stays on the tongue too long. We want the consumer to take a refreshing drink with good flavor and bitterness, and be able to enjoy multiple beers if they wish. Besides the hops imparting flavor and aroma, they also provide some protection against bacterial growth in the beer. But that protection is limited, because you would have to add a lot of hops to have a profound effect. Over in England, when they shipped kegs of beer to their colonies around the world in the old days, the beer was not pasteurized. So, for example, when they shipped to India, beer would arrive spoiled. By hopping at high levels, the beer could make the journey, and not be spoiled on arrival. This type of beer has become known as an IPA, which stands for India Pale Ale."

Harry smiles at Max and says, "Wow, that's a lot to take in and remember." Max chuckles and replies, "You asked! But I will be honest with you. I have worked with many employees over the years in the brewhouse. While they were all good workers who got the job done, most knew the how, but not the why. So, I encourage you to keep asking questions and learning, and someday maybe you will have the opportunity to advance yourself to a foreman position." Harry looks Max straight in the eye and tells him, "I will not stop at foreman, I want to be a Brewmaster!" Max replies, "Well now, you are very ambitious. Go for it!" Harry says, "Thank you again for all the information." Max pats him on the back and says, "Anytime, Harry, all you have to do is ask."

The next few years seem to fly by. Harry cannot believe that he has been working in the brewhouse for the last five years. There hasn't been a day where he didn't enjoy coming to work. Over the years, Max has taught him everything he knows about brewing beer. Joseph is still the filler operator on the can line. He hasn't changed much at all, and is still single. His favorite pastime seems to be drinking and getting into bar fights. But aside from that, he has been a reliable employee. Like Harry, he has not missed a day of work. Good old Uncle Otto has really flourished as the Plant Manager. His knowledge of the entire Miesbach Brewery is quite impressive. Fortunately, he is well respected by all the employees. Otto is direct and to the point, tough but fair. Everyone knows where they stand with him and he is known for pushing everyone to be the best they can be.

Jana is growing fast and is now five years old and ready to start kindergarten. Jana is the spitting image of her mother Emma, blonde-haired and blue-eyed, with a lovely smile. Harry and Emma could not have asked for a sweeter, loving child. It's early September 1941, and Emma is walking Jana around the corner to start her first day of school. Emma wonders what she will do with her time now that Jana is in an all-day kindergarten. Most likely, she can do her sewing business full time, to bring in some more extra income, and besides, it's something she really enjoys. Emma has even discussed the possibility of opening a small store downtown, selling clothes she has made and doing alterations. Emma and Harry love each other more with each passing day. They are so happy they found each other and look towards the future with boundless optimism. Unfortunately, life is going to take a turn that neither one of them expected.

## Chapter 6
# War

It's Friday night, November 14, 1941, and Harry and Emma are relaxing in the parlor. Jana has long since gone to bed and is sound asleep. When Emma tucked her in, Jana told her mother how much she loved going to school, and about all the friends she has made. As Harry and Emma sip their coffee, they are simultaneously listening to the radio and reading today's evening paper. The major topic of the day, as it seems to be every day this year, is the ongoing aggression of the Nazi's. Harry says to Emma, "There seems to be no end to this Schweinhund Nazi scum. They have already conquered Poland and France. They are bombing England all the time and a couple of months ago, they invaded Russia." Emma replies, "Being in America, it all seems so far away. Do you think it will come here?" Harry sighs and says, "I really don't know about such things. I just hope the government is prepared if it does." Emma says, "I sure hope they are, too. You know, something strange happened at school the other day. I usually talk with a couple of the other children's mothers, but suddenly they have become very standoffish, I think is how they say it." Harry asks, "Did you have an argument or something?" Emma replies, "No, not at all, but I thought I heard one of them say under her breath, something about filthy Germans. I know they are of British heritage, and we are of German heritage, so maybe that's their problem." Harry rises from his chair, visibly agitated, and raises his voice, saying, "Gott im Himmel (God in Heaven), we are Americans now! So what if we came from Germany? We hate the Nazi's just as much as anyone else." Emma gets up and hugs him, saying, "Calm down and lower your voice. Jana is sleeping. I didn't mean to upset you. Sit back down and finish your coffee."

After a little while, Harry says to Emma, "We can't control what other people feel about us. All we can do is go about our lives and set a good example, work hard and don't get into trouble." Emma replies, "I agree with you. Maybe in time they will accept me." Harry tells her, "You know, I was talking with Joseph yesterday, and he told me he was a little concerned because he could not get in touch with his Uncle Gerhart and Aunt Lena back in Friedrichshafen. He has written letters and sent cables, but has not received a response. The last time he heard from them, they wrote that the Nazis had taken control of everything. The Gestapo have spies everywhere, and they are always looking for any act of perceived disloyalty. He is very concerned about their safety, but I guess all we can do is pray for their safety."

It's now Sunday morning, December 7th, 1941 and Harry, Emma, and Jana are at their church for 9:00 a.m. Mass. Little Jana cannot understand what the priest is saying, because the Catholic Mass worldwide is spoken in Latin. However, she always enjoys the wonderful choir that they have. There is even a wonderful group of ladies, led by a very friendly woman named Rosie, who performs songs by playing the hand bells. After the Mass has concluded, the congregation goes over to the parish center. This morning is the monthly coffee and bake sale. There are all kinds of wonderful cakes, pies, freshly made donuts, cookies, etc. Little Jana wastes no time in asking for a freshly made donut, which Harry is happy to give her. Emma and Harry are each enjoying a large slice of apple pie with a piece of Wisconsin cheddar on top. The coffee is hot and everyone is having a good time. They recently met two other couples that attend the morning Mass that are of German descent. When they saw Harry and Emma from across the room, they moved their chairs to come over and sit with them. They spent the next half hour or so getting to know each other a little better, talking about work, talking about food, just having a nice, relaxed time.

The next evening, Harry and Emma are sitting in the parlor having some coffee and dessert, as is their custom. Jana has already finished her treat and is playing upstairs in her room. Suddenly, the music stops and the announcer breaks in to say, "Attention! Attention! Please listen carefully. The President of the United States, Franklin Delano Roosevelt, made an address to Congress earlier today. We broadcasted that speech live to our listeners and we will continue to replay it every hour because of its importance. President Roosevelt told Congress and the American people that Japan has attacked our naval base at Pearl Harbor, Hawaii yesterday. The attack has caused extensive damage to our fleet and resulted in thousands of casualties. The President calls it, "A date that will live in infamy." The President requested and received from Congress a declaration of war against Japan. Most people do not even know where Pearl Harbor is, but they know what war means. Emma quickly gets on the phone to call her parents to see if they have heard the news, which they have. Harry hears yelling outside and opens the door to see what's going on. People are running through the streets yelling that we are at war with Japan. The next few days are filled with trepidation by everyone in Sheboygan and people all across the country. Just when things couldn't get much worse, they do. All the radio stations are broadcasting the same alert, "Attention! Attention! Germany and Italy have declared war on the United States."

Over at the Miesbach Brewery, Otto is meeting with Frederick the Brewmaster. Otto, acting as Plant Manager, tells him, "We are really going to have problems running the brewery if the government starts drafting people, now that it seems everyone is declaring war on our country." Frederick replies, "I was up all night worrying about the same thing. War with Japan was bad enough, but with today's announcement, we have even bigger problems. Now it's Japan, Italy and the German Nazi scum! I was just looking at the ages of our employees, and I would say at least seventy-five percent of them are in their late forties and beyond. If we lose some of the younger ones to the draft, we should still be able to operate, although possibly on a more limited basis." Otto replies, "I agree with you. This is one time where an older workforce will work to our benefit. I will start looking at all areas of the brewery, including the ancillary products, and start planning for a worst-case scenario of losing a quarter of our employees. We may have to implement some mandatory overtime, if need be, to keep everything running." Frederick replies, "Thank you Otto. I will take a hard look at the brewing department and we will meet in a couple of days to discuss our options."

Otto gets home late that evening, his mind weighed down by the enormity of the problems that the brewery faces to stay in operation if they lose employees to the war effort. What will become of his family and friends in America, and back in Germany? As soon as he walks in the door, he heads straight to the bottle of schnapps sitting on the credenza. He doesn't see that his nephew, Joseph, is sitting on the other side of the room. Joseph says, "Uncle Otto, join me for a drink." Otto spins around and replies "Joseph, you startled me, I didn't see you there." Joseph looks at him and says "I made an impulsive decision today and I wanted you to be the first to know." Otto gazes at him and says "What have you done now?" Joseph takes another drink to get up his courage, and then blurts out, "I enlisted in the Army today, and I passed my physical. I cannot stand by and watch our country be attacked, and besides, those damn Nazis need to be wiped off the face of the earth." Otto goes over and hugs him and says, "Joseph, I am so proud of you. I couldn't bear it if anything happens to you. But that being said, I am very proud of you." Joseph looks at Otto and says, "I love you Uncle, please understand that this is something I must do." Otto smiles and replies, "If I was a younger man, I would be right there with you. Do you know when you have to leave?" Joseph nods his head. "Yes, Uncle, I ship out for basic training at Fort Dix, New Jersey, next Monday morning. I have to report to the recruiting station at 7:00 a.m., where we will board trucks to take us to New Jersey." Otto tells him, "Then I'll plan on a going away party for you on Saturday. We will have it over at Gruen's Restaurant." Joseph says to Otto, "That is very generous of you. I will certainly miss you, Harry, Emma, and Jana." Otto says, "I know you will, but we should go over to their house and break the news to them." Joseph peers out the front window and says, "I see their lights on, so I am sure they are still awake. Let's go over right now."

Joseph and Otto are standing on Harry's front porch and Otto knocks gently on the door, so as not to wake Jana. Harry hears them and immediately gets up and welcomes them in. Harry and Emma ask at the same time if something is wrong. Joseph responds, "Wrong? I think the entire world has gone wrong. But I wanted to come over to tell you some important news. I enlisted in the Army today, and I leave for basic training next Monday." Emma is shocked, but not entirely surprised, as she goes over to hug him. Harry shakes hands with Joseph and wishes him well. Harry says to Joseph, "Give them hell, and then come back home to us, my friend." Joseph replies, "I fear many of us will not be coming home, but it's all in the Lord's hands now." Otto then invites them to the going away party next Saturday.

At work the next morning, Joseph is talking to his friends while they are taking a break in the lunchroom. They are all relaxing drinking a fresh mug of beer they have just taken from the finished beer tank next to the lunchroom in the cold cellar. The chief topic of conversation is obviously the war. Joseph tells them the news that he has enlisted. Several of his friends are seriously considering signing up. Mandel, who they call Manny, has already done so, and will be on the same transport as Joseph. Before they leave to go back to work, Joseph invites all his friends to his party on Saturday at Gruen's Restaurant. Before he knows it, the next couple of days have flown by. As he leaves work on Friday, he realizes he won't be packaging beer again for quite some time. Joseph is apprehensive about going to war, but that only lasts a second. Immediately he is filled with rage and can't wait for his chance to fight the Nazi's. Joseph walks across the street to the tavern and stops for a few cold beers before heading home. He wants to take care of a few home repairs for Uncle Otto before he leaves Monday morning. No telling if and when he will be coming home.

All the guests that Otto invited have gathered at the restaurant to say goodbye to Joseph. It is a very good turnout, as it appears there are forty to fifty people present. Emma and Harry helped decorate, and there are American flags and banners all over the room. On one side of the room, Frederick the Brewmaster is having a good time conversing with Hanno, Kurt, and Wilhelm, who are Assistant Managers at the brewery. On the other side of the room, Harry, Emma, and Jana are sitting with Emma's parents. Leo and Alice came up from Chicago to say goodbye to Joseph as well. Otto calls out to everyone to please quiet down as he has something to say. He continues, "I want to thank all of you for being here to say goodbye to my nephew Joseph. As you may know, he leaves for basic training on Monday, and it may be a long time before we see him again. So, raise your glasses for a toast. Safe travels Joseph and may the Lord keep you safe." When the toast is done, they all sit down as dinner is served. The waiters bring out platters and platters of food, as it is a family style dinner. They are all of Joseph's favorites; wiener schnitzel, bratwurst, pickled cabbage, spaetzle, tomato cucumber salad. The food is top-notch and plentiful, as well as the Miesbach beer they are all enjoying. In the background, Otto has hired a local band to provide some background music. Once the dinner is over, the band gets decidedly louder as they belt out a series of patriotic songs. The night goes quickly, and it is now around 11:00 p.m. and the last guest has gone home. Otto is sitting with Joseph, Leo and Alice along with Harry, Emma, and Jana. Emma is holding Jana, as she has fallen asleep and Joseph is passed out at the table because he drank too much. Otto says, "Well, thank you all again for coming to the celebration, and also for helping set up the room. I think we better call it a night, and Harry, would you give me a hand? I think we will have to carry Joseph to the car. He's pretty out of it." Harry laughs and says to Otto, "No problem. This isn't the first time I had to help carry Joseph home, and it won't be the last."

It's a little after noon on Sunday when Joseph makes his way downstairs. Uncle Otto says, "Good afternoon, my boy. I was wondering when you were going to wake up. How are you feeling?" Joseph replies, "I know I drank too much last night and must have passed out because I don't remember coming home. But I feel pretty good, just a very slight hangover. Plus, I feel pretty excited about leaving tomorrow." Otto says, "Well, come sit down with me. I made a fresh pot of hot coffee, and some fresh kuchen from the bakery. Oh, and by the way, Harry and Emma have invited us over for dinner at 2:00 p.m. So, when you are done with your coffee, you better go upstairs to shower and get ready." Joseph smiles broadly and says, "That is so nice of Harry and Emma. I am really going to miss them while I'm away. And my sweet Goddaughter Jana too." Otto says, "Don't worry, I will keep a close eye on them. Alright, drink your coffee."

After a lovely dinner with Harry and Emma, they spend the rest of the afternoon and early evening telling stories and reminiscing about their life in the old country. It's now about 8:00 p.m. and Joseph and Otto say their goodbyes, and thank their hosts for the wonderful dinner and conversation. Harry and Emma embrace Joseph and wish him well on the adventure he is going to embark on. After they leave, Harry, Emma, and Jana are seated at the kitchen table. Harry tells Emma, "I have a feeling this is going to be a long war. I hope Joseph comes home to us." Emma smiles and says, "So do I. Come, let's all hold hands and say a prayer that Joseph is kept safe."

The next morning rolls around and Joseph is up early and raring to go. Uncle Otto has just dropped him off at the recruitment center. Otto says, "I love you Joseph, now you take care of yourself, and don't forget to kill some Nazi's for me." Joseph replies, "I hope I get the chance to, I don't know when we will be together again, but I wanted to thank you for all you have done for Harry and me." Otto smiles and replies, "It's my pleasure, now get going and make us all proud." Joseph boards the bus with all the other recruits and quickly spots Manny sitting in a seat towards the middle of the bus. Joseph says, "Manny, can I join you?" He replies, "Of course you can. I was hoping I would see you." Just then, the bus departs and Joseph and Manny realize that this is really happening. There is no turning back now. After about an eight-hour drive, they stop in Cleveland, Ohio at an Army base called Camp Perry. They pull up to the mess hall and are told to go in and get some food. On the wall is the ubiquitous mantra of all Army mess halls: "Take all that you want, but eat all that you take." After evening chow, they are taken over to the barracks to sack out. Bright and early the next morning, they board the bus again for the last leg of their trip to Fort Dix. It's now the middle of the afternoon, around 3:30 p.m., when they arrive at the fort. As they disembark from the bus, they are greeted by a screaming man and he says, "Get in two lines, you maggots. No talking and keep your eyes straight ahead. I am Sergeant Klineman, your Drill Instructor. You will only speak when I give you permission to speak. You will always address me as Sergeant." The D.I. then goes up and down the row, sizing up each of the recruits, and berating them for their size, weight, hair, looks, etc. Now it's Joseph's turn to be in the crosshairs. The D.I. looks at him up and down and says, "Well, you are a little runt, aren't you? What is your name?" Joseph replies, "Sergeant, my name is Joseph Vogler." The D.I. is incensed and says, "Vogler? That isn't some German name, is it?" Joseph replies, "Yes Sergeant, my parents were from Germany." The Sergeant says, "Do you hear that troop? We got a real-life fricking Nazi in our midst." Harry loses it and yells, "I am no freaking Nazi!" Pow! The next thing you know, Joseph is on the ground. The Sergeant yells at him, "I didn't give you permission to talk." Joseph leaps to his feet and says, "You can't..." Pow! Joseph is punched in the face again, mid-sentence, and is back on the ground. The Sergeant yells again,

"Shut your freaking mouth and get back in line and come to attention." Joseph's face is beet red, his eyes bulging out, fists clenched, but he somehow gets back in line and does what he is told. The rest of the recruits stand there staring straight ahead, not making a sound or moving a muscle.

The basic Army training lasted for a couple of months and was quite grueling. The troops would march, perform calisthenics, obstacle course, rifle training, hand-to-hand combat, etc. Joseph never seemed to have any problem with it, though. Joseph took to basic training like a duck to water. He just had no fear or physical limitations at all. He was the fastest runner, could climb ropes and go over walls like it was child's play. Joseph was blessed with excellent eyesight and coordination. During rifle training, he was the first to earn a marksman medal. During hand-to-hand combat training, Joseph was undefeated against the rest of his troop. The only one that could beat him was the Drill Instructor, and beat him he did. But as hard as he tried to break Joseph, mentally and physically, he could not. Joseph just kept coming back for more.

Manny, on the other hand, was struggling. He certainly was not the best runner and frequently fell behind the rest of the troop. Climbing ropes and walls was almost impossible for him at the start of basic training. He became close more than once to being discharged for his physical limitations. But, with the help of Joseph, Manny persevered. Whatever free time they had, Joseph would help work out with Manny, and encouraged him not to give up. That extra effort paid off, as Manny slowly but surely improved. He was able to meet all the requirements, just as the rest of the troop had. Finally, after a long couple of months, basic training had ended. After the graduation ceremony was over, they were back in their barracks, loading up their belongings. The Drill Instructor came in and had the troop fall in at attention. He then gave each one of them a copy of their orders, as they were to ship out immediately to wherever they had been assigned. The instructor did not speak to anyone except the last person in line, and that was Joseph. He handed Joseph his orders, snapped to attention and saluted Joseph, and being a man of few words, said, "You have earned my respect." Joseph saluted back, and at that moment felt so proud of himself. It had not been easy for Joseph, and he thought about how many times he I wanted to shoot that S.O.B., and now he saluted me! I guess you can't make this stuff up. As they left the barracks, each soldier departed to a different gathering point based upon their orders. Joseph and Manny have been assigned to stay at Fort Dix and were assigned to the motor pool. This turned out to only be a temporary assignment, because after a few months, they received new orders. It is now May 1942, and Joseph and Manny are in a troop transport aircraft and have been assigned to Camp Claiborne, Louisiana. They are to become part of the recently reactivated 82nd Infantry Division.

The next several months at Camp Claiborne have become quite important to the war effort. Joseph and Manny take part in many war game field simulations, as the Generals draw up attack plans. They easily discard scenarios that have no value and try to fine tune others that may have some value in combat. It is really quite the operation, with tens of thousands of troops from various bases taking part in the exercises. All of this takes place under the command of soon to be famous General Omar Bradley. However, during August 1942, the designation of the 82nd Infantry Division took a drastic change. The troops, along with Joseph and Manny, are shocked when it is announced that the new name of the unit will be the 82nd Airborne Division, the first division of paratroopers to be designated during WWII. With this change being made, the training shifts to learning how to parachute out of a plane. Needless to say, Joseph can't wait to give it a try. The training that Joseph and Manny go through to qualify to be a paratrooper is quite grueling. Besides the physical requirements, the candidates must show that they are not afraid of heights by completing obstacle courses high in the air. All along the way, soldiers are removed from consideration because of either being too old, not fit enough, or scared of heights. The successful candidates move on to the tower phase of training. Tall wooden towers of various heights are used to simulate various aspects of jumping. The last exercise has the soldier hoisted to the top of a 200 ft tower and then lowered by cable, which was attached to a parachute to simulate what it will be like to jump. After weeks and weeks of training, the moment of truth has arrived. Joseph and Manny, along with the other candidates, will make their first training jump from an aircraft. Many of them, like Joseph, have no problem with flying. Others, like Manny, are getting motion sickness and are nauseous to different degrees. But there is no turning back now. The instructor has them line up in the plane and attach their static lines, which will open the parachute for them as they jump from the plane. One by one, they jump from the plane in a timed sequence. Joseph is having a sensational time and is laughing and hollering on his way down. Poor Manny has his eyes closed tightly, as he silently prays to himself. The spotters on the ground count the number of chutes and confirm that they all have opened. As Joseph hits the ground, he lets his legs buckle, rolls to break his fall, and he quickly pops up and begins reeling in his chute. Manny and one other candidate have major problems, but all the others have landed safely. Manny, unfortunately, had locked his legs and one leg and one ankle have been broken in the fall. The ambulance that was on standby at the field has been dispatched, and the corpsman quickly takes Manny to the hospital. Whether he heals well enough to stay in the Army remains to be seen, but he will never be a paratrooper. Upon completion of training, Joseph is assigned to join the 504th Parachute Infantry Regiment (P.I.R.), which has recently been added to the 82nd Airborne Division. They are stationed at Fort Bragg, NC, before being deployed overseas.

Back in Sheboygan, Harry has been quite busy at the brewery. As Frederick and Otto had expected, between enlistments and the draft, they are running short-handed. Some of this is made up by the employees working overtime, which is not a long-term solution. Harry had requested previously to do cross training in some other areas of the brewing department, so now, after completing his normal shift in the brewhouse, Harry works his overtime in the fermenting cellars. As Harry has learned, the first step once hot wort leaves the brewhouse, is to cool it down through the ammonia chillers. The cooled wort is then aerated and left to rest for several hours in holding tanks, called starting tanks. During this rest period, additional protein complexes, termed cold trub, are allowed to settle out. The air that was added will provide oxygen to the yeast, which is needed initially, and will allow the yeast to grow and multiply properly during fermentation. If the initial oxygen concentration is too low, the yeast will not multiply properly, and the fermentation will slow down or even stop. This is termed a hung fermentation.

In the Miesbach Brewery, they are producing lager beer, and not ale. In making beer, the lager strain of yeast used works well at low fermenting temperatures, and will settle to the bottom when fermentation is complete. The production of ale uses a different strain of yeast, more similar to bread making yeast. That strain ferments well at higher temperatures, is fast acting, and rises to the top when fermentation is complete. Because of the differences in yeast type and fermentation temperatures, the flavor profiles of a lager versus an ale are quite different.

The cooled, aerated wort is pumped into the fermenter, along with the yeast. The ratio of yeast that is to be added to every barrel of wort is termed the pitching rate. The type of yeast, pitching rate, time and temperature of fermentation will have a large impact on what types of flavor compounds are produced, both desirable and undesirable. Once primary fermentation begins, the fermentable sugars in the wort are converted into alcohol, carbon dioxide, and heat by the action of the yeast. When the fermenter reaches the predetermined fermentation temperature, cooling jackets that surround the tank are activated, which will keep the temperature as constant as the technology allows. This is called attemporation, and it will help ensure a consistent fermentation, batch to batch. A typical fermentation takes about 96 hours in the Miesbach process. Several tanks per week are monitored for what is termed peak yeast cell count throughout the fermentation. As the yeast divides and multiplies, the number of yeast cells in solution will begin to increase, then reach a peak, and then decline as the fermentation finishes.

The carbon dioxide that is produced is initially allowed to vent to the outside atmosphere until the purity increases to a sufficient level, and then it is collected, further purified, compressed, and stored for future use. By using the carbon dioxide that is produced during fermentation, the brewery greatly reduces the need to buy it. In the Miesbach brewery, all the carbon dioxide used in the entire brewing department has been recovered from previous fermentations and not purchased from outside sources.

Another aspect of fermenting that Harry learned that as the wort ferments, the top of the liquid will foam. The foam is made up of yeast, proteins, and hops resins. It will precipitate out onto the lining of the tank above the liquid level. This dark precipitate is called brandhefe in German, and it will take hot caustic solution to properly clean it off.

Once the fermentation is complete, the lager yeast will settle to the bottom of the fermenter. The cooling jackets are turned on, only now the goal is to cool it enough to stop the fermentation, and to help the yeast continue to settle. The bottom of the fermenter is conical in shape, and the settled yeast will collect there. The yeast is drawn off first, and pumped to a vessel called a yeast brink, for storage and reuse in future fermentations. The fermented wort, which now contains alcohol, is now termed unfinished or "green" beer. At this stage of the process, the unfinished beer, while containing alcohol and many desirable flavor compounds, also contains some undesirable ones as well. The most prevalent one is a compound called diacetyl, which imparts a buttery flavor and aroma to the unfinished beer. During the next phase of processing, the unfinished beer is moved into cold storage tanks where it will age for several weeks, which is called lagering, German for "to store." During this time, the unfinished "green" beer will undergo many changes. What we are trying to accomplish in lagering is Clarification, Carbonation, and Flavor Maturation of the beer.

The Aging (lagering) cellar consists of many horizontal long storage tanks that are maintained around 50-55 degrees Fahrenheit. The Miesbach Brewing Company uses a very traditional method of cold aging its products. Because of its high cost and amount of labor involved, it is only used by one other domestic brewer. The first step in the Miesbach lagering process is the laying of long, curved, thin strips of beechwood onto the bottom of the tank. They have been boiled and rinsed to remove any flavor compounds. The wood strips will allow the yeast to settle on them, thus increasing the surface contact the yeast has with the beer over the three-to-four-week aging period. During this time, the yeast will degrade most of the undesirable flavor compounds produced during primary fermentation.

The beer, which has completed primary fermentation, and has very little fermentable sugars left, is moved into the lagering tanks. Then some freshly yeasted, unfermented wort is added to the lager tank. This is a process known as Kraeusening by some brewers. During the storage period, the yeast will ferment the fresh wort which will produce more alcohol. But more importantly, carbon dioxide will be produced which will naturally carbonate the beer. Initially, the carbon dioxide produced will be allowed to vent into the atmosphere, because its purity is too low. Eventually it will be placed on a common CO2 header, called the bunging system, which will allow pressure to build, thus carbonating the beer. Once it has aged sufficiently, has been carbonated, the clarity has improved due to settling, and the flavor has matured, the beer will be pumped off. The wood strips are then collected from the tank, rinsed, boiled, and then reused.

The next day, Harry is back in the brewhouse when his foreman Max comes to get him. He says, "Harry, are you working overtime today?" Harry replies, "Not today. Thankfully, it's wearing me down."

Max replies, "I know it does, but Frederick would like to see us in his office as soon as the shift ends." Harry says, "No problem, I will meet you there." Later that afternoon, Harry arrives at Frederick's office to find Max is already there, and they are drinking from a bottle of schnapps. Frederick says, "Harry, come in, join us for a drink. We have some good news to share with you." Harry smiles and says, "I like good news. Perhaps I will have just a tiny shot of schnapps." Frederick tells him, "Harry, I wanted you to know that Max is retiring next month, and I want to offer you the promotion to brewhouse foreman. So, think about it for a second, but the answer better be yes." Harry is ecstatic and blurts out, "I don't have to think about it. Of course, the answer is yes!" Frederick says, "Then it's decided. Now raise your glasses for a toast. Best of luck to Max on his retirement. You will be missed. And here's to Harry on his promotion. I will be expecting a lot from you. Congratulations and the best of luck!"

Harry can't wait to get home and tell Emma his good news. As he opens the door, Jana runs up to him and jumps in his arms. He twirls her around and says, "How is my big girl today? Daddy has missed you!" Jana replies, "I helped Mommy make cookies. Do you want one?" Harry smiles and says, "Yes, Jana, get me two!" Jana runs in the kitchen and gets the cookies and rushes back to Harry, with Emma following right behind her. He quickly eats one and tells Jana how good they are. Harry says, "Emma, there you are. I have good news to tell you." Emma looks dower and hands him a letter and says, "I took the liberty of opening it when I saw it was from the government. It says you have to appear before the draft board." Harry shrugs and says, "I guess we knew this would happen, eventually. Nevertheless, it's a bit of a shock." Emma looks at him and tries to smile, but she is visibly worried. She says, "You said you had good news. What is it?" Harry replies, "Something big happened at work today. I have been promoted to brewhouse foreman!" Emma is ecstatic as she embraces him, and asks, "But what happened to Max? Did he finally retire?" Harry says, "Yes, he has less than a month left, so I will train with him for a few weeks before he leaves." Emma says, "I am so proud of you, and by the way, do you think Otto knows?" Harry says, "I would assume so, but after dinner, let's take some cookies and go over and see him.

Later on, they all go over to Otto's house to tell him the good news, while they sit around the table having coffee and cookies. Otto replies, "That is just super. Frederick had told me that Max was thinking of retiring, but I didn't know he made it official." Harry replies, "He is leaving next month." He then asks Otto, "Did you have anything to do with me getting promoted?" Otto smiles and says, "I would have, but it was unnecessary. Frederick is quite impressed with your knowledge and work ethic. Harry, this promotion was all you're doing!"

The following week, on a Wednesday morning, Harry arrives at the Army Recruitment Center. He is directed to the storefront a couple of doors down the street. The Army has rented the space and is using it to screen the recruits, either draftees, or people who have enlisted. This morning, there are three to four dozen men seated around the room waiting for their turn with the doctors. After several hours of waiting, it was Harry's turn. The doctors evaluate him for all the normal things and tell him he appears to be in good health. The doctor asks Harry if he is aware of any medical condition they should be aware of, or if he is taking any medication. Harry explains that he takes phenobarbital to control brain seizures. Upon hearing that, the doctor immediately marks him as a 4F, unfit for military service. Harry is instructed to provide the doctor's name and address so they can verify his condition. But for now, he is ineligible to serve. As Harry leaves, he is a bit torn by his feelings. On the one hand, he wants to fight the Nazi's, but on the other, the thought of being without Emma and Jana fills him with dread. Before heading back to work, Harry stops home and gives Emma the news. She hugs him and says, "Thank God I don't have to worry about losing you." Harry replies, "I don't want to lose you either, but I feel bad that Joseph is in the service, preparing to fight, and I cannot." Emma says, "I understand, but we will all have a role to play in the war effort, so take solace in that. Now, you had better get back to work. I will see you tonight, my love."

The next few months bring a drastic change to the workforce at the brewery. It's now November 1942, and as expected, because of retirements, enlistments in the service, and draftees, the brewery is down almost twenty percent of its workforce. The problem is there are no more able-bodied men to hire. This is a problem affecting all businesses throughout the country. Consequently, the government has been motivating women to become part of the labor force. Signs have sprung up everywhere, trying to recruit women to go to work in the factories. The government is calling upon their patriotism to get them to respond. Free childcare centers are opening all over the country for any job classification. In addition, they are offering free transportation to work in a defense plant. Miesbach brewing can no longer operate profitably with restricted production and paying overtime, so they are forced to accept women into their workforce. This is a seismic shift in the culture at the brewery, and is especially true in the brewing department, where no woman has ever been allowed to work.

Today, Harry welcomes the two new women employees into the brewhouse. Rose and Ingrid are their names, and both are daughters of immigrants. Rose is black haired, brown eyed woman of Italian descent, her family coming from the town of Pisciotta, which is a fishing village south of Naples on the Mediterranean. Ingrid, on the other hand, has blonde hair and blue eyes, and her family had emigrated from Oslo, Norway. Harry takes some time to give them a tour through the entire brewing department. Harry gets a chuckle at how tired the ladies are after climbing the hundred or so steps to the top of the grain silos. After the tour is finished, Harry begins their training. They both prove to be hard workers and fast learners. After a couple of weeks, they are working independently, and Harry is very pleased. But as it usually goes in the brewery, things are going too well. For the first time since Harry was promoted to foreman, he comes out on the wrong side of the Brewmaster's temper. Harry is seated in the brewhouse office working on some reports when Frederick enters. He says, “Harry, do you have Rose and Ingrid working in the hops room?” Harry looks perplexed and responds, “Yes, Frederick, they have been fully trained and are performing all their duties.” Frederick’s face turns red and yelling asks him, “Do you let them go in the hops room when it’s their time of the month?” Harry is shocked and embarrassed and quietly says, “What did you say?” Frederick yells again, “Women are not allowed in the hops room when it is their time of the month. Their hormones will spoil the hops! You make sure that does not happen; do you hear me? " Harry rises from his chair and says, “Yes, Frederick, I will take care of it.” Frederick then storms out of the office, leaving Harry dumbfounded. Consequently, Harry had to switch around the job assignments, so only the men entered the hops room. All the hops that are needed daily are neatly packed in burlap sacks, marked for identification, and are left on the brew kettle floor for easy access.

Later that night, Harry gives Otto a call and says, “Otto, it’s Harry. I hope I am not bothering you, but I have to ask you a question.” Otto replies, “No problem. Tell me what’s on your mind.” Harry relates the story of not allowing the women employees in the hops room when it isn't their time of the month. Otto replies, “Oh my God, is he serious? For an intelligent man, I can’t believe he thinks such things.” Harry asks “Then it’s not true?” Otto laughs and replies, “Of course not. It’s some silly old wife’s tale from hundreds and hundreds of years ago. But Frederick is strange that way. He is very superstitious and hard headed. I am afraid you will just have to deal with it, as he is the owner of the brewery.” Harry says, “I have already made the arrangements, but I just wanted to know the truth. Sorry to have bothered you. Please come for dinner this Sunday. Emma would love to see you.” Otto replies, “It would be my pleasure. See you then.”

Sunday comes around and, as usual, Emma has outdone herself. Dinner was delicious. As they are seated in the parlor having coffee and dessert, Emma drops a bombshell on them. She says, “Yesterday, when

I picked Jana up from school, all the mothers were asked to gather in the gymnasium for a brief presentation before the children were released. There was a Naval Captain and a representative of the Manitowoc Shipbuilding Company. Basically, they are recruiting to find employees to work in the shipyard, building submarines and boats. They said the government would provide free daily transportation on a bus, to and from Manitowoc, which is about a half hour drive either way. Also, they will provide before and after-school child care right at the school, so Jana will be taken care of until she can be picked up." Harry is caught off guard and says, "Emma, is this really something you are considering?" Emma replies, "Yes, my love, I told you before that we will all have a part to play in the war effort. And besides, the extra money will be nice, as well. What do you all think?" Otto says, "I can't argue with the fact that everybody is struggling to find enough workers." Harry thinks for a minute and asks, "But do you think it's safe?" Emma replies, "They told us the shipyard is guarded by at least 50 soldiers, and security is tight." Harry interjects, "But what would you be doing?" Emma says, "Their biggest need is for welders, so I guess I would be trained for that. Just like Joseph said when he enlisted, I feel this is something I must do." Harry and Otto both shake their heads in agreement and tell Emma, "We love you, and if you feel that strongly about it, then do it!"

Within a couple of weeks, Emma has been hired and is riding the morning bus up to Manitowoc. As Emma looks around, she sees the bus is filled and is about three quarters female, and one quarter male. Emma is seated next to a thin brunette who has just told her that her name is Matty. Emma says, "That's an unusual name for a girl. Is that your real name?" She replies, "My parents immigrated from Palermo, Sicily, and my real name is Mattia. But they Americanized it, and everybody calls me Matty." Emma smiles and says "Well, it's very nice to meet you Matty, my name is Emma. Just so you know, even though my parents immigrated from Germany, I hate Nazis." Matty replies, "Then at least we have that in common. I hate them, too." As expected, the bus ride was a quick half hour from Sheboygan, and they were now at the gates of the shipyard. Security appears to be tight, with many armed soldiers on guard. As Emma and Matty enter the gate, the soldiers review their identification and allow them to pass. They are lined up and separated into groups depending on which type of job they will be trained in. The supervisor says to them all, "Quiet down. As I call your name, break up into your assigned groups. Group A, Welders, assemble over on my right; Emma Langer, Matty Migliore, Gertrude Hawkins, etc. Group B, Grinders, assemble on my left. Group C, Machine Shop, assemble in front of me, and so on until everyone on the bus had been given their job assignments. They then all left to begin their respective training classes. In the case of Emma and Matty, as they were to become welders, their training was intensive and long. But as their training progressed, they got better and better at welding, along with their confidence increasing. Finally, Emma and Matty successfully finished their training and were assigned to the construction of submarines. Emma was amazed at the size of the shipyard. Everywhere you look, there is something being constructed; submarines, ships, landing craft. With the many thousands of workers toiling away each day, it can only be described as organized chaos. But, somehow, despite all the challenges at the Manitowoc shipyard, it hits all the production targets the Navy has given it. As an extra perk, the company is lauded by the Navy brass, as having produced some of the best submarines in the fleet.

Emma was very apprehensive initially about the before and after-school day care, which Jana was attending. As luck would have it, those fears were totally misplaced. Little Jana loves the daycare, being able to play with all the other kids has been a good experience for her. Harry has been picking her up from school each evening on his way home from work. Usually, within a half an hour after they get home, Emma will arrive. The extra money she is earning at the shipyard has been a boon to the family. Realistically, Harry and Emma are both so tired after working all-day and making a quick dinner that, along with

Jana, they turn in early each evening. It's only on the weekends, when Harry is not working overtime, that they get to do some fun family outings. They always try at least once a month to take a drive down to Chicago to visit Emma's parents. And in turn, Leo and Alice will come up to Sheboygan every couple of months. Sometimes, they take Jana to the zoo, or out for ice cream. Once the weather warms, they look forward to picnics by the lake. After several more months, Harry, Emma, and Jana have fallen into a pretty good routine. But, as is true with everyone else in the country, there are certainly challenges. Between gas and food rationing, metal shortages, fear of attacks on American soil, and sabotage at the shipyard, etc., it certainly has been psychologically draining. But everyone tries to keep their spirits up and keep moving forward. Praying for the day when the war will end and everyone can return to their normal lives.

Joseph has been in training and patiently waiting for an overseas deployment, and his chance to fight. He finally gets his wish, when on April 29th, 1943, his unit sets sail for deployment in North Africa. After the perilous journey, Joseph and his unit set up camp just outside of Casablanca, Morocco. Joseph is surprised at how pleasant the weather is. It's a sunny dry day, with temperature around 70 degrees Fahrenheit. He thought that being in this part of the world it would have been much hotter. While the soldiers have little interaction with the locals, it is a bit of a culture shock. As they passed through town, they noticed that all the local women were veiled, as was the Islamic tradition, and they heard calls to prayer coming from the mosques. Almost everywhere they look, there are camels walking around and various foods being hawked by street vendors.

The next few months are spent training and practice jumping, after having been deployed further north of Casablanca. The unit's military precision becomes well- known and respected by the various allied countries' military who have come to observe. Finally, the time has come for the unit to be deployed, and a convoy of trucks is used to move the troops almost a thousand miles to the city of Kairouan,

Tunisia. From Kairouan, it is only a couple hundred miles across the Mediterranean to Sicily. On July 9th, 1943, the invasion by the allies of Sicily, code named "Operation Husky," began. This is the very first wartime deployment of paratroopers in United States history. Unfortunately, the beginning of the operation starts off badly for the paratroopers. Somehow, allied ships mistake the squadron of planes carrying the paratroopers as enemy planes, and begin firing on them. Dozens of planes and hundreds of soldiers are lost in a horrifying example of death by friendly fire.

Joseph's plane, while still intact, received some damage by shrapnel. A few of the paratroopers on the plane were killed, as was the soldier sitting directly across from Joseph. Finally, they are ordered to make their jumps, although things are quite confused at this point. Joseph and most of his fellow troops are able to land safely, but are scattered throughout the countryside. Over the next couple of days, many of the paratroopers were able to link up, and they carried out many attacks. Motorized German troops were attacked, phone lines were cut, German and Italian patrols were ambushed, various targets were blown up, all along the southern coast of Sicily. This widespread harassment of axis troops kept the enemy busy, as the beach landings of the main invasion force unfolded.

Joseph proves to be a fearless fighter, although some could say he was reckless. But because of his leadership and fighting ability, his small band of soldiers captured several dozen axis troops. He really is a crack shot and has no problem hitting anything he is shooting at. As they march the captives back towards the allied beachhead, one of them pulls a concealed knife and kills one of our soldiers. Joseph jumps into action, but instead of shooting the Nazi soldier, he gets into a knife fight with him. Joseph is much too fast and skilled for the Nazi, and he is quickly able to land some cuts to his body, and he drops to the ground. Joseph orders him to drop his knife in German, and the Nazi grimaces and lowers his blade. As Joseph steps forward, the Nazi lunges at him with the knife, but Joseph is able to jump back, and grabbing a hand gun he had taken off of a Nazi officer, shoots him dead. Joseph thinks to himself "I should have just shot him in the first place. I won't make that mistake again."

As they continue their trek, the paratroopers encounter a couple of more Nazi soldiers and attempt to capture them as well. Joseph, speaking in German, tells them they are surrounded, and orders them to drop their weapons. But they hesitate, and in that instant, Joseph shoots them both dead. The other captives are enraged, and as one of them runs forward, Joseph shoots him dead, as well. Joseph looks straight at them and, speaking their language, says, "Make one wrong move and you will end up like your friends. Don't test my resolve! Now, all of you, put your hands on your heads, interlock your fingers, and march forward." The next day, Joseph and his fellow paratroopers link up with General George Patton's Western task force composed of the armored U.S. 7th Army. Patton's forces had successfully stormed the beaches and landed the rest of his men and material. Off to the east, the British General Bernard Montgomery's Eastern task force has landed successfully as well. Shortly thereafter, Patton and Montgomery begin their advance into the island itself.

One thing Joseph begins to realize is General Patton does not like to fight for the same ground twice. He is totally hard charging and relentless in his attacks against the combined Italian and Nazi troops. Day after day, week after week, the allied troops advance as the axis resistance begins to crumble. They are quite fortunate, because prior to the actual invasion of Sicily, the allies carried out covert operations in order to deceive the enemy into believing the attack would be against Greece, and not Sicily. This operation was a success as Hitler ordered some of his forces to leave Sicily, and instead reinforce his defenses in Greece. Joseph and his fellow paratroopers fought long and hard, and on August 17th, 1943, the island of Sicily was now under Allied control. For now, Joseph and the remaining members of the 504th P.I.R. are sent back to Kairouan, Tunisia, to regroup and to prepare for the upcoming invasion of Italy.

The initial invasion of Italy started on September 3rd, 1943 and was led by the British Army, who crossed the narrow strait of Messina from Sicily to mainland Italy, to the region of Calabria, which is the "toe" of Italy. This attack was a diversion to draw the Nazi troops to the south. At the same time, Mussolini, the fascist dictator of Italy, was removed from office and arrested. On September 8th, 1943, it was announced that Italy had officially surrendered. However, many of the Italian troops never got that information and they continued to fight. The Nazi's were outraged at the Italian betrayal and it only strengthen their resolve to fight.

The major assault by the allies, led by the Americans, occurred the next day, on September 9th, with the major amphibious assault on the port city of Salerno, which lies just south of Naples, and about 300 miles north of where the British attacked Italy almost a week ago. The fighting in Salerno was quite intense, and the landing was in jeopardy of failing, as the Nazi's struck back ferociously. In an attempt to protect the beachhead, elements of Joseph's 504th P.I.R. was deployed from Tunisia to enter the battle. This time, the troops parachute in successfully and they quickly took up their positions. Joseph and the rest of the troops took the high ground on hills close to the beach. The Nazi's knew if they could break through the allied lines, they could force them back from the beach. Somehow, the 504th was able to hold on, even after wave upon wave of Nazi attacks, they held their positions. Finally, because of the allies resolve, artillery, heavy naval gunfire, and allied aerial bombardment, the overall Nazi assault across Salerno was thwarted, and the beach head was secured. Hour after hour, more and more allied troops and equipment came ashore to join the battle. The 504th had performed magnificently and was even awarded a medal for their accomplishments. However, it came at a very high cost. The majority of the soldiers were killed or severely wounded. Joseph himself was found barely alive by a corpsman, who did his best to stabilize him so he could be evacuated to a hospital ship for treatment. Days later, Joseph is laying in a hospital bed when he opens his eyes for the first time. Everything in his sight appears blurred, and in that instant, he feels searing pain, before he passes out again. His wounds are extensive, shoulder, right lung, arm, and both legs. It will be several more days before Joseph is conscious. Finally, he attempts to speak and he whispers to the nurse, "Where am I? How long?" She replies, "You are on a hospital ship; you have been unconscious for almost a week." With that, Joseph shakes his head and closes his eyes to rest. The pain is subsiding, but Joseph is totally exhausted. It will be some time before he will be able to function properly. It remains to be seen if he will regain full use of his legs, as the wounds are extensive. For now, all he does is rest, and pray that he can get back home to see Uncle Otto, and his friends, Harry, Emma, and little Jana.

After a few more days on the hospital ship, Joseph is deemed stable enough to be moved. He is transferred via landing craft to shore, and then to a recently captured airfield. From there, he is flown to England for further treatment and to convalesce. By the time he arrives at a military hospital located outside of London in the countryside, he has developed a high fever. One of his wounds has become infected, so they treat him with penicillin. During the next few days, Joseph is in and out of consciousness, and even when he is awake, he is delirious. Often, he mutters in English, then reverts back to his native German, then back to English. This comes to the attention of one of the other soldiers in Joseph's ward, who is just being released back to active duty. He stops by Joseph's bed to see if he is awake and lucid at all. The penicillin has done its work and his fever has broken. The young captain asked Joseph, "How are you feeling Private?" Joseph whispers, "Glad to still be here." He then asks him questions in German, and Joseph, who understands him perfectly, replies to him in German. After a couple of minutes, the captain wishes him well, and he tells Joseph he hopes to see him again soon. Joseph is perplexed at the conversation, but is too exhausted to give it much thought.

Over the next couple of months, Joseph's wounds have all heeled, and except for his legs, he is doing quite well. Every day he is doing some physical therapy and little by little that improves. By the time he is discharged, the only outward sign of his injuries is a slight limp. Psychologically, Joseph is filled with more rage than ever before. He has always been a hothead, but it appears he is losing his temper faster than ever. While he has been recuperating in England, he has been able to finally receive some mail from Uncle Otto and Emma, which improves his spirits greatly. In turn, he has written several letters back to them. Finally, Joseph is ready to be discharged from the hospital. He wonders if he will be allowed to return to his unit, or if he will be discharged because of his limp. As Joseph opens his orders, he is surprised to find it was neither one of those scenarios. He is shocked to find that he has been assigned to go back to the states, and he is to report to Fort Bragg and await further orders. He is flown back to North Carolina on a troop transport. Fortunately, the allies have achieved air superiority over the Atlantic Ocean and the flight goes without incident. Once he arrives at Fort Bragg, he waits patiently for his new orders, which come after a few days. Joseph is called into the Commander's office, and handed his orders, which are labeled top secret. The Commander tells him that he is to carry out his orders, but under no circumstances can he discuss them with anyone. Joseph leaves the office more confused than ever and asks himself, "What the heck is going on?" The next day, Joseph boards another plane and is transported to an unknown location. Once he lands, he is put on a truck with other soldiers and civilians, with orders not to talk with one another. In the truck with them are two armed soldiers who are guarding them. After a short drive, they arrive at their destination and are greeted by a young captain. Joseph thinks to himself, "Where do I know him from?"

The captain then addresses them, "I am Captain Anderson, Military Intelligence. Welcome to Camp Ritchie, Maryland." This group of recruits comprises 14 individuals. Eight of them are civilians, and six of them are military. Both the Army and Navy are represented. They are led into a building and into what is best described as a large classroom. After they are seated, Captain Anderson addresses them. "I want to welcome you all to Camp Richie. I know you must be a little concerned over the security arrangements and the cloak and dagger you have experienced. I will tell you it is all necessary and critical to our mission." Joseph raises his hand and asks, "And what is our mission?" Captain Anderson replies, "Well, Joseph Vogler, you are here for one reason, and one reason alone. You are all fluent at speaking German. Some of you were born in Germany and emigrated here before the war, or were born here to German parents. Many of the recruits here are Jewish, who escaped the Nazi's early on. As I mentioned, I am part of Military Intelligence, as is this camp. All the civilian recruits on the base volunteered to join us, even though they did not know the true extent of our mission. Military personnel were given orders to be here, and I expect you to carry out your orders without question.

As I said, you are never to discuss your mission here with anyone. That's friends, family, fellow military outside of this base. Tomorrow, you will join the other recruits to begin your training. Some of you will be trained as interrogators and you will be assigned to gather actionable intelligence from deserters or other captives. Some will be trained as covert agents and you will be sent behind enemy lines to work with the resistance in gathering intelligence. Your German language skills, as well as knowledge of German customs and attitudes, make you perfectly suited for our mission. It is now May 1944, and Joseph and his fellow "Ritchie Boys" as they are nicknamed, have been training hard the last several months. Some of the men have already been deployed, but Joseph has no information about where or what their mission is. There seems to be an increase in the sense of urgency to complete their training. They know something big is coming, but nobody knows what. Finally, Joseph is being deployed. He boards transports with many others that he has trained with and departs for an unknown location. Once the plane lands and the men disembark, Joseph looks around and says, "Well, it's cold, foggy, and definitely bleak. It's got to be England!"

Joseph and his fellow interrogators spend all their time either drilling and doing calisthenics, or role playing and practicing their skills. Joseph and his compatriots have been housed at the far end of the military base in a separate building reserved for them. It's Monday morning, June 5th, 1944, when they are ordered to assemble on the other end of the base. As they exit their transports, they are again greeted by Captain Anderson, who orders them to attention and says, "I need not remind you that you are sworn to secrecy. I am notifying you to be prepared to carry out the job you have been trained for." He then reads off a list of names, Joseph Vogler included, who are to board a separate truck for deployment. Later that evening, Joseph and the rest of his group, are put aboard a large ship. They can only wonder what is going on as they wait patiently. As it turns out, they don't have to wait long. The next morning, June 6th, 1944, the allies commenced the invasion of Europe, on what is known as "D-Day." As they cross the English Channel, Joseph and a couple of friends make their way on deck. They cannot believe their eyes, as there is nothing but ships as far as the eye can see.

The invasion goes slowly at first as the allied troops are pinned down on the beaches by heavy Nazi gunfire. Unfortunately, the casualties are heavy for the first wave hitting the beaches. Slowly but surely, over the next several days, the allies have succeeded in getting off the beaches and begin their drive inland. Joseph and his group have landed and taken up residence in an abandoned church. Almost immediately, a steady stream of Nazi soldiers are captured, or they surrender. It is then that Joseph begins the work he has been trained for. As we know, Joseph has a temper, but he is relentless in his interrogation of the captives. Sometimes he gets information in a few minutes, and sometimes it takes hours. They employ all kinds of tactics to gain information; straight interrogation, listening in on conversations, sometimes dressing up as German officers. The "Richie Boys" become well-known for their success in gathering intelligence from the captives, which proves to be invaluable to the invasion. As they are proficient at reading German as well, they can quickly evaluate any captured documents or maps. As the allies advance through France, and Belgium, and later into Germany itself, Joseph moves along with them, gathering information every step of the way. The war dragged on for almost another year until finally, on May 8th, 1945, the British Prime Minister announced to the world that the Germans had surrendered, and the war in Europe had ended. Later that month, prior to being discharged from the Army, Joseph finds himself back in England. He was awarded a Silver Star medal, which is the third highest award a soldier can earn, for his bravery at the Battle of Salerno. At that moment, although he will be scarred physically and psychologically for the rest of his life, Joseph is filled with joy and pride for what he has accomplished. He knows in a few days that he can finally go home and be reunited with his uncle and his good friends.

## Chapter 7

# Semi Golden Years

Joseph lands at a military base just outside of New York City. As his discharge from the Army is now official, he will have to find transportation back to Sheboygan. He hitches a ride over to New York City for a couple of days and takes in the sights. He walks through Times Square, goes to the top of the Empire State Building, rides the roller coaster at Coney Island. Now that he is off of wartime Army rations, he tries just about everything he sees. Some Nathan's hot dogs, ice cream, saltwater taffy and slices of Italian pizza. He had a wonderful time sightseeing, and everywhere he went, people saluted him, shook his hand, and thanked him for his service. The next morning, he arrives at Penn Station and waits patiently for his train to Chicago. From there, he can catch a local train up to Sheboygan. He sent Uncle Otto a telegram yesterday, informing him of his planned arrival on Saturday morning. Once he gets to Sheboygan, it is just a quick cab ride back home to Uncle Otto's house.

The train ride was long, with many stops along the way. Joseph spent quite a bit of time in the dining car, trying just about every type of liquor they had. It was well after midnight before he returned to his train car and was able to fall asleep. Suddenly, about four o'clock in the morning, Joseph wakes up screaming and in a hard sweat. A couple of other soldiers and some civilians rush over to his seat. One of them says, "Hey Pal, you alright? You screamed so loud you woke the whole car up!" Joseph's voice is shaking and says, "The Nazi's, they're advancing, we must hold them off." The other soldier replies, "It's ok, we get it, but there's nothing to worry about. The war is over. There is nothing to hurt you anymore. Now, why don't you try to get some sleep." Joseph looks around and regains his composure and says, "I am sorry, just a nightmare, I guess. I will try not to disturb you again."

The rest of the night is uneventful, and the train pulls into the Sheboygan Station around eleven o'clock in the morning. Joseph exits the train with the other passengers, but, because of his limp, he lags behind. Once he walks outside the terminal, he is greeted by thunderous applause from a large group of people. Joseph looks around at the crowd, dumbfounded. In the next instant, he recognizes Uncle Otto, Frederick the Brewmaster, Harry, Emma, and little Jana, and all his old friends from the packaging department. They all came to see him, and he couldn't be happier. One by one, he embraces them, or shakes their hands, and thanks them for being here to greet him. As he embraces Harry and Emma, he is shocked at how much little Jana has grown. After all the greetings are done, Uncle Otto makes an announcement and says, "Friends, thank you for coming to welcome my nephew, Joseph, home from the war. Please join us at the Prime Steakhouse for a luncheon in honor of Joseph." Otto has arranged for steaks smothered in onions and mushrooms, and all the sides, to be served. Joseph hasn't eaten this well since he entered the Army. As good as the food is, Harry has almost forgotten how good the Miesbach Dark Lager is, as he downs them in quick succession.

After dinner is over, Joseph, Uncle Otto, and Frederick, the Brewmaster, are off in the far corner of the restaurant. They are enjoying a glass of schnapps and a good cigar. Frederick asks Joseph, "Now that you are back, have you made any plans for the future?" Joseph replies, "I would like to take a few more weeks off to relax, and I have to see some doctors, but then I would like to get my job back at the brewery." Frederick is delighted and says, "I was hoping you felt that way. Whenever you are ready to come back, you just let your Uncle Otto know." Joseph shakes his hand and says, "Thank you, Herr Gambrus, it would be my honor." Then Emma strolls across the room with Jana in tow and says to them, "Please, come back over and join us. We are ready to cut the cake I made." Joseph replies, "Emma, that's so sweet of you. I always enjoyed the pastries you used to make. You don't have to ask me twice." After they have the cake, Joseph spends some time catching up with his friends from the packaging department. They tell him they still stop at the bar after work, and to join them anytime. As the luncheon comes to a close, Joseph again thanks everyone for the wonderful celebration. As he drives back to his uncle's house, he tells Otto how blessed he is to have such good friends and family.

It's been about a month, and Joseph is finally feeling a little more relaxed. He is still having some nightmares and sweats, but this week it only happened once. The weather has been warm and sunny and he enjoys taking walks through the park and around the neighborhood. Every weekend is spent enjoying the company of Harry, Emma, and Jana. It has been especially fun going with them on picnics over at the lake park. Joseph loves playing catch with Jana, and she wishes he could chase her around and play tag, but his injuries will not allow for it, as he still limps. Today is an especially hot summer day and they decide to go swimming at the lake. Joseph goes over to the bathhouse to change into his swim trunks. As soon as Emma sees him, she is shocked and filled with pity. She embraces Joseph and says, "I did not know your scars were so severe. I am so sorry." Joseph steps back and says to Emma and Harry, "This is the price I paid to defeat the filthy Nazis, and I would do it all again if I had to. All that matters is we are all together again. Now, let's go swimming and have some fun."

Joseph is finally feeling better and more positive, and he tells Uncle Otto that he would like to return to work. Otto explains to him that with the war being over, some of the women employees have decided to leave the workforce, and some have decided to stay. Otto has no problem hiring some new people to fill the open positions, as all the soldiers have returned home and are seeking work. Otto tells Joseph, "Before you left for the war, you were doing an excellent job as filler operator. Now, you have returned as a war hero. Frederick and I think we would like to reward you for your service and take advantage of your leadership skills. What do you think about being the can line foreman? Our current one has taken ill and will not be returning." Joseph is taken aback by the offer and replies, "Are you serious? I never imagined myself being a foreman." Otto says, "It can be a challenging position, but I don't think it's anything you can't handle. So, think about it for a minute and then let me know your answer, but it better be, Yes." Joseph replies, "I would like to give it a try, thank you Uncle Otto." He responds, "Fine then, it's decided. I will let Frederick know, and you can plan on starting on Monday. Currently, the brewery packaging department consists of a keg line, returnable bottle line, non-returnable bottle line that has just restarted as rationing has ended, a can line that has just restarted as well, and finally, the warehouse. Each line has a packaging foreman and a maintenance foreman assigned to it. As they are down a man, the bottle line foreman are running themselves ragged trying to cover both bottles and cans. They are relieved when Joseph reports to work, and they immediately set out to get him trained. Joseph gets off to a fast start, and everything seems to be falling into place. The only thing that disappoints him is that some of his friends from the packaging department seem to be a little standoffish, since he is now their supervisor. One of them, named Peter, even gets belligerent with him occasionally. But he will not let that stop him from running the can line the way it needs to be. He cannot let Uncle Otto and Herr Gambrus down.

Over in the brewing department, Harry has continued his cross training into other areas of the process. He is well versed in malting, brewhouse operations, fermenting, and lagering. Recently, he has been working in the Schoene cellars, as the Miesbach brewery calls it. Once beer comes off of chips from the lagering tanks, it still needs further clarification. Besides suspended matter, such as precipitated proteins and yeast, there are dissolved proteins that can cause problems and need to be removed. One of the issues that needs to be addressed in making a clear, pale colored, pilsner style beer is the phenomenon of what is termed chill haze. The beer will appear clear when the consumer buys it, but once it is chilled down and stored for a while, the beer will become hazy. Once it warms up, the haze will go away, thus the term chill haze. So, as the beer is moved from lagering to Schoene (which means to clarify), a fining compound such as Isinglass is injected into the beer. The Isinglass reacts with dissolved proteins to form a gelatinous mass that settles to the bottom of the tank. The chill proofed beer is then drawn off and moved to the last step in the process.

The beer will now undergo final filtration prior to packaging. After all the previous steps, there is still a considerable amount of yeast and suspended matter that affects the clarity and stability of the product. The beer that is drawn off from Schoene is filtered through a bed of diatomaceous earth, which, in the brewery, is known as Kieselguhr. These are the shells of microscopic crustaceans called diatoms, which are quite beautiful to look at under a microscope. They are of many shapes and sizes, but all have tiny perforations in their shell, which traps suspended material. Once the beer has been filtered through this media, it is stored in large tanks, termed "Finished Beer Tanks," where it is stored cold until being released and gravity fed to the packaging fillers. The beer cellar, where these tanks are located, is also known as the government cellar. The brewery must pay the federal government an excise tax on every barrel of beer that is released. There is a flow meter on the release lines that keeps track of the barrels of beer sent to packaging, which is reported to the federal government, and they, in turn, send a tax bill based on this number.

A couple of years go by and it is now July 1947 in Sheboygan, Wisconsin. Emma is still taking the daily bus up to the Manitowoc shipyards where she continues welding. With the war being over, things have slowed down and Emma is not sure how much longer she will be working there. Emma can hardly believe that Jana is eleven years old already. Child care for Jana is becoming difficult, so Emma may have to go back to doing her sewing to make some extra money instead. Harry is back in the brewhouse as the foreman, his cross training having been completed. While he is capable of working in any area of the brewing department, he is most comfortable in the brewhouse. Post-war sales have been very strong, and the brewhouse is running full production, and management is considering adding a third shift.

Joseph continues as the can line foreman on dayshift, and it is a daily struggle. Between being pushed to run the line at its maximum speed as much as possible because of the strong sales and all the equipment issues, there never seems to be a spare minute. Joseph is still single and has gotten into the habit of drinking at the bar every night after work. The alcohol relaxes him and helps him forget his wartime trauma. Unfortunately, it has become an all too frequent occurrence that Uncle Otto or Harry, have to pick him up and drive him home. But, somehow each morning, Joseph wakes up and makes it to work on time, ready to perform his duties.

Today starts out to be a challenging day on the can line for Joseph. The line has been down for a couple of days for routine maintenance, so this will be the first run of the week. As the first cans come off the filler/seamer, Joseph can see something has gone wrong with the seam. He can visually see beer foam squirting out of the seam where the top lid has been attached to the can body. Consequently, Joseph has to immediately shut the filler down. As bad as this is, it is actually a blessing in disguise that it was caught at line start-up. Sometimes, the seam can be just good enough that liquid or foam cannot escape, but the carbon dioxide can, resulting in flat beer. Once the cans hit the pasteurizer and heat up, it will only make the loss of beer and carbon dioxide worse. Joseph notifies the maintenance supervisor assigned to his line, and he quickly gets a mechanic who has been trained in seamer repair. After a little while, word gets back to the maintenance manager, Hanno Berg, and he joins them at the filler. Coming from the opposite direction is the Packaging Manager Kurt Hoffman, and his Assistant Manager Lewis Landon. There are now so many people milling about the filler platform that there is barely any room for Joseph. Lewis Landon is the first to lose his temper and starts yelling that the line has been down too long. He then turns his ire to Joseph and says, "Why did you break the seamer? Don't you know what you are doing? Look at all the time we lost, and all the beer we will have to throw out" Joseph, visibly upset, yells back, "I never touched the seamer, you know that only maintenance is allowed to do that, so why the hell are you yelling at me?" Lewis yells back, "You're in charge, you're in charge, everything that happens on this line is your responsibility." Just then, the good news came that the seamer adjustments have been made and production can start again. Just as quickly as all the managers appeared at the filler in order to "help", they quickly disappear.

Unfortunately for Joseph, after lunch, things go from bad to worse. There is a problem with the electrical system and the can packer has shut down. Consequently, the entire line has to stop, and the pasteurizer begins to cool. It took almost four hours to get the line ready to run again, and it is right at shift change. Again, Joseph's favorite manager, Lewis, was back out on the line, pushing everyone to get the line running. Joseph says, "You can't start the line yet. The pasteurizer cooled down. We need at least a half hour to bring it back up to temperature." Lewis yells back, "Go home, your shift is over and we will handle it. This line ran so poorly today what do we need you for." Joseph can't believe how he got yelled at again by Lewis, and mummers under his breath, "Someday I'm going to shoot that stupid son of a bitch." Joseph was right after all because many of the cans entering the hot zones of the pasteurizer did not reach the correct temperature, which means the beer will spoil quickly, as it was not pasteurized properly.

Joseph leaves work and makes his nightly stop at the bar across from the brewery. He is so upset after the terrible day he had. All he wants to do is drink and drown his sorrows. However, he remembers a conversation he had recently with Harry where he said, "Joseph, Emma and I are getting concerned about you. You're drinking way too frequently and way too much. Remember, after the flooding in Kelheim, when I was so upset and despondent. You, my friend, are the one who saved my life. Who knows where I would be now without your help? So, Emma and I want to be here for you. Maybe it's time to get some help before you drink yourself to death. Remember, your Uncle Otto loves you and needs you, just like we do."

After being at the bar for a few hours, and eating some pickled eggs and sausage, Joseph decides to call it a night. For the first time in a while, Joseph leaves to go home, only slightly inebriated. He decides to leave through the alley behind the bar because it is a shortcut home. As he leaves, he is confronted by Peter, who is one of his old friends from the packaging department. Peter says, "Joseph, I just want you to know what an asshole you are. I used to think you were a nice guy, but since you got promoted, you are anything but that." Joseph replies, "I don't know why you feel that way. I never give you a hard time at work, unless it is called for. Come on, let's go back in the bar and I will buy you a drink." Peter yells, "I wanted that promotion to foreman, but they gave it to you instead. That's only because Otto is your uncle and you are some kind of war hero." Joseph takes a couple of steps back from him and says, "Look, Peter, I don't want to argue with you. Can't we leave it in the past and move on?" Just then, Peter makes the fatal error of attacking Joseph with a knife he has concealed. Joseph quickly takes off the belt from his pants and uses it to defend himself. As Peter lunges at him, he is able to take the belt and wrap it around the arm holding the knife, and in one swift motion, he kicks Peter's leg out and he falls to the ground. Joseph gains leverage on him and drives Peter's hand, which is still holding the knife, into his stomach. Just as quickly as it started, the fight was over, and Peter lays dead in the alley. Joseph panics and throws his body into a dumpster. He looks around, and not seeing anyone, limps back home.

At the last minute, he goes over to Harry's house and tells him what happened. He doesn't want to get Uncle Otto involved, and he hopes if he is caught, it will not hurt Otto's position at the brewery. Joseph raps on Harry's door and waits on the porch. Harry opens the door and says, "Joseph, what is wrong? Why are you here so late?" He replies, "I need your help. I mean, I need Emma's help." Just then, Emma comes downstairs and says, "Joseph, I thought I heard your voice." He replies, "I am sorry to bother you both, but something terrible has happened. One of the packaging guys, Peter, attacked me with a knife tonight in the alley behind the bar." Emma says, "Are you hurt? Did you get cut?" Joseph replies, "I'm alright." He then sits in the chair by the door, and covers his face with his hands and says, "He attacked me, we struggled, and I killed him. God help me." Harry and Emma are shocked and in disbelief. Finally, Harry says, "Look, we are glad, obviously, that you are alright, but you said you wanted Emma's help, please explain?" Joseph says, "I put Peter's body in the dumpster, and hopefully it won't be discovered, but I can't take that chance. Can you call your father for me? He will know what to do." Emma does as she is asked, and calls Leo and says, "Father, Joseph needs your help. Can you bring a couple of your helpers? You know what I mean. There is a mess that needs cleaning up." Leo tells her, "If you are calling me, it must be a gigantic mess. We will be there in a few hours."

It's close to midnight when they finally arrive at Emma's. Leo goes into the house by himself, and his henchmen wait in the car. Joseph explains the whole story to him, when suddenly, there is a knock on the door. It's Uncle Otto, who says, "I have been worried when I saw Joseph wasn't home yet. I looked out the window, and I thought I saw you, Leo. What is wrong? Why are you here, and who are those men in the car?" Joseph stands up and says, "Uncle, please come into the other room so we can talk privately." After a couple of minutes, Otto, without saying a word, walks by all of them and leaves, crosses the street, and goes into his house. Leo asks Joseph, "Are we good?" Joseph replies, "Yes, he understands the situation." Leo says, "Alright, Joseph, give me the location and it will be taken care of. Now, the rest of you, go back to bed." The next morning Emma receives a call from Leo saying, "Tell Joseph everything is fine. It was so good to see you, Emma, although the circumstances could have been better. I wanted to let you know that your mother and I will come for a visit this weekend. See you then!"

Joseph returns to work the next day, but his spirit has been crushed. Fighting the Nazis was one thing, but having to kill a co-worker is another. What he was forced to do weighed on his mind all-day. Finally, the shift ends, and he stops at a different bar after work, one where no one knows him. He proceeds to drink himself into a stupor before passing out. The bartender gets his address out of his wallet and sends him home in a taxi. The driver dumps him out of the cab onto the front lawn. Uncle Otto hears the car door close and sees Joseph passed out on the lawn. Otto cannot handle him by himself, so he gets Harry to help drag him to bed.

The next day, Joseph makes it to work but before he left the house, Otto told him they needed to have a serious conversation this evening. Today turns out to be the best day he has had supervising the can line. They produced a record amount of packaged beer, quality was good with nothing out of specification, and no defective product. As Harry is leaving the brewery, he runs into his boss, Lewis Landon. Of course, Lewis has to be a jerk and instead of complimenting Joseph on a job well done says, "Joseph, I just wanted you to know your line ran very good today. What the hell do I need you for. The line can run by itself." Joseph says nothing and continues shaking his head as he leaves.

After dinner, the doorbell rings and Harry, Emma, and Jana are let into the house. Emma has Jana go into the kitchen for a treat while the adults talk. Otto starts out by saying, "Joseph, enough is enough. The drinking and the passing out has to stop." Joseph replies, "I know I need help, but what can I do?" Emma speaks up and says, "At the shipyard where I work, they have had quite a problem with people drinking too much and not showing up for work. What's worse is some of them come to work drunk and get hurt on the job. There is a program available to all the employees. It's new, and they call it Alcoholics Anonymous. We could see if they offer it in Sheboygan." Harry gets up and goes over to the phone and calls the operator to get information on where they have a listing for an A.A. group. He finds one at a local church. Uncle Otto says, "I will make time tomorrow morning to contact them and find out when the meeting is." Then Harry interjects, saying, "Joseph, plan on me going to those meetings with you. I'll be with you every step of the way."

A couple of nights pass, and Joseph and Harry arrive at the local church for Joseph's first A.A. meeting. As they sit around in the circle, the leader of the group asks them to introduce themselves and state why they are here. After several people go first, it is Joseph's turn, and he introduces himself as the others have. "My name is Joseph Vogler, and I am an alcoholic." Over the next couple of years, the program works well, and Joseph has not missed a meeting, and only slipped once and had one drink. Joseph has also recommitted to his Catholic faith, and makes it a point never to miss Sunday Mass.

Slowly but surely, Joseph's demons fade away and he becomes much calmer and happier. Joseph has even begun dating Emma's co-worker, Matty, from the shipyard. Matty is about five years younger than Joseph, and after Emma introduced them and they just seemed to be so enamored with each other. Emma and Harry are so happy to see Joseph finally smiling and laughing again. In fact, Joseph and Matty are so happy together, they are married within a year, on May 27, 1950. They are able to buy the house two doors down from Uncle Otto, staying nearby to Harry and Emma. Matty immediately becomes pregnant, and she delivers the first of her four children, including a set of twins, on February 23, 1951. It's a beautiful baby boy, whom they name after his father, and his nickname is J.J., short for Joseph Junior.

The post-war boom, as it was known, was certainly that. Production at the Miesbach Brewery has never been higher. It is so good, in fact, that they added an extra shift of production and are now running round the clock. Miesbach has become a very popular regional brewer, and they distribute their products all over the Midwest. Harry is still the dayshift brewhouse, but he had to come in early at 4:00 a.m. to cover for the midnight shift foreman who was out sick today. As things are running well in the brewhouse, Harry takes a stroll through the fermenting cellars on his way to the break room. As he looks up, he thinks he sees something hanging off the edge at the top of the fermenter. He decides to take a look and climbs up on the catwalk to investigate. He can't believe what he is seeing. There is a man and woman stark naked, having sex on a blanket. He almost can't contain his laughter as he runs off to find the fermenting caller foreman. Frederick, the owner and Brewmaster, was always apprehensive about a mixed workforce, but with the war, it made women working in factories commonplace. Harry thinks to himself, "Frederick will not be happy when he hears this one."

Later that day, Harry is back in the brewhouse office when suddenly he hears a loud explosion and his office shakes. Everyone stops what they are doing and tries to find the source of the explosion. There doesn't seem to be any fire or damage inside the brewhouse area. As Harry exits onto the roof, he can see smoke coming from the grain silos. The sound of fire engines and police sirens is coming from all directions. Evidently, one of the grain silos has exploded. This phenomenon does happen, although fortunately it is an infrequent occurrence. As the silo is either being filled or emptied, the grain gets agitated and it produces a grain dust cloud made up of very fine particles. This dust cloud is highly explosive and can be set off by a spark, static electricity, or even spontaneous combustion. Unfortunately, in this case, the fireman discovered a casualty in the rubble. The body was identified as a mechanic who had been assigned to work on the conveyor system. They have no way of knowing if the mechanic triggered the explosion, or was just in the wrong place at the wrong time.

The next day, Frederick the Brewmaster/owner calls a meeting with Otto the Plant Manager, and all the managers and supervisors from all departments in the brewery. Everyone assumes the meeting is just to discuss the grain silo explosion, which he starts the meeting off with. Frederick then continues, "I had intended to give you all some good news today, so notwithstanding the tragedy yesterday, here is what I wanted to tell you. The brewery is doing very well. Sales are the strongest they have ever been. I appreciate all your hard work in keeping everything running efficiently. I wanted to announce that we will be expanding the brewhouse. This will allow us to keep up with production demands and make it easier to brew new products. Now, what I am proposing will be a stark departure from our normal all-malt brews. Once the expansion is complete, we will brew not only with malt but also with what we call an adjunct, made up of either rice or corn. By using an adjunct, we can drastically reduce our cost of production, as the adjunct is much cheaper than malt. There is also a difference in flavor profile in the finished beer between an all-malt product and an adjunct brew. Since it will be a much cheaper beer to produce, we can introduce products at a different price point, and hopefully gain new customers. It is going to take a good two years to complete the expansion, so there will be a lot of construction going on. Be aware of this and try to keep your employees safe." Frederick says, "Now I know you are all thinking that I am a hypocrite. As I always said, we would never use rice and corn adjuncts, just barley malt. Well, never say never I guess, but the cost savings are too significant to pass up on.

Just as Frederick had expected, the brewhouse expansion took almost two years, and it's now fall of 1953. As Harry and Frederick tour the recent addition, Frederick says, "It looks like everything is almost finished. I think in a couple of months we will start making some test brews." Harry responds, "That is quite exciting, but I think we all have many questions about this new process. But, before we get into that, I wanted to ask, why did you install a stainless-steel kettle instead of copper?" Fredrick explains, "It was simply a matter of cost as we were able to install the stainless at a large savings relative to copper. However, before we start production, we are going to install some copper fins on the bottom percolator. Having some copper in the brew will help to drive off volatiles, and also reduce some unwanted yeast flavors that can develop."

Frederick explains, "I know you have questions about our new product, so this is what I am planning. I have decided to leverage my name, and call the beer 'Gambrus Lager.' In order to keep costs down, and provide a different flavor profile, we will have to make some significant changes. We will brew this beer with only 6-row malt, and the adjunct will be corn. Also, we will not use any imported hops, just the domestic variety. As you know, normally in fermenting, we allow the yeast to consume most of the sugars in a brew. Then, when we fill the aging tank with it, we also then add some freshly yeasted unfermented wort, which we call the Kraeusening process. The secondary fermentation that will take place will naturally carbonate the beer."

Frederick continues, "For our Gambrus Lager, we will be using an unfamiliar process. In this case, we will move the beer out the fermenter while there is considerable sugar left in the brew. We also do not recover any yeast from this fermenter. Instead, during aging, the residual sugars and yeast will provide for the secondary fermentation, and naturally carbonate the beer. This type of process we term a 'Green Fass', so you can see it varies from our normal Kraeusening procedure. I hope this helps clear up some of your questions."

Harry expresses his thanks to Frederick for the information on the new product, but he is quite apprehensive about how this adjunct process is going to work. He says to Frederick, "The normal mashing process that we have used all these years is quite straight forward. I am trying to figure out how we use the corn or rice adjunct in our process." Frederick explains, "We are going to use what is termed a 'double mash' system. As you normally do, we will have a mash tun full of malt and warm water. What's new is we will also have another vessel called a cereal cooker. In this case, the corn or rice adjunct will be added to the cooker along with water. We then heat the mixture up to what is termed the gelatinization temperature. The starch molecule in the corn or rice will absorb so much water, it will burst and the starch will be broken down into smaller molecules. We will then pump over some of the malt mash, which now has a very active enzyme system, into the cereal cooker. The enzymes will rapidly degrade the smaller starch molecules into sugars. Then we will pump the entire cereal cooker over to the mash tun and combine the two. The hotter cereal cooker mash will raise the temperature of the main malt mash, then heat can be applied to raise and maintain the combined mash at the proper conversion temperature."

As fortune would have it, Frederick's gamble pays off. Gambrus Lager is an enormous success, with sales soon eclipsing their flagship brands, Miesbach Lager and Miesbach Dark. Competition is fierce, trying to compete against the much larger brewers in Milwaukee, and St Louis. But Miesbach has a loyal core following all over the Midwest. By taking out advertisements on television, which are becoming very popular throughout the country, they are able to reach many new consumers. There have been many changes in the packaging department as well. Several years ago, post-war, the brewery switched their keg beer in wooden barrels to stainless-steel kegs. The sale of beer in cans has become so popular they have added another can line. Joseph continues to do well as the foreman on the can line, despite the Packaging Assistant Manager, Lewis Landon. Joseph has proven himself many times over the years, but Lewis always finds something to complain about. Joseph's wife, Matty, reminds him all the time to keep his temper under control, as the job is too good to lose. Joseph knows he has on the "golden handcuffs", so he just keeps moving forward, content knowing that he has a loving wife and children that he can go home to.

The can packaging line that Joseph is in charge of is designated line #35, so named because it was constructed in 1935. Following that naming convention, the new can line is designated as line #53, as it was constructed in 1953. The new can line is quite the improvement over Joseph's. The filler is much larger and faster, and can produce almost 35% more packages per shift. Obviously, the more they can produce each shift, the lower the cost, and the higher the profits for the brewery. Profits have done so well that Frederick Gambrus has become quite wealthy. He has built himself a small mansion in Sheboygan, overlooking Lake Michigan. He has also taken his family on a couple of month-long vacations to Europe, where he has purchased a home in Bavaria. In Fredericks' absence, the Senior Assistant Brewmaster, Horst Landt, is in charge. Harry enjoys working for Horst, because besides being very knowledgeable about the entire operation, he is just a down-to-earth person. Harry and Emma have become close with Horst and his wife, Bernadine. They enjoy having dinner at each other's houses, and occasionally they go to the theater together.

A couple of years later, during the spring of 1955, Joseph's wife, Matty, gives birth to her fourth and final child. She is a beautiful little girl whom they name Joan. After all these years, they decide to go with a more American type name. Joseph and Matty are extremely pleased to have a daughter, as they previously had three boys, Emil, Hans and their first born, Joseph Junior. Emma was extremely pleased and privileged to be asked to baptize little Joan. The last few years Matty had been working as a part-time welder, but with the birth of her daughter, Matty retires from working.

It's only about a year later that Harry and Emma's daughter, Jana, begins dating. Jana has been working since she graduated high school in the office at Miesbach Darling Ice Cream. She has met a young man named Michael Aquila (Latin for Eagle) at one of the company picnics. Michael works in the finishing cellars at the main brewery. He is tall, dark haired, and quite good looking. While Harry and Emma are not pleased that he is not of German descent, they are pleased that he is Catholic, and that he shares the same faith as they do. Actually, Emma and Michael hit it off quite well, as he is of Sicilian descent, and Emma has a love for Italian food. Michael has even made Sunday dinner for them a couple of times. For an appetizer, he made a "frizzell" a round loaf of bread cut in half with a hole in the middle, which is twice baked. It is then slightly moistened and covered with sliced ripe tomatoes, olive oil, garlic and oregano. For the main course, some pasta in a deep red tomato sauce with beef meat, meatballs, Italian sausage, and braciole. What's not to like!

It looks like Michael has won over Emma's parents very quickly. After about a year of dating, Michael receives Harry and Emma's permission to ask Jana for her hand in marriage. She quickly accepts, as she knew from the moment they saw each other, that he was the one. Harry and Emma could not be happier that their only daughter was going to be married. So, finally, the next year, on August 20th, 1957, Michael and Jana were married. The wedding is a wonderful affair with almost 320 guests attending. The steak dinner was delicious, as are all the Italian cookies that Michael's parents, Vince and Rose, have made for the wedding. Just as Emma had done when she was married, Jana carried on the tradition and they had a carrot cake with cream cheese frosting. The next day after the wedding, they left for their honeymoon. It was the first time either one of them had flown on an airplane. Jana had no issues, but Michael was a little airsick. In any case, they arrived safely and enjoyed a lovely week at a large hotel with a private beach in the country of Bermuda. The only issue they had was Jana got way too much sun the first couple of days and her eyelids swelled up, so she had to wear sunglasses inside and out the whole week. But as luck would have it, Jana became pregnant on her wedding night and gave birth the following year to her first of three children.

It's now the year 1958, and unfortunately, Frederick, who by now is in his late seventies, has had a heart attack. He has survived it, and after a long convalescence, has briefly returned to the brewery. He calls for a meeting with Otto, his Plant Manager, and Horst, his Senior Assistant Brewmaster. Frederick says "I wanted to thank you both for all the hard work while I have been laid up. The brewery has never looked or run better. As a token of my appreciation, I would like to present you both with a $10,000 bonus." Otto says, "This is most generous of you, Frederick." Horst agrees and says, "Thank you so much, Frederick, and I couldn't be happier for your support." Frederick looks at them and says, "As much as I love this brewery and enjoy working with you both, the time has come to make some big decisions.

My doctors have told me that long-term, I am going to have to slow down and take all the stress out of my life. They said if I continue on the path that I was on before I had the first heart attack, I will surely have another. But what's worse is, they said I probably wouldn't survive it. So, strictly because of my health issues, I have decided to sell the Brewery and retire. Otto and Horst are shocked at what they have just been told. Otto says, "I don't know what to say. Do you have anyone in mind that may be interested in buying it?" Frederick replies, "I know of a few companies that may be interested, who also have the required finances to be able to take us over. I will keep you informed of how the search goes, but for now, I am getting quite fatigued, so I will see you all another day. Hold down the fort for me, will you?" Otto and Horst assure Frederick that they will keep everything running, as they have been doing.

Frederick goes about contacting his many friends and acquaintances at other breweries and companies throughout the country. Once word gets around that he is interested in possibly selling the brewery, there is no shortage of candidates. One of his friends from the Brewers Association, that he has known for years, is Kieran Gilbride. He is the owner and Brewmaster of the Ballygar Brewery in Duluth, Minnesota. While most of Minnesota was settled by a lot of people of Scandinavian descent, there was a 10-15% Irish population in the Duluth area of St. Louis County. The Ballygar Brewery is well known in the Midwest for producing what is termed today as an Irish Red style of ale. The brew gets its characteristic red color from the use of a small percentage of dark roasted, unmalted barley. When mashing with this grain, and at a slightly higher pH, the red hues are extracted from the grain. Kieran Gilbride is looking to expand his operations, and the range of products he produces. Taking over the Miesbach Brewery gives him instant access to the lager beer market that is becoming increasingly popular. After some back-and-forth negotiations, they come to a mutually acceptable agreement. One of the stipulations, however, is that all the brewing department's employees, including Horst and Harry, are safe from firing. In the same vein, Kieran has agreed to preserve Otto's position as Plant Manager, and Horst will be promoted to Brewmaster. In reality, Kieran knows they are all too valuable to lose.

After the sale of Miesbach Brewing to Ballygar Brewing, the new owner, Kieran Gilbride, visits Miesbach about every three months. For the most part, he is pleased with how it is being run by Otto and Horst, and keeps hands off. Several changes were made to the operation and Miesbach Malting is now producing some roasted barley and specialty malts to Ballygar, which has reduced their cost of production. The other change was the forming of a Quality Assurance Department. Some tasks they are responsible for on the packaging side are: inspecting outgoing products, determining package fill levels, package carbon dioxide content, and package air content, as well as monitoring pasteurizer temperatures, checking labels, etc. The packaged air content is very important because it directly relates to the amount of oxygen that is in the package's headspace. Oxygen has a detrimental effect on beer flavor and aroma, so it must be kept to a minimum. The first technician in the new department is none other than Michael, Jana's husband, and Harry and Emma's son-in-law. Horst and Otto had a role, of course, in getting Michael transferred out of the brewing department. Because of working the entire shift in the cold, finished beer cellars, Michael was constantly sick. Hopefully, the department change will put him back in good health. He was sent up to the Ballygar Brewery for some intensive laboratory training in the basic Quality Assurance techniques used in brewing, packaging, and microbiology.

It's the fall of 1963, and things have been going better for Joseph at work. His boss, Lewis, has directed most of his anger lately at Thomas, the can line #53 foreman. Thomas is a 27-year-old graduate of a technical college, and has only been with Miesbach/Ballygar for about a year. It seems Lewis does not like people with a college education, presumably because he is jealous of them. There is much excitement at the brewery today, as this will be the first full scale production of the all-aluminum can, with a pull top. This is a revolution in the brewing and overall beverage industry. Aluminum cans have so many advantages over the old steel/tin cans. They are cheaper to make, and lighter to transport, and being thinner get cold quicker. With the recent development of the pull top can, it is no longer necessary to use an opener, which is a game changer. Both Joseph and Thomas start their production line, and after a few hiccups, both lines smooth out and run well, until late afternoon. As Joseph is returning from the warehouse, where he had checked the palletizer, he notices something wrong with the aluminum cans on line #53. He rushes to the front of the line as fast as he can and motions to Thomas to stop the filler. Thomas and Joseph go back to the pasteurizer exit and see that the bottoms of all the cans are turning a light black color. Thomas runs back to the warehouse and has them segregate all the production until they can resolve the problem. They then go to check Joseph's line #35, and find no problems with the can bottoms. Lewis gets word that the filler is shut down, and he makes a beeline for Thomas. As usual, he is screaming and says, "What the hell did you do now, and why are these can bottom black?" Thomas replies, "I didn't do anything obviously, but I put a call into the maintenance to check the pasteurizer water. The same date of cans is running on Joseph's line and they are fine. The cans are good going into the pasteurizer, but not coming out. I therefore assume there is something wrong with the pasteurizer water." As it turns out, if the pasteurizer water has too high of a pH, that will turn the can bottoms a black color. Within a few minutes, maintenance has the adjustment made, and the problem is corrected. Now it is up to Lewis and his bosses to decide what to do with the beer that is being held in the warehouse.

Simultaneously, with all the drama that is happening on the can lines, Kevin, the non-returnable bottle line foreman, is having his share of problems, as well. They have been having intermittent problems with the metal crowns dragging and gapping as they go through the device that aligns them all so they can be fed into the crowner and be affixed to the top of the bottle. Maintenance has found that the metal plate that the crowns rub against as they travel to the crowner has literally become etched due to the millions of crowns that have been fed through it all these years. Once the mechanic installs a new plate, the crowns move smoothly through, and the problem is solved.

Yesterday, Kevin was having a problem with the non-returnable beer bottles exiting the pasteurizer. Some of them were getting rusty crowns. Since crowns are made of metal, it is important that the water chemistry of the pasteurizer be correct. Normally, various rust inhibitors, also known as oxygen scavengers, are used to prevent oxidation to the crowns, and also to the pasteurizer itself. Just as Kevin's boss, the infamous Lewis Landon, arrives at the filler to discuss the rusty crown issue, Kevin gets injured. He has been making an adjustment to the high-pressure water jetter, which is sprayed into the top of the bottle in order to make the beer foam up and overflow, thus reducing the oxygen content in the headspace of the bottle prior to crowning. As Lewis screams, Kevin is distracted and, as he turns, he gets injured. The top of his pinky finger on his left hand has accidentally brushed across the high-pressure jetter stream, which cuts the tip of the finger off. Kevin yells out in pain, and Lewis is forced to take him to medical to get treated. Fortunately, Kevin is right-handed, so once he heals up, it won't interfere with his day-to-day life. All of this was so unnecessary, as Kevin learns later. It was Lewis who caused the rusty crowns. In a cost-cutting move, Lewis convinced his boss, Kurt, to reduce the amount of rust inhibitor being used. Why they did this in secret and did not inform their line foreman or Quality Assurance, remains to be seen. Kevin is so upset, he wants to bash Lewis's head in. He thinks to himself "What nerve that bastard Lewis has! He's yelling at me for something he caused, and I'm the one who has to lose part of my finger. Someday, I'll make him pay, and pay dearly!"

One thing you can always count on in a brewery is there is never a dull moment. On any given day, there are hundreds of tasks that need to be completed to ensure the brewery runs efficiently. On the flip side, there are hundreds of things that can go wrong. The latest problem that Michael, or "QA Mike" as he is known, is dealing with, has to do with a carbon dioxide tanker. A good portion of the carbon dioxide that is used at the brewery has been recovered from the fermenting process for cleaning and reuse. This is termed "preferred CO2", and all CO2 used in the brewing department is of this type. There is still a significant amount that is needed to be bought and used in the packaging department, and that type is termed "purchased CO2". Today, QA gets a call from the powerhouse that a CO2 tanker has arrived, and needs to be checked before unloading. Michael gathers his equipment and goes outside to start the testing process. He first gives the driver a long stainless-steel cylinder with valves on either end, and a knurled fitting on one end that matches up the outlet valve on the truck. The liquid CO2 fills the cylinder and flashes off to a gas as it exits. They do this for a couple of minutes to clear any oxygen from the cylinder, and then the valves are closed. The driver is supposed to open the relief valve on the truck to bleed away the pressure, but he forgets to. As he is unscrewing the cylinder, it shoots off the back of the truck like a rocket, and skims 40ft across the parking lot, coming to rest under a car. Thankfully, no one was in front of the cylinder, or they could have been killed. The CO2 from the cylinder is attached via a hose to a glass reservoir, and it flows through, removing any air until only the CO2 remains. Caustic is added, and the CO2 is absorbed. If the truck CO2 is very pure, as it should be, it will all be absorbed. Anything not absorbed is air which contains oxygen, and will appear as a bubble in the measuring device. On this truck, the purity appears to be within specifications. However, the second part of the test needs to be run. Michael attaches a clean tube to the cylinder and removes some CO2, which is bubbled through some cold filtered water that has no odor or taste. After bubbling, Michael tastes and smells the water. Normally, there have been no issues, and the trucks have been quickly released for unloading. In this case, the water has a distinctive aroma of rotten eggs, which is caused by hydrogen sulfide. Michael gets the powerhouse foreman, and they go back outside to inform the driver they cannot unload his tanker. Michael says, "We have a problem. The CO2 in your truck smells bad, so we will have to turn you away." The driver smirks and crassly replies, "This is some bullshit, screw you. I will just drive down to Milwaukee and unload at any of the breweries down there. They never do the bullshit tests you do here. Hopefully, I won't be back!"

Back in the brewing department, Harry, along with the other supervisors, are attending the daily department meeting with the Brewmaster. The first item on the list to discuss is that Horst is not pleased with the speed of the fermentation. It has been running about twelve hours behind where he would like it. One of the things they monitor is the growth of the yeast during fermentation. It should start out at the pitching rate, then increase hour by hour until it reaches a peak, and then decline. The faster the peak is reached, the faster the fermentation. Horst has been discussing this with the owner, Kieran, to see if he had any suggestions. He lets the staff know they will begin adding a small amount of a solution, made up of zinc acetate, to each brew. The zinc is a micronutrient for the yeast, and will stimulate a faster growth rate. This proves to be quite successful and becomes standard practice.

The other item up for discussion today is a problem they have with one of the aging tanks. This particular tank was determined to have a bad off-flavor note during yesterday's taste panel. It has a pronounced buttery, butterscotch flavor and aroma. This type of buttery flavor is caused by a compound known as diacetyl, and it is normally produced during fermentation at low levels. During aging in chip tanks, the yeast will re-metabolize this compound, until it has no effect on beer flavor. However, this compound can also be produced if the beer has been infected with a particular strain of bacteria called pediococcus. These are bacteria that have a spherical shape and appear as groups of two, with some as groups of four in a box shape, which is a telling characteristic. They brought a sample from the tank down to QA and had Michael examine it under the microscope, where he determined it had a pediococcus infection. This is quite serious if it spreads to the other tanks. Their only recourse is to dump the beer, and clean the tank and all associated lines with hot caustic. Fortunately, after the cleaning process, they were able to stop the infection from spreading.

After a couple of years, it's now 1965, and Michael and Jana are doing very well in their jobs. Michael becomes more proficient with his laboratory skills and Jana is now the office manager at Miesbach Darling Ice Cream. Their private lives have been just as rewarding, and they live several blocks away from Jana's parents, Harry and Emma. They have three young children who are growing fast. The oldest is daughter Melissa, and she is seven years old, a son Michael who is six years old, and the youngest daughter, Joanne, who is three years old. It's a quiet Saturday morning and Michael has just made a large batch of blueberry muffins. Michael likes to add some of the blueberry juice to the batter in order to turn the muffins blue, and the kids love them and think they are magical. Just after Jana leaves the house to go grocery shopping, the phone rings. Michael answers and the voice says, "Michael, it's Horst, the Brewmaster. I need you." Michael responds, "What can I help you with? Is there a problem at the brewery?" Horst explains, "I suspect we have another contaminated beer tank. Would you be able to come in this morning and check it for bacterial infection?" Michael thinks for a minute and says, "Well, I could, but I am babysitting the three kids, as my wife is out shopping. As long as you don't mind me bringing them along, I can be at the brewery in about an hour." Horst agrees and says, "That's not a problem. You just keep a close eye on them so they are safe." Michael then gets the kids dressed, and he calls his father-in-law, Harry, to ask if he can drive them over to the brewery, because Jana has their only car. It's Harry's day off and he is happy to help Michael out. Emma comes along with him, and they stop off on the way to buy the kids some candy. Once they reach the brewery, Harry and Emma monitor the kids while they wait for Michael to complete his task. He confirms that the tank is contaminated and calls Horst to give him the bad news. Before they leave, Michael puts a sample of yeast under the microscope, and lets the kids take turns viewing it, which they think is cool. As soon as they pull up at the house, Jana pulls in at the same time. She is so happy to see her parents and wonders why they came over. Michael explains what happened, and they both thank Harry and Emma for the help. It's a beautiful day out, so Jana decides to go on a picnic at the lake, and asks her parents to come along with them. Jana grabs some cheese, bread, dried sausage, fruit, and the candy her parents bought. A wonderful time was had by all, and they all agree that they have to do it more often.

The following spring, Harry and Joseph finally have one of their weeks of vacation at the same time, which has never happened before. They decide they want to do something special for their wives, so they decide to fly down to Florida. Joseph's and Matty's kids, who range in age from 11 to 15 Years old, will be staying at Uncle Otto's house while they are away. Joseph is the only one of the four that has been on an airplane before, having been a paratrooper. But that was a propeller plane during the war. None of them have ever been on a jet before. They fly from Chicago to Miami on a Boeing 727, which is one of the newest jets being used. Joseph cannot believe how technology has changed over the years. The flight was only a few hours long, smooth and quiet. They went all out and are staying at the Fontainebleau Hotel, right on the beach and is considered a high-class hotel. It has an excellent location and service, with delicious food, and nightly entertainment. They are even able to score some tickets to the Jackie Gleason show, which is broadcast from Miami. The days are mostly spent relaxing on the beach, with a little sightseeing thrown in. On one of the days, they rent a car and drive down to Key West, and on another day, they take a short tour of the Everglades. And as often happens when northerners visit Florida, they all get a touch of sunburn, so they have to be careful with that. Every evening is dinner, followed by a show, at the hotel or one of the local venues. Harry says to Emma, "Do you remember how, when we were first married, we would go down to Chicago to enjoy the nightlife?" Emma replies, "I miss those days so much. Well, we only have a couple of nights left, so we better make the most of it." They all are so happy that they came to Florida. They think of what it would be like to live there someday when they retire.

When Harry and Joseph return to work from their vacation, they both receive some interesting news concerning each of their departments. Over in packaging, Joseph's can line # 35 will undergo major renovations. It will get a new high speed can filler and seamer installed, upgraded conveyors, new pasteurizer and packer, almost a complete updating of the line, which is long overdue. The increased capacity will help the company keep up with increased demand for canned beer, which is becoming almost as popular as bottled beer. When the line restarts production after renovation, along with sister line # 53, they will utilize the latest advancement in can lid technology. The normal pull tab on the can lid will be replaced with a ring tab. Basically, the tab will have a circular hole to put your finger in, which makes it much easier to remove the tab. The one downside to these removable tabs is they cause a considerable amount of litter, and are sharp so you can be easily cut by them.

As far as the brewing department is concerned, Horst the Brewmaster, and Kieran the owner, make a major announcement. Kieran says, "As sales have been strong, we have to better utilize our equipment to maximize production. The most cost-effective way for us to do that is through the changeover to what we will term 'heavy brewing'. As you know, our current brews target a final balling of 11.0, or eleven percent sugar content. In heavy brewing, we will target a final balling of 15.0, or fifteen percent sugar content, and just prior to the finished beer cellars, we will inject what we will call 'Adjusted Water' to the brew. This is cold, carbon filtered, carbonated water, which has no taste or aroma, thus, achieving our normal final balling of 11.0 percent. This will, of course, require us to run many test brews once the new equipment is installed so we can make adjustments to the recipe. It is imperative that the taste of the final product produced through 'heavy brewing' is the same as the final product produced through our normal procedure." It takes quite a while to install the "adjusted water," system, and much trial and error to get the recipe correct. Of course, it's always two steps forward and three steps back with any new endeavor. The first of the "adjusted water," tanks that was put into service had a door seal failure. As the tank was full of pressurized water, it all rushed out, creating an internal vacuum, which led to air pressure crushing the tank. As it could not be repaired, they had to dismantle it with cutting torches and haul it away. A quite expensive piece of bad luck, to say the least. But finally, a year later, "heavy brewing," became standard practice at Miesbach/Ballygar Brewing.

It's late summer 1967 and Uncle Otto has invited Joseph and Harry over because he wants to share some news with them. Otto begins by saying, "You know boys, I'm seventy-two years old and I think it's time for me to finally retire. It has been a heck of a career at the Miesbach Brewery, but time is catching up to me, I guess." Joseph is the first to reply, "That is fantastic news. You deserve it after all these years." Harry chimes in, "Absolutely, you should. Have you given any thought to what you want to do?" Otto replies, "The first thing I want to do is take a trip back to the old country. It's been quite a long time since I have been there. You know, one of my greatest regrets in life was losing my brother, Gerhart, and his wife, Lena, during the war. When I was able to go back in 1947, their shop and house, and half the block for that matter, had been destroyed. I searched all over Bavaria for them, but to no avail, and I had to accept the fact that they had perished. But on the flip side of that, one of my greatest joys has been having my nephew and his family in my life. Harry, the same thing goes for you, as well. You are both like sons to me. Thank you for being in my life."

Otto makes the announcement of his retirement at work the next day, and a steady stream of employees stop by to wish him well. The following weekend, Joseph and Harry have organized a going away party for Otto. As Harry has an extremely large backyard, they decide to do the party there. A large tent is erected and kegs of ice cold Miesbach beer are brought in. Joseph and Harry spend the day grilling steaks and bratwurst, and serving beer. Emma and Matty take care of preparing and serving all the side dishes. Throughout the day, at least seventy-five of Otto's friends and co-workers have attended the party, including Kieran, the brewery owner, who came down from Minnesota. Kieran has brought a guest along, who he introduces as his brother-in-law, William. Later in the day, Emma and Matty bring out a large cake Emma has baked for the occasion. It's Emma's and Otto's favorite, carrot cake with cream cheese frosting. After they are done with the cake, Kieran asks for everyone's attention. He thanks Otto for the many years of hard work, and presents him with the obligatory gold watch. He also presents him with a large present. As he opens it, Otto is delighted to find a large ceramic Eagle, which is his favorite bird. Otto was surprised that Kieran would remember such a small detail as that. Later that evening, after the guests have all gone home and everything is cleaned up, Joseph's family and Harry's family all gather at Otto's house. Otto says, "Thank you all for this wonderful party. I really enjoyed it. I love you all!" They all reply, "We love you too, Uncle Otto." Joseph asks Otto, "When are you planning on leaving for your trip to Bavaria?" Otto replies, "I will fly out Wednesday morning, and depending on how everything goes, I am planning to stay for a month to six weeks. So do me a favor and monitor the house for me." Joseph replies, "Of course, everything will be taken care of in your absence. You just enjoy yourself!"

Come Monday morning, Joseph and Harry are back at work when the word comes down for all employees to gather in the warehouse for a meeting. Harry and Joseph assume it must be to announce Uncle Otto's replacement. Well, they were correct on that one. Kieran, the owner, opens the meeting by introducing the new Plant Manager to the employees. It is no other than William Jones, the man Kieran brought to Otto's going away party, his brother-in-law. Joseph thinks to himself, "What a sneaky, underhanded way to spy on the employees. With all the beer everyone drank that day, I hope nobody said anything to piss him off." That turns out to be the least of their worries, as William turns out to be a loud-mouthed, power hungry, shoot from the hip, "ready, fire, aim" type of guy. He is just the opposite of Uncle Otto and it only takes a couple days of William's tenure as Plant Manager for everyone to really hate him.

Later that afternoon, Michael, who has recently been promoted to laboratory supervisor, is waiting patiently for the lab tech to finish the latest set of samples from the can line. Joseph comes in and asks if the fills, airs, and CO2 checks are all within specification. Michael assures him they are looking good and have been that way all-day. Just then, the brewery's one and only female line foreman Chrissie, comes in. Joseph cannot contain his laughter as she walks up to Michael, and squeezes two cans of beer against her ample bosom and says, "Michael, do you want to give me a Balling!" Michael turns beet red and stammers, "Oh my gosh Chrissie, really? If you wanted me to check the sugar content, why didn't you just say that." Joseph pats Michael on the back and says, "Lighten up my friend, live a little." As Chrissie and Joseph leave the lab, Michael can still hear them laughing above all the noise on the packaging floor.

Just after that, Michael enters the QA taste room where his managers have been screening some finished beer tanks prior to them being released. As they have been training Michael to become a beer taster, they ask his opinion on the tank samples. Michael checks the six samples and says, "They mostly seem normal to me. For flavor, they are slightly sweet, malty, yeasty, hoppy, with a clean finish. For aroma, they are a little fruity, with a pronounced hops note. But, tank # 12 smells odd. I would describe it as smelling like Frito's corn chips." Immediately, his bosses realize that the tank is contaminated with caustic, and ask Michael to run the sample and check for sodium content. It turns out to be quite elevated, and upon notifying the brewing department, the brewers find that a valve failed, allowing caustic to be pumped into the beer tank. Consequently, the tank had to be dumped because of the contamination.

The next morning, Joseph and all the other day shift line are called into the morning packaging meeting. This is the first meeting presided over by the new Plant Manager, William Jones. He starts out complaining that he is not happy with the line efficiencies, and insults the previous Plant Manager for not fixing it. Joseph thinks to himself, "What the hell is this guy saying? Otto did a super job, and the lines have been running the best they ever have." William then berates the foreman and tells them they have not been doing a good enough job. He then puts them on twelve-hour shifts until they bring the efficiencies up to the level he demands. In just a few minutes, William has alienated all his foreman and destroying their morale. After he leaves the meeting, Joseph calls Matty to let her know the news about the overtime he is mandated to work. Later that evening, just before the end of his twelve-hour shift at 8:00 p.m., Joseph sees a couple of security guards escorting someone up from the warehouse. As they walk between the two can lines heading towards the front office, he sees the guards are escorting a beautiful blond young lady wearing pink hot pants. He learns later that she was a prostitute that the truck drivers were using. The guards threw her off premises and told her if she returns, they will have the police arrest her.

Now, as luck would have it, a couple of weeks into the twelve-hour shifts Joseph gets a reprieve for a few days. All the supervisors in the plant are being sent to three-day management training classes. Joseph just shakes his head, thinking what a waste of time, but a few days away can't hurt. The training is held at a nearby hotel in their conference room. The trainer Carol is a consultant that has worked at the Ballygar Brewery, and has been in a clandestine affair with William Jones. They have mixed up all the attendees, so they are with people from other departments. Joseph is happy to see that Michael is in his training group. The first exercise is what the instructor terms progressive relaxation, and is supposed to be different techniques to handle stress. She makes them all lie on the floor and do rhythmic, deep breathing exercises. She makes the mistake of turning off the lights, and Michael, Joseph, and half of the group doze off. They are awakened one by one, as the instructor kicks their feet.

The next day is just as comical, and beyond belief. They start the day's class with them all being asked to stand along the wall. The instructor Carol yells out, "Stand up straight, chest out, stomach in." As she comes over towards Michael, she stops at the supervisor next to him, who is named Tony. "She berates him and says, Speak up. What's your name?" He says, "My name is Tony." She replies, "Well, Tony, I don't like your attitude, you are not trying." Tony shakes his head and says, "What do you want from me?" Carol raises her voice and says, "Suck your stomach in, shoulders back." Tony yells back, "My stomach doesn't go in any further," as it hangs over his pants. Michael speaks up, "Carol, what's the problem? Tony used to be a sumo wrestler. They all look like that." Carol throws up her hands and walks away.

The third and final day turns out to be the ultimate embarrassment for Carol. She makes everyone put their chairs in a circle around her. Then each person has to take a turn and sit in a chair opposite her to do a role play. She has stated that she can teach them how to deal with any difficult or unruly employee situations. It's Joseph's turn to be in the hot seat, where he pretends to be an unruly employee. As Carol opens her mouth and tries to change Joseph's attitude, he stands up and throws his chair against the wall and says, "I don't have to listen to your bullshit. Where's my union steward?" Carol is taken aback and shocked beyond belief. Suddenly, the tears start flowing down her face, and she runs off crying. It's about an hour later before she returns, and she dismisses everyone for lunch. Now, everyone is thinking the same thing, "What a waste of time." At lunch, one of the brewing foreman orders a couple of bottles of champagne and charges it to the company. Joseph wonders how that is going to go over. The rest of the afternoon goes quickly, and Carol keeps everything low key, basically just reading out of a training manual.

Once word gets back to the Plant Manager, William Jones, that his mistress Carol had such a hard time at the class, he was not happy. But the last straw is when he got the bill for the champagne. Had it not been for the fact that it was a brewing department employee, whom he had no authority over, that person would have been fired. Needless to say, that was the last off- site training class the brewery ever had.

A few more months go by, and everything is still pretty crazy at the brewery. Harry is still fairly insulated because he works in the brewing department. Horst, besides being Harry's boss, is still a good family friend. Horst still treats everyone with respect and is a fair person to work for. He is pretty much the opposite of William Jones. Today, one of the Packaging Assistant Managers dared to disagree with William in the morning meeting, and was quickly demoted and sent to work in the storeroom. Joseph just keeps plugging along and doing his job to the best of his ability, but the constant pressure is taking its toll on him.

Harry and Emma have finished dinner and are relaxing in the parlor, watching some television on a Thursday night. The phone rings and Harry gets up to answer. It's Matty on the other end of the line who says, "Harry, I am worried about Joseph, he hasn't come home yet, have you seen him?" Harry replies, "No, but he told me last night that there was no overtime in his department this week. Do you want me to go and look for him?" Matty responds, "Yes, please, I am getting concerned. You know how tough things have been in the packaging department since Otto retired." Harry says, "Leave it to me. I will find him." Harry tells Emma what's going on and then leaves to go look for him.

Harry starts in the one place Joseph should not be in, the bar across the street from the brewery. As he enters, he sees Joseph seated in the back corner booth. As he approaches, he sees a mug of beer and a couple of shots of schnapps sitting on the table. Joseph looks up and says, "Did Matty send you to find me?" Harry replies, "Yes, old friend, she did. May I join you?" Joseph shrugs and says, "It's a free country." Harry asks him, "What's going on? What are you doing in a bar, after you fought so hard to get sober? This isn't the answer." Joseph looks up at Harry and says, "I have been sitting here for a couple of hours fighting the urge to drink. So far, I have been able to resist, but I really want to get drunk." Harry says, "I know you and the other foreman are going through a rough time, but like I said, this is not the answer." Joseph replies, "Then what is?" Harry thinks for a minute and throws out an idea saying, "You know, Joseph, you have kept yourself in excellent shape all these years. You need to find a way to release your frustrations. When Emma and I were downtown shopping last weekend, we passed some kind of karate or judo studio of some sort. I really don't know much about it, but Emma and I enjoy watching that tv show, The Green Hornet. You know, the one that has that karate guy, Bruce Lee? Maybe you could sign up for that and vent a little." Joseph thinks for a minute and says, "You know, during the war, we were taught some of those techniques for hand-to-hand combat. Maybe I will look into it. It actually sounds good." Harry says, "It's settled then. Now come and let me get you home. You've worried Matty enough." Well, look into it he did, and Joseph spent many evenings and weekends training. He got into it so much and trained so hard, he compensated for his limp and earned his black belt. Joseph may never be able to run, but he sure could fight. Matty and the kids, throughout his training, enjoyed going to watch him. Eventually, one by one, the kids all started training in martial arts and they, several years in the future, were also awarded their black belts. Matty, for her part, joined a group of ladies and a few times a week took what they called a kickboxing class, which consisted of the ladies punching and kicking large workout bags suspended from the ceiling. It was a challenging workout, and many friendships were made.

It's now Christmas week and Emma and Matty were hard at work in their free time baking all kinds of cookies and pastries. The plans are for Jana and Michael's family, as well as Joseph and Matty's family, and Uncle Otto, to spend Christmas Day at Harry and Emma's house. Jana, not to be out done, bakes some wonderful lemon cookies, and chocolate fudge nut pastry logs, to add to the dessert table. Michael is at work on Christmas Eve Day, and is looking forward to having a couple of days off. As he is walking through the Quality Assurance Lab, he runs into Frank, the pest control guy who takes care of the entire brewery. Michael has gotten friendly with him after being involved in some pest control inspections together. Michael says, "Hey, Frank, Merry Christmas. I'm so glad I ran I into you!" Frank says, "Same to you Michael, you ready for the holidays?" Michael laughs and says, "Yes, and here comes another five lbs. gained!" Frank laughs and replies, "I know what you mean. So, I hope all the pastries I brought yesterday doesn't contribute to that?" Michael looks at him incredulously and asks, "Pastries, what pastries?" Frank is a little agitated and says, "I brought five large rectangular white boxes of various pastries from that new Italian bakery, and left them with the QA manager for your department to enjoy." Michael says to Frank, "We never saw them, but when I was in the Personnel Department yesterday, I was looking out the window at the parking lot and the manager was putting some large, white rectangular boxes into his trunk." Frank can't believe it and says, "What a no-good cheap son of a bitch. I'm sorry you didn't get to enjoy any of the pastries." Michael replies, "Not your fault, Frank, but thank you anyway for thinking of us. Have a nice holiday, and I will see you in January."

## Chapter 8
# Descent

It is now Monday morning, January 5, 1970, when an announcement is made at the brewery. It says, "Effective immediately, there will be a freeze on hiring and on raises for the rest of the year. Management feels that with increased costs across the board, their profit margins are being squeezed. This is in addition to the fierce competition of the other major brewers. Miesbach/Ballygar have to pour a lot of money into marketing their products in order to compete. One area in which they can save some money is on can and lid production. In working with their can vendor, they are able to reduce the wall thickness of the can, thus saving on metal costs. They can also reduce the diameter of the neck of the can, which means they can use a smaller lid, which again reduces the metal cost. One of the other innovative things they started in order to reduce cost is an employee suggestion program. For any suggestion that is deemed worthy of being implemented, the employee receives a cash reward, based on the amount of savings. One of the areas in the brewery that is always quite expensive is the cost of water. Due to all the cleaning and rinsing that takes place, the brewery uses almost five times the amount of water then what actually goes into the package. There are many employee suggestions accepted concerning water usage that result in significant savings. This program becomes an enormous success, and results in savings of over a million dollars per year.

Unfortunately, management has decided to play hardball in their efforts to reduce the number of employees. The day shift general foreman, George, who has responsibility for all of packaging and the warehouse, has returned to work after recovering from a heart attack. After just one week, George is put on the midnight shift. In addition, he is mandated to work 12-hour shifts for the next month. Needless to say, after a couple of 12-hour shifts, George immediately retires.

What's more concerning for Joseph is, after all the years he has been a can line foreman, he and bottle line foreman Kevin are put on a performance improvement plan. Essentially, they are on probation and are in jeopardy of losing their jobs. After a year of increasingly ridiculous demands, suddenly, they are removed from probation. Joseph and Kevin are obviously relieved, and the only explanation they can come up with is that two other foreman have quit, and they need them now. Who knows what the rest of the year will bring?

But, as happy and relieved as Joseph is, it turns out to be a very challenging month. In a couple of weeks, Joseph is checking out the empty can rinser that feeds clean cans into the filler. He detects a noticeable aroma of chlorine, which he has never smelled in this area before. Turns out, the rinser water is carbon filtered to remove all taste and odor, and then a slight amount of chlorine is added to eliminate any bacterial growth. However, the chlorine pump in the powerhouse is out of calibration and is pumping twenty times the normal amount of chlorine. The lines are shut down, and the common rinser system is flushed with clean water before restarting production. The Brewmaster and the quality department taste samples of finished product to ensure there are no detrimental flavors or aromas present. Just as caustic and beer smells like Frito's corn chips, chlorine and beer would smell like a Band Aid. Fortunately, all production is tasted and found to be unadulterated, and released for sale.

The second major problem the brewery had occurred a week after the chlorine incident. For this issue, they were not so lucky, and a significant amount of beer was lost. One of the out-of-state distributors has notified the brewery that they have some wet cases of cans in their warehouse. Upon investigation, some of the beer cans are found to be leaking. But, all of them contain beer that is totally flat, as the carbon dioxide has leaked out. As the seam is formed, there needs to be a sufficient overlap between the top flange of the can and the lid. In this case, the overlap is far out of specification. Unfortunately, it is found they have almost two weeks worth of production that needs to be dumped. Until this point, a mechanic had been in charge of performing the seam analysis. But for whatever reason, either the checks were not done, or done incorrectly. In any case, the mechanic was terminated immediately. Subsequently, the task of seam analysis will now be done by the quality assurance department, and the frequency will be increased to twice per shift.

It's late April 1971 and spring has come to Sheboygan. The weather has been sunny and gradually warming. Things have been relatively quiet at the brewery for the last few months, but that is about to change unexpectedly. It's Friday afternoon, and an announcement is made that all employees are to meet in the warehouse for an emergency meeting at four o'clock. Everyone gathers and is made to wait for almost half an hour before management finally arrives. The anticipation and stress level has certainly increased with each passing minute. The owner, Kieran Gilbride, flanked by Plant Manager William Jones, and Brewmaster Horst Landt, starts addressing the employees. He says, "I have sold the Miesbach/Ballygar Brewing Company to an investment firm, something called 'Private Equity.' We expect the deal to close in just a few months. I expect there will not be any major change to the operation or to our personnel, so please stay calm and we will notify you as more information becomes available. Now, does anyone have any questions?" The first to raise their hand is one of the few female brewers, Frieda. Kieran totally embarrasses himself as he mistakes her for a man and says, "Yes sir, what is your question?" The rest of the workers try hard to contain their laughter as they all look down. After answering a few more questions, the atmosphere in the room turns hostile, as the employees are freaking out. Kieran cuts his losses and asks everyone to return to work, or to leave if their shift is done. Nobody believes that things will remotely stay the same. These types of corporate buyouts have become all the news lately. In fact, the firm that is buying them out has also made deals with four other regional breweries, to bring them all under one company, for a total of six breweries. The buzzword that is used in these types of buyouts is they will leverage the "synergies" of the various companies taken over. It basically means they will make money by consolidating manpower and try to get volume discounts on purchased materials.

After a few months, the buyout of the Miesbach/Ballygar Brewing Company is complete. They are now the property of Empire Capital, which is based in New York City. The employees always suspected in the lead-up to the final sale that nothing would remain the same. Unfortunately, their fears all too soon become reality. Within a month of the sale closing, Empire Capital sells off Miesbach Darling Ice Cream to one of the largest dairy cooperatives in Wisconsin. Fortunately for Jana, she can keep her job as office manager at the ice cream company, and the new owners are quite impressed with her skill at dealing with the customers. A couple of months after the ice cream sale, the last piece of the operation to be sold off is the yeast cake division, which is quickly purchased by one of the national bakers.

Selling off the subsidiary businesses is always the easiest way for private equity to make money, and is considered the low hanging fruit, so to speak. Some of the other changes they make are asking for volume discounts from the suppliers, and they start paying their suppliers in 60 days, instead of the standard 30 days. Through the elimination of the yearly summer party and the Christmas party, Empire Capital saves a little money, but it negatively affects morale. Every single aspect of the operation is vetted for cost savings, literally down to the amount of stationery supplies they use.

While most departments at Miesbach are seeing a reduction in staffing levels, the one area that does not is the business department. In fact, they have hired many new people and have greatly expanded. This is because they have made Miesbach what they term a system "hub." So now, with the help of the new IBM mainframe computer they have installed, Miesbach will assume purchasing, accounting, wholesaler support and inventory, etc., for all six breweries that Empire Capital owns. By doing this, they have reduced headcount by 35 percent in these areas.

Operational changes, however, take a little more time and planning to implement. The first major change the new owners want made is in the brewing department. Horst, the Brewmaster, has been asked to work with his counterparts at the other breweries Empire Capital has acquired. Their task is to eliminate the use of the wood chips in the aging process at Miesbach Brewing. This was a traditional method of aging beer back in Bavaria in the old days, and something Miesbach Brewing has always done. But it is a very expensive process, besides the cost of the chips, it is extremely labor intensive. Empire Capitol realized that nowhere printed on either the cans, or the bottle labels, did it reference the fact that the beer was aged on chips. It takes a year of trial and error, but eventually they eliminated the chips from the process. A much tighter emphasis on proper malting, mashing, wort boiling, fermentation, and lagering led to the outcome they desired, elimination of chips without changes to the beer flavor profile. Unfortunately for the brewing department employees, once this change was made, dozens of jobs were eliminated.

For Harry in the brewhouse, it actually becomes a non-stop cascade of changes and experiments in an effort to reduce costs. Recipes are tweaked to use a few percent more of 6-row malt instead of the more expensive 2-row malt variety. In the same way, the hop recipes are changed to use a higher percentage of domestic grown hops, rather than the more expensive imported type. In a little over a year after the takeover, a major change was made to the hopping part of the brewing process. They have been directed to stop using bales of whole fresh hops. Instead, they switch over to what's called pelletized hops. These are freshly picked hops from the farm that are dried and then milled and pressed into pellets. The advantage of this type of product is they take up much less space to store, they last much longer than fresh hops, and theoretically, they can use slightly fewer hops per brew to achieve the same amount of bitterness in the product.

Through all the constant changes at work, Harry just rolls with it. He tells himself all the time that the most important thing in his life is his Emma, daughter Jana, and all the grandkids. Emma had continued working as a welder for over twenty-five years. Once things went bad at the shipyard, she bounced around from factory to factory, sometimes working full time, sometimes part-time, and sometimes not working at all. Emma and Harry have just enjoyed a nice evening out, and following a delicious dinner, they listen to a live band playing in the park. As they take a stroll by the lakefront, Emma says, "You know Harry, I have always enjoyed my welding job, but I am thinking of giving it up and doing something a little less tiring." Harry replies, "I think we are stable enough financially, so it's fine with me. Did you want to retire totally, or just try something different?" Emma thinks for a minute and says, "I would basically like to retire, and maybe just do a little sewing occasionally. Maybe do some alterations of wedding dresses, that type of thing." Harry is very supportive and tells her, "Go for it. I think it's a fantastic idea. You know if I can just hold on at work for a few more years, I will retire also, when I turn 62 years of age." Emma smiles and says, "I can't wait for that day so we can spend all of our time together."

Over in the packaging department, there have been major changes made since the takeover. There is a big effort underway to improve training and empower the line employees to make some decisions on their own. The next major change that takes place is the announcement that the line foreman, such as Joseph, will now have to supervise two lines instead of one. So, with that change, they will have to eliminate some of the foreman. Joseph is worried that he could be on the chopping block. As luck would have it, several of them, upon hearing that they will now be in charge of two lines at a time, decide to just quit. So, Joseph ends up keeping his job, and is now in charge of both can lines. It turns out to be one of the most challenging things he has done, but, just like Harry, he thinks to himself, "If I can just hold on a few more years."

On the plus side for Joseph, they have also reduced the number of Assistant Packaging Managers. Joseph's nemesis, Lewis Landon, has been terminated. Instead of being unhappy about losing his job, Lewis is elated, as he immediately gets hired as a technical representative at one of the label companies. Lewis is still making a very good salary, but has none of the headaches associated with production. The improvement in his stress level and personality is quite profound that even Joseph could get along with him now.

On the home front, Harry's wife Emma has just received some troubling news. Her mother, Alice, has just phoned to tell her that her father has been taken by ambulance to the hospital. Emma puts a phone call into the brewery and leaves a message for Harry to call her back as soon as he gets it. Once Harry receives the bad news, he can get out of work an hour early, and they drive down to Chicago to the hospital. By the time they get there, Emma's father is in a room, but is in a coma. The doctors inform Alice that Leo has suffered what they believe to be a massive stroke. The doctors feel it is a condition he will probably not recover from. Alice, Emma and Harry are understandably devastated by the news. Leo is able to hang on for three or four days before he succumbs with his family by his side. Shortly thereafter, Leo is laid to rest in Saint Bonifacius German Catholic Cemetery. This is where he had the foresight to buy a couple of plots years ago, before they ran out of space. Emma and Harry convince Alice to come stay with them up in Sheboygan until she decides what she wants to do.

Alice initially was almost to the point of being despondent, but slowly, after a few months, returns to normal. Being around her daughter and the entire extended family has certainly helped her out. Eventually, Alice sells her house in Chicago, and moves in with Emma and Harry in Sheboygan.

It's now the spring of 1973, and Alice, who fortunately is still in good health, takes much joy in watching her great-grandchildren's activities. Jana and Michael have recently enrolled Melissa, Michael, and Joanne into the Karate studio where Joseph and his family trained. This was really one of the greatest things for the kids as they all lost weight and became very strong because of the intensive training. Almost as important, they achieved mental toughness and learned that there was nothing they couldn't accomplish if they worked hard at it. They take about three years of intensive training in order for them to earn their Black Belt. However, because of the rigors of this sport; running, jumping, kicking, and fighting, little Joanne developed some severe inflammation in her knees and could not train very much after she received her Black Belt.

Back at the brewery, Joseph and the crew have had their hands full with all the new packages they are producing. Gone are the days of just producing the standard 12 oz cans. While that is still the most popular package size, Joseph's lines also produce a larger 16 oz can, as well as a smaller 7oz can. This, of course, makes the can line operation much more complex, as the lines must be converted back-and-forth to run the different sized packages. Obviously, this puts much pressure on Joseph and the mechanics to make the change-overs in a precise and efficient manner, so downtime on the line can be reduced. This morning, Joseph gets a call on his radio from Michael over in the Quality Assurance department and he says "Joseph, we need you to shut down the filler and hold all the 16 oz can production from line #53." Joseph replies, "Freaking great, what's wrong this time? We have been running for about four hours on this package." Michael replies, "We just got word from the Brewmaster's taste room that the canned beer tastes very metallic, so they are shutting the beer line to #53 filler." Joseph goes about clearing the line of any remaining packaged beer and has it all segregated in the warehouse. He is also instructed to hold any empty 16 oz can pallets with the suspect production date he was running. So, they have no choice but to have the mechanics start converting the line back to 12 oz production. Both the brewing and quality taste panels verify that the finished beer tank tastes fine. It therefore has to be a defect in the can liner, or contamination of the can. The empty cans appeared clean and free of any drop in contamination, so samples of the defective cans were sent back to the can plant for analysis. It was quite remarkable what modern technology can do. They were able to examine the can liner under an electron microscope and found that they had many minute pieces of metal embedded in the liner. They were able to trace the problem to some rust particles falling into the cans and embedding in the freshly applied liner, as the can went through the curing ovens at the can-plant. All the affected can dates had to be destroyed, and all the hold beer at the brewery was dumped. As this was determined to be a problem with the material, the brewery made the can manufacturer pay for all the dumped product.

A couple of more years go by and Joseph and Harry are working hard every day, and trying to keep their spirits up. Long gone are the days of having that feeling that your job is secure and you will be able to provide for your family. They just always worry about what is going to happen next. One of the obvious changes in the brewery is the number of younger employees that seem to be everywhere. In fact, since the takeover, the average age of service for a Miesbach employee has dropped from 22 years to 15 years. It is quite obvious to everyone that experience and loyalty are not valued by Empire Capital. It all comes down to the bean counters in New York City trying to reduce cost at every turn, and no one's job is safe. Even the Plant Manager, William Jones, has been terminated and replaced with Walter Fischer. His transgressions appear to be Empire Capitals' displeasure at the pace in which he had reduced manpower in the brewery. So, you could say he got a good dose of what he had been dishing out to everyone else.

Over in the brewing department Horst, the Brewmaster has retired. The constant pressure to reduce overhead has taken the joy out of coming to work. To Horst, brewing beer is mostly art, with some science thrown in. To Empire Capital, it is neither of those things. Brewing beer is simply a series of predetermined steps to produce a product that they can sell and make an ever-increasing profit on. The new Brewmaster, Dave Morrison, is the first non-German to oversee Miesbach's brewing department. In fact, he is of English descent, and is an engineer by trade. He has bounced around at a couple of the other breweries in Empire Capitals network to gain some brewing experience.

The first personnel change that Dave Morrison makes is to offer Harry a promotion to become one of three Assistant Brewmaster's. Harry says, "That is a quite generous offer. Would you allow me to give you my answer next Monday?" Dave looks perplexed and replies, "Yes, but why the delay. Don't you think you can do the job?" Harry explains and says, "I can do the job, but as you know, one of the most important jobs an assistant will have is being a member of the taste panel. I have been on medication for many years that prevents me from drinking alcohol. However, I recently have undergone a series of tests and if they come out the way I am hoping, I'll finally get off of that medication." Dave replies, "I totally understand, you just let me know on Monday, and we will go from there." Harry gets the test results back, and it shows he is no longer having abnormal brain activity, so the doctor says he can start weaning off the medication. Monday morning, Harry enters the Brewmaster's office and says, "I have received news from my doctor that I will be able to drink alcohol again as I am going off my medication. If your offer of promotion to Assistant Brewmaster still stands, I would like to accept it!" Dave replies, "Yes, Harry, the job is yours. Congratulations! Now the first thing I want you to do is to go up to Duluth and attend a week-long taste training class that we are putting on at the Ballygar brewery." Harry is ecstatic and says, "Thank you, Dave, for this wonderful opportunity. I won't let you down." As soon as Harry leaves the office, he puts in a call to Emma and invites her out to dinner to celebrate his good news. They extend an invitation to Jana and Michael's family to join them also, and what a fun evening it turns out to be.

Dave Morrison wastes no time in implementing some more major changes to the brewing department, the first of which is eliminating the use of the hop pellets. Instead, they switch to what is called a hop extract, which is made by extracting the hop resins in the hop cone with liquid carbon dioxide. This produces a syrupy product that is cheaper to store, transport, and keeps its quality longer than whole hops or pellets. The hop suppliers learned how to modify chemically the extract so it does not allow the beer to turn "skunky" when exposed to sunlight. So, with the chemically modified hop extracts, the brewery starts producing something they said they never would, beer in clear bottles.

Dave Morrison and Empire Capital didn't stop there with the changes. They go about constructing several large stainless-steel storage tanks. The new Brewmaster asks Harry, "Can you guess what they are for?" Harry replies, "I don't have a clue." Dave says, "These tanks will be for the storage of corn syrup, which we will start using in place of some of the malt and other adjuncts we currently use." Harry is perplexed and says, "I know you can use syrup, but the elimination of more malt from the recipe seems like a radical change." Dave replies, "The yeast doesn't care where the sugar comes from that they will ferment; corn syrup, malt, rice, etc. It's all the same to them, and we cannot discount the significant cost savings we will achieve. Harry asks, "But what about the beer flavor, won't that be affected?" Dave says, "We will have an entire team of Brewmaster's and Assistant Brewmaster's, including you, Harry, that will work on making this transition successful. We obviously don't want to change the beer's final flavor profile that our customers have come to expect. We will also be introducing some new products that will be made completely with corn syrup."

Well, contrary to the assurances that the Brewmaster made to Harry about brewing with corn syrup and hop extracts, it has a negative effect on the flavor profile of Miesbach's beer. This became clear when beer sales leveled off and then began to drop. Long-term, this was a disastrous move they made messing with the established beer formula. As they learned the hard way, beer drinkers are very fickle. They expect consistency and quality in what they drink, and they were quick to pick up on the subtle changes made to the beer flavor. Consequently, because of the erosion of sales volume, the decision was made to close one of their six breweries. That volume of production was allocated to the remaining five breweries, who are now operating at above 90% capacity. However, in another attempt to save money, Empire Capital has changed advertising agencies, and even reduce some television ad buys. This turned out to be another example of shooting yourself in the foot, so to speak, as the new advertising campaign was less than inspiring, and did nothing to increase sales.

Harry and Emma have stopped by on a Friday night to visit Joseph and Matty at their house. Because of all the hours Harry and Joseph have been putting in at work, there has not been time for socializing the last couple of months. As they are sitting in the kitchen having some apple pie that Emma made, Joseph says to Harry, "Remember how we were able to get our vacations at the same time before, and we had that glorious trip to Miami, Florida? I have the last two weeks of my vacation this fall, in the middle of September, and I was wondering if by any chance you could get the same weeks off?" Harry replies, "It's funny you say that, because I was just looking at the vacation schedule the other day, and I also still have my last two weeks to schedule. I think September is wide open, so I think I can definitely be off at the same time. What did you have in mind?" Joseph says, "I want all of your opinions on my idea. So, I have always said I never wanted to return to Germany, but I have been thinking about it more and more lately. If we ever want to go, it will have to be before we get much older. What do you all think about a vacation in Germany this fall? We could start off by visiting Munich, as it will be Oktoberfest. Then we could visit Kelheim, where we grew up, and Friedrichshafen, etc." Matty is the first to respond and says, "I am all for it, on one condition. If we are going to Europe, then besides visiting Germany, I want to spend a few days in Italy as well." Harry, Emma, and Joseph think it's a wonderful idea to visit both countries. As the guys have Saturday off from work, they decide to go downtown to the travel agent and plan out a trip. While Joseph and Harry are a little apprehensive about going back home and not knowing what they will find, Emma and Matty are euphoric. They both have always wanted to visit Europe, and now they finally have their chance.

It's September 1975, and the start of their European vacation is at hand. Joseph and Matty's children are all young adults and perfectly capable of being on their own, but Joseph has told them to contact Jana and Michael in case they need anything while they are away. Emma's mother, Alice, who is still in good health, will stay with Jana and Michael at their house. The first part of their trip starts off with a flight from Chicago to New York City. After a short layover, Joseph and Matty, and Harry and Emma board a Lufthansa flight that will fly directly into Munich, Germany. Fortunately, the weather was pleasant, and they had a smooth flight across the Atlantic. At this time, the airlines were still serving a very nice in-flight afternoon meal, which they all enjoyed. By the time they landed in Munich, it was around 7:30 p.m. CST, which is 2:30 a.m. the next day Munich time. After retrieving their luggage, they grab a quick bite to eat at the only food stand still open at the airport. Then they share a taxi to the Hotel Brack, which is located only a 5 to 10-minute walk to the Theresienwiese, which is an enormous park square in Munich where the Oktoberfest takes place. After checking into the hotel and getting into their rooms, they are exhausted after the long flight and are asleep as soon as their heads hit the pillow. Because of the long trip and the time change, they are all noticeably jet lagged when they finally awake close to noon time. Everyone is famished, so they decide to go out and have a big lunch somewhere. There is no shortage of restaurants in the area, but all are quite busy because of the large number of tourists who are visiting the Oktoberfest. Joseph and Harry readjust their watches to match Munich time. It's close to 1:30 p.m. by the time they are seated and the restaurant is full of patrons having lunch and enjoying themselves. The noise level is high and many people are smoking, so the smell of tobacco hangs in the air. The first thing they ask the waiter, named Karl, is for some bread or rolls to tide them over until lunch arrives. The waiter is a jovial obese fellow and is happy to oblige them. The waiter says, "Have you decided on your order?" Joseph replies, "I would like to order for the table. Please bring us a platter of sauerbraten (marinated pickled beef), a platter of jagerschnitzel (pork cutlet with brown mushroom gravy), some spaetzle (small sauteed noodle dumpling) and pickled cabbage. Oh, and waiter, I would also like to order some schweinshaxe (roasted pork knuckle). I haven't had that since I was a child." The waiter replies, "We will get that out to you as soon as we can, but it may take a while. If you wish, I can bring out each platter as it becomes available, instead of serving everything at the same time." Joseph replies, "That would be fine. The sooner the better. Can we also have some more bread while we wait?" Karl replies, "I can see you are all famished. I will take good care of you." True to his word, Karl kept them well fed. The food is plentiful and absolutely delicious. Emma says to the group, "How many times have I made some of these same dishes at home, but they taste nowhere near as good as these." Harry chimes in, "I think your cooking is fantastic, Emma." She replies, "Thanks for saying that, sweetheart. I am just so happy to be here and be able to taste authentic Bavarian cuisine.

After a wonderful lunch, they decide to take a sightseeing bus, which makes predetermined stops around the city. They run at regular intervals so you can get off and enjoy what the city offers at that stop for as long as you like, then boarding again and moving on to the next stop. It turns out to be a lovely, sunny, fall day and the scenery is just outstanding. Depending on what part of the city you are in, you see anything from modern skyscrapers to some ornate 500-year-old buildings. Fortunately, most of the historic areas of the city were not destroyed in the war. What remains is called "Old Town", and is one of the most popular tourist destinations. While in this area of Munich, they were able to visit the "Frauenkirche", which is a large brick Roman Catholic Cathedral consecrated in the year 1494. As they continue to explore the "Old Town" area, they stop at "Viktualienmarkt," which is a very large outdoor market of stalls and stands that sell many kinds of local and international food products. When they strolled through the market, they purchased many types of Bavarian pastries. As they finish their third pastry of the afternoon, Emma laughs as says, "Oh, well, never drink a calorie you can eat." Harry smiles and replies, "I agree, but we are at Oktoberfest, so don't say that too loudly. People will think there is something wrong with us." As they continue their tour, they come upon the Marienplatz, which is a large plaza surrounded by many ornate buildings. The new city hall is located there and was constructed in the gothic style and finished in 1909. This building is a huge draw as it contains a Carillon or Glockenspiel, which plays music three times daily. As the music plays, its 16 moving figures, which are visible from the plaza, move and depict various historical events of the Bavarian royal families.

It's now early evening and as they are walking back to their hotel after a successful day, they stop to relax at a small nearby park. The next hour is spent people-watching and discussing all the lovely sites they had seen. After the large lunch and all the fine pastries they ate at the market, nobody was that hungry. As they leave the park, they pass a food cart that is selling bratwurst on a long roll. Each couple shares one, which turns out to be all they can fit in their stomachs. After returning to the hotel, they decide to have some hot coffee in the lounge before turning in early for the night. As they are discussing what to do tomorrow, Emma says, "We have a lot more traveling to do on our vacation, so why don't we stay close to the hotel and go over to the Theresienwiese and check out the Oktoberfest celebration?" Harry is the first to respond. "I think that is a wonderful idea, Emma. Now that I can have some alcohol, I can't wait to try out the beer tents. Oh, sorry Joseph, that was insensitive." Joseph smiles and says, "Don't worry about it as he hugs Matty. Stopping drinking was the second-best thing that happened to me. I am at peace with that problem and the cravings are long gone. Matty is all I need to keep me on the straight and narrow. So, while I won't be drinking, I will be enjoying the food, the music, and the scenery." Emma says, "Alright, it's decided, but I am so exhausted I am sure to sleep late tomorrow. Why don't we meet in the lobby around 11:00 a.m. and then get some breakfast before heading over to Oktoberfest? Harry, Joseph and Matty are all in agreement, so they go up to their rooms and call it a night. This turns out to be an excellent decision, as the extra rest is just what they all needed.

The next morning, they meet as planned and head over to a nearby restaurant for breakfast. The waiter comes over and gets them all a cup of hot coffee to start with. After he asks what they would like to eat, Harry replies, "Well, what is popular around here? We are visiting from the states and we would like to have a traditional Bavarian breakfast." The waiter replies, "Is that what you all would like?" Joseph, Matty and Emma all nod yes, and Harry also orders Kartoffelpuffer (potato pancakes) for everyone. After just a few minutes, breakfast arrives. It consists of brezen, which is a soft salted bread shaped and baked like a pretzel, weisswurst, which is white sausage made with veal, bacon and spices that is peeled and eaten with sweet mustard, and a bottle of weissbier, which is a fruity and spicy wheat beer. Joseph and Harry enjoy the weisswurst more than the ladies do, but overall, not a bad breakfast.

It's a short walk over to the Theresienwiese for the Oktoberfest. They arrive at the square, and they find the festival already has a large crowd in attendance. As they move through the area, they see it comprises over thirty tents, both large and small, with the largest seating, almost 6000 people, indoors. There is a lot of outdoor seating as well to take advantage of. It's quite easy to tell the tourists from the locals. All the German attendees are dressed in lederhosen if they are a male or a dirndl if they are female. Lederhosen are traditional shorts made of leather that strap over the shoulders. The dirndls are short traditional dresses that are adorned with a tie-on apron. Even how the apron is tied has significance and will tell everyone if you are single, married, or widowed. They decide to walk around the festival and see the sites as nobody is hungry or thirsty having just had breakfast. They decide to stop at an outdoor square that has been set up with a dance floor and an elevated stand for the band. The band is playing traditional Bavarian music and the dancers are doing the Schuhplattler dance. After watching for a while, the dancers have a few of the tourists come up on stage to join them in dance. Most of them have a problem keeping track of the steps, but they seem to be having fun, regardless. As Emma and Harry turn around to see if Joseph and Matty want to leave, they are recruited to go on stage. Surprisingly, Harry is a natural at it and he tells Emma he remembers dancing it as a child, and with his help Emma picks it up quickly. They do so well, in fact, that the dance troupe gives them a round of applause. As they leave the stage, Harry and Emma are quite out of breath and have to sit for a while before continuing on. Once they are up to it, they try to enter one of the nearby tents, but the powerful aroma of cooked fish hits them in the nostrils and drives them back. They have much better luck at the next tent, which seems to have a hunting theme. All around the tent there are mounted animal heads; deer, boar, etc. The aroma in this tent is much better as they are just preparing a roast pork dish called Schweinebraten and dumplings called Knodel. At the far end of the tent, they find something truly unique. It's a shooting range for crossbows. They all find it interesting and watch the shooters for some time. Once they decide to sit down, they order a couple of plates of food that the four of them will share. Joseph was not drinking, of course, so they just ordered two beers for Harry, Emma, and Matty to share. They were just amazed to see the beer maids carrying what looked like eight very large liter sized glass beer mugs at a time. The long table they were at was mostly local patrons, and our group, except for Matty, conversed with them in their native German language. The rest of the afternoon and early evening was spent at the Oktoberfest, people-watching, and dancing, and meeting many new friends, and of course, nibbling on all the delicacies for sale. As they did the day before, they go back to the hotel and get some coffee and discuss all they have done and seen today before turning in for the night. Tomorrow will be a big day as they are going to take a break from Oktoberfest and instead take the drive up to their hometown of Kelheim.

The next morning, they get up early and have a quick breakfast before heading out to Kelheim. The city lies about seventy miles north of Munich and should not take long to get there. The plan is to spend the day there and stay overnight before driving on to Friedrichshafen. It's a lovely ride through the Bavarian countryside before getting to Kelheim. Once they arrive, the first thing they do is drive to the outskirts of the city to see if the farm where Harry grew up on, is still there. As they approach the area, Harry remarks how most of the farmland has been replaced by housing and, to his surprise, he finds his farm is indeed gone. They then decide to drive by the site of the old Baumer Brewery, where they worked before the flood destroyed it. Harry and Joseph cannot believe how the area has been rebuilt into a thriving riverfront tourist area. By this time, it's around 1:00 p.m. and they decide to stop for lunch. As they drive through the town square, they are surprised to see that the tavern that Harry used to live above is still in operation. As they take a seat in the tavern, Harry says, "I can't believe it. This place hasn't changed in all these years. Emma, if you look up, that is where my room was. I wonder who the tavern belongs to now?" When the waitress came over to take their order, Harry asked her who the tavern owner is? She says, "My father, Walter, is the owner now. He inherited the tavern from his father, Heinrich." Harry smiles and tells her, "I knew your grandfather, Heinrich. How is he?" She replies. "Unfortunately, he perished during the war." Harry says, "I am sorry to hear that. When I was young, I lived upstairs and your grandfather always treated me well." She then says, "Happy to meet you, what can I get you folks to eat?" Joseph replies, "Bratwurst sandwich with sauerkraut sounds good." After lunch, they stroll through the town square, checking out all the shops. Their favorite is the chocolate store, where they feast on many kinds of delicious chocolates. As they continue their stroll through town, Matty asks, "It's such a beautiful sunny day. I wonder if there is a place to take a boat ride?" Emma says, "That is a really good idea. Let's ask someone if they know." As it turns out, it is a short drive down to the riverfront dock where the sightseeing cruise boats leave from. They are able to get on one of them and take a short 45-minute boat ride up the Danube to the Weltenburg Abbey. This is a popular tourist stop and the site of one of the oldest continuously operating Abbey breweries in all of Europe. They are known to produce one of the best beers anywhere, and have been brewing there for over a thousand years.

After having another delicious dinner, they are back at the hotel and are doing their nightly ritual of having coffee and recapping the day's events. Emma says to the group, "I know we were talking about taking a ride down to Friedrichshafen tomorrow, but what do you think of going to Zurich, Switzerland instead? According to the map, it's about a 4.5-to-5.0-hour trip. We can stop at Friedrichshafen on the way back to Munich!" Harry says, "I'm all for it. I hear the Swiss make the best chocolates in the word. Let's go for it. Who knows if we will get an opportunity like this again!" Joseph and Matty are in full agreement, and they all look forward to their next adventure.

The next day, the drive to Zurich is wonderful, and the scenery is spectacular. The view of Lake Constance followed by the majestic Alps mountains is fantastic. Once they arrive in Zurich, the first order of business is to get some lunch. They find a local restaurant and are treated to something they have never had before, a traditional Swiss fondue. Harry and Emma, along with Joseph and Matty, are seated at a round table with a pot of hot gruyere cheese in the center. The waitress explains how they are to take the extra-long forks and spear a cube of crusty bread to dip into the cheese. She also recommends either a glass of dry white wine or some hot tea as the perfect accompaniment. After lunch, they begin their sightseeing through Zurich, fortunately they dressed properly as the weather is cloudy and the temperature around 59 degrees Fahrenheit. Their tour of the Lindt Chocolate factory was quite fascinating, and the samples were delicious. But as fun as that was, what they really enjoyed was walking the Limmatquai, which is a shopping area along the river Limmat which flows out of Lake Zurich. They stopped at many of the numerous small chocolate stores in town and tried well over a dozen different chocolate confections.

It's been a wonderful day of sightseeing and it's now late afternoon and they decide to find a hotel for the night. The group travels to one hotel after another, until on their fourth try, they find the Hotel Kindli, which has just had a cancellation. The location of the hotel is in the center of Zurich and very near to "Old Town" and the Limmatquai. After checking in and freshening up, it's time to go find some dinner. After a short walk around the corner, they find a small neighborhood restaurant with a wonderful old-world décor. After they are seated, Joseph asks, "Waiter, what is the house's specialty?" The waiter, named Steffen replies, "Our most popular dinner entrée is the zuri-gschnatzlets, which is veal sauteed in cream, white wine, and mushrooms, and is served with a side of rosti, which is a cross between a potato pancake and a hash-brown as you Americans call it." Dinner was, of course, wonderful, just as all their meals have been on this vacation. The portions were large, the veal was tender, the sauce flavorful, and the wedge of rosti was crispy outside and tender inside. After dinner, they decide to take a taxi back across the river to the Limmatquai. The temperature is a little brisk by this point, but they decide to sit out at one of the cafes overlooking the river. Matty is the first one to say what everyone is thinking, "Wouldn't it be something if we could live this way every day?" Emma replies, "We have a good life in Sheboygan, but if we had the chance, I would love to live someplace warm, and be able to travel. There are so many places to see." Joseph and Harry smile and nod in agreement, and as they look at each other, they are both thinking of how to make that happen. Once they finish their coffee, they duck into a chocolate store for something to bring back to the room, and then hail a taxi back to the hotel.

The next morning after breakfast, they head out on a 2-hour drive to Friedrichshafen, Germany. They are not planning on staying overnight, just a quick stop on the way through. Joseph, who is driving, says, "I would like to drive by my Uncle Gerhart and Aunt Lena's old house. I wonder if any of it is still standing after the war?" Harry replies, "Your aunt and uncle were the best. I miss them as well." As they arrive, it takes Joseph a few tries to get his bearings, but he finally finds the correct street. Joseph says, "Harry, look over there, isn't that where their house and shop were? Half of this block has been rebuilt." Harry says, "I think you are right. I remember walking over to that little corner tavern down the block, so this must be it." As they leave, Matty says, "Joseph, if you remember where they used to attend church, we could stop and light a candle and say a prayer for them." Joseph and the others all agree and drive a couple of more blocks to the church they attended. When they were done there, the next stop was to where the Zeppelins were made prior to the war. It was the same situation again, as nothing remains of the old factory and Hanger. They decide to stop for lunch and Joseph and Harry take turns reminiscing about their escape. Emma and Matty were quite shocked when they finally confided in them of how they had just been arrested by the Gestapo, and Wolfgang was able to kill the Nazi so they could escape. They also told them of their identity change, and jumping off the train, and the Zeppelin flight to the states. Emma and Matty finally had a true understanding of how dangerous it had been for them and how it was a miracle they had survived. After lunch was finished, they bid Friedrichshafen goodbye and took the two-hour ride back to Munich. They want to get back early so they can pack and relax a little before they fly out in the morning for their last stop of the vacation, Rome, Italy.

They have an early flight out the next morning, which should take less than a couple of hours. Matty convinces everyone to skip breakfast in Munich and instead wait till they get to Rome to eat. After arriving at Rome's airport, they grab taxi's and meet at the hotel. As it is still early, their rooms will not be available until later that afternoon. So, the front desk holds their luggage and tells them to come back after 4:00 p.m. The first order of business is to get breakfast before seeing the sights of the city. As there is no shortage of restaurants and cafes, it is a simple matter to find a place to eat. Around the corner from the hotel is a corner café that has pastries displayed in the window. Emma says "Bingo! Those pastries have been waiting for us." They start out enjoying a delicious sweet ricotta filled cannoli which has a very crispy outer shell. That is followed by a pasticiotti, which is a round custard filled pastry with ribbed sides. These are enjoyed alongside a hot cup of espresso. After enjoying the pastries and people-watching for a while, they decide to board a sightseeing bus. As they will only be in Italy for three days, they will tour the city and try to see as much as they can. They spend the rest of the day taking a couple of different tour buses to all the normal tourist stops; the Coliseum, the Trevi Fountain, the Vatican with St Peter's Square and the Sistine Chapel, all of which are the most beautiful and interesting things they have seen on their European trip. For their lunch, they all enjoyed a street vendor food called "suppli," which is an oblong rice ball that has been mixed with sauce and ground meat with a piece of mozzarella inside, rolled in egg and breadcrumb and then deep fried, simple yet delicious. The amount of ornate historical architecture is just everywhere they look, whether it be a building, a fountain, statues, or a square, each one more beautiful than the last. Emma and Matty have taken so many pictures they have run out of 35mm film, so they have to stop and buy more, at the substantially inflated tourist price of course.

It's early evening and everyone is getting quite hungry and just want to find a nice restaurant to eat and relax after a long day of seeing the sites. They have to wait a little longer than they planned, as unlike back in the states, restaurants in Rome rarely open for dinner before 8:00 p.m., although you may find some in the more touristy areas. Emma is adamant that she wants to eat at a small trattoria that is off the beaten path, as she wants to sample some authentic cuisine. They find just the place up a small side street four to five blocks from their hotel. This is a small trattoria that does not even have tablecloths or a printed menu, quite the opposite of a typical restaurant. The trattoria holds only twenty tables and is a true family affair. The hostess is the owner's wife and the wait staff are his children. Their waitress tonight is a lovely, dark haired beauty named Giovanna. Harry says, "That is a lovely name, I thought I've heard of a 'Joe vanni' or something like that." Giovanna laughs and says, "Yes, Giovanni with an 'I' at the end is the male version, and Giovanna with an 'A' at the end is the female version." Harry replies, "Thank you for explaining that, but can we get some menus to look at?" Giovanna says, "No menus. What we have is on the chalk board over there." Matty says, "Alright, Giovanna, we want to have a typical Roman meal, what do you suggest?" She replies, "We will start you out with an antipasti platter consisting of roasted red peppers, fried eggplant, fresh mozzarella, and pecorino romano cheese. The first course will be tagliatelle pasta with bolognese sauce. The main course will be veal saltimbocca which is fried veal cutlet topped with prosciutto and marsala wine butter sauce. It will melt in your mouth. We will top the meal off with some espresso and a dish of flavorful gelato." Everyone nods in agreement and Matty says, "That sounds great, let's have that." Giovanna says, "Perfect, I will get the order in, and I will deliver the antipasti shortly." The dinner was every bit as delicious as they hoped it would be. As they walked back to the hotel, they were amazed at just how busy the streets were. There were many street vendors hawking anything from food to souvenirs. Once they get back to the hotel, they decide to call it quits for the night. Tomorrow will be another long day of sightseeing, so they need to get some rest, especially Joseph, as his bad leg is hurting.

The next couple of days in Rome and the surrounding areas are truly magical. They took a side trip down to Naples, which is a little less than three hours south of Rome. They toured the city and took a bus to the nearby ruins of Pompeii. Matty, who is of Sicilian origin, is so happy that they stopped in Italy as part of their vacation. As they stop for lunch at one of the pizzeria's, Matty remarks, "This Neapolitan style pizza is fantastic, round and thin with a crispy bottom from the wood-fired oven, and cut into wedges. The Sicilian style pizza that I grew up on was the opposite. My mother always made it in a rectangular pan and it was very thick and cut into squares." It's now early evening, around 5:30 p.m. as they stroll through the town. They come to a large piazza and there is a festival going on, with singing and dancing. As they find a seat to enjoy the entertainment, Matty and Joseph go over to some street vendors to purchase some snacks for the group. As they return, Emma says, "What did you buy for us? Matty replies, "Well, eat these while they are hot. It's a fried piece of pizza dough sprinkled with sugar they call pizza fritte. We also bought a pastry called sfogliatelle, which is a crispy layered pastry. After enjoying the festival for a few hours, they continue strolling down by the ocean front. It's around 8:30 p.m. when they decide its' time for dinner and they find a restaurant overlooking the Mediterranean Ocean. They are seated by the window overlooking the water, and the moonlight reflecting off the ocean is truly beautiful. The waiter asks them if they know what they would like and Matty says, "I'm the only Italian of our group, or more specifically, Sicilian, but I think we would all like to try a traditional Neapolitan dinner. The waiter smiles and says, "Then I think you will enjoy a plate of our famous spaghetti alla puttanesca, which is made with sauce, garlic, black olives, capers, and some spices served over spaghetti." Emma replies, "If everyone else is agreeable, let's try that." As it turns out, everyone enjoyed it and, on the side, they had some crispy Italian bread which they dipped into olive oil. It was quite a starchy dinner, but filling and delicious. As the waiter comes back, Harry asks him, "Dinner was delicious, but what does spaghetti alla puttanesca even mean?" The waiter replies, while laughing, "It means spaghetti in the style of the whore," as this was a popular dish in our red-light district in the old days." Harry and Joseph just look at each other, as Matty and Emma laugh uncontrollably. They are all thinking the same thing, "What an adventure this has turned out to be." After dinner, they head to the hotel as they have an early bus trip back to Rome in the morning. Unfortunately, they had to pay for a night at the hotel in Rome that they could not use, but they felt it was worth it as Naples was so charming.

They are now back in Rome, and decide to spend the afternoon enjoying some street vendor food and checking out the many museums and churches in the area. They are all blown away at the many paintings and sculptures that are on display from the likes of Michelangelo, Raphael, and DaVinci. The beauty and level of skill needed to produce such masterpieces are truly amazing. For dinner tonight, they decide to go to a restaurant, and instead of a regular meal just feast on several varieties of pizza which tastes so much better than anything they have had in the states. Afterwards, they spend some time in the local square enjoying some espresso and people-watching. As they discuss all the wonderful things they have seen on vacation, Emma says "I hope we can come back someday. I know there is so much more to see that we don't have time for." Matty says, "Yes, the next time we come, if possible, I would like to go to Palermo, Sicily to see where my people came from." Harry responds, "You know Joseph and I will turn sixty-two next spring, maybe it's time to seriously look at our finances. Working at the brewery is certainly not what it used to be." Joseph replies, "I agree with you Harry, I think we have to make a change in our lives sooner rather than later. But for now, we better get back to the hotel, as we have an early flight tomorrow and another long day of traveling." The weather was good, and the flights were smooth as they returned home on a Saturday night. At least they will have a day to rest up before returning to work on Monday, as they are going to need it.

Upon arriving at work Monday, Joseph sees his friend Kevin, one of the bottle line foreman. He asks, "What's been going on around here Kevin since I left for vacation?" Kevin responds, "Well, you won't believe it, but Walter the Plant Manager was promoted to corporate headquarters, so now we have another new Plant Manager. He's called a meeting with all supervisors today at 4:00 p.m." Joseph says, "Here we go again, somebody new that's out to make a name for himself, at our expense." Kevin replies, "I have no doubt in my mind that it won't be any good for us." As expected, the new Plant Manager, whose name is John Dorfman, started complaining about the line efficiencies and all the equipment breakdowns. So along with the Brewmaster they inform everyone they are to start twelve-hour shifts on Tuesday. As they leave the meeting, Kevin says to Joseph, "I think this is just another ploy to force people out so we can be replaced by cheaper new employees. Joseph hooks up with Harry, who was at the meeting only on the other side of the conference room. Harry tells him, "I really don't relish going home and telling Emma the news. She is going to be pissed off." Joseph agrees and says, "Matty, also, we just got home from a fun vacation, and now this. Well, let's go home and face the music." As expected, Emma and Matty are livid, and they both basically tell Harry and Joseph the same thing. At this point in our lives, we want to be spending more time with you guys, not less. Do what you have to do for now, but things must change.

The next day over in the Quality Assurance department, Empire Capital has requested a half barrel of each of their four principal products be shipped to New York City for the annual Plant Manager/ Brewmaster meeting which will take place next week. To ship them, each half barrel is loaded into a large cylindrical drum, packed with dry ice, and then sealed. As draught beer needs to be kept refrigerated, the dry ice should suffice for the journey, as they will be air freighted overnight to its destination. Several weeks after the meeting took place, the brewery is contacted by the airlines. They are trying to find out the exact nature of every item that was shipped on that flight. The airline explained that there were several pets that were present in the hold on that flight that had died under mysterious circumstances. As far as any of the office people knew, it was just kegs of beer that were shipped and that's what they told the airlines. It wasn't until word got down to the QA Department that packed the kegs, that they realized it must have been the dry ice had warmed and turned into carbon dioxide gas and escaped the shipping containers, which suffocated the animals. From that point on, only frozen freezer packs were used to keep the shipment of kegs cold.

Still in the Quality Assurance department, Michael, who normally works in the Brewing and Microbiology sections, is instead covering the packaging lab due to vacations. The female lab tech, Lisa, has just finished checking the non-returnable bottle line air content, and it is found to be out of the limit of salability. Michael notifies Kevin to shut the filler down and calls the warehouse to hold all product back to the last good check, which was two hours ago. Almost immediately, Kevin, his boss Tom, and Tom's boss, enter the lab with some samples to recheck. As Lisa is running the samples, Tom is pressed up close behind her and is looking over her shoulder. They're all yelling trying to intimidate her in reading the result to their benefit. Michael goes over and asks them all to calm down and step back and let Lisa finish the checks. Michael verifies the results and tells the packaging people the hold stands. They storm out of the lab and go out and make adjustments to the filler. After rechecks verify the problem is corrected, the line is allowed to restart. Michael recalls the first time he supervised the packaging lab, and that day held twenty pallets of beer. Tom was irate and stood in the lab swearing at Michael with his face beet red and fists clenched tight. Michael at first was totally intimidated and was going to rescind the hold and release the beer. But the more Tom yelled, the madder Michael got, and he blurted out "Calm down Tom, you are right. I see your point." Toms' fists unclench as he says, "You do, I'm glad to hear that." Michael replies, "Yes, Tom, twenty pallets was wrong. Make it forty." At that, Tom glares at Michael, turns and walks out without a word. The next morning Michael is called into Tom's office and thinks he is going to be fired. Instead, Tom shakes his hand and hands him a mug as a gift and says," I like you Michael, you had the balls to stand up to me. Good job." Michael leaves his office and breathes a gigantic sigh of relief.

At the end of the shift Lisa is very upset and stops in the Personnel department to lodge a complaint. She tells them that Tom had his body pressed up her backside, and she feels she has been sexually harassed. This is something that is just starting to be addressed as a problem in the workplace, and laws have been passed to stop this type of harassment. Lisa saw a news report about this recently, so she felt empowered to lodge a complaint. Tom was reprimanded and forced to personally apologize to Lisa, which was really all she wanted. Of course, Kevin's bosses are not happy about the hold beer, or the harassment complaint that resulted from it, so Kevin gets blamed for both and they berate him mercilessly in the next production meeting.

Joseph and all the other foreman have been on twelve-hour shifts for over a month and are on the brink of exhaustion. Finally, John Dorfman is happy enough with the progress they have made and takes them off the extended shifts. Fortunately, they are coming into the Thanksgiving four-day plant shutdown where major yearly maintenance is performed. Joseph couldn't be happier to have a nice long weekend before starting the grind again. Harry's twelve-hour shifts had only lasted a week in the brewing department, so he is not anywhere as burned out as Joseph, but he will enjoy the break just as much.

The long weekend was just what Joseph needed, spending time with the family and having an American turkey dinner. Joseph and Matty had invited Harry and Emma along with Jana's family. They had a full house for sure and put on a few pounds, but it was so nice having everyone together, which is getting harder and harder to do.

The following month it's the week before Christmas, and Joseph is hard at work, but the can line is not running well because of multiple packer breakdowns. In the production meeting, the Plant Manager, John Dorfman, starts berating Joseph and says, "What do you mean the packer on line #53 broke down again today? It broke down yesterday. Why are you breaking my packer?" Joseph stammers and replies, "I wouldn't put it in those terms. We are running that packer non-stop at maximum speed. It's inevitable we are going to have issues." John raises his voice more saying, "Issues, I don't pay you to have issues. Be more proactive and get your ass in gear." He then turns to the maintenance manager and starts yelling at him saying, "Get your mechanics over there and find out what the hell is going on and get it fixed once and for all. Don't you or Joseph come in here tomorrow and tell me that packer is not running." Now it's Kevin, who is foreman on the non-returnable bottle line's turn. Kevin starts out discussing any safety issues which is their procedure saying, "We had an employee slip and fall on the ice and snow in the parking lot this morning on his way into work, he slightly sprained his wrist when he fell, but he is alright, and we did not have a lost time accident." The packaging manager is irate, and red faced and says, "This is winter in Wisconsin. What the heck is wrong with that guy? He should know to be more careful when there is snow and ice on the ground. You get the hell out of my sight and go down there and tell him to his face that I said he is stupid." Kevin doesn't know what to say, and that infuriates the boss even more and he yells again, "Don't make me repeat myself, you heard what I said, now get out!" Kevin rushes out of the room and locates the individual who fell, named Denny. After relaying the message, Denny wants to go punch Kevin's boss out. Kevin struggles with him and is able to physically restrain him. Kevin tells him, "Calm down and just suck it up, it's not worth losing your job over."

Over in the brewing department, things are not much better for Harry. It is just a constant battle, as all corporate wants is more ways to cut costs and increase profits. The problem the company is having is that as sales have fallen, they have reduced the capital that needs to be reinvested into the business. As the equipment ages, it needs more and more maintenance to keep them running. A major issue Harry is trying to solve currently is a strange aroma that has developed in a couple of beer tanks, best described as a plastic or new shower curtain smell. It was so pronounced, the beer tanks had to be dumped. Consequently, corporate has been putting much pressure on the brewing department to fix the problem, as they can ill afford to be dumping more beer. Word has come down from on high that heads will roll if they lose another tank. It takes much digging into every facet of the process, but Harry is able to find the cause. The fermenting area had a problem where some yeast that should have been recovered from a completed fermentation and chilled down immediately wasn't. Instead, it was allowed to warm up and sit for an extended period before it was moved to the refrigerated yeast brink storage tanks. Fortunately, all the yeast that is used is tracked as to what fermenter it came from, and how many generations it has been used. Harry was able to dump the remaining bad yeast before it was used to ferment any new brews. Consequently, proper yeast collection procedures were reinforced with the brewers and no further problems were found. Harry thought he would get a pat on the back for solving the problem, instead he got a kick in the ass. Dave the Brewmaster, blamed him because he oversees the brewhouse and fermenting areas. Harry says, "Since we are short an Assistant Brewmaster, I can't be everywhere checking on everything at one time." Dave replies, "I understand where you are coming from, but the reality is this. Corporate has made it clear they don't want excuses. So, if at any time feel you are not up to the challenge, you let me know and I will find a replacement." Harry leaves and can't believe what he is hearing and thinks to himself, "After all these years I have to be talked to like that. Can this place suck any more than it already does?"

To answer Harry's question to himself, if this place can suck any more than it already does, the quick answer is yes it can. It's 4:00 p.m.

Christmas Eve, and all the employees are called into a meeting in the warehouse. The Plant Manager, John Dorfman, gives them all their un-Christmas presents, courtesy of Empire Capital. He says, "There has been a change to the amount of vacation time we are all able to take. Effective on January 1, 1976, instead of a maximum of four weeks of vacation, it will be reduced to three weeks. In addition, everyone will be required to pay in $10.00/month towards their medical insurance. As you know, sales have been sluggish, and that is why corporate is making these changes." Suddenly the employees start to chant, "Union, Union, Union," as John Dorfman runs out of the warehouse.

As Harry and Joseph leave the brewery, they see each other in the parking lot. Joseph says, "I don't know about you Harry, but I turn 62 in January, as you do, and I am thinking of calling it quits sometime this year." Harry replies, "I totally agree with you. Can you believe they want to cut a week's vacation, bunch of cheap S.O.B.'S?" Joseph says, "Yes they are, but the worst part is how they treat everybody. We bust our ass every day, but lately, I can't seem to do anything right. Oh, and get this, I heard a rumor that they are thinking of getting rid of more packaging foreman. Instead of having two lines to cover per supervisor per shift, it will only be two supervisors per shift." Harry agrees and says "It's the same thing in the brewing department, same rumors, empower the employees, and get rid of the foreman. But, you know, I was thinking the one thing we should not do is to go home and tell our wives that they cut out a weeks' vacation. They will go nuts, and I just want to have a nice Christmas." Joseph says, "Totally agree, let's just keep it to ourselves, and besides, it may be a moot point if we do indeed retire."

It turns out to be a wonderful, joyous Christmas and New Year's. Everyone's children and grandchildren had so much fun baking cookies and opening presents. It really kept Joseph and Harry's spirits up having a few days off and being able to spend time with the family. As happy as Harry and Joseph are, they are apprehensive about what the new year will bring.

It didn't take long for tragedy to strike, as a few days into the new year, Emma's mother, Alice, suffers a massive heart attack and passes quickly. Poor Emma is devastated and really needs Harry to lean on. Harry asks for a few days off to help with the arrangements, but he is rebuffed by his boss and told that Alice was only a mother-in-law so he could only have one day off. As Harry protests that decision, his boss says "Hey, Harry, where do your priorities lie? Is it with the company, or not?" Harry is totally irate, but holds his temper and says, "After all these years I have been loyal to the company, you ask me where my priorities lie? Well, it's simple. My loyalty is to my wife, my daughter, and my grandchildren. I will take the one day, but I'm not happy about it." Fortunately, Joseph's Uncle Otto, who by this time is eighty years old, but in fine health and his mind is as sharp as ever, volunteers to help Emma with all the arrangements. He turns out to be a godsend, as Harry has been working long hours and is only allowed the day of the funeral off from work. A few weeks after Alice is laid to rest, it's Saturday January 24, 1976, and Harry and Emma are out for breakfast as Harry has his one weekend a month off. Emma says to Harry as they enjoy some hot coffee while waiting for breakfast to arrive, "Harry, we can't go on like this. You are working all the time and I barely get a chance to see you anymore, and I never should have had to rely on Uncle Otto's help. I'm not mad at you, but since my mother died, I feel empty inside, and I need my husband." Harry replies, "I love you Emma and I want to be with you, as well. I will be honest with you, not getting enough time off when Alice died was the last straw. I am seriously thinking about retiring this year." Emma is so happy and replies, "I don't care about the money, I care about you. Please see if you can make it happen this year, the sooner the better."

Unbeknownst to Harry and Emma, Joseph and Matty are having the exact same conversation. Matty says to Joseph, "I'm happy you have the day off today. What do you think about going downtown later and take in a movie?" Joseph replies, "I would love to. It's been a long time since we have gone to one." Matty continues, "You know I were thinking about it last night. All of our children are grown and out of the house and thankfully independent. Have you given any more thought to possibly taking your retirement.?" Joseph nods and replies, "It's all I think about lately. Financially, we are doing fine. The house is paid for, and we have money in the bank. If I were to retire after I turn sixty-two in a couple of days, I can get social security and a pension, as I have enough years in with the company. I was thinking of waiting until later this spring to turn my retirement papers in." Matty says, "Then we are agreed. I can't wait to spend the rest of our lives together."

The following month Harry has celebrated his sixty-second birthday and is also trying to figure out when he wants to retire this year. Before work one day, Harry and Joseph are talking, and they both decide to put their retirement papers in before the end of the current week, with an effective date of June 1st. They figure that would give the company plenty of time to hire and train their replacements, if they were going to be replaced at all. Before they have a chance to turn in their papers, Empire Capital, in another bid to reduce labor cost, makes a huge announcement, "Effective immediately, any employee who wishes to put their retirement papers in within the next ninety days, and effective before the end of the year will receive a one-year severance." Empire Capital knows they can replace any of the older employees with young people just entering the workforce who will work for much less money. They don't care about all the experience they are losing if the bean counters see they can reduce overhead. When Harry and Joseph hear the announcement, they can barely contain their glee. Harry seeks Joseph out on lunch break and finds him in the cafeteria. Harry says, "Finally, something has gone right in our favor! We were going to retire anyway, so why not turn in our retirement papers today, only make it effective at the end of the month." Joseph replies, "Heck yeah, the sooner the better! Do you know how happy the wives are going to be? Let's skip lunch and go over to the Personnel Department right now." Harry replies, "Let's do it, and tonight, why don't the four of us go out to dinner so we can tell Emma and Matty the good news."

That evening as they are having dessert after a splendid dinner at their favorite restaurant, Emma says, "Alright you two, you have kept Matty and me in suspense long enough, what is the big news?" Harry and Joseph reply at the same time and say, "We put our retirement papers in today, effective the end of the month." Emma and Matty are so happy they leave their seats and hug and kiss their husbands. Afterwards, Emma says, "As soon as you retire, why don't we take a trip back down to Miami, Florida for a vacation? Remember how much fun it was the last time we went?" Everyone agrees that some fun in the sun is what they all need. However, the best laid plans don't always work out.

The next morning as Harry and Joseph arrive at work, they are called into the Plant Manager's office. As they both enter, they find John Dorfman talking with the Brewmaster Dave Morrison. John looks at them and says, "So you two numb skulls want to retire? Didn't it occur to you to give us a heads up on what you were planning?" Joseph replies, "We figured with the latest announcement from Empire Capital, it is what you wanted." Dave, the Brewmaster speaks next, "The fact is, you two do not have the proper mindset that Empire Capital is looking for, and you do not fit in with our long-term strategic objectives." John Dorfman says, "You will be allowed to retire sometime in the next six months. We will tell you when, now get out of here and get back to work," As they leave, Joseph says to Harry, "Schweinhund, they are lucky I don't have my knife, or I would gut them like the pigs they are." Harry replies, "Calm down, calm down, don't do anything you will regret later. We may have to wait a while longer, but it is going to happen. We are so freaking naïve to think anything around this place is going to be easy. I am sure what they are doing to us is not legal, but we don't want to miss out on the year's severance. Come over to the house after dinner and we will give the wives the news." Joseph says, "Alright, I will see you tonight. If I don't get arrested for murder first."

After dinner, Harry and Joseph tell their wives the latest. Harry says, "We have good news and bad news from the brewery. The good news is, they accepted our retirement paperwork. The bad news is, they won't let us leave for up to six months. So, we will have to put our vacation plans on hold." Emma says, "This sucks big time. Forget about the vacation, I just wanted you out of there sooner rather than later." Matty is not so eloquent, as she uncharacteristically starts swearing with every bad word she knows. Joseph grabs her in an embrace and holds her tight saying, "It's your turn to calm down. I was so mad I was going to kill someone today. But we will just do what we must. At least now there is light at the end of the tunnel." While everyone is visibly upset, they soon calm down and Harry and Joseph agree to just face it like any other of the challenges they have dealt with in their lives.

As it turns out they don't have to wait as long as they thought. Empire Capital decides it needs to plan ahead and set things up financially, so they will meet their second quarter targets which runs April-June. Consequently, it is now near the end of March when Harry and Joseph are again called into the Plant Manager's office, only this time, besides the Brewmaster, the Personnel manager is also there. They tell them that this is their last day of employment, and they are officially on retirement. Harry and Joseph are shocked as they thought it would be at least another three months. Harry says, "It's been a great career, lots of ups and downs along the way, but I always felt fortunate to work here." Joseph is not so forgiving and says, "I am thrilled I am officially retired, because I don't care to work here another day. Empire Capital does not have the proper mindset and does not fit into MY strategic objectives." The Personnel manager intervenes and says, "Everyone, let's try to stay positive. I know this is a stressful time for everyone. But, both of you have a stellar work record and we appreciate all your efforts over the years. As a token of our esteem, we would like to present you with this retirement gift." They both receive a medium-sized box, but before they open them, two security guards appear at the door. John Dorfman says, "Harry, Joseph, thank you again for your service. These guards will now escort you off the premises."

Harry looks at Joseph and while smirking says, "Well, my friend, I guess we are getting the perp walk."

As they leave the brewery, Joseph invites Harry and Emma to come over the house after dinner and they can open their retirement gifts and discuss what they want to do next. As they sit in the parlor, they have some delicious blueberry pie that Matty has made, topped off with French vanilla ice cream. After Joseph finishes his second piece of pie and their coffee, it's time to open their presents. Joseph and Harry both laugh as they unwrap a ceramic eagle statue with our names engraved on the front base. Joseph says, "OMG, this is the same gift they gave Uncle Otto." Harry replies, "This is quite an interesting gift, to say the least." Emma says, "Maybe we can put it on the mantle above the fireplace?" Joseph interjects, "Or maybe put in the yard to scare the pigeons away?" Harry adds, "Oh look! They spelled my name wrong!" After a good laugh, they discuss plans for a vacation and decide since the weather is still cold, they will take a trip down to Miami and stay for a couple of weeks.

After a short time to make the arrangements, they arrive in Miami, and they spend the first week just lounging on the beach or resting in their cabana. At the beginning of the second week, they are at dinner one night and Emma says, "I was thinking, what would our lives be like if we could live in Florida full time?" Joseph replies, "But, what about Jana and the grandkids?" She replies, "Don't get me wrong, but as much as I would miss them, I think a change of lifestyle would do us all good. Besides, we can visit each other during the year and talk on the phone every day if we wish." Joseph says, "Matty and I were talking about the same thing last night. Maybe we should spend some time this week and see some open houses. Once we find out prices, taxes, and fees, etc. we can make a more informed decision." Everyone agrees, and after some searching, they each put a deposit down on a house in a new community that is being built a few blocks from the beach just north of Miami. Emma and Matty make a point of calling their children and letting them know what they have done, as they want to see if the feedback is going to be negative, in which case they will ask for the deposit back. On the contrary, the children are happy for them, and encourage them to make the move while they are still healthy enough to enjoy themselves.

It's now the day before their vacation will be ending, and they will fly home to Sheboygan the next morning. As they sit in their adjoining cabanas, Emma says, "You know, I would have thought the brewery would have put on a going away party for all the employees who took retirement. I mean, look at all the years you guys toiled in that place, it's the least they could do." Harry and Joseph look at each other and smile. Emma says, "Matty, why are these two idiots sitting there with stupid grins on their faces?" Matty asks, "Alright, out with it! What's so funny? Harry replies, "Well, there is a going away party scheduled that we were invited to." Emma is surprised and says "Well then, when is it? I think you guys deserve to go." Harry and Joseph both look at their watches and Joseph replies, "When is it, you ask?" As they both laugh hysterically, Harry blurts out, "It started half an hour ago!" Emma and Matty are shocked, and Emma says, "What the hell is wrong with you? Why didn't you tell us? We could have planned the vacation differently." Harry says, "Emma, actually, we planned it this way because we didn't want to go to it in the first place!"

"So now, what's the plan?" the girls ask. Harry replies, "It's simple. Hey beach waiter, bring my friend Joseph here some cold soda and for the ladies and me, let's try a bucket of ice cold bottles of that Anheuser-Busch Michelob Beer!"

The End.

Made in United States
Troutdale, OR
12/18/2024